THE PROTECTORS TRILOGY:
BOOK ONE

By Arial Alexis

Happy Birthday
Kayla !

Follow your dreams when

ISBN: 978-1-329-38287-9

To my family, for being the greatest supporters of my dreams. To my mother for always patiently listening to my stories, my father, for reminding me to stop and have fun, my sisters Destin and Trinity, for the hours of entertainment and inspirations, and my brother Robbie, for always believing in me and being just as awesome as the characters I write. I love you all.

When Fantasy is Reality-
Fiction is Fact-
And Sci-fi is Who
And What you are...
Welcome to our normal.

Prologue

I had long before forgotten to want to be shocked when situations like these did not faze me. In the first few weeks I had looked for the thrill of the chase, hoping that if I came close to death, if I put myself in the way of what should have been terrorizing then the wall between my consciousness and the empty void of what was presumably once my empathy would crack, and something, an emotion, an action done of compassion, some sign of my shredded humanity would eventually break through. I had gone as desperate as jumping off a building, savoring the artificial freedom of the five story free fall. Yet when I opened my eyes, the only thing that had changed was the sky, tinted yellow with the coming sunrise. Mostly uninjured, it dawned on me. Pain is a reward, a reminder that we are still alive, a fuel to find something better, and an honor I hadn't earned.

When those weeks had passed, so did that slight reason to hope. If you live long enough in the dark your eyes will adjust to it, along with the rest of you. The idea of an escape was no longer imagined. The thought that perhaps one day I would not have to force myself to move or act was forgotten. I was doomed to this. But a remedy, to feel a single emotion, for a thought to be more than an observation, for my anger to be directed at more than myself, for hate or fear or even the slightest taste of joy to at least be able to be faked… The idea such a thing as that could exist was all that kept me going. Even if I could not heal myself, there had to be something that could.

I was brought back to reality when the gun shifted, taking aim at my chest.

Let's get it over with.

What side are you on?

I tried to rationalize, knowing this couldn't be reality, but it was far from a dream. The creeping cold against my back was real, beyond any argument my subconscious made against it. A steady pressure held me at my wrists, chest, and ankles. The darkness offered me no other answers, all I knew was what I felt. Worse than the feeling of helplessness, was the sorrow and rage that came with knowing I had failed. At what, I didn't know. I only knew the fire in my chest and the cold at the pit of my stomach was caused by something, something I knew I had to find, if only so I could escape it.

I opened my eyes, remembering that the darkness was one of the things I could control, and looked down. Then I realized why I couldn't move. I was strapped down. I didn't even notice that the steel bars of the restraints were cutting into my skin, not until I saw a small line of blood dripping from my numb fingers.

Before I had time to think, a bright white light burst forth from every possible direction, blinding me in an expanse of glowing emptiness. Loud, mumbled voices pierced the constant, electrical, droning of the wall of machines I had seen surrounding me.

The last thing I remember before it went black was being taken captive by a fear so consuming I knew it was only a matter of seconds before my heart stopped beating. And pain. Lots of pain. Coming from nowhere, hurting everything. Yet, in the midst of this, I felt *alive*. More alive than I had ever felt before. My whole body hummed with energy. My eyes went blurry and red with blood before everything was cut with

2

pristine clarity. Each white, fluorescent light above me was surrounded by a dim rainbow, every flake of dust made visible in the resonating glare. The minuscule dents in the ceiling were gashes, and all the shadow's darkest points were revealed. The energy that had been sending sparks down my spine ignited, searing through me. A sharp, penetrating sensation lit each cell in my body, making even the softest sound of blood pumping through my head a thought drowning roar. I tasted the metal that laced the air. I could feel everything that touched my skin, the faint powdery substance blowing through the too-clean atmosphere, the beads of hot sweat rolling down my forehead, and the pressure settling over my whole body that threatened to collapse my lungs. The weight quickly grew heavier.

Too heavy.

I was a man seeing the world for what felt like the first time, and as I lay there, my pant-like breathing labored, my head pounding to the rhythm of my heart, and my vision going black, I realized that no single man was meant to see it this way.

The Apparent Beginning

Green eyes rimmed with glasses staring down at me was the first thing I saw when I opened my eyes. They belonged to pudgy man who kept demanding answers to meaningless questions in a voice that was both nervous and overly animated. A woman appeared, her manner mirroring his, and put her cold hand on my forehead. I was so lost in a fog of what I can only describe as extreme exhaustion to question who they were, even as he quizzically eyed me over, his pale mouth continuing to silently rant.

I must have blacked out then. I don't remember anything else.

A bright orange bio-suit walked slowly across my vision, carefully carrying a small container. Others stood at the base of one of the four white washed walls surrounding me. The screens above them displayed profiles, dozens of them, pictures taking up nearly half of each screen, but one of a man with black wavy hair and blue eyes seemed to stand out more than the rest. He looked vaguely familiar. Large, bold capped red letters "PROJECT TREASON" was displayed at the side of each screen. The words written in the charts underneath the ominous titles were blurred.

◆

I rolled my eyes at the crowded bedroom. Subconsciously I knew that this must be my room, everything was familiar, and at the same time everything seemed just outside of my grasp, like when you know you are dreaming and you should wake up soon. The only problem was I couldn't wake up. The pale green walls remained where they were, holding up worn out football jerseys and numerous medals. In the farthest corner there was a cluttered bookcase covered in dust and trophies. A desk supported a sleek computer screen, countless magazines, and a framed picture of a kid around fourteen with jet black hair, black eyes, and pale skin standing next to the people I remembered from the living room.

I sat up quickly and instantly regretted it. I felt too dizzy and lightheaded to move; my head spun for longer than I thought it should have - *even if I do have brain damage*. I suddenly remembered hearing that. There had been a doctor, he had said I had been in a motorcycle accident, that I had snapped a tree in half or something, and the Harley was nothing more than a metal pretzel. My brain was the smoothie that came with it.

Is this going to be permanent?

I didn't know the answer, only that I was starving. The house was silent, and the sun was barely high enough to cast a shadow, leaving to assume they – whoever they were – were asleep. I went to go pillage through the kitchen and stopped as I passed the large refrigerator. The mirrored door held an unbelievable image. A pair of deep onyx eyes set in equally dark circles stared back. I shuddered at their emptiness. Shaggy, straight black hair framed the somber face of a young man. A body belonging to a professional wrestler stood over six feet tall and seemed to consume the entire surface the door.

I knew it was my reflection, but felt nothing when I looked at it, not even the desire to feel something.

The man was suddenly standing behind me, to the side of the unknown person in the mirror.

"...You've got school starting in an hour." He muttered, his eyes unwilling to meet mine after his unexpected approach had scared away what was left of my sanity. With that he wobbled back into the living room, a cup of coffee in one hand and a remote in the other.

School.

I didn't think about it – allowing whatever was left of my unconscious memories to guide me through the day. The tattered school ID in my wallet was the first thing I dug out, finding my name scribbled beneath the scratched lamination. When I left my room again, there was a note on the counter, a reminder that I had a psych appointment that afternoon, and that I would be taking the bus. When I got there, the building marked with nothing but two stories of red brick and black letters over a double door entrance, everyone treated me like I was new, which I figured, at least as far as I was concerned, I was.

But even then, I couldn't help feel someone was always watching me. I had actually debated real paranoia, but regardless of how close I came to fitting the condition, I wasn't scared of whatever it was, just aware. I did not tell the mousy man I was told to sit in a room with for an hour a day any of this. I did not speak to anyone actually, not unless I had to. It wasn't worth explaining that no matter what I did, it remained; hiding in the corner of my mind, telling me something was wrong, but I never knew what or how to fix it. That's why I liked to avoid the strangers who called themselves my parents, my house, all of it.

I honestly do not remember when it was that the fog lifted, it felt like it could have been years. It's ascent was gradual, until one day they told me the shrink would only have to see me once a week, and that my memories would start returning soon. I didn't believe them, but anything, even a false pretense of belief, was better than existing as I had been.

◆

I was running, windowless doors flashed by, yellow signs on the white washed walls raced by past me. Black smoke floated above my head and down the deserted hallway. Loud shouting erupted from behind. Men and women in bright orange suits ran after me holding small black blocks in their hands. "BREACH! SECURITY BREACH! PROJECT TREASON-SECURITY BREACH!" shrieked hidden speakers. The yelling behind me increased and the smoke grew thicker, making it harder and harder for me to breathe. I kept running...

I jumped out of my bed to the infamous buzz of my alarm clock. Another nightmare. *TGIF.* I thought sarcastically. Some days were easier than others. Some were solely highlight by the fact another day alive meant another day to figure out how to disappear. That day was the later. I wasn't sure what was worse, the fact I couldn't remember my own birthday or that the motorcycle I had bought myself for it was scrap metal, leaving me to ride the bus to school.

"Hey..." She said warily when I didn't greet her, sitting next to me.

"Hey." I said minimally, scooting over to give her massive backpack room. She too was the victim of vehicular absence, but in her case it was a deer that had been the cause of it.

"What's up?"

I shrugged.

"You okay?"

"I'm *fine*, Mary." She may have been the only person at the entire school I considered a friend, and the only person in the free world brave enough to sit next to me, or even more so, poke fun with me, despite the twenty inches in height and hundred pounds between us, but her care free personality was useless that morning. I hated the nightmares.

"Well I know *that*. But are you okay?" She cocked an eyebrow.

"I said I'm fine"

"Oh, so now I'm the bad guy for trying to help?" She sharply countered. I looked back out the window. "Brad..." She warned.

"What?"

"Come on. You know you want to tell me, you'll feel better." She nudged my shoulder, trying to get me to look at her. "You can't win on this, so you might as well just tell me."

I didn't want to tell her in the first place, much less read the reaction that'd play out her behind her hazel eyes if I did tell her. *It's not like I have anything to lose....Well, actually I do. She's the only .*

"You ever feel lost?"

"We all get like that." She said thoughtfully, her voice dropping an octave.

"Not like me."

"I swear if you don't cut out this ridiculous brooding tortured teen act and tell me what the heck is wrong I will-" I turned towards her. She stopped, the serious of my glower silencing the irritation in hers. "We all got things going on with our past or whatever. It's no excuse to be mean." She hissed, crossing her bare arms over her tank top.

"I wouldn't know."

"That you're a jerk?"

"Yeah" I gave her that one. She smirked. I was forgiven. "And about my past."

"What about it?"

"I don't remember much...I got in a wreck." I explained to her dazed expression. She frowned. "I don't remember anything about who I was, am, but everything else is fine."

"Is that even *possible*?"

"Apparently." I had already researched it, but the doctor who came to the house every few weeks remained adamant that I was fine, that I would remember soon, that nothing was wrong. I never believed him, but I found myself less driven to prove him wrong.

The bus stopped. Her expression was tense.

"Meet me after school."

Trace

"That doesn't make any sense." She fussed, shaking her head for the thousandth time.

"I know." I said dispassionately, leaning back on the metal mesh bench, one of the few that surrounded the outdoor lunch area. I crossed my arms, squinting in the Florida sunshine. "The shrink and the doctor both told me it's all in my head. Psychogenic amnesia – caused by the stress of the crash. They said it's a fugue state."

She pulled out her phone, looking up everything I had said. Disassociation, loss of personal identity, caused by factors unrelated to physical trauma, popular in pop culture fiction, Wikipedia had it all laid out.

After a minute or so, she looked back up to me, sizing me up against her quick introduction to neuroscience. "Well…It explains a lot I guess." She rubbed her palms on her shorts, attempting to fight the damp humidity before looking back up at me. "Dang Brad, I knew you had issues, but I didn't know that *no* baggage is just as bad *as* baggage."

"Thanks."

"You know I didn't mean it like that!" She swatted at my arm. "They said it's not permanent."

"Yeah."

It still sucks though huh?"

"Sucks sugarcoats it just a bit."

"I bet…And your parents? How are they coping with this?"

"I don't know them." I helplessly lifted my shoulders in a shrug.

"Yeah. You're right. I can barely deal with mine, and we were close...once." She sighed, running her hand through her shoulder length hair. "So you really don't remember *anything*?"

I couldn't hide the small shudder.

"You do don't you?" Her voice took an ominous tone.

"I don't know."

"What is it then?"

"Nothing." I leaned over, elbows on my knees and head in my hands.

"That sure narrows it down." She wasn't letting it go, making an exaggerated 'huff.'

"...I don't sleep. At all. It's a fight just to shut my eyes. I'm constantly ready to jump somebody. It's like I'm on edge of snapping – *all* the time. There's never a moment where I don't feel like something it wrong, like I'm being watched."

"Paranoid much?"

"Do I have a reason not to be?"

"And you aren't on anything right?" She frowned, clueless to the fact my sobriety was the only thing convincing me I might still be sane.

"Unless they're slipping me steroids, no."

That make her laugh, her eyes once again assessing my stature.

"Huh. Well, I know a few guys who need a good jumping, if you're interested in letting out some roid-rage." She laughed to lighten the mood. I smirked, even if the comment had raised questions. I wasn't going to ask her, but I didn't like the idea that she knew 'a few guys' that were on her bad side. She was oblivious to this, once again looking at her phone. "It says addressing the cause helps people come out of the, uh, oh- fugue thing. We've addressed it so, do you feel

11

better? Any sudden memories of freshmen year coming back to haunt you?"

"Not really...But it was nice talking to someone about it." Having someone else know made it seem less like I was losing my mind.

"I'm always here."

"Thanks."

"You're welcome." She said happily, throwing her backpack over her shoulder. "I have friends picking me up today – you want a ride home?"

"No, I'll walk."

"Suit yourself." She started to walk away. "Wait!" She spun around. "I forgot with all this but I'm throwing a party tomorrow night and I know you're committed to this lone wolf vibe, but maybe getting out will help? Loosen up, dance, smile for once? Might as well make a few memories while you're waiting for the old ones to come back, right?"

I won't hear the end of it the rest of the semester if I don't show.

"Fine."

I'd forgotten about how my every move was monitored and my strict ten o'clock curfew until I got home that day. When I passed the man named Ben – even in my head I could not all him my father – in the living area, he looked up from a laptop only long enough to see I wasn't running straight for my room.

"I'll be out late tomorrow." I said minimally, keeping my eyes down. Just being in the same room as him left me feeling like I was covered in hives.

"Alright." He said impassively, returning to his typing.

I frowned.

That's it?

I would have thought less of it if he wasn't so obsessed with knowing where I was at any given moment. My phone would ping at random times when he'd locate it, and there was some GPS tracker designed for parents to find their kids hooked on my back pack. I had dismissed that because I had been, according to them, a troublemaker, with the drag racing and subsequent wreck supposed to be proof of that. I didn't question it when he would stare at me like I was growing horns on my head. Or, when the woman who I knew I should have called mom but could barely look at without feeling guilty – not that I didn't know her – but that I had no desire to – would fuss over everything I did. If I ate, they'd say what, if I left, they'd ask where, if I never left my room, they'd probably be fine with it.

In hindsight I should have paid more attention in biology when we learned how genetics work.

♦

Freefall

I stood in Mary's house's large glass entryway, staring at the text telling her I was there. Had her neighborhood not been under construction, the cops would have been all over it in less than a minute. As it was, her mostly undeveloped road provided a private drive. Red plastic cups were already strewn across her porch and freshly mowed yard. A couple dozen cars were parked along the street and in an empty lot next door. The frame work for another six thousand square foot mini mansion loomed behind them. I would be surprised if it lasted the night.

"You could have just come in. I thought you'd ditch." She said, leaning against the newly opened door, cup in hand.

"I might. I didn't expect all this." I glanced over her shoulder.

"Yeah, I went overboard. I know." She explained over the shouting coming from behind her. I was relieved to see she was still mostly sober. I realized I wasn't fond of the fact she threw house parties. No matter how little I actually knew about her, I knew she was fragile, her tough, unconcerned façade barely going deep enough to be called superficial.

"And your parents?"

"Out – somewhere in Tallahassee for a business thing. Don't worry, no one is getting busted, come in already."

We stepped inside. She'd not lied when she'd gone overboard. She'd understated. It looked like the entire upper class had shown. She nimbly squeezed through the throng that crowed the hallway. Once they noticed me standing there they started to part. She grabbed my wrist, leading me towards the back. It got quieter the farther we were from the speakers.

14

Beneath the swaying bodies and mess, it was a nice house. I didn't plan on sticking around long enough to be a part of the cleanup crew, but I knew she would definitely have her work cut out for her.

She introduced me to five or six people, even in the chaos playing hostess.

"I'll be back down in a bit, you good here?" She tried to smile, her gaze tight.

"What's up?"

"Nothing! Go enjoy yourself for once!" She motioned back towards the living room, smiling for real now, before disappearing up the stairs.

Now what?

I slunk back towards the corner. My stomach seemed to rise into my chest and my entire body vibrated with the base pounding in the background. That feeling had a weird sense of déjà vu attached to it, but the music was good. The people in the house moved in packs, three or four of them migrating into different rooms or out into the yard at any given minute. But their restlessness was nothing compared to mine. The feeling of being watched was gone, if only because I was backed into a pair of walls and no one around me could possibly care to wander why, but there was something else. I caught myself counting the bodies, listing who was where, identifying who would be the ones to go the craziest and who would be passing out. It wasn't a game of profiling, I did that every day, there was more to it, a label I would unconsciously place on each of them, one I did not know how to recognize at the time.

A few songs had played when a muffled yell pierced the overwhelming roar of the music. No one else seemed to hear it.

I paused when I realized it had come from the second story. I didn't let myself think. I wasn't sure what I was thinking. Or if I was. I just moved, shoving my way towards the stairs, hating every second that it took to reach them and the even longer time it took to throw people off them so I could fit by.

I found Mary curled up, hiding in the corner of what looked to be a guest bedroom. She clutched her shoulder, hiding her face in the wall. I was beside her, the twelve steps between e doorway and the other side of the dresser lost somewhere in the bloodshot haze surrounding me. .

"What happened?" I demanded. She looked up at me, frantic eyes wide.

"I- Sam he...he-" Her voice broke. She lifted her hand to her face, her wrist swollen and red. I looked around to make sure no one had followed me, but I wasn't hoping to be alone, either. A part of me wished he had stuck around. *If he is still here I could kill him – no I would kill him.*

"It's okay Mary." I said softly. I scooped her up, standing. She was too tired or in too much pain to protest.

There was only three things I could clearly think. First, take her out of that room. Next, clear the house, even if it meant calling the cops. Third, find the SOB and beat the you-know-what out of him.

I found her room, in some part of my head surprised to see the girlish, antique poster bed and frills everywhere. I laid her down as lightly as I could on the soft blue bed spread. Her dark eyes were blank, though I could tell from the small shudders that raked her at every muted sob that she was indeed awake, even if she wasn't fully aware of what was happening. *For all I know, she's drugged* – but I didn't let that alone take the blame.

"It's going to be okay." I swore over the still resonating boom of the base blaring downstairs. Someone stumbled past the entrance to her room, stopping when I glared over my shoulder. "Get lost." I ordered, and by the time I had taken a step they were halfway down the stairs.

After I had made sure the room was empty and the rest of the floor was vacant, I ran down the stairs, knocking a few people over them in the process.

16

"Party's over." I said flatly, standing on the third step. No one moved, but they did yell a few things in reply. *"Get out!"* I ordered, launching myself down to the floor, not caring who got shoved in the process. That worked better. There were still people too drunk or too oblivious to know I wasn't messing around, but those who did know got their friends out one way or another, even if a few were dragged by the hood of their jackets. Half would not look at me again, the rest stared in a mixture of fear and resentment that they felt it.

I wanted to tear somebody's head completely off. I *could* have done it too. I *wanted* to do it.

"He already left." I told myself as I shut the doors, locking the dead bolts. I had a thousand plans of what I had do to him when I found him, but first I had to call her parents. That was going to be a lot of fun. I hated ratting her out, at least as far as the party went, but I was in no condition to come up with a lie convincing enough to cover up the massive mess her house was in, and there would be no cleaning it before they got home the following afternoon. Mary's – injuries – were another issue. If I left the house as it was and took her from it, there would be an even greater aftermath. Last thing she needed was for them to come home and think she was missing. At the time, calling them seemed easier.

I called her phone, finding it in that same guest room, knocked under the bed. There was no lock on it, and when I swiped it to the home screen there were four unread messages. They were from a contact listed with a < and 3. I opened them, scrolling up before I let myself read it. The first from that day was a reminder she had sent about the party – asking him to come. The last, from only three minutes prior, was from him.

Don't pretend u didnt want this –"

The phone screen cracked beneath my fingers.

I shook my head, gulping past the stone at the back of my throat. I went to most recent calls, finding her parents four lines from the top.

I tapped the number.

17

The shattered screen made the texting difficult, but I could not face the idea of calling them.

Come home. Going to ER. Not serious.

I hit send, debating how big a lie the last two words were.

I turned it to silent, slipping it into my pocket as I ran back up the stairs. When I opened the door to her room, she was sitting up, staring at me, the bruises on her arms and around her throat worse. I couldn't spare myself the torture of thinking about how those weren't the only wounds. The only thing I wanted more than to get her safe and then kill that guy, was to go back and undo that night.

"...I need to take a shower." She whispered, looking towards the door on the other side of the room. She didn't move, and even we had had spoken, it wasn't to me. I went next to her, leaning down so my face was level with hers. She stared at me for nearly forty seconds before she suddenly blinked, leaning back the smallest degree. "I need to take a shower." She repeated, but it sounded as if it was the first time she knew she had spoken it. I slowly nodded, even if I knew it was a bad idea.

I helped her up, letting her grab onto me rather than I touch her. Her detachment from her actions was only rivaled by my own, but I knew I wasn't the one in shock. She let go of me when we reached the door. I told her I would be outside if she needed me, and listened as the water turned on. The humidity of the room rose, steam seeping from beneath the door. Her breathing had remained even, for the first twenty minutes. The phone in my pocket had not vibrated once in that time, something that would have worried me had it not been a relief.

The water stopped. The curtains were drawn back. There was a shuffle of feet against tile. The door opened. She walked past me, her head down and her arms locked around her waist, the tie to her robe trailing behind her. She sat down on the corner of her bed, cradling her wrist in the palm of her opposite hand.

"Mary, I'm going to take you to the hospital, okay?"

There was no answer.

◆

Her parents sat across from me in the waiting room, a few broken fingers and cut foreheads keeping us company, witnesses to the murder her father was about to commit. He didn't trust me, and the judgment was mutual. The text I had sent was delivered at 10:37. It wasn't read until nearly an hour later, and he hadn't responded until twenty minutes after that. I hadn't expected him to charter a helicopter, but he had spent more time attempting to call and yelling at who he thought was his daughter over text than it took to drive from Tallahassee to where we were. When he'd arrived to find me the one holding her phone, and had been told by the doctor that Mary was exhibiting symptoms of Acute Stress Disorder, I had become public enemy number one. That was four hours ago.

Mary's mom was a nervous wreck. She would pace around the room, ask an unfortunate passing nurse a few questions, wring her hands, and dejectedly sit back down. I had learned that Mary's kid brother was at a sleepover, the reason for him not being there, or knowing what was going on. I figured it was best that way.

"So, how do you know my daughter?" He asked as casually as he could.

"School." My head hung in my hands, the migraine leaving me nauseous and irritable beyond reason. I had already accepted ibuprofen from a concerned nurse, before her parents had arrived and turned the entire night staff against me. It hadn't helped.

"You're a senior?"

"Sophomore."

"*College*?" He asked, shocked.

"No."

"...Tell me again what happened." He demanded, his tone disguising it at a peace offering, as if the prior eight times I had explained were utter lies. Which, in part, they were, but there were reasons to that. Sam was my problem, not theirs, or even hers anymore.

"Look, I told the doctors, I told you, I was at the party when I heard her yell, I saw she was hurt, told everyone to leave, called you, and brought her here."

"Nothing else happened?"

"No." My stomach returned to stone and fire raged in my throat.

"Well it seems rather...odd how you were the only one to help her. Why didn't one of her friends bring her?"

"Emmalyn would have been there – she is the one who has been picking up Mary from school." Her mom agreed, her tone equally panicked and pleading.

The realization hit me like a giant, almost ironic clap of thunder. They really thought *I* was the one who'd hurt her and I was trying to cover it up

"I was the only one sober enough to drive." *Even if I do feel like I'm facing a hangover worthy of an award.*

"Brad?" His voice sounded overly loud.

"*What?*" I snapped, not caring if he knew I was irritated. He wouldn't shut up.

"If she tells us anything different-"

"When she wakes up you can ask her yourself. All I did was help her get here." I regretted my decision to call them nearly as much as I regretted staying downstairs earlier that night.

Her mom spoke up, perhaps recognizing the fact I was in pain too. "Alright, we will ask her. It'll be fine. Why don't you go home? I'm sure that you parents are worried sick about where you are."

You have got to be freaking kidding me, right?

"I'm fine." I said through my teeth.

"Well, did you tell them you're here?"

"They know my number. If they want to know where I am, they'll call." *They probably already found out anyway.* The locating alarm hadn't gone off all night, which was more suspicious than if it had blared every hour on the hour.

"Thank you for helping her Brad." She whispered. My eyes widened. It was the first time either of them had something that was a demand. "It means a lot to us you know. I can't even imagine…" She choked up.

I nodded.

Steps echoed down the hall behind us, coming from her room to the waiting area. We all stood up at once.

"She is awake now if you want to see her, but take it easy. Her... fall, left her pretty shaken." The concerned nurse glanced at me, but I was at the door before she could say anything else. Mary had a brace on her shoulder and an ice pack on her forearm, above where a cast was set from her palm up. The mark on her face had faded by the time I had gotten her there. When her eyes met mine, there was still a detachment between what she saw and what was real, but at least she was seeing again. The side of her mouth twitched upwards in a faint attempt at a smile, but it fell as soon as I felt them behind me.

"Mom, Dad? *You-*"

"I texted them from your phone on the way here." I stated.

She looked between her parents and me, her warning glower landing on me. We knew exactly what everyone thought. I figured she'd told the doctors if they looked for a better excuse than whatever she'd given them, she'd file a personal infringement suit, since she was eighteen. She was smart like that; she knew how to locate and work a loophole,

21

but I wished she wouldn't have, for the doctors at least. What the nurse had said was enough for me to keep up the charade.

"Honey, are you okay? Oh my poor baby girl. Ooh-what happened sweetie?" Her mom threw up the words. She went and held Mary's hand, the one not in a cast, unable to hug her from the bruises that covered the exposed parts of her skin.

"We will protect you." He shot an accusing glance at me.

"Oh no – no I told the doctors – mom really I'm fine." She begged me with her eyes to keep my mouth shut.

"How'd this all happen?" Her father glared at me.

"I had just got out of a shower and I guess I tripped over something on the stairs. I think I was trying to ride it – the rail – like Jonny does. I don't know. I hit my head on that stupid bannister. Mom, really, I'm okay, I was just out of it for almost the whole ride. It freaked me out but docs said I don't have a concussion though, so that's good." The only flaw in her story was that it was a lie. Her expressions, her tone, her body language, all so perfect I nearly believed, and desperately wanted to. "...I'm okay now. Really. I was just frazzled, that's all. I didn't want you guys to find out about the party and when Brad said he was taking me here I just kind of snapped, I mean I know this means spring break it out. I'm really sorry – I guess karma comes fast. I shouldn't have thrown that stupid party." She rolled her eyes.

The nurse saw her dad's wheels turning. "She's on quite a bit of pain killers and needs to rest, Mr. Summers." She cut in, her voice stern. The unspoken agreement was made. If he lost it, he got kicked out.

"Can we talk about it later?" Mary faked a yawn. They nodded. "Before I pass out could you and mom go and get me some food? I'm starved." They nodded again, after looking to the nurse for approval.

"Brad would you stay?" She asked, her voice softer. Her dad was instantly on high alert, but didn't challenge her. I held the door open for them. They were not appeased my halfhearted attempt to get on their good side.

"Would you leave too?" She directed her question at the nurse.

"I don't think that's a go-"

"I know how to work the call button." She snapped, furious for a brief moment. Miffed, the nurse stuck her nose in the air, taking only enough time to give me another cautionary glower.

"You didn't...?" She asked cautiously, once we were alone. Her eyes were punched out holes, dark, tired.

"How you feeling?"

She didn't answer. I picked up a chart hanging at the end of the bed, thankful that funding and privacy were low in supply in small towns. I felt myself frown. When I finished reading, she ducted her gaze from mine, attempting to push herself higher up on the bed, wincing when her bruises proved to be too vast to allow the movement.

"Yeah well, ten bucks says you look worse than I do." She tried to cover it up, her voice still strained.

I doubt it.

"That bad huh?" I played along.

"Well are you sober?" She fought to keep the conversation off her.

"Obviously."

"You don't look it." She quipped, her eye brows dashing upwards.

I walked over to her, not willing to play her game anymore. She looked away, cowering. I lightly touched her cheek, where the mark had once been. The pretense fell, as a shadow across her face followed suit.

"Thanks...for, uh...being here, Brad." She whispered, her voice course from having to push its way past the monster

23

strangling her from the inside out. "I don't know what I would… have done without you."

"It's going to be okay." I said again. *I'll make sure of that.*

"I want to believe you." She shuddered. She leaned against my shoulder when I knelt next to her, her chin pressing into me when she looked down at her hands, the cast a horribly cheery shade of pink. "You asked what happened?"

"You don't have to say anything."

"I know. But…I need to. I really am out of it and I keep seeing it over and over and it won't stop." She shook her head, raising her palm between her eyebrows. "No – no I'm okay. I'm okay." She sighed, taking a shaking breath before she continued. "He uh…I invited him over – but I wanted to end it. I thought the party would be a distraction – something to keep things from getting…getting out of hand. He – I – I didn't…I tried to-"

"Don't." I stopped her, taking her hand in mine. "You didn't do this. *He* did. Don't tell me – don't even think about it. Do you understand? It is going to be okay. He will never hurt you again." There was a finalization to my vow that even I hadn't fully appreciated.

She hurriedly nodded, pulling one hand free to wipe her puffy red eyes. "Memory loss doesn't seem so awful."

"Listen to me, Mary. In eight weeks, when that cast is off, you will never have to remember any of this. It will all be gone. You will be fine."

"But what about you? My dad – No one saw anything? Dammit! I was so stupid! I should have never-"

"No one knows." My voice was level. My thoughts, clear. Precise. As if everything was falling into a preprogrammed plot my subconscious had spent years practicing for, every cause, consequence and variable streaming into a single, seamless flow of influence, where the universal rule of action and reaction weren't influenced by any outside intention or emotion. There was no doubt, because even without a plan, the fact I had already made up my mind to act took away any indecision. He would never hurt anyone again.

"You aren't going to tell *them*?" She squeaked.

When I didn't answer her right away she flipped out, pushing away from me, wincing as she did. "No! You can't! They'll freak out! I can't handle that!"

"I won't." I said quietly.

Maybe it was what I said, maybe it was how I said it, but if only be instinct alone she read the scheme behind my stare with twenty-ten vision.

"But, you've got something else in mind don't you?"

"As if you'd expect me to do otherwise." I muttered.

"...*Please* don't."

"He's going to pay for this."

"Brad no. It is no big deal, really. I'm...f-fine." Her words were halting, heavy.

"No. You're not. Not yet. He hurt you and he is not going to get away with it."

Her tired, confused eyes widened.

I exhaled and tried to calm down.

"Tell me where to find him." I finally stated.

"*Please* forget about it." She was begging. She might've gotten up to yell at me had she been able to.

"No."

"Why not...?"

"Why are you trying to protect him?" I struggled to keep my voice low, calm, for her sake, but the question had cornered her, because that is what she was doing, protecting him. He'd done more than scare her, and the fractured wrist would heal sooner than the worst of the damage, and no matter what her reasons were for remaining silent, silence never leads to justice. Justice was the farthest thing from my mind, but it keeps similar company with revenge.

"You won't do anything *too* stupid?" She asked cautiously.

"Just trash his car, and knock him around for a bit." I tried to make it sound as innocent as possible.

"You better not get in trouble, ok? You can't-"

"My costs are irrelevant." I said slowly, each syllable hiding the deluge of heat rushing in my blood.

"...I won't let you do that just because of me." She sighed, cowering as her memories assaulted her all over again.

"I'm supposed to sit here and do *nothing*?" I resisted the urge to yell even louder. *She can't be sane. Not that anyone would expect her to be right now...*

"Not nothing. Just be here. Stay okay? I-I can't let something happen to you."

"No."

"Why *not*?" She shook her head, her eyes glossy.

"He's not getting away with this. I'm not going to be made helpless because you're afraid of him. I'm not – I can handle him myself, and you'll never have to see his face again. What else do you expect? You won't tell the cops."

"*No*! My family couldn't, I can't." She stammered, for a moment frightened that I might even think of doing that.

"Then let me do this."

"No."

I licked my lips, preparing to switch tactics. Tears lined her eyes, her hands grasping the sheets in shaky fists. Her tan skin was pale, almost gray. She was near breaking, and as horrible a thought as it was, the edge she balanced on could tip in my favor.

"I can always find out from other people. I'm only asking your permission to give you the benefit of having a part in it. So...?" I pressed.

"I don't want you to leave." She nestled into my side, her eyelids heavier. I put my arm around her, resting it on her good shoulder, and was relieved in a way I can't describe when she didn't flinch or draw away.

"It isn't like I won't be coming back." I argued, aware of how tired she must be. She would have to give in soon.

"Promise."

"Yes."

"You still have my phone right? It's in my notes."

"Thanks."

Her dad's yet-to-shut-up voice echoed down the hall. I got up.

"Be safe Brad." She whispered, lying back down. "No stupid remember?"

"Yeah."

I left before her parents rounded the last corner. I did not even pause to notice the pieces as they fell into place. The first thing to draw me out of my schemes was on the short drive back to my house, I started to feel different, as if I had swallowed gallons of ice water. The cold sensation seeped in to every corner of my body, making my hands and legs quickly go numb. The migraine at the base of my skull and radiated down my entire spine. Every nerve in my body endured a constant throbbing.

Driving like a maniac and nearly blinded, I somehow made it home. I stumbled through the door, unable to keep my balance. I couldn't think or even see straight, much less walk.

"Brad, you feeling all right son?" Ben was standing in the hallway, holding a cup of coffee, not at all surprised. I was not surprised at that. The early morning news played in the background.

"I'm fine."

"Is Mary feeling better?"

Of course he knew where I was.

"She's fine. I'm going to bed." It was closing in on six in the morning and the indescribable, overwhelming pounding I felt intensified as I staggered to my room, using the walls to keep me upright. The frozen sensation I had known so well was replaced with a low, hideous burning in the pit of my stomach.

It grew hotter with every step I took.

I fell on the bed, burying my face in a pillow. I was suddenly so exhausted that even breathing hurt.

The sun had yet by the time I was able to clearly enough through the fog of pain to know something was wrong. I pushed my hand under my chest in a feeble attempt to get up and go back to the hospital. My arm gave way as I fell back into the sweat drenched sheets.

I drifted in and out of consciousness for what felt like days. Nightmares plagued my dreams, but when I woke up, I could never remember what they were about, only that I had desperately wanted them, and this strange, incapacitating illness, to end.

◆

I sat up slowly, expecting to be dizzy, but when the lightheadedness never came, I was relieved. The pain had vanished, crystalline clarity occupying where it once had been. I argued that maybe I had caught something in the waiting room and didn't think twice over it as a left my room. I walked out of my room into the kitchen, out of habit taking a glance at the computerized calendar on the front of the fridge.

Tuesday? I'd slept for two days. Had I not already been racing to put together the next hours, I would have cared more about what had happened in the past forty-eight.

I checked my pockets, finding her phone still in my pocket, its battery still clinging to a few percent, enough to find Sam's address in her notes. I deleted it as soon as I had it memorized, as well as his contact information and her text and call history, getting rid of the last evidence tying her to him. Then, it was time to deal with him.

Existence

I pulled up in front of a large building belonging to the community college, went over my plan again, checked the clock to make sure the majority of the students would be out for lunch, and then I walked up to the first kid I saw. It was a small college, maybe a few hundred students, so my odds of finding him were pretty good, but I didn't want to waste time.

"Do you know Sam (bastard's last name)?"

The guy's eyes widened and he scanned me over. He seemed to be amused at my question, though it wasn't funny.

"Does he owe you money or did he just hook up with the wrong guy's girl?"

My hands flexed.

"...So the latter?" His voice trailed off at my glare.

"Do you know where he is or not?"

"Hey, okay I get it, chill." He continued, a bit more serious. "That's him over there." The kid pointed to a guy wearing a red, tight fitting t-shirt and baggy black shorts, his back turned towards me as he was leaning against a mud splattered truck.

"But you didn't hear it from me ok? I don't want any trouble."

"Yeah."

I stalked over to him.

"You're Sam?" I challenged the tall, rough looking blonde. He looked like the type of guy no sane, normal sixteen year old would ever want to get in a fight with, but at the moment I wasn't very sane and I wasn't a normal sixteen year old.

"What's it to *you*?"

"I'm a friend of Mary's."

"What do you want?" He glanced to his friend behind him, the confidence in his smirk laced with a twisted sense of satisfaction so potent it made my stomach churn.

"I want you to own up to what you did."

No, I want him to pay for it.

"Man, you don't know (anything)."

"I know you hurt her."

"And you think showing up here trying to get me to (freaking) say sorry proves you're some kind of (freaking) saint? Screw you kid! Just going to (freaking) walk up like you own the whole (freaking) joint? What the (hell) does it (freaking) matter to you? Get out of my (freaking) way!" He kept going, more expletives flying.

I felt it first at the back of my throat, as if I'd swallowed fire, only I had no desire to breathe it out. It sparked at the top of my spine, coursing down to its base until every nerve in my body was an extension of its flame. Every fiber of my body was screaming at me to fight him. Then someone started chanting it, and I only then noticed the crowd of people that had gathered around us. They formed an impenetrable wall of bodies that vibrated with excitement, sensing with the accuracy all adolescents seem to inherit that there was something volatile about to happen that they wanted a piece of, and whether they partook of it or stood by didn't matter. *Great, we've got an audience. I'm not going to get my face plastered all over the web... Do I have a choice?* I did, but running was not one.

He made his choice the same moment I had mine, taking a glance to the crowd before lunging at me, his right arm swung back before flying forward with misapplied force. I moved out of the way with what felt like hours to spare. He continued to throw more and more punches, all of them going out in hazardous patterns and landing in different directions, none of them making contact with anything but air and the flash of camera phones .

"(Coward)!" he snarled. "Throw a (freaking) punch!"

I did.

I had hit him straight in the gut, the impact marked only by the sensation of my fingers molding into the sudden softness of his body. His face contorted into fear and pain before he flew over twelve feet, sliding across the turf for another four.

From the attoseconds it had taken for my brain to send the signal for my hand to close in a fist, and lasting well into the seconds passing in that aftermath, I had ceased to think. My actions were controlled by a pure, mindless rage. I went to the truck he had been leaning against and kneeled, hooking one hand under the front bumper, the other on the front axil. I shifted my weight back, and stood up, lifting it from the ground as I turned, before tossing it, sending it flying twelve yards, only to land upside down, totaled..

I came back to my senses about the time the crowd realized they weren't being punked.

What did I just do!?

By instinct, I knew to run. No one else had even moved by the time I was slamming the door to my father's car, forcing the key into the ignition and flooring the accelerator before taking my first breath since watching that truck impact the ground.

When the torrent of my confusion and fight or flight rush had passed, I realized it was storming. Bruised, pregnant, thundering clouds rolled in over the roof of my automobile. Blinding rain poured down in thick sheets. I was afraid if the visibility got any worse, I would have to pull over, but I realized that I could see fine. I knew I should have been freaking out. Problem was that I wasn't. I went over everything, the pictures and memories flying through my brain at speeds I hadn't known possible. I came up with over a hundred possible explanations for what had happened, but most were just wishful thinking. I had thrown a truck and no amount of adrenaline could explain that.

I pulled up in front of my house and quickly got out of the car, slamming the door behind me, turning back at the sound of breaking glass to see the driver window shattered. I cursed and ducted inside the house, grateful that it was unoccupied. I went to the kitchen, hoping food would settle my stomach. I caught the edge of the corner with my shoulder and felt the drywall crack. I paused at th

I felt a sharp, stinging pinch in the side of my neck.

The light around him made his features too dark to see, but I knew the stranger's face. His eyes were nearly yellow, his orange hair looking more like a ring of fire around his skull with the white glare behind him. I tried to sit up, realizing after a few long, confusing moments that I couldn't move. I glanced down, seeing the reason why. I was restrained – *Just like in my nightmares*. The only difference was that I was now held down with large wire ropes, a pair across my forearms, shins, and chest.

"How do you feel?" He sounded like I was listening to him from under water.

Nothing.

"Well I assume you wouldn't be coherent right now. There are enough tranquillizers in you to put down an elephant." He seemed amused. "But you can hear me, so we will just have to settle for that now, won't we?"

Did he say he gave me drugs? How did I get here? Where is here!?

I jerked against the wound steel ropes.

He didn't jump back, but I saw his body tighten with the instinct to.

"Don't think you can try that again, as much as I had like to let you out and see what you're really capable of, I can't do that..." He lowered his voice. "Not yet at least. I am as curious of you as you likely are of me, so let's introduce ourselves, at least in part. I'm the only person alive that's able to explain why there are dents under your fingers."

I hadn't realized I had been clutching the sides of the bed so hard I had bent it. I nodded, having already tested the strengths of the ropes and knowing I was outmatched. If he had the answers I needed, I would gladly delay my escape to hear them.

"See? I knew we could get along better than that. So, where to begin? I'll spare you all the years spent at GEMSEC and the dozen private companies I went through before…shall we say, ended up here. I was studying on how to enhance the human body's attributes when I stumbled across a- well I cannot take all the credit. I had a brilliant nanotechnologist working with me when we were able to claim any kind of success. She is gone now, but that's a story for another time. We were both deadest on the blending of our fields, and you are the proof of just how accurate out predictions were. You are also the outcome of what happens when a third party takes its turn, just enough where its defensive properties become far more...*eccentric.* The results of hers and mine programming would be much more intrusive than originally planned, and carried a much lesser chance of success, mind you.

Within a decade, it was ready."

I scowled.

"You want to know what it was, yes? The perfect blend of science and nature – and as the third party deemed, it would create the perfect weapon by erasing, diminishing, or covering the human body's main structural, physical, and emotional flaws. We only had one problem, how to make it become activated within the human frame. Nanotechnology had never been paired with genetic engineering on a level past sheep fetuses, to make it human compatible would take time. They tried everything on the variation of animals we'd been testing a prototype on. Soon after, they began the hunt for human specimens. One who was young, strong, without any genetic flaws or mental weakness, and who we believed could withstand the painful transition."

He glanced down at me for the first time.

"We found seventeen, the youngest was six, you were fifteen." He paused, expecting me to deny it. I was too drugged up to do more than blink. "We deduced a holistic approach. Nano-shells are microscopic sealed capsules that are injected through the blood stream and are carried by specific proteins to key points throughout the body. From there, our science bloomed, and we watched in awestruck wonder as its offspring came to flourish - but only on you. I cannot say I was surprised, you seemed the most headstrong, if will played any part."

The realization was painstakingly slow in coming, due to the massive amount of sedatives, but when it came, it was a tidal wave.

Those nightmares were *memories*.

"They were ecstatic until they realized that the serum had not given them the desired effects, beyond superficial physical changes and hormonal anomalies. In defeat, my superior and our investors decided to destroy all of the trial's participants and start over, which I did, except for you. You actually escaped. I'm still unsure how, but you almost burned down half our base." He chuckled. "It was quite the little task finding you again. You, *Brad,* are special. Do you like your name? It stands for 'Biological Reengineering Acceleration Devices' –the serum filled nanos you were given. To keep you safe, I placed you in a new home with two of my best employees posing as your family. It was simple enough. All I had to do was invent some accident. New kid, new town, people are so trusting these days it was almost too easy."

Nothing. No thoughts, no feelings, no fear…*Nothing*.

"I believed given time you would be able to activate the traits I had designed to go into the serum's original chemical buildup. I was pleased to hear you had adapted well to your new life, and..." he leaned next to me "...even made a new friend."

Mary. A brief flame of fear and anger ignited.

"Don't worry about her. She'll be left alone. You see, as far as my superiors know, she does not exist, and neither does your little tryst into civilization. It was my own private experiment, to see what you would do. I never would have guessed it was throwing a motor vehicle!" He laughed loudly and turned his head as he heard someone yelling in the next room. "We shall have to finish this later. ...I have got big plans for you."

The light was no longer hindered in its glare, once again the only thing I could see if I opened my eyes.

I waited for what felt like hours for the fog around my brain to dissipate. Knowing I had little time before I was drugged again, I began figuring out my escape. I wasn't scared, not even nervous. I had done it before, and this time, I knew what I was capable of, more than I believe they did. But how it ended did not matter, I was completely *numb* to the possibilities of my unbalanced fate.

I only knew one thing: I would not become their 'perfect weapon'.

It took a long hours for me to realize that I could get out of my confines if I focused on breaking the bolts of the bed and not the wire ropes. I pushed against the railings and smirked in twisted satisfaction at the sharp complaining squeal of the bending metal. Apparently, my captors had also yet to learn the true extent of my strength. I sat up and scanned the room. Nothing had changed. The walls were lined with different machinery that what I remembered from my dreams, the room was smaller, no bigger than twenty by fifteen feet. The single door could have belonged to a school, not like the military bunker vault I felt it should have been. Even so, I ran as fast as I could, my memories useless. This was not the same place I had been before.

The air was wet, sappy, like a pine forest. Not a medical prison.

There was a flight of stairs ahead of me and then I was on it, running upwards towards a door rimmed in light. I raced out of the building, pausing only long enough to turn around and see a hole in the would-be barricade belonging to the seemingly abandoned shed, no bigger than a three car garage. I didn't question why there were no guards this time, or why nothing and no one had tried to stop me, I just ran.

Dread

"Brad? What are you doing here? What's going on!? Where the heck have you been?! Why do you look like that?" She demanded, the words shrilling hissed on a single breath. She grabbed my shirt, pulling me inside, shutting the door behind her.

"I was running."

"At *two* am?"

"I need to disappear." I could have taken the time to sugar coat it, but time was something I couldn't spare. It'd been at least three hours already. I had run until I had hit the interstate, and had kept running.

"What are you talking about?" Her expression changed from surprise to fear. "What did you do?! Where have you been the last three days?!"

Days...?

"I can't explain right now –"

"Why not?" The hand not in cast went to her hip.

"Once things settle."

"What *things* Brad? Last thing I know you leave me alone in a hospital and now you're showing up here freaked and looking like you've been through hell but you won't tell me *where* you've been or *what's* going on and I'm supposed to just roll with this too?" She struggled to keep her voice down.

"I swear, when I can, I will tell you everything." I had absolutely no intention of telling her about being held prisoner by "'Dr. Evil' (lame, I know, but it first thing that I thought of while running) and company."

"You better. Keep quiet. My family is asleep." She cast a glance at the stairs, her dark eyes betraying whatever memories wounded her, before quickly turning into the dining room.

"Are you okay?" For a moment it seemed bitterly ironic, me asking her if she was ok, knowing she wasn't, and knowing I was far from it. With some underground bio-warfare company having me on their most wanted list, she wasn't the only one feeling haunted.

She didn't answer. My stomach fell when I saw the faint shadows of her remaining bruises lining her arms, regardless of the darkness and their healing, to my eyes they were blotches of ink staining her light tan skin.

"*Where* were you Brad?"

"I can't-"

"Yes, you can, you just won't and I don't understand why. Was it Sam? What *happened*?" When she turned to face me she looked skeptical, worried, and worse, she'd been crying. "Is that the reason you are running away? Did something happen?" Her voice shook in fear. Her eyes ran over me.

"Kind of..."

"Dammit, tell me! I can't take this! They won't even let me near a computer and I had no way to call you and I don't know what's going on! Why won't you tell me?!"

I was next to her before she could yell any louder.

"I will tell you, just not right now, okay?"

"I don't understand! Why can't you–"

"It's better for you to not know. You're safe now. Just trust me." As careful as I was, I could feel her cringe when my hands landed where his had once been. I immediately loosened my grip, though I couldn't bring myself to let her go, not with the way she hugged me back. A tiny glow of enraged regret and fury somehow managed to kindle on the sheet of frost covering all I was.

She eventually nodded.

"...I trust you."

She let go first, wiping her eyes.

"You really have to leave?"

"Yeah."

"Where?"

"I don't know."

"Can't I come?" She pleaded.

"No. You can't." I stammered, taken aback.

"Why not? I can come with you and we can leave this whole screwed up town behind us. Let's just go. I'm eighteen. I can't stay here!" She stomped her foot.

"Because it isn't safe." I growled. "This isn't about Sam; it has to do with what I was *before*."

"Do you remember?" She asked, shocked.

"No."

"Then I don't see why I can't come." She pouted.

"I'm not letting you get hurt again."

"You're not making any sense."

"I know. Whatever – whoever I was before is in trouble, okay? And I need to get out of here, before it catches up to me. That's all I can tell you for now."

"...You're serious." I nodded. "But you'll call me, and tell me everything? And I'll see you again, right?" I nodded. "So what? You need cash or something?" I nodded again, unable to deny the fact that 'running' wouldn't get me far enough fast enough. "Ok...stay here." She went upstairs, this time without a second thought. A handful of moments later, she returned, walking quietly down the tall steps. A black sweatshirt hung over the curve of her cast.

"Thanks." I took the small, rubber banded roll of cash from her.

"It'll get you far enough."

"I'll repay you later."

She rolled her eyes, trying to smile. "I was saving it for spring break... I owe you."

"No you don't, just don't tell *anyone* I was here." Her eyes widened with suspicion. "For your own sake, don't ask." I repeated. I studied her for a moment, looking for anything more than fear and pain and worry. They were all there, but the one I dreaded to see wasn't. There was no weakness, and because of that, I knew she would see to it we both made it through this. "...Be safe."

"Be careful, Brad."

I started towards the door.

"For my sake." She whispered.

Before I did something even more stupid than going there in the first place, I ran out, feeling her quizzical stare drilling into my back. The ice re-froze, making it easy to lose focus.

I bought a bus ticket to the farthest city my money could buy and rode the whole way in silence, glaring at the fabric of the seat in front of me long enough I half expected it to spontaneously ignite. My only plan was to hide, for however long I had to. I tried to feel, I would have settled for being cold, but I was *dead*. I had run long enough that I should have been struck with heat sickness and over exertion. I hadn't eaten in who knows how long. Or truly slept. Yet, nothing. Not the meant to be comfortable seat, not even the cramped, recirculated air bothered me, despite the woman failing to sneak a cigarette behind me. Every thought I had was influenced by the thought before it, all of them stemming off of the memories of the last week, but my present circumstance, and what was to come, were nonexistent. Nothing else could find standing. The outside world I could still see, still hear, still touch, but I could no longer *feel*. It no longer affected me.

An unwanted epiphany occurred.

It would create the perfect weapon by erasing, diminishing, or covering the human body's main structural, physical, and emotional flaws.

Did he mean that I had no sense of feeling? I tried to override that with other explanations, but it was inevitable. That numbness wasn't from shock. Or ATSD or PTSD. Or being high out of my mind on whatever drug they'd given me. It wasn't a temporary coping mechanism, or a survival tactic.

It was permanent.

◆

Obscurity

Months could have passed; I don't know how long. Time became an irrelevant and maddening force, because I could not grasp its passing, and it never seemed to end. I hunted the city's streets, searching, still lost in the caverns of my strangely detached and unpredictable mind. The world turned grey, hardening into stone, losing its warmth in sync with the disintegration of whatever shred of humanity I had held onto, all of it slowly fading into the backdrop of icy oblivion. The memories that had led me to the place I was were quickly lost in the reality of what I was becoming. Even when my own strength sought to destroy me, and everything and everyone I came close to, and my heightened senses threated to drive me insane with the constant noise, I could always count on tomorrow, and in that was my curse. It would never end. Each sunrise brought me closer to the steep, unforgiving edge of madness and each night offered the tempting chance to leap over it.

The consuming darkness was a virus, and once it penetrated, it spread, choking out the now emaciated ethics I had once held so dear, and dampening whatever waste of hope I might have clung to that there was a cure to this, that normally could one day be achieved.

I ceased to live my life and simply began to exist without noticing. Without the needs once necessary to my survival, for even the nightmares of my sleep were soon rare, I lost the desire to endure altogether. None of it mattered. Yet, I found myself walking every night, never staying in the same place longer than a few hours. It was an unconscious quest through the hordes of transparency, all of it to find meaning.

◆

I knew he couldn't see me. The black clothes I wore hid me within the shadows of the buildings surrounding us. His average appearance and unlikely apparel of a suit that looked like it had been through a wringer sent my mind through a habitual analyzing of the situation. *No one comes to this part of the city unless they are looking for trouble.* I included myself in that thought. He was no older than thirty, but the sun blotched skin on his hands and his face made him look older.

I listened closely to the faint, echoing noises, already having lost immediate interest. The drunken cursing and shouting from the red-light district a block over reminded me of my ability to still get headaches. The sound made me focus, tuning it out, trying to only pay attention to what was immediately around me. My breathing stopped when I heard what I was sure was a small *heartbeat* coming from the luggage case the man had only moment before removed from the trunk of a hurriedly retreating taxi.

I felt my mind tense and body tighten with it.

I did another assessment, this time ignoring everything on the surface. His stance said he favored his left leg. Possible weakness in the right knee. His eyes were twitchy, nervous. He was far from a trafficker. I wasn't going to be dealing with someone with experience.

He never saw me coming.

"Who-" he barely whispered the word before the realization that he had been caught quickly set in. He actually tried to *run.* I was standing in front of him before he was able to go more than a few feet, jumping down from the last steps of the fire escape. He pulled out a small gun from his coat pocket.

"Get back." He warned. His voice was all but intimidating. I tossed it out of his shaking hand with no more than a flick of my wrist. He tried to run again, this time releasing the handle of the cloth suit case and making a dash towards the direction his cab had gone. I grabbed his shoulder, spun him around, and hit him once on his forehead with my own. He blacked out, his eyes rolling to the corners of his mouth, his heart beat dropping dramatically. I felt a smirk play at the corners of my mouth. I would like to tell you it was because I was happy that I had stopped him and subsequently that I kept him from doing whatever he'd planned, but it wasn't. I liked it period, being better, being stronger. The only speck of satisfaction I had with this curse was that no one could stand in my way. I wasn't the one running now.

I stalked towards the case and pulled the zipper down. I hadn't smelled blood, and the evenness of her pulse said she was uninjured. Both amazement and fear crossed her face when the dim yellow light above us crossed it. She couldn't have been older than eight. I gently peeled the tape off of her mouth and untied her hands, some previously untouched switch in my head flipping to a different setting at the terror in her wide eyes.

"Are you hurt?" I asked. I had déjà vu and tried to not remember why.

When the realization hit her that she didn't have to fight anymore, she started to cry. I picked her up, carefully since I still hadn't mastered just how much force I could exert. She clung to me tightly, her frightened tears muddling whatever she had been trying to say. With my free hand I grabbed the man by his arm, dragging him with me. Her face was hidden in my shoulder, and she was asleep in less than a minute.

I walked the miles back to the closest police station, glaring at anyone who noticed us, not that they would have done more than just stare. Some people are infamously afraid to step up, afraid of a situation or of their perceived powerlessness in it, but whatever their reason, they became more like animals than conscious beings in the moments that most counted. If you were to go running up to someone and beg them to call 911 and they will just stare at you, and if you screamed for help they would ignore you. Give them a cold stare on the street and they will forget you after five minutes. Those happened to be that type of people.

I had tried to avoid the cops or any type of law enforcement, for good reason up until then, but if anyone could help her get back home, I had figured it would be them. I knocked on one of the side doors to the downtown headquarters, calculating just how long it would take me to bolt once they had her, and what route I would take to disappear.

An older officer holding a cup of steaming, white topped coffee and a donut opened it. The ironic nature of the situation failed to amuse either of us. He dropped the coffee in shock of what he saw. I personally would have done the same thing if it had been me staring at what appeared to be a massive figure of a man around twenty or so, wearing all black, and gloves, holding an unconscious little girl and dragging someone else behind him.

"She needs help." I stated simply. I would have set her down and run, but I wanted to make sure they knew where to find her previous captor.

"Oh my...! Sara come here! It's Lauren! Oh-my-gosh! Come in!"

I walked into the lobby and gave Lauren to one of the female officers, who had her in the back faster than the first man had been able to pick up his jaw from the ground.

I didn't let go of the man, who had yet to stir.

"I found her in his suitcase." I dropped him, his torso hitting the ground with a resonating thud. Two of the officers came forward and picked him up, dragging him down another hallway. Someone made a call for a medic.

The officer who had opened the door made call on his radio, then turned to me.

"Sir, I had like to have an explanation for you having Lauren and bringing her here like you did." He was attempting to stay calm, the sweat on his forehead and the rush of adrenaline lacing the air giving him away.

"Right time, right place. Bad luck on the perv's part."

"I've called her parents; we're sending a patrol car to pick them up. They'll be here in a few minutes." The round faced female officer, Sara, had reinterred. She glanced over at me then at another man who had positioned himself to my right.

The exits were blocked off.

"What do I do about him?" She tilted her head towards my general direction. My heightened senses were coming in handy for once.

"He stays. Book him as a witness." He looked at me, "You will stay here until we get this all on paper, yes?"

"You can try." I wanted them to know that I wasn't easily held captive anymore. He cocked his head. "If you want me to stick around its going to take more than a guard dog." The guard dog stiffened, and stalked over, cuffing my hands behind me, almost trying to get me to resist while his body reeked of instinctual fear his mind would never admit to. The other two protested his extremism, but they kept hands by their holsters.

The cold metal stung my wrists.

He retreated a foot back, pretending to get something off the counter behind him.

I flexed my hands, staring at the one who seemed to be in charge. The handcuffs cracked, landing in a pile of clinking metal at my feet. I smirked. It wasn't the first time I had done that.

"You *broke*-"

"I can do a lot more than that."

There was a bang when the back door swung open, two officers dragging the kicking and screaming kidnapper into one of the holding cells. When the belligerent man saw me he fell perfectly still. Once the door shut behind him, the cops turned back to me, just as I had been about to run.

"I guess I can't book you on manslaughter."

"If I had wanted him dead, he would be."

"…Understood. I'm Lieutenant Jim Locker. I want to thank you for finding Lauren. She went missing yesterday night – and from what I understand SVU didn't have any leads. I can't imagine what could- Well she is safe, thanks to you. You'll still have to be questioned of course, but we won't make things more difficult than they need to be.."

My only thoughts were how to get out without getting tazerred. I didn't know if I would feel that and didn't plan on finding out.

"I mean it, son."

I stiffened. The last person to call me that was a stranger who I believed to be my father against every reason I had subconsciously made against it. And it was a reminder. A reminder of the lie I had lived, of what had gone on within that lie, and how it had ended. A reminder that no matter what, I was literally wired to be a killer.

"If you ever need anything, once this all is settled I mean. You look like you could use a decent meal." He handed me a small, white card with his address written on it. When I didn't accept, he placed in on the corner of a desk that stood close by.

I didn't like reminders.

"Her parents are here." Another, younger policewoman came in, followed by a couple who clung to each other, both of them dismissing me the instant Lauren came running from the back, leaping into their opened arms with shouts of excitement to pair with her parent's laughter. I tried to use the reunion as a way to sneak out. The police knew I would, widening their stances in the doorways, hands conspicuously closing around the handles of their weapons.

Her face between her parent's chests, I heard her say, "You saved me, like a superhero." I doubted anyone else had noticed.

48

I ran out of the closest door, pushing the cop blocking it out of my way. I heard him yell out at me, and the sound of a dozen tromping footsteps followed. Leaping up to the fire escape twelve feet above me, I crossed three blocks jumping from ledge to ledge until I slowed down, looking for a place to hide out until the streets – and even more so – my thoughts cleared.

It hadn't been an explosive epiphany, but a quiet one, with no massive change, only the realization of how it could all be rearranged. A little girl had provided me the answer. I was made to be a weapon, to kill and control people, to be a tool, used for no more than the will of whoever welded me, or to whatever whim possessed me. In all, I knew I had been made to fight wars, to *win* wars, and I knew that still held true, because no amount of optimism or self-acceptance could override physical and mental mechanical and chemical programming. But, the war I knew I had to win was the one within me. I knew what I had to do in order to save this last fiber of mortality that had escaped from being obliterated.

Become a "superhero."

Give or take.

Fallen

I cursed when the man's partner pulled out a handgun, highlighted by the single ray of streetlamp seeping in above the door. I judged the distance between us. One stood five feet in front of me; the other was advancing from behind, his racing breath hinted with the snickering laughter of impending victory. I heard the pocketknife click into place, the action almost simultaneous with cocking of the loaded pistol. I did the analysis without thinking. My strength was not the issue. I could easily overcome them. It would take me all of one second to spin around, launch myself at the second fugitive, relieve him of his knife, and knock him out, another half a second to throw the switchblade at the first one, with any luck severing his fingers, making his aim less than perfect. I debated going for the gun holder first, but one little misstep, one wrong judgment on his likely reaction time, and I would be shanked at the least.

At worst, dead.

Death wasn't something I looked for, though I thought about it often. It was hard not to, when so many lay lifeless around me. Not at my doing. It was the one thing I reminded myself when questions of my fake sense of morality were raised. I was too late sometimes, and even that, of all things, as horrible and painful it should have been, failed to bring a rise from me. It was just a variable, a nameless component in the blood stained statistics that made up the underbelly of the world that I called home.

I had long before forgotten to want to be shocked when situations like these did not faze me. In the first few weeks of hiding in the city I had looked for the thrill of the chase, hoping that if I came close to death, if I put myself in the way of what should have been terrorizing enough then the wall between my consciousness and the empty void of what was presumably once my empathy would crack, and something, an emotion, an action done of compassion, some sign of my shredded humanity would eventually break through. I had gone as desperate as jumping off a building, savoring the artificial freedom of the five story free fall. Yet when I opened my eyes, the only thing that had changed was the sky, tinted yellow with the coming sunrise. Mostly uninjured, it dawned on me. Pain is a reward, a reminder that we are still alive, a fuel to find something better, and an honor I hadn't earned.

When those weeks had passed, so did that slight reason to hope. If you live long enough in the dark your eyes will adjust to it, along with the rest of you. The idea of an escape was no longer imagined. The thought that perhaps one day I would not have to force myself to move or act was forgotten. I was doomed to this. But a remedy, to feel a single emotion, for a thought to be more than an observation, for my anger to be directed at more than myself, for hate or fear or even the slightest taste of joy to at least be able to be faked... The idea such a thing as that could exist was all that kept me going. Even if I could not heal myself, there had to be something that could.

I was brought back to reality when the gun shifted, taking aim at my chest.

Let's get it over with. I shifted my weight to the balls of my feet, preparing to lunge.

Gold light cascaded down the once dark warehouse walls. I and the 'transporters' dropped to the floor, blinded by the overwhelming brilliance.

No sirens.

It wasn't a spotlight.

No static of radio signals.

It wasn't a sting operation either.

51

I listened harder, my breathing, theirs, a cockroach scurrying back into hiding, and a heavy thudding – louder and more powerful than anything alive could make – filled the air. It was steady, until a helicopter or a plane.

Drones? DEA has drones now?

I forced myself to my knees, squinting in the glare. A women's silhouette was made clear through the gold haze. The outline of her eyes, a thin black void surrounding each of their identical almond like shapes, held me and my thoughts in place.

◆

Everyone has been given the Gift of Life...
The choice of its Path is yours to make...

The pure ecstasy coursing through me caused the intensifying smolder underneath my skin to grow ever brighter. The learned-habit of inhaling the atmosphere around me caught in the midst of my all-consuming-heat-light-joy.

I lessened the frequency of light and energy, recalling their sensitivity to my radiation. I did not want to injure them. I placed my hands against the two, pulling their power into me. They collapsed, the electrical pulses down their bone-sheltered-spines lessening against the force of my own. I smiled in shaded-dark gratification. I had not forgotten all of my instruction, and he had been truth-spoken, it would work on humans too.

I looked over at the human-man half raised from the ground. Immediately I averted my gaze, for he was staring at me with such disbelief-amazement that I questioned-doubted again my reasons for this display. His life-light was that of one prepared to fight-face-danger and remained so for longer than I believed it should or *could* have. Hesitation clouded my consciousness, reminding me of every warning. Such a

52

variance from the laws-of-the-race was a condition I had not prepared for, even when I had felt the variation in his power some measure of this planet's concept of time before.

"Are you well?"

He gravely contracted the collagenous-muscle-fibers in his neck, his head dipping downwards in what I recalled was a sign of agreement.

"What do they call you?"

His energies were focused, as if distraction was impossible, yet he glanced down at the half-lit weapon one of the other beings dropped when he had fallen. I dared to have met his eyes, cold, they were beautiful in a strange-unreal way.

"Black Dagger."

I found myself mimicking the facial movements they used to express amusement. "I am called Stargazer." I told him, knowing how well the term fit me and glad to say it, to know myself once more.

"How're you doing that-?" He looked down at the dusty-grey floor. I had not noticed that I was making myself an opposing force against the earthen-ground. It explained the sense of floating.

"Oh." I stammered through the catch in my power. I ceased the release of power below me, its absence making my physical form succumb to gravity. In the midst of my unbalance I noticed that he was about five inches taller than me and twice as broad. I let my mind's sight trace him, judging his reaction. The levels of power, both kinetic and potential, remained unchanged, the steroid and protein based chemicals rushing through the eons of his veins, though already hundreds of times higher than others of his kind, were equally stable.

"What are you?" He asked, his voice low. It was not the responses they called fear or curiosity that lead to this question. As I looked, I saw nothing had led to it, for his internal modus had not altered once.

"You would call me an 'alien'" I said quietly, ducking my eyes in the-manner-I'd-gleaned-from-human's-minds. I laughed within my thoughts at the absurdity of having to stare at the ground, as if I could not see him perfectly without the aid of what he would see to be eyes. But, this was what humans did when revealing themselves, as I had in using such a term to describe what I was, as absurd as it was to assume planets were boundaries. I had learned the term in a confusing meeting with a group who claimed my markings were a 'costume.' In the wake of the encounter, I learned to make myself appear as human as I could, studying thousands to master reactions that would be expected of me. Such I practiced then.

"...Explains a lot." The corners of his grimace lifted just slightly. The sudden shift in his tone was confusing, but I smiled in return.

"You believe me then?"

"You're not human, so I don't see a point in disbelief. And I'm alive, so coming in peace applies, I'm assuming."

"You are not far from the truth, Black Dagger."

"You're glowing."

"My surface reacts to my energy." I explained in simplest terms. I was surprised that he didn't seem more disturbed. *He must be used to the "unnatural"...The imbedded codes his body runs by are organic, but not entirely...* The evidence was so blatantly obvious I almost overlooked it, but the reality was sure, he was by no means just any mortal man. I had allowed my power to brush against over a million of these beings, and not one had help my attention for more than a few moments, until his existence became known. He was so drawing that it startled-frightened me, my response so purely-human it was nearly incapable of belief. I had never felt that before, in this world or the galaxies I called home. It was the strangest thing I had ever sensed, but stranger still I did not run or counter it. Greater than my nature was a hunger, a curiosity to test myself and defy all reason-caution for the sake of knowing what none dared to have asked.

"So that's what I heard…Did you kill them?" He directed his stone-onyx eyes over to his prey. Garnet-hued unrest still clung to the edges of his power, but its source remained in the shadows, drowned out by the unmoving grey that surrounded him.

"No. No, I would never take life." I was quick to defend myself, though in my haste I forgot that this race used inflections in the tone of voice rather than the shade of another's aura to determine such emotions, leaving it as a flat declaration. He seemed to not notice.

"Could you have?"

It struck me as anomalous that he had failed to ask me why my presence was, and why I had come to his aid, instead seeking such an answer as that.

"…No more than you would have been able to. I merely absorbed enough of their body's active-kinetic-energy that they fell asleep. They shall wake up, given enough time."

"No point in waiting for that. I'll drop them off to the cops." He lifted his shoulders a hair's breath, flicking his gaze over me, his thoughts stalling in preparation for my reply.

"How do you plan on transporting them there, if I may ask you?"

"Walk."

This is madness, I told myself, even as another part of my entity argued against it. I grabbed a long piece of blended-steel-metal off the ground. I put enough of my energy into it that it glowed slightly and laid the men on top, magnetizing them to it. He watched without response. It was something I had grown used to with the few humans I had encountered, but his was the only one to affect me.

"Do you want to follow, or would you rather wait here?"

"I'm not patient." His assessment was of blatant observance.

I could have told him that if I could circle the Earth before he could notice that I had departed, but I wanted him to come with me. No - I wanted to go with *him*.

"This is giving off the energy I gave it so it may fly over the earth. I could make one for you; however you shall be safer if you hold on to me."

A- No, Stargazer *you have finally lost your intellect. Vivimerea have mercy.*

"Come with me now." I held out my hand. He was so skeptical that I grabbed his, not giving him the option to say no. We flew out the warehouse's wide-wooden doors. I waited until we were just over the city before I leveled out my flight path. Black Dagger was holding on tightly on to my arms with the strength that would break a lesser being. I had never become conscious of my touchable nature in the manner I was in that moment. It was not his body that had drawn me into this vastly over-populated-power-bleach place, but it was what held me there.

However surprised he was, he had not been frightened. *...You* are *different*

"What in the world?" He whispered coarsely. I smiled. I was not of his world; the ironic statement had been amusing. The city lights beneath me formed hazardous patterns as I flew past them. I looked down at the millions of energies and felt the world turning beneath us.

"What do you think?" I slowed my speed so he would be able to breathe well enough to answer. The fact I asked versus simply seeing was another silent oddity.

"How can you do this?"

Once more, I tried to simplify what I had done. "I push the energy fields that surround us beneath me in order to fly this slowly. Otherwise, I would put off my own waves, and go much, much faster than this, though I wouldn't try that carrying a human. You could get hurt if we were to crash or collide, for I am unfamiliar with your hazardous-crowded-skies."

Acuity

"I'm not entirely human." Despite the accepted truth, it stabbed at my core to hear myself verbalize it, even *her,* who most obviously wasn't one at all, a fact I reminded myself was meant to alarm me. Yet my only response was to what I was, not what she was. I had recited it innumerable times in my head, but... *To hear myself say it makes it all too real.* I looked down at Stargazer, a name I assumed held about as much legality as the one I had chosen minutes before.

A pane of her long, slightly wavy copper tresses hid her face. She seemed to be ignoring me.

"I will not let go of you." As if I intended to a few hundred feet above a solid concrete jungle, or in general.

"I will not put you in danger." She said. Her was voice all *but* unyielding.

"I won't get hurt."

She shook her head slightly, her hair formed rolling waves of metallic strands. In desperation for a thrill, I heard myself say, "Please?"

She turned her head and smiled slyly. She had *stars* in her eyes; bronze, eight pointed stars surrounded by perfect gold coins, no irises were present.

"Very well, but recall that you requested this." Heated air rushed up at me from every possible direction. Walls of light surrounded me. They flickered with increasing frequency until everything became a vague drum of expanding white and gold.

"How fast are we going?" I yelled, I think. I could barely hear myself over the roar in and around my head.

"What you would call, nine hundred miles per hour." She was not yelling, but I could still hear her smooth voice perfectly over the thudding air. The atmosphere stopped suddenly and everything became normal again, depending on how I chose to define normal. We hovered about fifty feet above a building, descending slowly. "You're not hurt?" She sounded worried.

I shook my head. It hadn't cracked the wall, but it had made me feel the rush, and that alone left me breathless.

"Forgive me, but I've never flown a human before." She seemed to be self-conscious. With how tightly I held on to her, I didn't doubt it.

"Not completely human." I reminded. She landed on a roof, I couldn't tell which one. I let go of her and went, very unsteadily, to sit down against one of the cement walls surrounding the edges. She sat down next to me, and even though I sensed that was probably the first time she had ever done so, she executed the thoroughly human action flawlessly, her knees under her, hands in her lap. I could feel her drilling gold eyes against my chest, and reason spoke that she saw more than a black shirt.

"Explain."

"What?"

"How you are 'not human.' I know of many forms of life, but you say that you are not what I know that you indeed are, Black Dagger."

"I -" I decided to show her first. I had never talked about the origin of my abilities. I tried very hard to avoid even thinking about them. It was easier to pretend they just were, that I just was, that I had manifested out of the dry, recycled air in that Greyhound bus without a tie to the world.

I picked up a metal, solid pipe that was lying on the next to me and bent it, then crushed each of the sections, one by one, between my pointer finger and my thumb. I tuned down my hearing so the sound wouldn't leave me with a migraine.

She watched with wide, shimmery-eyed interest, but no fear.

"I have never found something I can't break, or at least bend. I can apparently go flying at nine hundred miles per hour, and I've never once felt any large amount of pain...recently anyway. When I get hurt, what should take months to heal takes about a week. I've jumped off buildings, gone without sleep for a week, and gone without food for even longer." I flexed my hands, admitting how stupid that must sound to her. I had explained how I did what I did, but not why, and she seemed to be waiting for the whole truth. "...I am everything that I fight against, what I look for in others, that lack of humanity, is what I battle within myself. The only way I win is if they lose."

I rightfully expected her to look scared. She should have run – she should have left me there; she should have done anything except what she did. The tips of her fingers brushed the back of my free hand, electric shocks running up my arm. Her eyes were soft; the stars pulsed, reaching past the gold. Her hand reached for the metal. It instantly melted between her fingers, pooling on the roof, leaving only a small, white-hot glowing puddle in the palm of her hand.

I blinked when she shook it off as easily as if it had been water.

"Do you think yourself alone in that battle, Black Dagger?" She asked in a light tone. Her lined eyes met mine again and she smiled faintly. A question she would not ask burned in her angelically carved features.

"Forget it." I muttered, looking away. *If the things I can do don't upset her, fine, good actually.* I didn't hold as much hope in that same reaction should she learn *why* I could do them.

My mind blanked when she leaned over to me, her face only a handful of inches from mine, so close that I could feel the intense heat she radiated. It hit my skin in waves, each more noticeable than the last. *Heat.* It was then that I saw I was feeling, that heat, and even though it wasn't much, it instantly made me want more. More proof that I was alive – and not simply existing inside this seeming indestructible shell. More of the heat. More of her.

"Will it be easier for you if you *showed* me?" She placed a burning hand on my exposed forearm, fingers locking into my skin in a compelling hold. I gulped. Needless to say I was still a teenage guy, her, the most beautiful, stunning woman I had ever seen, and somehow I had *dismissed* it a second later. The rush of being this close to her was replaced with a different sort of instinctual response.

Something was off.

I'd long since realized could sense a threat. Everything in me screamed to throw her off, to grab her shoulders and force her down, rendering her theoretically helpless under my weight. I could see it, see her beneath me, her waiflike features contorted shock, hands locked into fists as she powerlessly resisted, golden chest heaving... The idea of trying to capture her in all her obvious power and breathtaking brilliance was both enticing and, I suddenly mused, almost terrifying.

But she looked as if she was *worried*. The flowing ocher gold of her black lined eyes pressed into me, as if she saw more than I did when I found the courage to look in the mirror.

"How-"

"Close your eyes." She whispered, and I found they had shut before she'd finished speaking, without any direction on my part. "Focus on what you are trying to say. Do not be afraid of what you may feel, this is what it means for me to know you." A wealth of heat passed over me when she moved in closer.

I cringed as the repulsive memories filled my previously shady mind. I watched with my mind's eye as they flipped through themselves, too fast for me to recognize but a few. I saw enough to know she, somehow, had instantaneously seen all. They stopped moving only a few days before the present.

I opened my eyes. Hers stared back.

"I know you now."

She retreated a foot back. Her voice was slow and thoughtful at her next words.

"You were reluctant to show me how you became the way you were, and I can comprehend why, You have strengths beyond your ability of comprehension and you decided to not use them selfishly, but for the good of your kind, of your home. You took vengeance for those who were powerless. You defied those who claimed to know you. You fled when they dared interfere with your destiny. ...You're your own path chooser." By the end, she was smiling. I couldn't understand how seeing what she saw could make her smile. Or glow for that matter. "In many of those we are the same Black Dagger." She whispered happily.

"*You* weren't created in a lab."

"Neither were you. Though it is true your very make up has been altered, you were *created* by means of a process that even I have yet to fully grasp, a process that should be..." She searched for words. "Impossible? ...And simply because I wasn't created to be as I am now, doesn't imply I wasn't well trained to be what I am. Who we are was not altered by means of what you call science or even instruction"

"Who trained you? For what?"

She paused, if only for a moment, her body becoming utterly motionless. "Someone who I trusted, before I realized that my path could no longer follow his, for whatever I choose to do with the knowledge and power. Same as you."

"So you think. Mine was a straight ticket to hell." Why I felt safe with her knowing all that she knew, I understood. I wasn't the only one with a secret that could get themselves killed, or worse. Even Dr. Evil would trade in a hundred 'Perfect weapons' for the chance to get to her. Knowing I had something – *someone* – who he wanted, even if he knew nothing of her, gave me an odd sense of pleasure.

"So I know." She corrected – her voice firmer. "We are all responsible for our own choices. You chose to do the only thing that seemed to be logical to you, to run, and it was that choice that lead you here. I chose to leave my place of origin in the universe, which lead me here. The actions we have taken are no longer weighted against our respective pasts, because that were chosen in the moment of the action. By this alone, can you judge whether or not what you have done is justified. But these are words that must be learned." She abruptly stood, flowing to her feet. "Do you have a position of habitual dwelling?"

"No." I admitted. I couldn't remember the last time I had slept in a real bed either.

"Does not matter, do you wish to fly with me again or can we walk?" She looked at me, her eyes calculating.

"Walk." I said, admitting that my head still spun. She smiled. In a flash of light, she was at the building's edge. *Wouldn't my memories have told her my jumping limit?* I thought, even as I walked over and at the much too far away ground. Her hand closed around mine. And she leapt off.

It took me a very long and harrowing millisecond to see that she combated gravity with enough force to soften our landing.

"For one without fear, you seem to worry a lot." She laughed, soundlessly touching the pavement. Her hair settled around her, framing her face perfectly. Normally, I would have argued that worry and awareness were two different things, but not with the way she laughed. I could only smirk. She grinned back and began walking.

I glanced at her between steps. If I looked away for too long she'd disappear, because she shouldn't existed. Every fiber in my altered brain, a brain that sought only to find reason and ways to overcome the world, knew she was without reason and not of the world to begin with. And even if she was in fact real, and I suddenly hated myself for this, she should have been living in someone else's dream, not my nightmare.

"Have you done that before, look at people's minds?"

"It is what taught me how to behave here, what was expected of someone under the assumption to be human. Every word or motion I make is a mirror to what I have seen. …What happened to the female at the beginning of your memories?" She whispered a few minutes later, her voice deeper than before. I almost wished I had lost step.

"More than I like to remember." I said, explaining why that had been hazy. I had gone long enough without reliving it that it must have sunken deeper than the rest. She slowly nodded.

"Does that happen…often?"

"Unfortunately."

A low mutter escaped her lips, the language escaping me. "…What are more acceptable customs then?" She hurriedly changed the subject, meeting my eyes.

"I wouldn't know."

"But I only trust you to answer." She said, the sudden confusion of her voice drawing what was left my attention. "It seems this kind each has their own interpretation of light and dark, and it would be my honor-privilege to learn yours."

Like that pipe, I melted. I did not know it then, because it was only logic she had asked for, and it was all I had to give. I told her everything I could think of. Her quiet reserve and extraordinary outlook on life was so…*new*. She was beautiful in a way her body betrayed her for. As much as my eyes wanted to absorb her appearance and marvel at her presence, my ears soaked up her replying words even more so. She didn't look with any preference, but would see for what was, much like I did, except she would see a layer of natural sugar coating on it. And for once, that didn't irritate me. Her reasoning was sounder than even my own, even if I refused to admit it at the time. I would 'put up with' the lecture-that-wasn't-meant-to-be-a-lecture if that meant she'd stay longer. I didn't like the reality that the moment she left, things would fall back into their places. She'd take her heat and her light with her.

I had not taken my gaze off of her, but out of habit I knew exactly where we were and who was around us. A cop car's siren was four blocks behind us, a crying baby in the building to my left, every sound, smell, and appearance was cataloged and judged by its potential to be threat. The few out on the streets made quick notice of her, and even quicker notice of me, but even then I was eager to get out of sight.

She eventually led me to a small motel in an older part of the city. She stopped by a bush near the entrance and placed her hands against it. I thought my mind was playing tricks on me when it *disintegrated* under her hands, and was replaced by a lump of what appeared to be fabric. She put on the brownish-green, long sleeved dress to cover her gold, glowing skin.

We walked through the front door. The first thing I noticed was the darkness. A balding man sat on a small chair behind a bared off section of the dingy room that hadn't seen fresh air in a decade. He jumped up at our unexpected entry. He stared over his blood shot, alcohol puffed cheeks at her and then glanced at me.

I wonder if she has any idea how humans see her?

"Uh, what can Ah do yaw' for?" I didn't like the way he only addressed her, even though I didn't blame him. *How is it I already act like I hold some kind of claim in how he watches her?*

"We need two of your rooms." She had darkened her tone to match her well-portrayed character.

"Two hours?" He glanced at me again.

I wasn't fond of the conclusion he'd jumped to.

"Two rooms."

"Well how long do ya'll plan on staying cause' Ah gotta' bunch a people coming in here soon and Ah don't know if my regular rate will end up having to go up yaw' know 'cause a room availability and all'a that." He was a bad liar, and I heard his heart rate go up. Not that I had relied on the last part alone.

I was going to say something, but she stopped me with a quick, stern glace. She stepped closer to the barricaded counter top and held out her hand. She was holding a perfect sphere of …*Gold?*

"Will this suffice for the night?" She asked. The man balked. We both had no idea who – or what for that matter – we were gawking at.

"Uh…Look mah'issy, Ah don't wantta any trouble ah'right? Ah gotta' good gig going on here and Ah don't want the fuzz and all to'a come snoopin' ah'round…" He gulped, eyes darting towards me, before inevitably falling back on her. Except now, they were worried. "Da' streets ain't gotta rep for being too nice to someone so purty…Maybe you should just go on'a home. Your parents are sh-urely worried by now gurl."

I blanked. She did look young, but not *that* young. But I was biased, and I fully admit it.

I found myself hatefully agreeing with him. No good could come out of her staying with me. What small amounts of control I did have slipped easy, and she was far too precious to be allowed anywhere near me, or that place. *And maybe this planet in general.*

"No trouble is intended nor anticipated. I can take care of myself, don't you fret." She handed the sizable gold piece to him, flashing a dazzling smile. It would have won me over. I saw him debating a few seconds…accept a fortune and give us rooms or say no and miss out on enough cash to buy a yacht.

"Well'a, I guess, ya'll can take rooms seven and ten." He winked. I glared.

"Thank you."

Luminescence

I waited till we were out of the operator's earshot before I spoke. "*Where* did you get *gold*?"

"I made it." She opened one of the rooms and strode in, leaving me in a warm and honey scented trail of confusion. "I am apologetic for the condition of the place, but no other would have accepted my payment. I wish to remain as anonymous as possible, for the present time, as I will assume you also desire on the account of your pursuers? He wouldn't dare report us, fearing his reward be taken in as means of…evidence is the word, yes?" I nodded. She took my stark silence as a demand for answers. She hadn't been far off. "My people have done it before. We have even made our homes here out of those materials. We have a passion for objects that make their own light and we surround ourselves with them as much as we possibly can, Black Dagger. We made our tangibility from such things." Her voice was guarded.

She stood a couple feet in front of me, but the space didn't change the heat I could still feel coming from her, neither did it bury my desire for more of it.

"This" She raised her hand in the air, curling her thin fingers, keeping her dim eyes down. Her copper tinted nails flashed in the low, dust scattered lighting. "Gold. Nothing else. Even what I feel, I feel first with my mind. Then my mind tells this body what it should feel, so quickly sometimes it is easy to forget the two are separated. Nothing I am will change. What you see, what you felt, it is only a mask."

"*How?*"

She glanced up at me, confusion in her cinnamon tinted eyes.

"I do not know. We needed substance to become physical in nature; the ground on which you walk offered it. So we took it. When it became a part of who we are, we stayed here, for a time at least. The place known to your legends as 'El Dorado' was the last of our Earthly dwellings."

"What?"

My habit of one-word sentences had never been questions, before her.

"My...lineages built it, the "city of gold" as it is now called. They would visit the Earth until the shrinking world became too hazardous, when rather than being worshiped as gods or made rulers, they were hunted. ...We consider all life sacred and to remain they would have to protect themselves, in the process the likely killing of humans. So they left." She explained.

"Aliens *did* build the pyramids." I frowned at how I was unable to appreciate the obvious awesomeness of this. *Only a mask...* I repeated in my thoughts, surprised at how clearly she saw not herself, but at the way she'd so plainly stated *me*.

She paused, her expression betraying the fact she was raking a brain for the reference, and it wasn't necessarily hers she was searching.

"...No."

"Why though?"

"Build a dwelling here?" She asked perceptively. I nodded. "They had some things in common with humans. Energy, we are made of it, so are you to a small percentage. That made them able to get along well enough to support a bond, though actual bonding was prohibited." She added. "Your race had things my people wanted, things they traded their power, essence, and energy for."

"Are there others? Or are you alone?"

There was little pertinence to how I rightfully expected him to react; there was never true change to his energy-light-life. Where there should be shock, fear, even awe, there remained only acceptance. A strange graying fog dulled even that small spark, to the point where had I not witnessed his excitement-aliveness during our flight, I would have thought his body inept of change.

I was lost in thought over how this man, this *human*, could get me to answer all I had.

"I am the first to return in four hundred years."

"Why did you come?"

I could sense how he'd been building up to that question. I studied his energy, and then met his coal-stone-onyx eyes. The force they gave was deep. Too deep, as if he could already see through me.

Except such things are impossible, are they not? The old lesson resonated in my mind. *"They hold little perceptiveness Child...They're thoughts and wills are weak. Their eyes are blind to the hearts and minds of others, and are shaded from ever perceiving the ultimate truths. They live their short lives in search of a meaning they cannot find in their days, a meaning that escapes a great number. Even those who claim to see more than others, those who have been given insight we as a race once shared conversation with, often fall from their place back into the droning hordes that continue to suffocate the smallest light of wisdom within them by the fog of senseless wandering of their existences. There is rarely a soul willing to admit its subjection and submission to the fact all things are not as what many see them to be."*

...Have I been taught ancient lies?

"Stargazer." He said quietly, judging my vacant expression.

I quickly translated my thoughts to words he might understand.

"I believed that the lives I could save here would mean more than what I could have done at my former home. There was nothing there. I am a 'princess' if you will...Though it isn't in the same sense that the word is used here. We give the title by what our energy is and how it relates to the others of our kind, by what my formers were once called. What my starters did in coming here, in hopes of living among the humans, among your kind, is seen as treason now. For me to seek to right what became of their original time here, I would have to be cut off from the rest of my kind. Our laws change slowly, but they do change. And I defied them. The elders held no power over me, something they hated deeply, because they could not force me to stay. In that I have chosen to banish myself." His eyes widened. His lips formed soundless words. "Please do not mention what I have spoken any further. I have accepted my choice." He nodded. "Thank you."

"You won't show me?" He cocked one eyebrow, the question lying deeper than his words.

"No."

"My mind isn't the greatest thing to hang out in." He smirked, crossing his arms.

"There are chapters of my past that are not privy to any but the one who witnessed them with me, and for me to show you these things would put your life at risk. It is not your consciousness that is dangerous, but my own."

"...Will you stay here-on earth?"

"I will remain here." I assured him, the softly spoken vow hiding the mountain of untainted conviction. I was not going back

"Good." He said, but I could not decipher more from his words, body, or mind.

"You should sleep now Black Dagger." I murmured, recalling the race's necessity for unconsciousness, and his own lack of it.

"Will you still be here in the morning?"

70

"I shall."

A nightmare unlike any other before it tore unmercifully at my persecuted mind. I was trying to fight off what I could not see, and escape what did not exist. People surrounded me. I was frantic; no one else was seeing what I was or feeling my fear. They were as shadows, with blank eyes, deaf to my shouts for them to flee the dark mass coming towards us. Then the crowds disappeared, but the terror remained, and no matter how hard I fought or how fast I ran, it won.

Warm, golden honey washed over my thoughts and the nightmare was quickly dissolved into nothingness. A soft voice filled my newly freed mind. "Sleep peacefully" it said. I listened to its gentle order.

I woke up slowly, in my ease forgetting that this would have been the first time I had not bolted into consciousness with the fierceness of a gunshot going off in my head. Sunlight filtered through the cloth window shades and brilliantly highlighted the millions of minuscule dust pieces floating about the room. Of all the trouble I had gotten in and the many things I had broken when learning how to control the side effects of my altered DNA, the one perk I enjoyed was being able to see things clearer, in both ways. It made the world ugly, stripping away any forgiving masks, and made me ugly towards it, but what little beauty I found, most of it discovered the night before, I treasured more dearly because of it.

I rolled over and paused in all consuming marvel. I had never seen her in the light.

An involuntary smile spread across my face.

Her copper hair cascaded far past her waist, a slight wave at the end. Her hands were folded in her lap, and a small, caramel smile adorned her face. Her eyes were bright, glowing. When I finally let my gaze fall from her face, I saw she was floating just a few inches above the foot of my bed.

"Good morning." she said softly. She must have seen my surprise. "I beg your pardon for the intrusion, but you were giving off so much negative energy last night and I was obligated to make sure you were well."

"That was *you*?"

She smiled.

"Thank you." *I wish she'd been around last year. -Not only for the nightmares either.*

"You're welcome."

I got up and walked towards the small table that sat in the corner of the room, more or less clueless as to what to say. I knew I was supposed to have questions, but I did not ask them, not from lack of a desire for answers, but for the fact that none of the answers I could hope to get from her mattered to me. She was still there, she wasn't some spy sent to find me, and she had said she would stay. These were the cornerstones of the triangle she sat in the center of, each of them a support to everything about her I understood.

Which I realized was very little to begin with.

I stared at the air beneath her. That would take some getting used to.

His rise in energy was unanticipated, he'd not slept long for a human, but he said that he was different than the others, the unmistakable evidence of that I was then learning quickly.

"What is it you are doing?"

He was sitting on top of a flat, chipped carbon-plant surface that was held up two feet off the ground by matching wooden-built-chipped rectangular rods. I had assumed it was a humans' 'table', but he had been sitting on it.

"Today? First get breakfast, after, I don't know. I'm not used to company."

"I want to help you." I posed, knowing how easily he could not let me. I could persuade him, I knew that well, but I sincerely wanted him to want me without the ploys I once

72

practiced. My path had crossed his for a reason, and I would do anything to find out *why*.

"Do what?"

"What you were doing last night, facilitating the actions to keep your kind safe." I had planned that conversation, the words and expressions I would use rehearsed over a hundred times within my thoughts, yet every idea I had vanished the second I had opened what he saw as my mouth to speak.

"You want to *help* me?"

"…Let me explain, what may not be evident to you now Black Dagger is that I am purposeless. When I became aware of your existence, and then when you allowed me to see you, I understood the darkness that breeds from inaction, and I refuse to be a part of it. Your kind has seen some of the greatest acts of violence, war, and self-destruction known to any life form, but they are not the only ones who fight this. I was without the ability to lead or change the ideals of my own, but here I believe I, we, can. In every piece of your history I have gleaned these last months it was always a solitary force that changed the direction of society, that altered what had been. You believe what you do belongs in the shadows, a force of darkness consuming the equal bearers of damned fate around it, but I think you are wrong in that logic. Whether or not you will have me, I do not know, and I will not beg you of it, because I simply do not need your permission. I ask to join you because I believe that where I falter, you are stronger, and where your own perception fails you, I can see clearly. Together, you will not be forced to hide, as I will not rely on the eyes and minds of strangers to relay the world to me as one of it. If this is a reality you wish to witness, then let me help you."

"Why? Why would you even care?"

"For the very same reason you care, the logic by which you do it, Black Dagger. You think of it as retribution for the sins of your very existence, but I know the truth. You have come to enjoy it, to hold the power to change the course of events around you and alter them to your will, but by a miracle of rarity, you have chosen to alter them in the best ways you are capable of understanding. You do not ask yourself questions over your own actions, you do not slave over the answer to what is moral or good, you simply act, without doubt, without guilt, you take what is yours and you use it without asking permission to exercise your own abilities and reason from those who have no right to offer such authority. You have merely taken it as your own.

Such is the same as I have done, though the places from where I come cannot be changed by me, thus my being here. I never thought to meet one of this race who bore my same drives, nor did I expect it to take form in you, but I am pleased it has, and in the interest of serving both our purposes to their fullest, we would be better to do what we have sought for ourselves together. These are my reasons for asking you if I may join you in this."

"You understand that a couple of thugs aren't the worse that comes with this?"

"If I had wanted my existence to be spent lounging without care I would not have stepped foot on this planet."

"All right."

"You consent?" She asked excitedly.

"I cannot stop you." I half expected to wake up on some deserted roof anyway, only to find the last, amazing twenty-four hours had been a dream, a good one for once. Or that I was finally dead and I had somehow had gotten the 'up' ticket issued, and she was a beautiful, though mentally deranged angel.

"That, Black Dagger, you could not." She smiled… and started glowing again.

Overcome

We were then in the heart of a 'midday stake out' on an old fire escape close to the metropolitan's main 'black market' area. I hated the cold-consuming-darkness of the city's alleys, but it was efficient enough, and despite my assurances that his desire for absolute anonymousness were without grounds, his habits-of-action were hard to alter. I found myself continually intruding upon his mind for the explanations of his strange tactics, and though I never voiced my opinions over them, I remained constantly prepared-power drawn for anything of this world or mine that might hinder our 'work'.

Such was the reason I had waited this long to speak. If he was to act as one with only one motive, the presence of what lied directly ahead of him, there could no longer be presences behind him bidding for his attention. True to the name he had given himself, and the nature of such material things related to it, he needed honing, and precision. For much of what he recalled he had been flung about by every drive he encountered. If I was to learn how to help him, he needed to be controlled by his own words first.

"You should go see him like you said you would." I told him quietly. It wasn't the first words I said, but they were the most thought over.

"What are you talking about?" His eyes were half shut, his head leaned back against the weathering-red-bricked-human-built-wall behind him. His energy was stable-unmoving and to my utter disbelief, in the steadiness of its existence, it was overpowering. I had not believed such to be possible at first – no power stood still, even that which appeared to be without motion was in fact always moving, the very power-matter-cluster they called the solar system I could feel rushing through the expanses of space even then. Yet he stood still.

"The law officer I saw in your memories, you said you would visit him and you have failed to as of yet." I also had known how he avoided anyone he had met, but only in the time before my appearance. Another thing unexplained, another thing I dismissed in knowing that it was unexplainable. He was unexplainable.

"And?"

"Then we should go to him, as you agreed to before." I glanced over, watching his power-form-expression and his cold-onyx eyes.

"I didn't agree, and it's been months."

"I do not understand these concepts of time as you see them. I have been with you for three of these so named months, what of this?"

"It is a long time to leave someone waiting, to us."

"He is waiting then?"

He lifted his shoulders, looking away from me.

"Do you understand why you have to do this?"

"I understand that if I don't you will not stop talking about it until I do."

I wanted to laugh. It was not the first thing I had used the human-act-of-pestering to urge him into. The first had been to get a true place of residence, something that had taken nearly seven rotations of the Earth to accomplish with his insistence that it was unneeded-unsafe.

"This is true, and as that is, I am going to go this dusk and I will very much like to take you with me Black Dagger."

-It was times like those when I regretted letting her in my head.

"Fine, but we just go and we leave." She'd a knack for getting what she wanted. I normally didn't mind it. I was used to women with that capability.

"All I asked for."

"One condition." I said flatly. "Do not tell him anything about me, not my name, where I use to live, anything. I don't want the, well, company to… to track me here." I was haunted by that possibility, I had yet to know if they were still searching. Another thought, something I had forgotten since the first night, amid the endless array of success her ability to read minds had done to my hunting habits, reoccurred. *And what happens if they get to her?* I clenched my jaw shut at the silent, muted rage at the possibilities of what could happen.

"Whatever disrupts you, you are not alone in facing it." She whispered. It was the little things like that, her comforting murmurs, the way she would touch my hand or that innocent yet tempting smile that left me facing an even bleaker reality.

"That's what I am afraid of." *Well, as 'cautiously aware' as is possible for me.*

"I do not comprehend."

"What if I'm *not* alone? They could have expected me to run – planned for it – wanted it even, and I'm too blind to see their plans. You agreed – it was too easy to get away, with what I remember for. I don't know what they are capable of Stargazer, of what they could do to you if they were to find me. It isn't safe for you. These people aren't just some crack dealers or cartel – they aren't what we deal with every day, they're organized and-"

She laughed.

"And completely unaware of my existence and your exact whereabouts. I would know if it was otherwise. They are not tracking you, not internally through any electronic device, I would know, as I have said before. We have spoken of this a dozen times, and at each instance you forget that no matter what I appear to be to you, I am not what you see, or what they might assume me to be. Do not worry, remember?" She turned to look at me directly. Her hand passed over her face. "Just a mask. What I am, what I know, they cannot understand nor tame. I have no weaknesses commonly known to this race. I am, as you say, invincible."

"You don't know what they can do."

"I know what *I* can do. I was exceedingly well trained for many of your years, and am quite capable of taking care of my and mine. …Perchance my allowing your ignorance to my power isn't as beneficial as I once thought?" She asked in a way I saw as rhetorical.

"You're sure?"

"We did not spend what you call centuries of perceived time being worshiped as gods simply because we are pleasing to gaze upon." Her eyes flashed, a warning smirk flicking across her lips.

I consented.

She was right in the fact I had very little knowledge into what she was. The night before I had watched four people hit her with multiple rounds of ammo, and had stared in shock as the bullets stopped inches in front of her, falling to the ground like rain. Literally. She'd melted them. I had realized soon after that there was a puddle of metal at my feet too.

The moment she had immobilized them, I had relieved them of their weapons. In that same instant I had reached for their necks, starting to knock two of their heads together hard enough to crack bone, the exact outcome I had desired. She had known that, and in a sudden break of passivity over my actions, appeared between them and I, grabbing my arms and locking them behind me faster than light. She wasn't trying to physically to hold me there, but the fact I wouldn't break free from her as long as I kept my artificial instincts at bay had held me captive, saving them from a few concussions.

"No." She had said, without any perceivable tone.

"They tried to shoot you."

"We are not their judge." She had muttered, releasing my wrists, with a glare stern enough to light a match. I'd growled under my breath before accepting her childish silent treatment. She had only been speaking to me again as of recent, but her soundless battle didn't seem to be directed at me. I didn't know if going to see the Lieutenant was her form of penance I was supposed to pay, or hers.

"We should speak to him first," she broke my train of thought, "and after, you need sleep before tonight. The streets will be quite enough to go sooner rather than later."

"I'm not tired."

"You haven't allowed yourself rest for three sunrises. This is enough for now. I have looked through nearly every mind within my ability to reach from here, and none of them have the information you sought regarding the arson last night. We can do nothing more here." She said strict enough to deny any chance of any argument. I got up off the rusted metal stairs.

Stargazer was already putting on her "civilian" clothes, their purpose was to hide as much of her skin as possible, should she drop her guard and start glowing. The floor length, long sleeved scarlet dress made my head swim in the same color. The mechanical guard belonging to that cursed part of me had faded, allowing what small amount of human tendencies I left to gradually resurface. That left me both a little hopeful, that the fog was slowing waning, and aggravated, because it was her warmth that was doing it. Human tendencies aren't nearly as acceptable when in the presence of one who seemed to lack them.

I only changed because I couldn't walk around in a mask and gloves without looking odd. Even in that city. I did shades instead. She also had a pair of gold sunglasses to hide her eyes. I left my black cargo pants and shirt be, they were inconspicuous enough on their own.

I jumped down the three stories to the sidewalk where she was waiting and made a quick look back up to we'd been; no sign of us was left behind.

We walked amongst a large group of rushing-anxious humans, hiding in the anonymous crowd. The crashing thunder of their consciousness's threatened to overpower me as I took the liberty of absorbing the powers behind the thoughts-feelings-emotions, calming those around me. I smiled when it took the desired-taught effect, the multitude of colors and powers ceasing their endless cascade and the air ceased to vibrate with the humming of their bodies.

We kept close to each other as we walked, though neither by conscious effort, for finding him was as easy for me as his eyes were capable of counting every window below when we would fly over the city. It was without thought. Black Dagger was head and shoulders above almost everyone there. His power stood out amidst theirs like a dark beacon, reminding me of my far off encounter with what this world calls 'Black Holes'. He too drew me in with more force that I saw possible. Only this time, I didn't fight back as hard as I once did. I often found myself seeking shelter within his unknowing mind when the thoughts of too many beings or even the thoughts of one, frightened or overcame me.

We were in the same lobby. The brick walls still smelled of the years when smoking indoors was the norm, and the lingering scent reminded me of the last time I had been there. That time, *thankfully*, there weren't any cops blocking every exit...yet. I could feel the tick in my head start counting off, the fight or flee desire building with every moment I lingered there. I had learned in that far off high school class room, was that this was called the Sympathetic Nervous System, and whatever they had done to me had sent it into overdrive, in turn ironically driving out whatever shred of actual sympathy I could hope to muster.

80

"Wait here." I told her. I walked over to the female officer behind the counter. I recognized her, but I knew I remained nameless. "I'm looking for Lieutenant Locker."

"Well hola to you too."

"We need to see Locker."

"He's busy now. I'm Officer Gonzalez; can I help you with something?" She cast a quick glance at Stargazer. She was noticeably stunned, her mouth going slightly slack. I didn't know how anyone could react differently.

"Can you give him a message?"

"What?"

I was acutely aware that Stargazer was now standing right behind me.

"Tell him that Lauren's friend is here to see him." It took me almost a full second to come up with a coherent answer, though to her that was nothing to bring attention to. Officer Gonzalez looked at me oddly, but left to find the Lieutenant without questioning my request.

Another one, a young guy straight out of training, judging by the precision of his posture, took her place, his hand hovering over his radio. One call and the doors would lock.

I could feel the walls closing in. Even she was lost in the siege that brought up all of my barricades.

Her hand seized my wrist, the other closing around my fingers, forcing my fist to open against her palm.

"Be present." Her eyes expanded, growing a glossier gold in the white lights. Just like a few other times before when she said similar, normally as I woke up from a nightmare to find her next to me, or when the numbness seemed to consume everything, making it even harder to fight, to feel, and she seemed to sense it and intercede, my only response was silence.

Officer Gonzalez walked hurriedly through the hall, her deeply tanned face beading with a slight dew of sweat.

"If you'll follow me." She stammered, flustered, knowing eyes on me. She led us down a short hallway and into room not that much larger than a dozen feet across, the brick walls continuing to mock me with their unmovable presence. Lieutenant Jim Locker stood in the doorway.

"Thank you Rosie. Come in, please." He shut the door and locked it securely behind us. Somehow that did not help me. Stargazer sat down in one of the two chairs, motioning I should do the same. I wordlessly refused, standing to face him.

"I didn't tell her– she remembers you now, but don't worry – Lauren made it very clear what happened. Of course I know you don't like the idea of being here regardless – But – Thank you for coming. You will be glad to hear that I have kept our last, err, meeting to myself, like I thought you would have wished, so you are still under any suspicion, well, anything that I'm aware of, but you know I only go so high up." He was giving me the answer to every question I half cared to ask in a single, worried stammering of a sentence.

"Thanks." I muttered.

"I see you didn't come alone?"

"Celeste." I nodded to her. She smiled, her indistinct eyes focused on his thoughts rather than his face.

It was silent for a moment, the kind of silence that reminds you how annoying lack of words can be too.

"Now, I don't want to prod, but do you happen to be responsible for that unexpected gang bust that happened late last night? They are clueless as to how they all landed on the chief's doorstep...begging to give their confessions and be booked...I've never heard of anything like that. Half of them are wanted for distribution and the other half are being held on possession. They confessed to it – everything we had – all of it, just to get off the street." His eyes were wide with expectation, the sweat gathering on his forehead causing an annoying shine under the white lights. We knew the rumors.

"We." I corrected him, flicking my hand to Stargazer. He looked over at her in astonishment. She smiled to him once more, lifting her hand and turning it outwards as if to question his shock. He quickly looked away.

"...I see. Forgive me, young lady, Celeste I mean, I am trying to understand all this."

"I am afraid understanding who I am will prove nearly impossible in the short amount of time we have here, Lieutenant Locker. However, because you helped him those months ago, I shall aim to do my best to answer anything you may ask." Her voice ended in a final, long ringing note.

He shook himself out of his daze, retreating behind his desk. Only then did I sit down.

"Well, I guess I should ask why you're both here. Have you decided to finally share a tip with us eh'?" By his rapidly increasing heart rate, he was nervous, but he did his best not to show it, smiling with perfect posture and looking between her and I without preference to one or the other.

"We have decided to take you up on your previous offer." She answered. He frowned, his expression guarded. He was trying to figure out how *she* could possibly pose a threat to *anyone.* She looked perfectly harmless. I left out 'normal' on purpose. No one who looked like her could be normal by any means. "Please, do not be frightened. I know you fear us, but I assure you we are not dangerous, not to you, or to anyone who holds themselves in an upright manner. We are simply here when needed." She held her seamless bearing, the dress shifting as she crossed her legs. "Forgive my bluntness, but do not be fooled by my appearance, as you now believe me to be but a girl caught in the crosshairs of a single man's conquest of self-justification through vigilantism. I can assure you both my standing in this situation and the belief that drives it is just as much my own as his, and we together, stand in this. I am far from a bystander in a private rebellion, but rather, you might say I am the fire in the Molotov cocktail he throws." She purred, narrowing her black rimmed eyes. "We as a whole, and I in my own, am not one to be trifled with, humanity will relearn that lesson soon enough."

We gulped, for completely differing reasons.

"We will do our best to assist you in your endeavors, and in turn I would ask of you to extend the same mutual understanding to us. There may come a time when the proper authority of this world will have to be called upon, and as you have been honorable in your time as an officer of the law, and have taken neither bribe nor privilege, I would like for you to be the one we will go to with such requests. That said, I also recognize that there are certain forces that are against his and mine existence, and your alliance with us, should you choose it, will put you at risk. I will be expecting such, and you will not be without our protection should there come a time when you need it, and if steps were to be taken against you or your family that required you to remove yourself from the common eye, you would be provided for beyond needs. Knowing these things, would you consent to being our ally within these walls?"

She grinned pleasantly, waiting for a response without the slightest sign of doubt to what he would say.

"…I …I would be honored. But I have a few more questions."

"Of course." She dipped her chin, glancing to me.

"We cannot talk much here – Supper. Come by tonight, around eight?"

"I can't promise an ETA." I muttered. I wanted to leave. I was more uncomfortable than I thought I could ever be, for feeling nothing at all. "But we will be there, at some point tonight. Right now we don't need more than eyes and ears inside the station. If the FBI or CIA or whoever else is getting in on us moves a few agents in or there is any other activity you know about, we only need the heads up." I said quickly.

I then heard hushed whispers outside of the door.

"Who are they?" "I don't have the slightest idea." "The guy looks familiar right?" "I don't know, maybe they're the contacts from upstate." "Or the undercover agents we placed in the lower east side last month." "The woman doesn't

look like she is a cop." "And she would be way *too easy to recognize."*

"They are not to be dealt with Black Dagger." She whispered for my ears only.

We definitely needed to go.

"Yes, of course, I understand, but I'm afraid if you stay any longer, someone may wonder why you are here." He apparently wanted us to leave too. I didn't feel the need to confirm his suspicion.

"It would be better for them if they didn't." I said before getting up. I could have been covered in fire-ants and I wouldn't have noticed a difference; every nerve in my body demanded I recognize the threat and face it. Ignoring it was beyond my ability. My control was cracking.

"Thank you for your understanding and cautiousness with this matter. It isn't often I meet one I can trust and it isn't something I hold lightly. You are truly appreciated, and I am at your service whenever you might need me." She smoothed over the brief but unsettling conversation.

"Of course, Celeste." He seemed worried about something, possibly *her*. "Be safe now." He added.

I left. From the sound of her steps, she followed close behind me.

◆

Trigger

"That was too close." He snapped, stalking farther ahead of me, not bothering to explain his former ten-earth-minute silence as he had unknowingly-to-himself searched for a place-without-witnesses. The shadows of the cold-dark-asphalt echoed his even darker light, reminding me of the precarious resting balance within him.

"I do not understand your dread." I said calmly, matching his pace.

"If you ever make me go do something like *that* again, I'll run. I *swear* I will. I'm not showing tonight. I can't stop you from doing what you want – but I can't go. I won't. We got way too close. We can't risk that. Someone could have heard us. It could be a trap." His ice-edged words were that of a man cornered with no escape and seemed to slice-severe through the air

"You gave him your word."

"I'm not going."

"What is it you fear, Black Dagger? I have seen you take on men with your mineral-metal guns and you are afraid of an older-human-police official? Or do you fear what he might have planned – even though his thoughts were without malice or ill intent? Is it his superiors, or the letter named associations this country is seemingly guarded by? No – I will answer for you, it is not these." I questioned him at his pale yellow-grey tinted energy, waiting for some sort of response and received no answer. "You cannot live forever with only your own 'awareness' as your companionship. You will go mad with this, with a fear of the unknown as your only comfort. If you do not hold yourself to your own promises, what then are you? Nothing. For one without honor and those to hold you to it and enjoy life with you is like a galaxy without light. It can never be complete. You cannot rely on your fears of the past for your only concern. You must discontinue acting as if it is the end of this world when you face that which seeks neither your aggression or dismissal."

He stopped walking, turning back to face me, his hands bound with the same fierce tightness as the aurora around him.

"I wasn't afraid of him, and you know nothing about what it feels like to have your world end." His words were bitter, accusing. "It isn't something *you* would want to be reminded of either Stargazer." His black eyes matched his soul.

"Do not assume what you do not know." I cautioned, feeling my surface cool.

"What do I know then? I know you can't ever shut up about how things are so precious and sacred. I know you can do whatever you want, but never actually do it. It's all just one big game to you. You think you can polish all the pain away until all we see in our scars is our own reflection. That's not how it is. Not everything is as easy as you see it! You can't act like it will all get better. It *doesn't*! And people aren't 'inheritably good'. We're all dark, one way or the other, we're stained. This is the real world – *my* world – and nothing has ever or will ever make it any better. It'll be hell till it ends. You can't act like it isn't, you can't expect to save it either – you can't save me, so *quit* trying to. We aren't meant to save whatever good is left, we are just here. Like everyone else we are here and I can't pretend that in the end I'm not as helpless and imbedded with this as anyone else. I'm worse, I am the epitome of it, so stop lying to yourself and stop trying to save me any the rest of us from it." He glared for another long moment before looking away. "...And you can't pretend or expect me to imagine that either of us is safe, I'm not – and in that you sure as hell aren't. What we're doing is pointless. No matter what we do, nothing will ever permanently change. See that – before it hurts you. You can't fix it. If you don't like how things are, you're freer than anyone else to leave."

"…I know there's darkness here, everywhere. I know what pain is, what fear is." I lowered my tone to match the shade of my power, knowing that the only thing capable of showing my thoughts to his kind were words.

"Then you should know better."

"You think I don't know that this existence is meant to be a test? You think I am naïve to what is happening? I above all creatures understand what is real. I do not lie to myself over what I see, I *choose* to see it differently. What we do, it does matter, for without one action, there can be no reactions. You are deceiving yourself, what you face…you are creating it where it does not exist."

"It doesn't matter how you see it, it doesn't change what it actually is! Either we fight until we die or we fight until we no longer see worth in dying for it. There is no other way. You cannot save me from that."

The dark expanse of him remained motionless in the dim yellow lighting in the alley's shadows. I fought back at what he'd said. It wasn't his voice, or his soul, that had nearly shouted those venomous words, and that comforted and frightened me all at once.

I took his hand and flew up into the sky, unable to stand the idea of leaving him alone in that place, even if it did mean I had to touch him, to know what it was in him that had said those things. I rose up to over the city in order for me to not have been taken by the humans as more than a large-flying-bird. Black Dagger was holding on tightly to my waist, his skin cold stone. I felt both suppressed anger and frustration running through him. I flew fast enough to get us to our top-floor-apartments near the center of the city within only a few minutes.

She landed lightly, though I had already let her go the instant we were near enough to the ground for me to step away as quickly as I could. Her hand caught my forearm, and with more strength than I thought she could possess, she held me still.

"Wait." She begged. I looked down at her for the first time. Her pleading, dark eyes were glowing, something in that light once again seeping into the cold mass inside of me. "I do not know what made me speak the things I-"

"Stop."

"Dagger-"

"No. You have nothing to apologize for." I stated, hardly able to speak. How could I have made her understand that every normal human response I wished to give had been callused by the physical inability to care? By an eraser to every part of my brain capable of empathy, and actions to darken every corner of my soul? How could she understand that everything I did or said was a constant battle, one I often lost? How could she see that the strength my body possessed had not been lent to my mind? What could possibly help her comprehend how hard it was for me to care enough to do what we did? Much less put up with her indescribable compassion that I caught myself thinking of as beneath me, regardless of how I was more often than not a receiver of it?

I stared at her helplessly, knowing that a single siren below or the sound of a phone ringing on the floor below or a traffic helicopter overhead would send me back into the calculated cage within my thoughts. Those few moments of silence were the only freedom I knew.

I embraced him, unable to withhold that desire any longer. I felt his stance soften under my unwavering grip. Even as my body fit against the hard-soft edges of his, the aura of my energy conformed to his – more than should have been possible. A thousand thoughts clustered around a single awareness as I held him for that moment that was an eternity.

"I never want to hurt you. But you have to *understand* –" He said, holding me tighter, so that I hovered even further above the ground. He did not continue, and I did not need to wonder at why.

"I understand."

"I don't see how."

"You don't have to." I let him go, the shock of my power returning to me so suddenly that it made my vision haze. "You should sleep." I advised, knowing my voice could not betray my emotions. He would want to be by himself, so that the pressure and distraction of my presence could not keep him.

"Stay close." He said, same as he always said when he left me alone. I smiled and nodded. I knew what he intended. I watched him until he left my physical view before watching him with my mind.

Why all of this? Why the reaction his words brought over me? Why this silent, screaming longing for-that-which-I-do-not-know-nor-see-a-way-to-understand? What sort of self-made-mental-fiend has possessed me into these things? Even the stars above me laughed at my blindness to what was so clear that the very world saw it before I did. The ground trembled when I passed over it, the air shook. They dared not approach such energy as mine, energy all too scandalously ready to change into something so rare and beautiful, yet terrifyingly unstable.

I tore my eyes from the sky. *I have broken every vow, even that which has made me what I am. Even my thoughts are mimicking his, my actions, my emotions. Or lack of those, now that I can think clearly again. Had I been correct-in-thought I would have undoubtedly run, lest I confront him with more than words. Or not spoken at all. All these things that separate me from his race, these lines that dare not be crossed are being blurred. The essence of what and who I am is morphing in front of my sight.*

My name, my identity, this world has been at work erasing since I arrived. And he is making it all so easy to forget, to want more of this, to want to lose myself in this world. No. Not in the world. In His World. He said so himself. This is his world.

How easily I might fall from this ledge of fear-knowing-uncertainty and find myself caught. If anyone had spoken as he had, he would have faced retribution, but I am all too willing to forgive him, to promise things I am not even sure are in my power to promise. I have bonded myself with my words. My actions prove them. My thoughts restate them… Would it be so impossible to tie myself not only to this world, but to its creator?

Regardless of that-which-I-do-not-and-might-not-ever-know, I am here..

And so Stargazer has begun.

Broken Boys

"Oh...come in!" The round, smiling woman in the wooden doorway was the Lieutenant's wife, Anna. She seemed perfectly at ease with us, which given the factors that her husband had been on the edge of panic earlier, made the hospitality all the more hair raising. I had already scanned the neighborhood: outside the city, suburbs, close circuit security cameras at the gas station on the corner, which we had avoided. No one was out on the street to have seen us land. Had there been any variable I could convince her was worth leaving over, I would have bolted right then.

The front door closed behind us. There was two inches of particle board between me and the outside. The air smelled like garlic. Anna smelled like flowery perfume and Biofreeze. Her heart beat was slightly elevated.

She led us to a neat, nicely furnished living room. The Lieutenant sat in a large, greenish gray recliner in the corner. He stood up immediately at our entrance.

"You came!"

"Yes." I said without details.

"Obviously there's no one from the force but me here, but if you need to look around I underst-"

"We did."

"Oh, good. So you know this is just a friendly dinner but I have to say...of course, I know it is just dinner. Sorry, I keep forgetting I'm not supposed to be interrogating you. ...But I do hope you will be willing to give me a few answers. Well I will go and grab our food and you three can get to know each other a little better, so, uh, I guess I will see you in a minute." He smiled slightly, awkwardly, as if anything could top his faltered speech. He left out of a sliding glass door at the back of the house, I couldn't see it, but I heard the sound of metal on metal and glass on metal.

"You'll have to give him a little patience, he's trying very hard to understand, that's all. I guess the whole city is. Oh, please have a seat." Anna motioned with her hand towards a sectional couch that took up most of the room.

"Thank you." I said. I made a point to keep my voice from being too even. She just smiled wider than ever and sat down on the end of the sofa. She and Stargazer started talking right away, of what I don't remember.

My eyes fell to the small amount of space between us, and I inwardly shook my head at how she could stand to be in the same room with me. The memory of the auburn pain I saw in her eyes, if only for that brief moment, her pleading with me to simply *look* at her, something I had trouble not doing on a regular day, was still sharp in my mind. I wasn't feeling regret or guilt, I was reduced to the one semblance of an emotion I had to give, fury, at myself for being unable to feel those things.

"And how old are you dearie?"

I come back to full consciousness after hearing the question.

"I am sixteen of your sun's seasons old."

I was ready to punch myself in the gut, after replacing my eyes to their sockets.

"*Really?* My goodness-gracious, aren't you too young to be running around with-" she stopped when she felt my eyes. Apparently, she'd forgotten I was there.

She deserves a medal for that.

"He's only seventeen months older than I." Her tone was slightly heavier, like she saw an unspoken remark.

"You're both *teenagers*?!" She shook her head in disbelief, her short cropped, rolled hair flying into her cheeks.

"As if anyone else is crazy enough to do what we do." I said and couldn't help but smirk at my own dark humor.

"Oh I thought, well I assumed- That is so young! Jimmy told me about you." She looked over at me, "and I never would have thought that you were both so young. You're just *children*." She complained.

"No 'child' ever, has seen or done what we have and none should ever have to."

Her face fell, showing the rebuke I gave her.

"I'm sorry...but it's just my son isn't too much older than you and I could never see how the stories, and the news, it just isn't possible for anyone – of course he is not...typical. From what Jimmy said, you should not be considered normal either." She tried to explain. "I know I'm not supposed to ask you questions but I just don't understand how it's even possible."

"No worries or grudges are in any form of attendance. We are doing what we must do, we are more than equipped to manage it, and we revel in its fulfillment. That is all that bears consequence." She attempted to smooth any newly ruffled feathers, possibly her own. She placed a warm hand on my back, I noticed out of Anna's view. My feathers were instantly unruffled.

"Come and get it!" The Lieutenant called, ending the discussion before Anna could ask for any more details. Anna rose first, Stargazer and I followed slowly after her. We'd almost rounded the corner into the dining room when Stargazer stopped moving, her stillness as that of stone. A confused, scared expression dashed across her face.

A faint humming filled the room, her body its undeniable source.

"Star...?"

Jim and Anna noticed her strange state, and what I had called her.

"What is she doing?" He asked cautiously. I ignored him.

She turned her head towards a hall that latched on to the kitchen. She walked unsteadily away from it, one small step at a time. Her hands shook and her dark eyes darted, before falling still. I looked in the direction of Stargazer's newfound stare. A small, misshapen, pale boy in an electric wheelchair appeared in the doorframe. His unnatural features told me he was a victim of some type of genetic disorder. I was unable to tell his age. His overly rounded head leaned over to his right side, his thin fingers stopping the pressure to the controls that propelled him forward as his almond shaped eyes widened at her glowing stature. Stargazer took a step towards him. Jim was instantly in front of her, a hand raised.

"Step aside please, Lieutenant..." The tone of her voice shocked me.

It *rang*.

"I think you n-need to le-leave." His voice quaked with fear. She placed her hand on his shoulder and pushed him back. I was too stunned to go to his or her aid, but he was the one needing it. He clutched his wife, stunned in fear on the couch. She knelt down to get face to face with the kid, who other than freezing in shock had not yet responded to her. I walked up behind her, my feet moving on their own accord.

"You are broken." She told him, her tone again like honey. He nodded vaguely. "Do you wish to be made whole, Zachery?" He nodded his head again, that time more aggressive than the one before it.

"What are you *doing*?" I silenced Anna with a quick glare. *I have absolutely no idea.*

She placed her hands on him, one on the top of his head and another at his heart. The humming in the room increased. The glasses in the China cabinet behind us began vibrating, a light bulb over the stove exploded, and the ceiling fan began to

95

spin above us at a violent speed, all the while she glowed like I had never seen her do before. The outline of her body expanded and condensed at an increasing rate until she was a blurred, contorted, ring of pure, shining, heat giving light. A flame. The heat I had become so accustomed and addicted to threatened to choke me. The air shimmered with it, the temperature high enough to burn my face. My body shuddered with her energy, but she was not the only one who had changed with its force. His skin glowed and his outlined frame seemed to expand and change as well, although it was not a flame he became.

As unexpectedly as it had happened, it stopped.

The room was dark, cold, silent. Then there was Anna's gasp, followed by Stargazer crumpling against the carpeted ground, her previously pulsing eyes rolling back into her head. I grabbed her, falling to my knees in time to catch her. Her skin glowed brightly and was near a hundred and forty degrees, hot enough to begin to burn mine.

"Star" I shook her lightly. Her eyes shot open. She quickly looked around the room. A flicker of an unidentifiable emotion crossed her face. She pushed herself up with one hand; her lapse of weakness passed. I turned some of my attention back towards the guy. I, if I had not seen him before, would not have recognized him. He looked perfectly *normal*.

"Thank you." He said, a few tears running down his seemingly sun tanned face. She turned towards his parents.

"He is well." She told them serenely. I'm sure they would have thanked her as well, if they had not been hysterically crying. She turned around to face me, placing her then shockingly cool hand against the back of mine. "Let us go."

"Thank you so, so much." The once illiterate boy spoke again.

"You're welcome. We will see you soon." She smiled, dipping her head. Her eyes were gold. He returned the grin before being buried underneath his parents.

She closed her hand around mine, hurriedly urging me towards the door. "...We should leave."

-BD- SG

"Are you sure you're okay?" He asked me again, his thoughts repeating the image of my physical form losing itself to the pull of the Earth's gravity. Even if the image had been equally unnerving for me to see through his eyes, the lapse was far from the fatal or wounded truth he deemed it to be.

"For the final instance, I am well. I have never done that before, it took more of me than I had expected, but I, like that young man am in perfect health now." I explained. His concern was touching, but was getting exasperating. He had not ceased to inquire over my state since we had left the Lieutenant's dwelling, and though the tint of his power had remained unchanged in its conflict-battle-ready shade, it had diminished in the last minutes we had been sitting the roof of our two-apartments'-imitation-rock-man-made-building. We would sometimes reside under the sparkling light of his – *our* universes' stars, for hours, in perfect-content-silence..

"How did you do that?"

"I do not know. I have learned of my people healing humans of their many terrifying plagues." Black Dagger's only slight response at that was understandable, though he waited for me to continue. "I was never taught how to do this, however, and I have never seen it done... Yet, I cannot explain it perfectly, except that when I saw him, and I saw that there was a fault in his being I had the ability to alter, it is as if I knew all along such capability was within me. I did not question its existence, even if it frightened me. My energy burned brighter than it has in years, demanding that I give some to that boy, not giving me a conscious choice but to submit – Everything that makes me, my power and my mind, knew what to do, yet I still do not understand fully."

97

I pressed my palms together, the fear I dared not show still coursing through me.

"You did it though." He lay down on the roof as he spoke the compliment. He used his arms as a brace for his head, crossing them behind it. At my assurances of being well, the last of his battle fever had gone, for to him the act had been overcome the moment I was able to identify the causes to it. Such is the way of reason.

I ran my eyes over him. The lean-hard-soft surface of his body showed underneath the thin, dark covering her wore. I studied his life-light-halo, awed by the way it moved, the way it conformed when it hit mine, changing ever so slightly as our unseen bond mixed.

I recalled that I must speak.

"This is true, but I do not know of any great side effects that might present themselves over time." *What might I have wrought?*

"Like glowing?" His eyes matched the sky, both reflecting the light they beheld, though one saw the city, the other saw me.

"Yes, like glowing." I consented, smiling at his jesting, and then continued. "I will have to check on him soon, because I may have overlooked that which I should have seen. I do not believe that the one who trained me in my ways knew I bore this ability, else I would have been instructed on it. Or if it was known, or even common to all of my kind, why is it I knew nothing but legend? These are the fabled waters your race claims that have never been crossed, and I am the ship whose masts are driven by winds and forces greater than the beams holding it in place..."

Other than my fear, another matter weighted me, making the unnaturally coming movements of my physical form seem heavy and tiresome. I had been contemplating that the entire flight back; I had even gone to the extent of slowing my speed to have more time to think. Fruitless time. My thoughts never roamed far before he reined me back into him,

98

my mind and willpower included within his all-consuming noose.

"Dagger?" He turned to face me. "You are broken as well."

I knew my lack of expression could not mask the absence of a reaction within me, if anything, it was a mirrored image of it, once that's image was too perfect to what it hid.

"What they did...to me...they made it where I can't feel...Not in the way other people do. What you see, that's only a glimpse." I paused, staring at the fists my hands hand clamped into, my skin crawling at the jeopardy of speaking everything I had fought to not voice into existence. "When you stopped me, the first time, remember?" I didn't need to look at her, I could not make myself do it. She remembered the same as I did. It had been a five weeks or so since she had appeared, and had she not, I doubted that pimp would have been breathing behind the walls of a cell. We had him pinned with the murders of two of his girls, both under fourteen, and the seventeen year old brother of one of them. Adding his name to the list of casualties had not been a second thought. "...I wanted him *dead*, Stargazer. You saw it, before I even knew I had given in, you put me to sleep. But it's not enough. I want most of the people we meet dead. I want to know they are not hurting anyone anymore – but that's just a justification." I exhaled, grinding the concrete beneath the heels of my boots. "At first, it was aimless, I was aimless. Rage. I don't have a better word. If I could have killed myself I would have – you saw that much – but I realized that I might be able to control it, to use it without it destroying whatever was left of my humanity. If there is any redemption for the devil, it's that he only has power over those who have entered his territory of darkness.

That's why. Don't you get it? Why I fight – why I do this – I have to. Moral conquest be damned, I *need* to. They made me a weapon, and I can't – I can't control when it goes

99

off, only where it aims. And even then, you know, you've seen it, how I lose control. Every single minute I am taking account of every threat around me, of how to eliminate them. If I don't, every second I leave it undone it undoes me. You came here with the noblest of altruism as your offering, and I...I seek to feed an insatiable blood lust."

"I am familiar with these things, Black Dagger." She said even softer.

"You knew?"

I didn't look up, not at first. She didn't speak until I did.

"You thought about it for a brief second while I was in your mind, that first night. I distinguished you had not wished to tell or show me under any circumstance, so I did not speak of it, such I have held to until now..." She ducked her head and stared at the general direction of downtown. The lights were blocking out the stars over the city, her golden outline lost in the smoggy haze. "I see the presence you say you are both slave and master over, and I have not run from it."

A minute passed. It became clear she refused to say anything more until I did.

"That makes it easier to explain." I muttered, some of the pieces falling into place. Her eagerness to get me to do things that seemed pointless, to speak when silence would have been perfectly acceptable, to answer questions that held no apparent relevance, she was making me face what I had been attempting to bury. "You could have told me."

"I did not believe it was not important for you to know that I recognized the existence of what you deem to be your only truth." She answered, her voice slow and pensive. Her head slowly turned to look at me. A shadow crossed her face. "I have spent these phases of the moon attempting to understand what it was they did, because in your mind, the very neurons of it, I can see where the areas of what people believe morality to come from, where the heart of humanity is designed to lie, have been altered. There are shadows where light used to be, and valley's of empty space where mountains

100

once stood, but if it is true, that your mind and body have been changed, where is it could these things truly come from then? I have not found their source, and though it may have been hindered, I do not believe they were able to eradicate it either."

"That's why you understand."

"No!" She shouted, moving in a blur, suddenly sitting in front of me. I stared at her, startled at her reaction. "It has nothing to do with what I know – I *understand* because I know you. I know *you*. Not what you say they made you. Not the version of yourself you see. Not what the world makes you out to be. Not what you think I perceive. I know *you*, the part of your being that could not be changed. They couldn't take away your soul – Your *soul* makes you *feel* – makes you who you are, not what they did, and not that I can see the evidence of it. That is not why I understand. It is not why I care, why I need you more than I should, but your *soul* is. The thing that separates your kind from any other creation, the thing that my people envied so much they thought taking on human form would allow them this indestructible, indescribable force. They were blind to the fact only you – only your spirit – is the entity most valuable, most unattainable and *indestructible*. The same entity that brought me and keeps me here is the same that they could not ever extinguish. I do not understand because I grasp at the ways you call science of what they did, or because I have seen your past, or even tried to aid you in taming it, I understand because I know that you are above both of these things... You are not broken from the acts of mankind; you break yourself with the way you see who you are."

Her face was eerily still, hiding the human like passion I had glimpsed not a moment before, her seraphic features seeming incapable of the excitement that had gone as far to have changed the air. Tears gathered at the corners of her amber eyes, evaporating as soon as they appeared. I had not known it possible for her to cry.

She turned away, her skin ceasing to reflect our city's brilliance.

"We all have run from something, Dagger, but what you fear most, that thing inside you by which no metaphor or phrase can make sense of, you are at war with, but you are not fighting without an ally."

Underneath every artificial instinct that plagued me, the one telling me to find something to hunt, the one telling me the alarms going off below us were a warning, and even one whispering that she herself was one, the desire to hold her, to feel her skin on mine, and look into eyes, to do whatever it took to see them gold, was stronger.

"You fixed the last broken boy you found." I stated.

"Yes?" She said with curious apprehension as to why I was changing the subject.

"Then you can fix me."

In a single, fluid motion, she rose to her knees, her hand on the side of my face. The heat of her touch was only surpassed by the fire in her eyes.

She kissed me softly, her satin lips folding against mine. My hands were on her arms, her warmth growing as she shifted her weight further towards me, arms around my neck, her deceptively soft contact breaking whatever bind I still detained reality with.

When I was forced to breathe, she grinned, resting her forehead against mine. I smiled back, bowing my arms around her. A sense of peace, unlike anything I had ever known, came over me in a deluge of a single abrupt awareness – an overwhelming, meant to impossible epiphany.

"I can try." She promised.

Atypical

We had invested two weeks into gaining the intel needed to find this particular runner. I wasn't about to screw it up. I was a creature of habit, just because there had been other options, like going with her in the sky verses hiding in a truck, didn't mean I would take them. I wasn't going to risk losing track of them again.

The silence was comforting. We'd not been discovered in the two hours since we'd been trailing him. We'd planned to confront them before they had gotten the chance to leave town, but there had been too many innocent variables involved. The people we were after were on a politician's pay list and a Cartel head's hit list, and the contradiction made this all the most dangerous. How big they were, we weren't entirely sure, but as soon as we had learned they were going to be coming through our city, we had set things in motion to put an end to it.

I scanned the energy readings on the earthen ground, taking note of the rising and falling intensities of their life lights and of the increasing electrical-pulse-friction in the air of the storm soon to come. It would not hinder us, as everything seemed to be in perfect order, although Black Dagger was not happy with his hiding place. He had decided to go get himself in the most amount of possible danger imaginable, as I had been forced to allow for lack of an acceptable way to prevent it.

The large-white-wheeled-moving-machine stopped in front of an abandoned air hanger. A man with a racing heart from the substance he had recently taken was let out to open the doors. That was what we had been waiting for, a 'drop point'. Mounds of man-made-chemical-'drugs' the vehicle carried were here to be sorted and separated for distribution. It was up to us to cease that from coming to pass.

The engine shut down a few moments after the van had come to a stop. The heat of the tail lights faded. I shifted my position, knowing that it was almost time. Each individual particle of dust landing on my skin felt like an ember, the sweat at the back of my neck cold. The muscles of my hands twitched, mirroring the ones behind my eyes.

"Get moving." I heard a gruff voice command.

The vehicle shuddered as a door was slammed shut. Crunching footsteps followed.

I punched the torso belonging to the dark, stunned face that had just opened up my hiding place. He flew up in the air a few feet and landed on some deteriorating crates with a thud. The other passengers were slow to react. I waited.

It was her turn.

Six men surrounded the back of the vehicle, all guns raised. I had only a moment to act before Dagger became 'mincemeat,' or so his own thoughts found darkly amusing. I placed my hand against a piece of metal and charged its atoms so it would attract all the others of its kind within a few yards before I tossed it up in to the air. The sound of clanking-solid-malleable minerals echoed, the mass falling to the ground, covered in an assortment of belts, keys, gear-turning-watches, and guns. The criminals wheeled to turn to face me, pausing, completely unaware of my identity and power, their minds defenseless for a brief moment of unguarded surprise. Consuming their consciousness with my own, I walked up to each, passing the open ends of my power in the palm of my hand over their bodies. They froze to the ground, rooted in their steps. A tremor went through me at their combined thoughts, forcing themselves upon me as a single-unstoppable

104

assailant. The darkness, the deceit-hatred-pain, all these things surrounded me a cloud of cold dusk. The golden tenor of my consciousness grew shady, my body refusing to follow my mind's frantic command for escape.

"You get close enough and their pain and their hate becomes yours, and if one were to take on too much, they will die. Their darkness, it is our only weakness, their only power over us. Their minds, if strong enough in their twisted wills, will infiltrate our light, and like a virus we will find that the seeping ice of our fear and our succumbing dimness will only grow, choking out our sanity in a slow, traumatizing-tedious hurting unlike anything else. Our minds, polluted by their angst and the troubles they bring upon themselves, losing sight of what and who we are, will deteriorate, leaving us without power or light or reason. Whoever dared to venture into their voids would be made aimless, consumed by the weight of that world and its cursed inhabitants."

The unwavering voice resonated in my mind, the lesson I cared to not recall all the more soul-fearing now. In my panic the truth presented itself as a newborn star, volatile beyond reason, was the realization that they held me there in the same way I held them, each of us fighting a battle we could not win.

"Star." His fingers locked around my wrist, yanking me away from their presence. I stumbled back, feeling the ties of their combined consciousness threatening to knot within me. His focus and his resolve cleansed me from their chilling thoughts, leaving my power without the holds that had bound it for that terrifying moment. Though the wounds from their latching on remained, leaving me to flee to Black Dagger, burying my mind into his in a desperate hope of escape.

Only then did I see the world again.

His black eyes glared into mine, the hard lines surrounding them lessening when he saw the foggy glaze fade from my soul. He took a step towards me.

"I am well." I spoke the words with haste, drawing my face into a smile, knowing the appearance of human compliance would comfort him.

I walked behind each one of them, cuffing them as I went. Although she'd immobilized their bodies, their mouths were a different story. I would have preferred to end the streams of cursing with a quick blow, but she was against using any "unnecessary violence" after an incident in Louisiana where I had thrown a serial rapist/killer the FBI had been hunting and that we had found, into a cement wall. He'd suffered head injuries, but survived, after she had healed him enough to keep him from dying from cranial hemorrhaging.

The press, with the help of the police we had brought him to, said that it had been an undercover operative working with the police whose tip had led to his eventual capture. What they didn't put in print was that he hadn't been alone when we had found him, and there laid the reason both the cement and his skull were cracked.

I looked up at the current lot. It didn't matter how their stories got told, as long as I never had to see them again.

"Pick how you want to go to jail – her way." I pointed to Stargazer. She stood about a foot back, her hands twitching at the concentration and force she applied to keep them still. I knew this many people was about her limit, but she hadn't said anything. She didn't have to. The fact they were still mentally aware of their surroundings proved it. "Or mine." Their eyes widened. It was a trick question, but it had become an unsaid joke between us. Nine out of ten chose the way involving the curvaceous goddess, regardless of gender. As far as picking me had gone, few had ever chosen mine, and those that did had been the witnesses of the few instances when her seamless peace would slip, and she would be the one they cowered from.

"Enough of you all." She growled, and released her hold. They fell to the floor as one; the profound cursing resumed whole way down. She placed her hand over each of them, putting them to sleep.

"Six down. A few thousand to go." I said, chuckling in shaded satisfaction.

"*Incredibly* amusing."

She once mentioned that I had taught her sarcasm.

I scanned the front of the car, looking for leads. The drugs had gotten in somehow, and the source was the real problem. As for the people who ran the product, it varied. The major gangs were always in question, and then the Mexican Cartel had a route through the city, but a new factor was always a possibility. Catching the latest 'kid kingpin' before he went big time was easier than taking on an entire business, drug lord, or a country for that matter. Even she had a hard time seeing who they really worked for, since there are about a dozen 'middle men' involved at any given time for the larger operations. It didn't matter if it was guns, drugs, people, construction scandals or fake disaster relief, the same technicalities applied. Our best chances were to cut off the legs if we had yet to find the head.

I scrolled through a few of the cell phones that had been in the front of the van, the texts all frustratingly vague, and those that were decipherable were worthless.

"Three-hundred kilos and half a dozen runners and not a single damn one of them knows who they work for?" I muttered, glancing up to her. She paused, one of the bodies she had been loading into the back of the van lying over her arm.

"I did not look...yet."

"We aren't flying?"

"There is a storm coming." She flicked her eyes to the darkening sky, visible through the rusted roof's holes.

"We have at least an hour before that hits."

"I am aware of the time, but tonight we will not be flying."

"Why?" I hated driving. The cameras on the stop lights were too easily hacked into.

"Why must you know?" She accused, her tone taut. I cocked an eyebrow, reminding her that my conscious attempt at 'caring' was new to me too. I didn't care. The fact we were driving was only an annoyance because it triggered my need for absolute security, a need she knew the reason for. If we drove, there would be surveillance cameras. I had to reason there was a motive behind her changing our methods. A motive that I *should* care to hear. Even if empathy was beyond me, I recognized the cues to give it. The explosive monster within me was sated by our work, and in the absence of his constant howling for release, I could heed more than just his hunger.

"Of course." She sighed. "I can trust you."

"There a reason you shouldn't?" I didn't know if it was a question she had said. I had liked to think it wasn't.

"...It is not that, but I fear you must know this. I am susceptible to dark energy. Not in the sense that their life force is dark, but that their lack of light draws my own into it. It affects me when I let my barriers down too far, or am overwhelmed. I was taken off of my guard this night, and I do not want to be in contact with them anymore. Not physically. Not with my power-essence. I do not even want to see them. I am faced with it nearly every moment, it is only when I lose sight of myself that I am susceptible. I am not one to be threatened...It would not be justified to them if I were to retaliate for my fears when they are mindless to their effects." She confessed, hands clasped in front of her. "But I fear that if I am to be forced to touch them again Dagger, to look into their minds tonight, it will fall upon you to see them there. So I refuse to do it."

"Dark energy?"

"Their souls lacked light, creating a vacuum so great that the conscious bearing energy that is my mind and unseen existence got caught in it."

"If you were to be around it long enough?"

"It would take a significant amount of time, even by this world's standards of such a concept, for it to be of any permanent harm." Her words were emotionless, her body held rigid with the force she fought to contain. She glared at their faces, now drooping with their exhaustion, before shutting the back of the van, shaded dents in the metal left where her hands had been.

"How long exactly?"

"I do not know, I came to this world without knowing nearly a grain of sand to the greatest of deserts of what I first believed I knew, and whatever knowledge once borne unto this soil regarding those of my kind has been lost."

"What would happen, if you stayed too long?"

"I do not know, entirely." Her hands closed at her sides. "Why is it you need so many particulars about the things I wish I was not?"

I stepped over a fallen, rotting beam, standing close enough to her to feel her heat waver when she realized my reasoning from whatever hasty analysis she gleaned from my thoughts. My hands closed around her arms, drawing her stunned face to mine.

"You said it. Dark energy. What does that mean? That you will have to leave when it becomes too much? That you're in pain? Why would you want to do this if it is the one thing that can hurt you?" I would not be a source of her pain. I was tainted, but she something that the world and I had no right to touch, someone who should never be forced to suffer with those of us damned to this.

The light returned to her eyes.

"I am not in pain." She hummed. "They cannot hurt me. Not when I am with you."

"My energy can't be that bright."

"It is not a matter of the measure of light."

"You're *susceptible* to the dark, but you're stupid enough to stay here." *To stay with me.*

"Stupid?" A hint of defiance lit the word, and her expression.

"If you're at risk. Yes."

One of them stirred, his moan seeping through the closed doors.

"We'll talk on the way back." I said in a way that made her see that she wasn't batting her eyelashes out of that discussion. This time, I was going to be the one to force her to speak. She flicked her eyes between me and the sky, before climbing into the front of the van, the door closing behind her with a shudder. I followed suit. I had given her ten very long minutes to speak first, a gift she didn't accept.

"Will you have to leave?" I forced the words out, gripping the leather steering wheel tighter, mindful to keep the pressure on my right foot even against the gas pedal.

"No. I will not leave this world, or run from it, and I am not a coward who flees at the first shadow to cast its presence over the sun."

"And if it gets too much?"

"It won't." She said simply, crossing her legs beneath her skirt, a human action meant to placate me.

"Then what was *that*?" I didn't look away from the asphalt, because I knew if I did my control wouldn't hold.

"I let them, as you would say, get to me. That shall not happen again."

"Next time, when there are twenty, or more, and I'm not right there to make sure you're sane, how am I supposed to think *that* won't affect you?" It wasn't the thugs I was taking into my reasoning. It was the idea that she had a weakness, one that could be used against her, something that I could not spare her from.

She touched my hand, running her warm fingers over mine, my grip involuntarily loosening.

"If you entertain such notions of darkness, it will consume you Dagger. This is what I mean when I say I will not

110

allow myself to be taken off of my guard again as I was this night. This weakness is not the omen you believe it to be... And if you still think you deserve to know more, you are most certainly right, but regardless of right and wrong, I will not place my burdens on you. You will not carry *my* weight." The metallic twang in her voice ceased, only to be replaced by a soft, still whisper. "I am here. I will be here in the morning. I will be here for as long as you still wish it. Nonetheless, there are things, perhaps as far as decades from now you will learn that might force you to change your sights, and when that time comes, we will be left to bear equal yokes, none heavier or harder to carry than the others'. That is all, Black Dagger. I cannot let you see me as I know you; I beg of you to trust me when I say it is for your own good."

I hadn't realized I had ceased to accelerate until the car stopped. Thankfully, the road was four lanes, and the honking of other drivers was unable to be heard over my roaring thoughts.

"It ever occur to you that telling me might be for your own good? I can't protect you if you won't-"

"This is not something you can shield me from in the way you think you are able."

I fell silent and began driving again. Had I thought I had a chance with reasoning with her, I would have. But the facts she held behind her beatific façade were sealed with more than words. The lightening above us intensified, its thunderous applauses rattling the car. Her gold face was lit with its power, drastic shadows cast over the slanting shape of her cheeks. She was unearthly still, her gaze down, hiding the color of her emotions.

"Don't scare me like that."

"I frightened you?" That brought her back, her brows raised in surprise.

"...As much as I can be."

She turned to me, reading my expression with her eyes and whatever else with her head. "I am sorry. I can't know

111

what my reactions will be – I do not wish to see you suffer for it." She apologetically smiled. "I do not like being this vague, but I don't know how to expound certain aspects of what I am…I am not used to having to exemplify my thoughts aloud. So much of how I think and feel is not in words. I am still learning what is to speak such things, a trial we seem to bear equally."

I took one hand off the wheel, holding it towards her in an invitation. Her pensive eyes lightened as she buried her face in my shoulder, wrapping her arm around mine. I saw the glimmer of her mind in mine, something that always left me breathless. Slow moving scenes of the last hour clung to the corners of the small portion of her consciousness that was visible. The distortion of the memory was frightening to us both. Tendrils of self-moving shadows were still caught in knots. She tried to break away, separating her power from theirs. Her light flickered as she battled against the force even I could feel. I focused only on the road ahead of me, forcing my thoughts to go blank, allowing her to come in further, feeling her warmth nestle deeper into me, as if to hide from the remnants of them.

Thank you. She murmured.

"Vivimerea so help me…" She moaned a partial hour later. She weakly pushed away from me, attempting to sit up. She leaned against the black leather seat, loosely staring up at the felt ceiling.

"I'd offer you an aspirin, but I doubt it would help." I studied her face, looking for signs of something more serious than whatever was her equivalent of a headache, keeping my peripheral vision of the pedestrian traffic, making a mental note of the 'business' corners we'd visit later.

"No, I suppose it would not." She attempted a laugh.

"Are you okay?" In three words I somehow managed to convey the entire gathering of all my newly created doubts.

She smiled. "Yes. I am."

"If that does happen again-"

"It shall not."

"Other-"

"I know how to escape it now. It doesn't matter how great the force is. I do not have to fight it, but flee from its clutches."

"But-"

"I learned from my mistake Dagger."

"And I-"

"You cannot hurt me as they did." She laughed at my irritation, a shining gold eye disappearing behind a charcoal line when she winked, smirking at her obvious replication of human actions and at my irritation. I didn't like having my sentences finished for me as much as she liked to do it. But I didn't have time to retaliate. We were already at the station.

I left the thugs in the car and walked over to the back door of the police headquarters, ignoring the rain still pouring down. She stayed close, both of us recognizing that this was a risk, as was any confrontation we took without knowing all of the variables. If the chance was not taken from the outside, but within me, there would be no quick aerial escape to safety as we were forced to take many times before. I had learned to recognize the signs of when the creature inside of me was scratching at its cage, and the door was too easy to open if I gave in to the overwhelming easy nature of surrender to my synthetic instincts. But, recognizing the signs did me little good in stopping their progression, once the door was opened it was not possible to shut it, not until every threat I perceived was neutralized – by flight or by force – and it was a sober reality to discover that her light didn't always win over the darkness the beast cast.

I nodded to her, letting her know that for then, it remained contained.

I texted the Lieutenant on my latest burner cell, simply saying 'here'.

Within a minute he stood in the lit doorway, his pulse racing, epinephrine coursing through his veins with the same urgency as the air forced over his vocal chords. "Go! You have to go – Hurry – before someone sees you. Quit staring at me like I'm losing my mind! The city has everyone on the force looking for you and you show up here without a warning – I can't put a stop this – It's over my head. You need to get out. *Now*."

Let me handle him Dagger. She watched me, waiting for my acceptance. She was then completely drenched and glowing faintly from the power she'd drawn in preparation against the elevated levels of his stress. The raindrops glinted like diamonds in the moments before they struck her, turning into steam that rolled off her skin.

I nodded, setting my jaw.

"I can assure you, as of right now no one within a mile of any direction knows we are here, now please, explain to us what has changed, Lieutenant." Star questioned him softly.

"It's not just us. That's what I'm trying to tell you. They found the pattern – you're too concentrated here – they know you're linked to this station and they have the whole city on lockdown-"

"Who?"

He stepped back, throwing his hands in the air.

"Pick anyone! We've lost jurisdiction on every case you two are suspected of being involved in. I'm under a bus – we've got more suits than uniforms in there and that's just the FBI. Look, I'm not afraid for you two but my family - this is getting too big."

"Who is the leader of the group currently pursuing our whereabouts?"

"An agent from DC. That's why you need to lay low."

"The guy is in there?" I asked.

"Don't-"

114

She walked to the door, not needing any type of signal to know what I wanted. The rain, though still soaking me, had evaporated off her in the moment she got out of it. The Lieutenant watched, helpless, as we passed him, stuttering more warnings.

"Keep me level." I warned her. She nodded to my unspoken gratitude, the satin skin of her palm growing warmer as the persistent chokeholds of my suspicions evaporated under her unearthly touch. I followed the sounds of the muffled shouting, the voice foreign to those I had grown to recognize inside the building. The smells of smoke and commercial cleaners gave way to department store cologne as we climbed the stairs, stopping outside a door with no window to see what was behind it.

"The Captain and the agent have been at it for an hour."

"Stay out here until I call you in." I told Locker.

Regardless of how it ended, we didn't need witnesses. He balked at first, startled by the request, but consented in an accepting step back to the way we had come.

"They are never going to believe me when I tell them a couple of dressed up vigilantes did this! The public is demanding action – Washington is. This cover up is not going to hold and I know this department knows something."

"We've told you everything-"

"No! I am not going to be made out to be a (...) for ('crying out loud') in front of the (random board of suits who signed his checks)! This clusterf…" his voice shriveled like the last of his dying bravado when I opened the door. In the moments of brief silence that followed I saw the room and its inhabitants clearly.

There was the man we can't name for his own safety now, with skin whose color had taken on a shade reminiscent of rotten milk. His suit was nice enough to show his profession but simple enough to make him still able to blend into a crowd. The small orange hairs stuck to the bottom of the pant legs suggested he owned a cat. The wrinkles in them betrayed the suitcase he had arrived with. No ring, only a thin line of slightly paler skin along the base of his left ring finger. Brown hair slightly grey at temples, died at the top, clean shaven; from the pace of his heart and state of appearance, early fifties at most. Manicured nails paired with botox in between his brows – *elections coming up, hand shaking, photo ops with different candidates. Higher up than just a special agent.* Slight impressions beneath his eyes, our work was apparently complicating his.

As detailed as my observations were, I knew Stargazer had the ability to go deeper than what was superficially observable, I also knew digging deep into people's heads was one of her least favorite parts of what we did, and as it seems, the one threat to her, meaning unless I asked, I was on my own here.

It wouldn't be a problem.

"You're..." He quickly spoke up, only to pause in fear.

I picked up a large, metal stapler and crushed it in my free hand.

"Real?" I finished. He gulped. The other man in the room, who I had summed up in the first two seconds to be nothing more than a helpless passerby in all this, likely some over schooled public relations 'Spinner', had fainted.

He stammered, falling back two steps at a time, his hand falling to his side and laying on the desk, his eyes darting to the top drawer.

Out of the corner of my gaze, she smirked.

Not that it makes a difference for us, Dagger.

She appeared at his side, opened the drawer and picked up the gun, offering to him, the barrel pointed at her chest.

He stared, stunned.

The gun melted in her hands, the red hot metal dripping down her fingertips. I remembered the first time I had seen that little trick, and his response was nothing less than what she'd wanted.

"Whoever is your superior, tell them what you have seen, and what our intentions are. We have never killed, nor have we failed to turn in anyone we have found to be guilty to the proper authorities. Even when you have failed –"

"And if they are released because the prosecutors can't do your job well enough to put them away even when they're hand delivered, then we will just get them again, and again, until you and every other degree slinging red-taper can get them legally. We aren't going to sit around waiting for due process when a hundred other people get robbed, raped, murdered, or stolen in the time it takes to fill out a single sheet of paperwork. You want to do it the 'right way'? Tell your people to stop giving parking tickets and prosecuting low level one timers and start doing stake outs. Otherwise don't think you have any right to come and intrude on our lot in this, or think you hold any power to say what we're required to do. We don't owe you or the government or this country anything –"

She continued where I had stopped, and his silence I rightfully suspected was her doing. "What we do is on our terms and under our own conscience and it is not limited to this city or this nation, nor is it controlled by either. Know this: your guns, your position, and your associates mean nothing to us. The only reason we are here is on behalf of Locker, and his department, who have done nothing to hide our presence or aid us in our pursuits, and in such you have no means by which to charge them. If you place this city under direct control then we will set it free, and we will start by removing the ones holding the chains."

"You're not in any position to be making demands!" He defended, oblivious or just too stupid to see the fact I hadn't been asking for his input.

"We're not making demands. We are telling you, right now, if you want to waste time trying to stop us, go ahead. You won't win."

"This is our statement." She murmured. She took my hand, sensing the fraying ties that held down the monster that wanted to grab this guy and everyone in the building whispering over our insanity and their own cowardice and shake them until their heads spun back into place.

We turned to go and made it halfway down the stairs before Locker stopped us.

"It's not over you know."

"We know."

"It's just going to get worse. We've had to drop over a dozen cases without witnesses – without you both. And with everything we're doing being watched…this is not going away."

"We will, if needed, testify this instance, only as a gesture of good will towards this government's justice system. However, this will not be asked of us again unless we offer it. As he said, it is not in our place to judge those who we cease in their doings, that is upon your prosecutors shoulders. I take it you all did not get to where you are by failing to bear such burdens."

He sighed.

"I can't promise it will help much, but thank you."

"We will be there." She assured him. When she failed to ask over what case or when the hearing was I knew she'd done me a favor and gotten what we needed to know.

"Tell the DA no press."

"Thank you again, both of you, for everything." He stared at her, film covering his eyes. "If either of you ever need-"

"Well there is an automobile full of criminals outside and you may want to take this one?" She hinted.

He smirked, shaking his head in disbelief.

Righteous Council

We cut out way up the dirty-granite-steps of the courthouse, fenced in by flashing cameras and screaming-pushing-humans. Black Dagger kept his hand securely around mine, our closeness only adding to their screeching demands. The clicking lights were dying stars, blinding me with their hazardous-flashes-artificial-energy.

"Focus on me." He cautioned, aware of my growing unease. His hand rested against my back, trying to create a barrier between the world and I. I vaguely nodded. I did not enjoy crowds such as this, when everyone's energy was directed towards my own in a never-ceasing assault. Anonymity had offered us, me, the sanctuary to exist in areas of dense-human-contact without such a unseen battle. Without it, I struggled under the supernova of their combined consciousness.

We were told to behave as best as possible. I tried to recall what Black Dagger and I had discussed about the human-in-charge-of-our-case the night before, finding my thoughts difficult to contain as my conscious power was battered by so many outside forces at once. He had made me promise him to keep the nature of identity undisclosed, after nearly three measured-time-hours of debate. I had protested, using every logical argument to be found, but when all reason had been set aside, he was trying to get me to understand his rightful 'awareness' that we were not without worthy enemies here. As hard as it was, I had submitted, something I found myself regretting when they again and again dared to grab at us for meaningless questions.

"You are certain that is the exact order events?"

"Yes." She said flatly.

"And what were you out doing at the time in order to witness such events?" He cocked his head in confidence.

I wanted nothing more than to get that beady eyed creep out of her face and bring her home. The seat I was in could have been inlaid with my own version of kryptonite and it wouldn't have made a difference. I was powerless, and I despised it.

"We were merely out walking…the city has a certain beauty once the sun sets." Her infusing charisma brought an expression of wonder over the court.

"And you expect this court to believe you were able to subdue my clients, Celeste, with a mere case of coincidence?" He thought he'd her at that. She made a point to let her contact covered eyes narrow, even beneath the false coloring they darkened to nearly black. It was as furious as I had yet to see her, but it was the stillness of her anger that was its greatest threat. No one knew the dynamite they danced in circles around while carrying torches.

She answered, which opened up another flood of questions regarding our lack of respect of the city wide curfew, of our trustworthiness, our honesty, our account of how we had happened upon the robbery. Cross examinations followed, a dozen 'objections' and enough manure based arguments to fertilize the Sahara.

She did not ever break the surreal stillness of her face, her eyes locked with mine whenever they were not on the jury.

◆

He smiled at me; it was a halfhearted smile, one weighted not by unease but mischief.

I reached out my consciousness to his.

Do not do what I know you are planning.

Why not? It isn't like there are cameras in here. It's better than you doing something.

Please, I do not wish to cause harm to anyone when I retrieve you out of the high-secured-psychological-institution they will most likely put you in, and I am not going to enjoy having to track you down when your Modifiers find you afterwards.

Star don't go there —

I am sorry, I should not have voiced that, but my views remain unchanged. If we do this, we must be prepared for any ramification. I am willing to undertake such a risk, and am not in fear of what would come from it, are you?

I'm tired of hiding.

I know you are. We have spent too long in the shadows.

I won't overdo it.

It is your choice, Dagger. It was your wish that the extent of our abilities were to remain without solid proof of their existence, but if we are to declare our prowess, should it not be in sight of everyone?

The muscles of his jaw tightened, the nod too slight for anyone but I to notice. The next partial hour was endless, and the proceedings went on in the manner of the paper-powered courts until we were dismissed.

◆

"What did you say in there?!"

"What part do you play in this?!"

"How do you respond to the 'vigilante' statements?!"

121

"How do you plan to…?"

"What do you say to the allegations against you?"

"What are your names?!"

"How do you explain the numerous accounts of special abilities belonging to both of you?"

"No comment." I hissed, taking her by her side and drawing her closer to me. Too much direct contact with their energies would leave her 'power drunk,' which was a lot less funny and a whole lot more dangerous than it had sounded the first time she had described it to me.

We had pushed halfway down the crowded steps before she turned around to face me. She grabbed my hand, letting her smoldering eyes speak. I wrapped my arm around her waist as she tilted her head towards mine, meeting my smirk with her own. Whether the roar was the paparazzi's yells or the sound of blood rushing through my body, I will never know.

She smiled before launching us up into the air at an untold speed, leaving the combined clicks of over sixty cameras beneath us.

We landed in a park a few miles away, far enough that no one would think to look for there but close enough that she could still listen in on the action if need be. We had sat beneath a large, old oak tree in silence until some very, very brave kid with smart phone came snooping. After a few minutes I realized it wasn't the pretty girl that he was ogling at. He knew.

"Can we go *now*?" I asked her again.

"Wait, he is working up the courage to ask you for your approval to give the photos out. He is afraid you might say no and take away his device." She explained.

"Don't tempt me."

"Do not be so overzealous in your cautions, what is one boy's photos in the wake of the thousands that are now being published?"

"Anyone close to us is at risk."

"As that is true, I see no reason for him to be included. I think if you would be just a little less *ominous*, he might come speak to us."

That was every reason to *leave*.

"Hello." She called over to the red headed boy, half exposed behind a bush.

"Star what are you getting at?" I knew, I just wanted her to know I didn't like it.

"Come with me." She got up, pulling me along with her.

She led the way towards the kid. He debated on either running away in terror or falling over dead in shock, but somehow landed on sitting there with the most stunned of blank expressions. She got down on her knees, her long, thin skirt forming small hills of sapphire colored fabric around her. "It is alright. We do not wish to hurt you child." She purred and held out her hand. The kid eyed it warily, and then took it. She pulled him and herself up to their feet with one fluid motion.

She was glowing.

"Sup'?" I asked him, trying to assure him I was not quite as scary as I looked. At least not right then.

"Hi." He half squeaked.

"What is your name?" She asked, as if it was the most normal conversation ever.

"I'm, uh, Terry."

"Hello Terry, I am Stargazer, this is Black Dagger. How old are you, child?"

"Almost ten." He said, obviously proud of the fact. I wondered why he was alone, and then questioned whether or not he really was. There were five human heart beats within three hundred yards, all of them old enough to have been his parents. They were stable, for then, meaning his absence was unnoticed. If that changed, we need to leave.

"Did you wish for a photographic capture of us?" Star beamed.

The kid looked like he saw Christmas morning, the next generation PlayStation, and a real life Pokémon all at once, but what had struck me as odd was how she bore the same expression.

"Really!? You'd let me?! I saw you guys on the news and then I saw you here and-and I wanted to talk, but I-I didn't know if you were…nice." He stared with undeserved wonder and amazement. "You want to see right?" He hurriedly handed over the phone, complete with slightly cracked screen in the corner. It had nearly a hundred pictures on it of just us, from every angle he could have possibly gotten it from.

I looked at the small-digital-device.

"I would like copies of the past-viewing-mirrors for myself." I said to the little-sun-freckled human. I kept my mind on the edge of his, watching his thoughts. I was amazed at how simple he saw things, at the purity of his rational and the effortlessness of his beliefs. I wanted nothing more than to keep him that way, to protect his innocence, to promise him a life free of pain. In that moment it was what I wanted more than anything, and I knew I could do it, but there is a greater pain than watching innocence and knowing the injustice to come and being powerless to stop it. It is called 'should' – because regardless of my ability, it was not my place. I could have hidden him away and taught him things beyond even the greatest of worldly comprehensions, but he was not mine to take nor to teach.

Then I will simply protect him, if I cannot save him.

"Thank you guys so much! How awesomely cool is this! Oh everyone at school will go crazy when I tell them!" I liked how the boy's face dented when he smiled, the great heights of his joy and the brightness of his life unspoiled by obscurity. "I can't believe this, real live super-heroes!"

124

"Just don't go telling everyone until after we leave, got it?"

His energy suddenly changed to one of surprising sadness. "Oh well...I texted my dad before I talked to you guys. See we were all here for his work's barbeque and I ran off when I saw you so I had to tell him where I was and..."

Black Dagger handed him back his cellular device. The boy's hand took his possession back with shaking-wavering fingers.

"You know computers?"

The child eagerly nodded.

"Leave these on thumbdrive under that tree tomorrow. We will pick it up once the park is clear. ...Thanks." Dagger said roughly. The young, joyous human smiled wider than before.

"Will I see you guys again?"

"We will see you again, though you may not see us." I said, knowing that as much as I may want those things, his life wasn't meant to intertwine with mine more than it already had.

I left with him just as I felt the energies of adult humans arriving where we once had been. I looked down and saw upturned, shocked faces staring back.

-BD- SG

We were all the rage ever since Stargazer decided to take off in front of live recording cameras. I had not approved of that particular exploit, once the blood had returned to my head. I had agreed to demonstrate a bit of what we were capable of, if only to gain some respect from the general population, but I had not intended for her to be the one to do it. I hadn't wanted it to become the most ground-shattering event since Pangaea split.

Since we were suddenly Prime Time material, when we caught people we had to make sure they were real criminals and not just reporters trying to bait us into an interview. Four times it had happened, once with a business guru staging his own mugging who was in cahoots with a cop wearing a body cam who 'was nearby', another was a politician who 'happened across a horrifying scene and came to the aid of the unknown vigilantes'...I'd nearly lost my head over that. Cutting the brakes on all the interns cars and having them causes a pile up that shuts down nearly six blocks and would have put fourteen people in the ICU had Stargazer not been there isn't a political move, it's a criminal one. The other two were a reporter who pretended to take his office hostage in exchange for an interview, and last was a day time talk show host who tried to manipulate us into appearing on air by promising to 'show the real story of your miraculous feats behind the shady rumors you must so hatefully despise' after we had "saved" him from a fire he had set to building where he filmed.

We hopped cities every few nights, always returning to our own but never staying longer than it took for me to sleep and for her to learn as best as she could where we would be most needed when I woke up. Within a month, we had publically gone international, our actions in other countries brought to light with the same haphazard attention to detail as anywhere else.

Only Star was content with our public status. She said the more the world knew of us, the less likely they were to try to do wrong for fear of our retribution. I had yet to see evidence of that. It seemed the more the media fed off us the less it paid attention to the real news, not that it had ever paid much attention to begin with, but we certainly weren't helping. To help bring the craziness down a few notches, we decided we should just give a universal statement, a single message to put everyone in their places and declare our purpose, and subsequently, deny them any hope of us ever sitting down with Oprah or the Today Show.

We delivered them to the home of the New York Times editor. The next morning this ran across on the front page:

126

BREAKING THE SILENCE
City's 'Protectors' Give Statements to Editor's Wife!

Excerpt: "Wife of the Time's editor, Janice E. Marks, says that the two, so called 'protectors' by many of the public, brought a small packet to her door last night. Although she admits to have blacked out in shock caused by their uninvited appearance, she "swears it was the same kids on the news and at that court house." We have yet hear any direct reports or verifications of the encounter and the two have not contacted us to any further extent to verify.

Printed on the packet's contents were hand written statements. The New York City police department had run the evidence through unnamed databases and conducted dozens of tests, but nothing surfaced that our staff was able to learn of before the envelope and its contents were seized by government authorities. We still do not know who these 'Protectors' are, where they came from, or why they have chosen to give us their comments now.

The packet's enclosed statements are as follows:

"We're on your side but don't stand in our way. -Black Dagger-"

"We seek only to shield those in peril and rid this world of darkness, and to those who choose to hide in it will soon face the light of a thousand suns. -Stargazer"

The two, now having given their names as Black Dagger and Stargazer, have been reported to be responsible for over four hundred arrests in the last four to five months, though reports are indefinite and have not been officially accounted for by police task forces in the dozens of cities they have been reported in. Personal accounts of their actions have tallied in the thousands, with more reported every day.

In addition to recent documented footage we have a few eye witness exclusives that claim they are capable of unimaginable…."

The newspaper article continued to elaborate on almost every one of our many nights out, except the few that involved our accidental (or forced) cooperation with the CIA or the FBI or one of the many other acronyms your taxes pay for. I was wary of them, I admit it, but only because of Star. Dr. Evil was at the back of my mind. They could guess who I was, but knowing my identity and which city I was in on any given night, and then actually finding me, were two completely different things. With Star I could be in Detroit or Chicago one hour and Atlanta the next, leaving them no breadcrumbs to follow. Therefore, the government was my main safety concern. The very organizations that begged on their knees for our help would also do anything for her "abduction" if they were to ever learn the truth of her existence. Or if they already knew, which I didn't doubt, they were just waiting for the opportunity to take her, a chance I wasn't willing to give them.

She told me after I had expressed my concerns that even if she were to ever get caught, finding a way to completely kill her was impossible. I couldn't help but bring up her dark energy encounter. She had only looked at me, smiling and shaking her head. *"If the day comes when you find out my protection for yourself, you will know everything."* She'd said simply, leaving me standing dumbstruck and irritated in our apartments' hallway.

Golden Dawn

Since the Lieutenant's son there was another side of what we did. Stargazer had not gone a single day without performing some sort of what the people called miracles. She healed and helped everyone she saw, regardless of who they were or what the risk was. Whether it was a woman dying of cancer or a guy out of a job with a family to support, she would always found a way to make their life easier. Be it handing over a lump of gold to the inner city pastor trying to raise money for a youth safe haven or granting the wish of a kid on a playground and sneaking a soldier home for an hour to see his little girl's birthday party. It didn't matter what it was, to her a need was a need. Taking out the bad guys, as cliché as the thought was, was something I did well. But her philanthropy was alien to me, her belief in a better humanity a cliff's edge of contrast to my own reasons for action. My silent presence was the only support I offered, and it was unspoken between us that she had not expected or asked for more.

It was a few months after it had begun that she had posed as a patient's sister and snuck into a hospital, with me following her, a bit less flashily. I had got in as an ER patient with head injuries. It was the easiest thing to fake and I always like I am coming out of a fight. We had already hit a hospice on the other side of town that morning, so I didn't expect us to be there long enough to come up with a better story.

Once I slipped out of the main waiting room and the gut-churning scents that went with it, I caught a glimpse of her walking down one of the halls, her hands out at her sides, a soft glow around her palms the only hint to the 'life-light' she permeated the atmosphere with. I lost her a minute later when a family appeared from an elevator, hiding which turn she'd taken. I had to redouble my steps, and nearly crashed into a nurse near the ICU, where I had guessed Star would be.

The whole floor reeked of death – sweet, rotten, slowly consuming death. A quick glance through the small window in the door revealed white washed walls, nurses in ironically cheerful pastel scrubs, and beds whose occupants were more machine than human. The fact Stargazer wasn't there was not a good sign.

After a hurried apology to the nurse and pretending to be lost, some backtracking later I found her in the burn unit, marked by the smallest but most daunting of little blue signs. There were only a few rooms occupied, and only one had no one standing outside of it. When I entered through the mirrored glass door I saw that she was leaning against the short white bed, as if her body that never tired was suddenly overcome.

She made no action to show she knew I was there.

I looked at the girl lying in the bed, the source of the room's sickening scents and ominous presence of fate. She was a total wreck, her full body wrapped in white gauze, stark red blood seeping through in parts. I could smell the other people on her, beneath the tinge of burnt flesh and antiseptics, the cadaver skin that lay in between her wounds and the bandages. Tubes looped in and out of her like a roller-coaster at Six Flags over hell. A whirring machine forced air into her lungs. The faint, weak throbbing of her heart, marked by sharp beep from the monitor to the side, left a rock in my stomach.

I placed my hand on her shoulder.

She turned, looking up to me in shock and sorrow. Her star-studded eyes that had darkened into a deep chocolate grew ever dimmer when she saw the understanding in mine. I pulled her against me, locking her in my arms.

"...I don't think that I can." She did not cry. Even her voice was the most calculated of even tones. Yet her fingers knotted in my shirt and her arms locked around me. It knocked some of my breath out, but she needed me more than I needed air. "She is dying, Dagger, and I fear...I fear I cannot save her."

I tilted her chin up, running my thumb over her cheek. "She's..." I couldn't finish that. I had no choice but to see this for what it was, a horrible tragedy and an end that couldn't be stopped. I wasn't allowed hope anymore, but damn me if I denied her of it. "People have lived through these things before you. She could make it out of this." I tried to comfort her. She felt horrible when her efforts proved fruitless or she was too late. She would spend hours staring, just staring, not at anything, not even at the sky. She would only come out of it when she got wind of 'another matter worthy of our attention.'

"I know." She buried her face in my chest, her nails clutching my back. "I have the knowledge to save her, but if I do not have the strength..." She sighed and turned to face the severely hurt, guessingly teenage girl.

She seemed to look worse than before. Her eyes flickered rapidly underneath her bright red, blue veined eyelids. Her face was swollen, her leathery skin, what little of it was not hidden, was nearly yellow. It was impossible to tell what she might have looked like before. I, in my serum 'fixed' head, knew exactly how much of her surface was burned and it was amazing she was even breathing, even if on a machine. Almost ninety percent of her was burned, sixty of it second degree and the remainder third and fourth degree, from what I could tell from the bandaging and lack of it. She would be fortunate for just another hour. Another minute even. If fortune is what you could call being forced to live. *And I think* I'm *unlucky... poor kid.*

"If we belong to an endless universe then so too are we endless." She whispered, one of her hands was placed on the girl's head, the other on her heart. She took a shallow breath. "Even so, this will be much greater a feat than any I have done before. You will need to shield your eyes, I cannot promise I will be able to monitor my light."

"I'm right here." I touched her shoulder, kneeling next to her. She put up a false smile, the copper tint of her fear saying more than she ever would.

"Thank you…but you should not touch me either. If I am to do this, I must be as I am, void of what you see to be human. There will be no barrier to shield you with, and though I can keep my radiation contained, you mustn't be here, not this close, else you may bear scars as she does."

I grimly nodded, lifting my hand.

She looked back at the girl.

"What are you doing?!" Someone yelled out. I spun around and saw a woman and a male nurse running towards us through the open doorway.

"I'll be outside."

She nodded, her eyes and attention never leaving the girl.

"What're you doing in there? Let us by!" The suddenly purple faced man yelled to me.

"I can't do that." I kept my voice low and monotone, trying to keep him calm. Star needed time.

"Move out of the way or I'll call security! That room is sterilized! No one allowed in-no one!"

… This is my gift to this race. I sought knowledge by my own will and power by my own might and by my own choice I am offering it.

I pressed my hand lightly against her. I took all of her hurt from her, pooling it in my being. Her fear was immense, and though she was unconscious, she did *feel* it, and she frantically wanted it to end. Her seemingly sedated mind was scrambling for an escape, crying out in a broken voice for rescue from this torture, for not every nerve had been seared-sealed from the pain she had suffered and continued to. I drew all the energy-power as I could from within me and transferred it to the young-female-human. I could feel hers and my own

132

bodies for a split-passing second, the searing-breath-stealing pain of our injuries bringing us both on the verge of surrender. Our hearts hammered in protest, each beat harder and more strenuous than the last. Our minds sparked and spat a thousand sudden thoughts, all of them directed at every throbbing cell that made us, every desperate prayer of deliverance. I let the ties to my physical form evaporate as our lungs roared to life, the machine useless now that so much power was being forced through our veins. Our burns manifested into the flames that had given birth to them, igniting for the last time so that they might die and heal. Our skin crawled as it molded over the open and raw expanses of our flesh, absorbing the foreign cells as its own in its quest to mend what was broken. Our bones shifted as our muscles' fibers were aligned in harmony. Our tongues tasted the blood; our eyes saw the purple haze of what seemed to be the cloud we desperately sought to yield into.

A strand of a doubt crossed my thoughts, that this was deeper than I had ever been, that the doubt itself seemed to have not come from my own mind, or even hers, but she needed more. She was still in pain. She was not yet whole. She needed more of me, and I found myself giving it without restraint. As her mind cleared, mine became ever more hazed.

I struggled as my force was draining too quickly for me to have power over it and watched helplessly as the girl began to heal faster and faster, like a spark that burns the brightest, my desire to heal her ignited and burnt out in fleeting moments. An eruption of escaping light exploded from within me, too great to only leave through my palms, pouring out of every energy path within me, so that I was nothing more than a vessel. For a fraction of a moment, I was the light, I was the power in her and in the room, my body was still, my soul in all but in nothing, my eyes looking into my eyes, before the light was consumed by her and the world crashed back into place with a thunder unlike anything of earth that began within me, rocking the foundations of my matter as if an entire universe inside of my being had collapsed upon itself. Through my dying ties the world, the smallest reflection of it crossed over into this realm, before everything came shattering down.

In a jolt, I returned to the shelter of my tangible form. I felt myself melt onto cold-serialized-blurred flooring, the acidic embrace of nothingness all too willing to accept me, and I wished for nothing more than to be able to see him again.

The white room was gone as I lost my sight.

I looked at the man as he yelled even louder. "That girl is in serious condition! She needs immediate care!"

"Please-please you don't understand! I don't understand! What do you want? I need to see her!" She cried as he had pulled her back in fear, meanwhile frantically clicking a small pager while a light went off overhead.

"We're here to help her."

An explosion of sound and an invisible wall of power went off, jarring the walls and our minds with its force. The glass shattered *inwards*, taking with it the air that had been in the hallway and dragging everything from the chairs that lined it to our bodies towards the epicenter of the quake. A sweltering heat burned against my eyes, forcing me to look away. I fell to my knees, overcome with the power of the hammering energy, losing my hearing and control over my body for what was perceived as hours.

I jumped to my feet the moment I could feel the ground underneath me and ran back into the room. It was all I could do to not fall out at what I saw. She was lying on her back, unconscious on the white-speckled tile floor. Her arms were spread out; her fists curled slightly, as if she had tried grab hold to something before she'd fallen. To the eyes of anyone else she would have been taken as dead for lack of breath, but it was not her stillness that brought me to my knees, but her dimness. Her body, nearly ripped clean with the force of the explosion, was pale, her face shallow and sunken. In a blur, I drew her icily cold form into my arms.

"Stargazer." I begged, silently praying she would open her eyes, that her mind would brush against mine, that anything would happen to prove she was okay. *She could die.* I thought unbelievably. I held her tighter, the truest of fears having stabbed through that wall the moment I had seen her. It was unlike anything I had ever thought to be, and the moment it came to existence it never truly left.

She took a shaky breath, knowing I would see it as a sign of life and her ability to show it. I laughed softly, drowned in relief.

"It's all right sweetheart." I panted, as much to soothe her as to comfort me.

Her head lolled against me, her body sinking further into my grasp. I grabbed the blanket off the floor, once belonging to the bed, and wrapped her in it, knowing that time was slipping. *Secure her. Get out. Evade security. Get her safe. Get her home.* Over the crashing urgings of my frantic thoughts I heard the woman start hysterically crying. *Get out of here. Get out now.*

I held Star closer and rose to my feet. I then saw the girl for the first time. Her body was restored, with nothing but porcelain skin visible behind the singed bandages. She had begun to wake up, choking on the tubes that had helped her breathe; her unscarred hands pulling at the now useless wires in her arms and at the bandages around her throat. The man was trying to help her while a suddenly appearing aid was attempting to keep the woman from losing it.

"Freeze!"

Damn it.

"Turn around slowly." A stern voice commanded. Three guards were at the doorway. "Put the woman down." The same voice ordered me again.

I gently put Star in a chair, gulping at how easily she conformed to its harsh edges. Her head fell over the armrest, her hands hanging motionless, dragging against the floor.

Get her safe.

I heard the faint clicks of their guns. Either they knew who I was or they didn't, the variable didn't change the chances of getting shot. I wasn't concerned, I could dodge fast enough to keep it from being fatal, but it would slow me down.

"If you all know what is good for you, you will let me go."

"Put your hands up!"

"I will ask you again to let us go."

"Get down on your knees! Now! Hands where we can see them!"

One of them had the guts to take a step towards her. I grabbed him, throwing him by his shoulder back into the others.

"*I dare you.*" I growled, stepping between them and her.

The youngest, a kid who was no more than a year or two out of high school, whose eyes had belonged to Star alone, dropped his weapon, his ankles shaking in an attempt to hold him upright as his O2 levels dropped. The rest looked into the room, following the kid's blank stare, first to Stargazer, and then to the girl, who was still trying to regain freedom from the machines. The microscopic shards of glass lay in a ring of diamond like sand around her, having stopped when encountering the source of the blast.

The guards mouths fell open.

I turned around and picked up Stargazer, crushing her against me. I ran out of the room, too worried to find satisfaction in the way they had hurriedly parted from my path or a faint thought of relief that they hadn't followed. Yet.

"It's okay" I assured her, ignoring my own doubts and the fact she was not conscious.

I loped down the stairs, afraid if I took the elevator they'd turn it off. Breaking out through the roof wouldn't have been a problem any other night. But not that night. I wasn't trying to make a point or capture a target. I was getting her safe, and any risk was too great of one.

I listened to the sirens getting closer. The low echoes and engine sounds betrayed the presence of SWAT soon to be arriving beneath us. I ducked into the next floor, running towards the window at the end of the hallway. Swarms of red and blue lights were sweeping the alleys. They had yet to fully surround the building. I had forty seconds before they did. I kicked the double-pained glass, its shattered pieces hitting the ground a moment later. I jumped, Star curled up securely against me, taking the shock of impact in my knees. Twenty seconds. Our apartments were too far. My options were limited to somewhere that could be reached by foot. The best one available to me was a hotel a quarter of a mile from the hospital, far enough that it wouldn't be included in the first sweep and tall enough that no building near it would see us on the roof. She was only safe when hidden.

We were halfway there when her eyes slowly fluttered open, a small gold slit in the dark shadows covering her face. She offered a tiny smile so innocent and pure that I had no choice but to return it before she once more fell against me.

I climbed up the fire escape's stairs, after having to jump onto a dumpster to reach them. The memories of every weakness she'd ever shown me, her whispered confessions, startling outbursts – all these told me one thing. She was not going to be taken from me by some super weapon making psycho. No. She was too smart for their traps. Dark energy, no matter how dangerous, could not hurt her unless she lost focus. And she rarely ever let her mind drift for long. All these things we faced every day were not lurking in the shadows, waiting to eliminate the light that threatened their existence. The only true pain of hers I had ever witnessed was something I had caused.

I held her closer, dew settling over her cool, dusted honey skin. The calm face belonging to the seemingly fragile woman I cradled against me would never again doubt herself in this world. I would not let her go, not now, not when in the moment she needed me the most was when I consented to the absolute truth that I needed her. She'd brought the dawn, she promised understanding and hope; she'd given me peace and comfort. She gave everything she was, no matter what it did to her, to share this light. And there she was, her hands dimly grasping me even in her sleep. I was not willing to let this sun set. Not when it was only now being allowed to rise.

-BD-SG

A soft-soothing energy burned behind me. I was leaning against its hard-soft source. His heart formed a captivating-mesmerizing rhythm that vibrated throughout the surrounding air. His breathing was different than other humans, less urgent. The rise and fall of it reminded me of the expansion of what this world calls solar flares. I could have stayed there for forever, listening to the tantalizing sounds of his life.

"Good morning sleepy head." He said happily, sensing my slight movement. I shifted my position so I could see his face. I was shocked at how much effort that small movement took and how tired I was after, as if this body had suddenly taken on the traits and not the appearance of human tendency.

"...How long was I cataleptic?" The faintest rays of new-light illuminated the farthest, building scattered sky east of us, the stars fading into the massive-space-called-the-universe.

"About twelve hours." His was weighted with a heavy, droning tone.

"I do not know what happened." I admitted, taking hope in his lack of fear-unrest. "Is she well?"

"She is."

"I did not hurt you – or anyone else – when I lost control, did I?"

138

"Just the walls from the explosion, nothing that can't be fixed."

I felt my gaze widen. I had not realized that had been external. If it was as isolated as his words suggested, my dread was greater than called for. I glanced down to my body, answering the question as to why I felt bound by more than his hold. I felt myself begin to glow, but did not allow it.

"I need to go back and try to understand what happened, and speak to her."

"Not until you rest." He tucked me against him, embracing me so carefully I couldn't help but smile, even in the face of the irritating truth of his observation of my helplessness. It was all I could do to inhale the words to speak, and even going into light seemed like too great an effort.

"Very well." I studied his striking-captivating face. Large, almost triangular pieces of space-black hair fell over his mask and eyes, a dark halo around his contoured face. He felt my eyes resting on him and turned just as I reached up and undid his mask. He always wore it, but there was nothing from which to hide when we were alone. My fingers brushed against his shagged hair, his cheek, his eyes, his lips, memorizing his body like I had his mind.

He shook his head, smirking at my marvel-filled wonder.

"You're still out of it." He accused.

"Perhaps."

"So long as you're okay." He said, remaining passive as a way to soothe me, hiding his previous fears. I smiled. How could I not be 'okay'? He leaned towards me before pausing, as if to question if this was what I wanted. I looked into his once stone-like-eyes. A new light, like none which I had ever seen before, illuminated their darkest depths. I slid my hand to the back of his head, feeling his arms sweeping me in a slow, decisive motion against him, our lips meeting in anticipation, each of us forgetting the world we hid from for this endless moment. I heard his racing heart rate skip a few beats as he dared to hold me tighter. Finding strength through his overcoming touch, I wrapped my arm around his neck, attempting to hold him in return. The breath of his life filled me, and for an instant, I thought of what it might be like to be a part of it completely. If it was anything like this, how beautiful it must be.

"I love you." He whispered.

My mind fell quiet, as if the entire expanse of my consciousness ceased. All that existed was his colorless face, lit by the rising sun, his onyx soul-fire eyes, his hands as my only support in this world, and his light lending warmth and strength to mine.

"As I love you." I swore to him with every essence of me agreeing. He caught my wrist and smiled, the farthest corners of his eyes creased slightly. I lifted my chin, inviting him back. He kissed me again, softer this time, gentle when he pressed his cheek to mine. He whispered my name, and hearing it as if I had never heard it before, I started to faintly glow, not realizing the action left me even more exhausted than holding him had.

"Let's go home." He urged, feeling me mold into him with the viscosity of a cloud.

"No."

"You want to stay here?"

"With you." I breathed, feeling then corded bonds in arms grow securer around me.

And in that moment I had no choice. I would be here, and if he wanted, I would be with him, forever. There was no other way. He took too much of me, too much had I been willing to give, too much had he stolen without permission, and in that, I would never be whole again. Without ever becoming his, he owned enough of me to bring me to my knees, and somehow, I was at peace with this. Surrender seemed such a flawless tactic, for rather than fight a tide and drown, I found it so much more satisfying and perfect to slowly wade into it, letting it take me out into the deepest of his soul's depths.

I laid against his chest, my ear to his heart, his hand in mine, and together we watched the world evolve into a gilded dawn.

Both of my identities were then held in it.

Aerial, Past, & Present Views

"You're impossible to speak to when you are being this blindly obstinate. I am perfectly capable of handling myself." Her voice carried from the other room.

"For someone who can barely walk." I said, shutting the bare fridge with a loud thud, forgetting for the eighth time there wasn't food in her entire apartment. I didn't trust her to not find a way to lock me out if I were to leave to go to my own. I didn't trust her to be alone, either. She was too eager to prove me wrong.

"Why will you not listen to reason?" She complained.

"I am – I'm just not listening to yours." I said, returning the spacious, airy living room, the only source of light the floor to ceiling windows lining the wall. The place had come furnished, built to look like some postmodern art guru had once lived in it, hence the chairs and a barren black book shelf in the corner, and the ridiculously long, white lounge sofa she decorated. We hadn't chosen it for its charm, even if it had been the nicest of the three main hideaways we had, but for the security system and privacy the two segments of the top floor offered.

"All we have done is sit here as helpless as children watching the world as it gossips over our inaction, and scurries about in a panic over things they are capable of handling but in terror of taking the responsibility for, and you are allowing it. Even if it were true that I am still unable to aid you, you have subjected yourself to these walls. You're being …pig headed." She accused, unable to hide the smile from her voice at the end.

"Maybe. But you're still not going out. I don't care how strong you think you are. The only thing you're up for, like it or not, is to be bait. And I'm not taking that risk. So shut up." My tone made it sound more like a warning and less like the empty threat we knew it was.

"I am, as you say, fine – see for yourself?" She stood up, her mauve dress clinging to her. I smirked. Before she caught on, I swept her upwards, setting her back on the couch, holding her there. If she could get out, I might reconsider. She'd guess as much.

"No, you're not. You're my prisoner and consider this apartment your prison until you're well. I'm not letting you go too far again. The risk of getting caught is higher since we've been inactive, everyone has their ear to the ground trying to find us and if you're compromised we–" I paused, feeling her hands run up my back, her narrowing eyes a playful warning.

"I'm *your* prisoner?" She purred, the gold curve of her throat tightening. Her fingers caught in the collar of my shirt, pulling my willing body towards her. "Have you ever wondered what could have been so desirable about *this* form that an entire civilization took it on at their own will?" She smirked.

And then I was on my back, staring at the ceiling with a mixture of bewilderment and a broken ego. About the time air returned to my lungs I realized she had played me. She smiled when I looked at her, my stunned expression matching my thoughts.

"Do not think too highly of yourself Dagger, for I am not the only one capable of being compromised. I might have to prove you wrong every now and then." In a very human manner, she winked.

"That was not fair play." I had nailed the 'bait' analogy, but I hadn't planned on being the one who fell for it.

"Same as it is not fair to impose the boundaries of your faith in my abilities as their actual limits, even if I am...laid up." She grimaced at the word.

"So you admit it."

"…Perhaps, but despite my limitations, did I not just pass your so called test? It is not as if I used anything against you any human woman might not possess. You may be different than others, and have greater control as you say, but you are far from immune. Thus, I am not as helpless even in your eyes."

I pivoted forward, landing on my knees, my face level with hers. "Wrong."

"The fact you were the one on your back says otherwise."

"It has nothing to do with what you think. You are the sole thing that manages to break through me and I refuse to let the world get to you when you are weakest. Hate me for it if you want Star, even if we both know I have no way of physically keeping you here, but I will not consent to you going out there and putting yourself at risk. Not right now, not until I know that if it came down to it you would be able to get out, no matter what the cost."

She laughed, looking away from me and out of the windows.

"That is but another lie you believe, to think I am not held here. As you wish, I will not seek to return to our calling before I am able to meet it with the same conviction and capability as before." She looked back to me. "Have you found her yet?"

I shook my head. I hadn't tried to, beyond a few phone calls from a burner cell and a five minutes at a reception desk.

"Don't worry, we will take care of it."

"But I must rest first," she said, animatedly rolling her eyes.

BD // SG

144

I felt her honey-like consciousness wash over my mind. *Do you wish to fulfill a forgotten promise?* A series of memories, pictures, bits of conversation, and even emotions surfaced from within my almost forgotten memories. She withdrew.

"Why now?"

"Because if you are to find the strength to overcome the demons in our present, Dagger, there can be nothing in your past to hinder it."

"None of that matters anymore." She didn't buy it. "I don't even know where-."

"I know where she is." Her face betrayed a story she'd yet to tell me about.

"I couldn't do that to her now that… We would know if that company had- if she had gone missing." I stammered, trying my best to implement some sort of emotion into my brain's artificial need to flee the threat. "Star, I don't think *I* can handle that." I admitted. Reminders were always a touchy subject.

"She was different for you then. She was not faked."

"What am I supposed to say? I can't exactly explain this all away." I asked, defiant.

Her hand holding mine tighter, reminding me of the previously forgotten contact, she whispered, "I will do my best to make this easier, but in all the expanse of what you perceive as time since, it has not been laid to rest, and if you cannot gain peace, it will always follow you. Your own reasoning will argue in favor that unresolved is the term preceding to chaos. Dagger, I would not ask this of you if I did not know she needed you. You must trust me in this."

"Not tonight. I need to think, to plan what she'll want to know." The faint unease he held was only a shadow of the feeling welling up within me.

"Of course."

"Detroit?" I questioned. I wanted to do something, anything that would release the tension.

"And Memphis." She reminded me. A random and widely public appearance by us would send enough of the night life running back into their holes to let the police, at least those that hadn't been paid off, make headway. It wasn't as tactical as I had wanted, but we rarely left without incident, and if I couldn't run from the prospect she had brought to life, ridding the world of a few of its own issues was a close second.

She pulled me up against her, drawing my hands around her hips, preparing to take off. I no longer felt the need to go chase someone down.

-BD- SG

She could have 'flown' to New York City in a matter of seconds, but to do that she would literally have to become her true state, a manner of energy that made it impossible for me to accompany her. She had first done that with me watching her, slowly becoming transparent and then simply vanishing. She'd still been there by the wave of heat that washed about the room, her mind remaining just on the edge of my own. Her consciousness had not changed in the slightest, even though her body was gone. She had rematerialized only a few inches in front of me, brightly glowing. Other than that, she'd showed no other signs of her former "transfer of conscious states".

As it was, we'd been flying for less than a handful of minutes and didn't have too much longer to go, from what I calculated from the wind speed and the changing terrain below us. I judged how high we were from how clearly I could see the ground.

"Catch me." I said as I let go, the initial thrill sending my pulse as high as I was free falling from. Air rushed up at me with a lung crushing, bone shattering force. I turned my body downwards, putting my hands against my sides and my legs straight. The sense of pure aliveness charged within me,

146

sending sparks through every nerve inside of me until the rush was all I felt. I didn't give into the urge of self-preservation until I was close enough to the ground to count the rows in the farm below. I was just about to call for Star when I felt her soft arms wrap around my torso and gravity's intense pull on me begin to lessen.

"The next instance you feel the need to test theories of space and time, perhaps you should give me a proper warning." I nestled my face between his head and shoulder, locking my arms so that should his carelessness-desire-for-exhilaration overcome him again he could not act on them so readily. If that failed, I had dropped our altitude and had slowed down considerably, lessening the temptation.

"Next time." He put his cool hands over mine. They didn't stay feeling cool for long, my power-force drawn to his with the same ferocity that had lead me to his side. "I wonder if paratroopers ever get used to it." He panted. I was confused at his terms and he noticed somehow. "Military." He explained, taking in air faster.

I simply nodded.

I personally didn't like much of the humans' governments, no country seemed to grasp full understanding, and the one where we spent the majority of our time then was no better. Escaping me completely, they did do some things well enough to apparently be permitted to continue, but I had no such form of régime and would not submit to theirs. It was to my utter horror-complete-revulsion-disgust how they allowed the killing of their own kind who had yet to have been allowed to live. I thought long and hard over ways to completely annihilate that altogether and was forced to realize that it was a conscious choice these creatures made.

"I see...we will be landing shortly."

He nodded, as we had previously agreed to not enter the city publicly. It would not have been our first time there, however, we were not entering as its protectors. The call of anonymity manifested in the hoards who rushed through its streets was to be our guide, and it had to be answered quietly.

Disbelief

I stood outside of an underground club. Not hipster underground, literally underground, some tripped out basement of an old construction warehouse in the middle of Hell's Kitchen. A line of people, almost a hundred bodies long, stood waiting to just get in to the door, regardless of the fact that the large building behind them was anything but inviting. She had left me there alone twenty-two minutes prior, giving me the chance to scope the crowd and make a note of everything I heard from their conversations from the graffiti covered wall I stood against across the street. The police could have filled every holding cell for three precincts on possession charges alone. I wasn't listening for information, even if my habit I had categorized much of what was said.

A rush of heat against my right side betrayed her presence.

"No police other than one a block up and DEA undercover – the woman who keeps glancing at the bouncer. No one has said anything. You're sure that she's here?"

"Yes."

I looked over at her, caught off guard.

"I assumed blending in would be in our best interest this evening? It seemed everyone here blends in by being lurid with their apparel. It is close, yes?"

I must have nodded.

She smiled, looking back to the building. "There are four hundred and thirty-five people inside, not including her. It will take me a moment to locate her definite position upon entry. There are security cameras inside, you would be wise to leave your solar-shielding glasses on, though I will do what I can to disrupt their feeds. I fear I will be sorely distracted once we enter, I will need you as close to me as you can be. As for passage…He will not accept the paper-money you have, it's not enough, but..."

"But?" I dreaded the 'but' she slipped in whenever she planned something I wouldn't approve of.

She walked to the front of the line. A huge bouncer, and I nearly found a piece of humor in the fact that even I could appreciate his stature, guarded the door. Her steps in shoes that looked impossible to stand in regardless had been purposefully unsteady, but the ploy didn't end there. She put her hand of her hip, the painted metal bracelets clinking as she leaned her weight on one foot and tilted her head slightly in my direction, her eyes hidden behind mirrored shades.

"Can my friend and I get in?" The girly squeak that rang from her lips left what little amount of shock I could feel blatantly displayed on my face.

"Come on darling." The guy approvingly ran his eyes over her. Had she not been staring directly at me with the words "shut up" written behind her glasses, the trick would have ended there. As it was, he opened the door and let the both of us pass through. I heard a few, yelling complaints from the people in line.

"Nice." I said sarcastically, over the noise.

"I did not feel like pressuring his thoughts, as this will take all of my concentration." She explained, her head turning over the room.

I hate parties. That one was no better than any other. It was bigger and louder, but that was it. The music vibrated throughout the room and the strobe lights lit up parts of the crowd, including us at one point, causing a dozen heads to turn when the white light lit her pure gold skin before we were once again hidden in darkness. I had a sense of dread at what I wished I wouldn't soon find, but then that terror was pushed down when the majority of the guys in there noticed her.

Then I was just ticked off.

I scanned the room's extreme-flashing-rotating-changing energies. What I felt was *unreal*. Some of the people burned with such force that I knew the source of their vigor-life was not natural while others were near unconscious, yet still their bodies moved. The drug-of-humans'-light seemed to block my mind from body. My power began to spin and I started to feel 'lightheaded' as more and more humans' energies changed and morphed it extravagant high and unbelievably low levels.

The clothes I wore, chosen to match the locations attire, did little to hide my surface from the contact of so many pressed around us, but then there was only him. He had one hand on my arm and the other directly on my back within a moment. He pulled me against him, shielding me with his arms. The cool-calm-compress shocked me from my daze, only to bring me into another one, one where what should be cold is ever smoldering.

"You okay?"

I nodded.

"Do you see her?"

I need a minute to concentrate. His presence was soothing, but not helping my focus.

Can I help?

No, not with this, I am just going to find her by searching through each one.

I shifted through the people, looking in their minds for their names, their memories. I found her after a few minutes, though I was not looking forward to what he would do. When I opened my eyes I saw him searching for any piece of information he could gleam from my features, a truth I was not eager to share.

151

No. Not true.

Shattered glass and spilt drinks surrounded her on the circular table. Her jeans were so tattered they practically nonexistent. Her thin tank top clung tightly to her even thinner, pale body. Her bleached white hair was a chopped up mess, hiding what little of her face I could see from where we stood. I was scared to so much as move, for fear that I see more of what should not exist. The sweet little thing who had been the only sole brave enough to befriend me in that long passed life was gone, in her place a stranger equal to the one I had become.

How could she ever...

I see as well. Star said, her hand brushing against my forearm.

She wouldn't have noticed my arrival even if I was wearing a sign. She was totally smashed, the alcohol seeping through her pores like hell's perfume, and I didn't want to know about everything else she'd probably taken. Even if I could nearly see it – like a rotten rainbow mist over the entire room.

"Mary." I said loudly. She stopped dancing. I saw her look around to see who had called her. She finally thought to look down, her hugely dilated, cloudy eyes meeting mine. "Come down." I held out my hand. She looked at it and then at my face. Her eyes widened even further before she passed out, falling limp at her knees. "Damn." I hissed. I caught her, turning my sight to Stargazer, whose somber, worried countenance spoke of things I had rather not learn. She stepped next to me, her hands running over Mary's languid, dangerously thin body.

She will be all right Dagger, but I cannot help her here.

Where then?

◆

152

I cracked open my swollen, burning eyes. The blinding light gave me an instant headache. I reminded myself how much I hated the morning after. And the night before. *I'm passed out in the bathroom. Oh* (freak) *my head hurts...*

I opened my eyes a bit more cautiously. The piercing light had mercifully vanished. It was dark and cool. I was on top of something soft, not a tiled floor, like I had appropriately thought. *Huh, this is a first.* Even if the guy had an apartment, I wouldn't still be in it, and I was way too comfortable to have been left on someone's couch. Or worse, still in the club. And my roommates weren't blaring music, so I wasn't home.

I was warm as well. I was wearing someone's jacket. My first thought was that the guy, whoever he was, had forgotten it when he left me at this surprising nice motel earlier that morning.

Then I fully registered what – *who* – I saw and not just what I had felt.

I hadn't been tripping. He was there.

He is supposed to be dead! He's dead!

Feeling my stare, his eyes locked with mine. I felt my heart stall. My racy, half formed thoughts centered on him. He looked so different. But it was him. It had to be. I caught myself thinking he was almost sexy. *Him- sexy! I'm dreaming! ...I don't want to wake up either ...I miss him...I hope I don't wake up before I tell him sorry... He needs to know...W-O-W I am so tripping. Then where the* (freak) *am I? Hold on! WHY IS HE HERE?! HE'S DEAD!*

"Brad?!" My voice was a raspy yell. *Man my head hurts bad...*

"She is not well." I heard a woman say in a hushed voice that rang for too long in my head.

I tried to sit up. I couldn't even find my arm to move it.

"I can see that." He snapped, never moving his lack of expression. "...How do you feel?" *He* asked me calmly.

What? How? He isn't dead? He was there...he's here now... Am I dead then and she is an angel? I actually considered that quite seriously, even trying to figure out how I made it in there and what exactly I had OD'd on. *At least...I hope it was an OD.* (Crap) *this will kill Jonny...But I can't be, right? My head freaking hurts.*

"Brad?! Where the (freak) have you been?!" I tried to sit up again. I could have been on a boat and the feeling wouldn't have changed. A pair of really hot hands grabbed my shoulders, gently lifted me up, and leaned me against the plush backing of whatever I sat on.

"Mary, don't yell. You will only feel worse." His face never changed, like he was wearing a mask.

Is he even real? Nothing's making any sense! "Brad? You're dead! I'm dead! You're *dead*!"

"Her mind is replicating her words." I looked over at the chick. The faint amount of light had reflected off her dress and her, her fake tan the best I'd ever seen. *What is she doing here? He is dead!* The room morphed into a fuzzy haze for a long minute. When it refocused, I saw he was sitting on funny looking couch and the unbelievably stunning woman stood next to him. Even as zonked as I was, she was still mysteriously daunting. And his eyes were blacker than I remembered, but I never had just looked in just his eyes before.

"Mary it is okay, you're safe now, and no one is going to hurt you again." He said slowly. *Why is he talking to me like that? I am not a kid, I can understand him, I think.* "You have to relax for just a minute. She is going to help you get better. It will be okay." He put his hand on my shoulder and squeezed lightly.

He sure feels real.

If my brain was functioning properly, I might have listened to him. But I doubt it.

The too gorgeous woman knelt down in front of me, her eyes never meeting mine. She put her hot hands on my face. I tried to not flinch. Something seemed to stab at me. I grabbed her wrists in terror. "What the (freak)? What're you *doing* to me?! Brad, get her off! Help me!" I cried. The woman let go, looking like she was the one who had been stabbed at. I frantically looked at Brad and then back to her. Her features were perfectly composed and oh so very pretty that it made me uncomfortable. I hadn't seen her before, but it wasn't the first hallucination I'd had. It was the first with a chick in a club dress that costs more than my rent, but Brad was always there.

"Trust me Mary. She won't hurt you." He faintly smiled, moving his hand to one of mine. I held it tightly, fearing if I let go, he'd vanish.

"Okay."

She touched me again. I recoiled. *I'm probably still flying' anyway and none of this is even real... I haven't said sorry.*

A haze came over my eyes, my head, soaking into all of me like a steam room at the bottom of my stomach, followed by everything going clear. I realized that my eyes had been shut and I opened them, cautiously. The goddess stood behind Brad. He'd moved to the side of whatever I was sitting on. I looked around the room for what felt like the first time. We were in a hotel, a really nice one to say the least. The pale cream satins were all so inviting. I wished it was real, that I could go crawl into that big chair in the corner, and stare out the window, listen to him tell me his stories, stories of his life, his *life*, a life I hadn't ended. I would never have to wake up, never have to leave this beautiful palace for my screwed up reality. Never have to feel dead again...

"...Brad?" I asked hesitantly. *I'm sober... Somehow.*

"Hello Mary." He said and smiled slightly. *This is way too much.*

"How... The cops said you were dead! You were killed in a car crash! I saw the pictures! Why are you here? How're you alive? You said you'd come back! Why did you leave me?!" I nearly wept in frustration.

Her eyes locked with mine for a split second before *she* looked away. She touched his shoulder before leaving to the other side of the room.

I gulped, panting for breath, searching his blurry face for anything.

"I'm so...sorry." He whispered, and I knew he was. His black eyes were like thunderstorms, rolling and flashing, rumbling with anger and remorse and God only knows what else. "...Mary, what have you done?"

"*What?*"

"What are you thinking? What happened? What the hell *happened*?" He was close to frantic at the last question. The woman turned towards us, but I wasn't paying attention to her. I was seeing him, standing at my door, watching him run off.

Tears welled up in my eyes.

That same thunderstorm he faced had rained down so hard it'd drowned me.

"You're alive...You're here." I chocked. I threw my arms around him, not caring how much it would hurt more when I woke up, not caring about how wrong this was. "You're here." I sobbed, crawling into his lap. *I can hold him can't I? We're both dead anyway.*

He stroked my back, trying his best to soothe me. I clutched his shirt, burying my tears.

"Yes I am Mary. And you need to listen to me, okay? You can't keep doing this to yourself." He hugged me for a moment.

"What happened to you? I thought I killed you. You were in a crash and it killed you – they said it did. Why didn't you come back? I thought I *killed* you. I'm so *sorry*."

"No." His voice hardened. "Don't think that- it had *nothing* to do with you." He said quickly. "I'm here, I'm alive, and whatever it is you think you did, you didn't. I had to go, but I'm alive, I'm fine." The way he said all of that, it was like he was reading a script.

I made myself let him go. If this was real, I couldn't let him feel how sick I was. *It'll only hurt him more.*

"What happened?"

He looked over at the woman. I looked back at him, waiting for my answer.

"Mary, I wish I could tell you more, but I can't." I gave him a look saying the he better tell me a good reason as to why. "Not yet anyway... Just know I'm alive okay?" I nodded, none of that made much sense.

"Yeah..." I wiped my eyes, unable to contain my tears.

His hand suddenly cupped my face.

"No one is going to hurt you anymore." He whispered, the heaviness of his brow forcing my eyes to sink into his.

"But I h-hurt myself a lot too..."

This doesn't make sense! I inwardly screamed, even as I found myself letting my arms fall. *Real or fake, dead or alive, he deserves to know I got myself into this too.*

I heard him suck in a breath. I hung my head further, letting him hold me.

"Mary..."

He grasped my hands, staring at my mutilated wrists. I had never gone as far as to consciously attempt it, always leaving it to what I called chance whether I woke up from the numb oblivion. The Grim Reaper apparently had a restraining order against me.

"...I didn't know what else I could do. Everything hurt so much and you were gone and... And it just *hurt*." I pulled away, guilt and fear coving over me in a wave of exhaustion. Even thinking about it made me hurt more. Whatever they were, the things that lived in the shadows, they had eaten me, slowly at first, settling into their new home, before taking little bites that sunk deeper the longer I let them live, ripping and tearing and shredding until nothing of any perceivable value was left. Only a void. A mannequin – hollow – faceless.

"I...I looked for an escape...But they lied. It didn't help... Nothing helped. No one understood! I messed up and it messed me up and it killed you! They said I killed you! It just *hurt*!" I bit my tongue to keep from bawling again. It didn't help. I wept into his hands, falling into them like crutches.

"Can you?" He asked, not to me.

"What's going on?" My voice trembled.

"We're going to help you Mary – She is."

"How?" I mumbled, afraid to look up and seem pain or condemnation in his black eyes. *Hadn't I just said no one but him can help me? Did I leave out that part?*

"The less you know, the safer you'll be." She murmured. I pushed myself up, glaring at them. I hated that phrase. The less I knew the more lost I got.

"She won't hurt you, I promise."

"Uh uh- not happening Brad. Just let me be. Let me live with this. I deserve it." I muttered, shaking my head.

"Mary-"

"No- you can't make me! I deserve this!" I stated and started to get up, scrambling for the edge of the plushy cushions. I would under no circumstances leave, but I would lock myself in the bathroom.

He grabbed my arm, not tightly, but the chances of me getting away were nonexistent.

I couldn't make myself talk. He didn't ask for my permission this time. She knelt in front of my again, her fingers running over my arms, her dark gold nails tracing each of my scars, before her hands moved to my head and one on my chest. I sucked in a breath and stopped thinking. *Even if it's real...*

Her right hand closed around my heart, never letting go as each of its dull beats became drum hammering in my head. Her fingers at my head probed through me, tickling, and digging, turning over parts of me that I had forgotten by nature or by force. They locked on something, hidden in the obscurity of my subconscious. I convulsed when they closed around something too dark to see, gasping at the searing hole it left when she yanked it out of me. She dove back in, and though I knew she was being gentle, it hurt like taking a flat iron to a sunburn. I shuddered when she latched onto a black, twisted tree, its roots pulling parts of my body, memories, and thoughts with it. Liquid sunlight rushed into the hole it left behind, cleaning away the grimy edges as it forced life into me.

All the while honey covered my mind, soothing the burning and the searing, leaving behind a sheen of optimistic lacquer. Then the light flooded in with it. Everything was lit up and as if they were running away from it, all the pain, and guilt fled, and finding no shadows to lurk in behind or places to hide until the next time I was alone. I realized they no longer existed.

And then it was dark, cool, calm. The darkness was tinted red, and I realized it was my eyelids that I saw. I opened them to see I was lying down again and he was smiling. Like really, happily, practically goofily smiling.

"You're not high are you?" I accused, shocked to hear my voice clearly.

His smirk widened and he motioned towards a mirror next to me.

I went to pick it up and stopped. My arms were a creamy tan, the pale blue lines running under the smooth skin without any signs of what I had done to myself. Even the burns were gone. My nails were long again. My eyesight was lucid.

I snatched the mirror, laughing in shock at the face that looked my at me, her wonder as apparent as what I felt. I was me again. My hair – my eyebrows – even my teeth – It was as if the last nineteen months hadn't existed.

"*How?*" I sobbed, tears spilling over my cheeks.

"You believe in angels?"

I started to shake my head, but then remembered seeing him in that bedroom, promising me it was going to be okay, scooping me up from that rancid pit of my existence and taking me away from it all, and changed my mind.

"You just met one."

"Seriously."

"Seriously." He repeated. I shook my head, smiling. *Who freaking cares? I'm me again – He alive! What does it matter how all this happened?*

Under-Stars-Trees-Skies

It so happened that I only thought that. I spent the better part of the next hour demanding every answer I could think of, still struggling to understand how deep whatever she had done had gone, for even my head to be clear again. For the most part, he responded to anything I asked. He told me about the night he left, the bus ride, the first few days of wandering, the city where he'd gone, and finally who, at least in part, she was.

"Where did you find her? Guarding an ancient mausoleum?" I probed, expecting a laugh and settling for an attempt of a smirk.

"No. She found me actually."

"And you won't tell me who she is?" I knew I fought a losing battle. He'd not given up on his Biblically proportioned alibi, and for all I knew and cared, it was the truth. Still, there was more to it, and I was not going to waste any of my regained clarity. As I expected, he just shook his head.

"But you are with her, though. So you do know. You just won't share. What is it then?"

"What is what?" He seemed to blank at the question. I was still dealing with the same basic Brad.

"Serious, casual, you can spill to me." I winked at him. For whatever argument I made to myself, I found it easy, to still remember my savior, my refuge, and yet witness the distant man before me and remember the so called angel who had yet to make her presence known again. Brad was my good guy – period. I trusted him, and I wasn't going to let common sense or rational doubt get in the way of that.

161

He smirked and rolled his eyes.

"What? Angels can fall right?"

"I don't know... it just is what it is." Something he said made him smile a little bit again. That made my wheels turn but I kept my thoughts in my head. I thought they were safe there.

"Okay...How long then?" I fed off this conversation, off anything that didn't relate to me. Where he'd been, what he'd done, everything and anything, as long as it wasn't about me.

"Uh...well I've *known* her for about..." He counted off on his hand. "Well, a year. I don't keep track of time well."

"But you managed to track me down...How did you know where I was?"

"She told me a few days ago."

"Oh." I hadn't expected that. Not that I had thought of what to expect over anything he had said so far. "Where is she?"

"Getting you an apartment."

"What?! Brad! You don't have to-"

"Yes, I do. So you can put up a fight over it, since you're back to your pain in the butt self, or you can shut up and let us take care of you. I owe you, so count it as payback. You'll have a place and a paycheck by this evening."

I just gaped at him.

"You're some sort of government operative aren't you? I knew it! You probably shot me up with a bunch of stem-cells, right? And I was asleep for weeks? The hotel is a set up – right? There's cameras and I'm going to wake up in my apartment without knowing? You'll delete the video because I figured it out. And she's some genetic perfection project and you're the bodyguard, am I right? No way you're seventeen! Ha! You-"

"What makes you think that?"

162

"Everything. Even explains Miss Freaky-make-everything-better-while-looking-like-a-goddess."

His eyes widened.

"I take it I outsmarted you."

"You're close."

"Really?"

"More or less. But I'm seventeen. That hasn't changed. And I wasn't anything but a kid with brain damage, until you saw me last."

"You looked messed up that night." Messed up was a general term, one where the specifics weren't needed. We'd lived through it, we didn't need detailed reminders. Sometimes the past is best remembered, not relived.

"I was."

"You still haven't told me what happened Brad. I know I don't deserve answers but I need them, okay? I need to know why everything went up in smoke like it did, why you left. All jokes aside, how am I back? How are you here?" I didn't get up from the bed, but I wanted to. I wanted to lock the door and hold him there until he told me everything. I wanted room service too, but that would wait.

"When it's safe, you'll know. But it isn't. Not yet." There was no compromise in his tone.

"Fine." I growled.

"You can ask anything else, just not about that." He tried to pacify me, flashing a smile meant to look boyish. He didn't pull it off, but it worked. I laughed, throwing myself back into the bed and staring up at the ceiling.

"I can't believe it. I know I need to, because I've tried to snap out of it and I can't so it has to be real, but it just doesn't seem it. You know? I want to strangle you and hug you until you suffocate and I can't decide which. At least tell me why you haven't gotten a haircut. Going for the 90's grunge look, or are you just lazy?" I smiled, nearly crying at just how easy this was.

He mumbled that he was lazy, and that he didn't own a mirror.

I rolled my eyes.

"Well do you at least eat?"

He picked up the phone next to the bed and made an order for one of everything on their menu. I nearly disowned myself for letting that shock me with everything I had witnessed in the last few hours.

When it arrived, we ate, and I ended up passing out halfway through a cheesecake and a mostly one sided conversation. I woke up a few hours later to find him still there, still sitting at the foot of the bed, picking up the answer to the last question I had asked as if I hadn't been in a food coma for the better part of an afternoon.

She came back, eventually, smiling to him and nodding in my general direction.

For some unknown reason, his face grew more serious.

"Mary, will you do me another favor?"

What does he want now, me to sign the official secrets act?

"K...?"

"Don't...don't go back. I'll be around, I'll keep an eye on you, but you have to swear to not go back to that. I know what happened to you, I was there. It didn't kill you, so stop trying to kill yourself because of it. " He watched me carefully.

"Oh." I avoided his eyes. I knew what he had seen, or had a good enough idea.

"If you go back to what you were, you've let him win. And I can't save you like before. You're free now. It's done. It's gone. Forgive yourself, don't forget but don't focus on it, any of it. You have to face yourself, you have to overcome this. There is nothing more. Just darkness behind you. You have to get out of it. You can't stay. Go to college like you wanted, or something, anything other than this..." His voice shocked me, the monotone breaking at the end. He stared at me, pleading with me with a silence that could have been torture if I let it continue any longer.

"...I will." I promised him, my voice shaking. I got up, needing a moment alone, despite my lingering fear of his disappearance. I had just found the kitchen when she came from behind me, her towering stature leaving my jaw slightly slack. She had changed out of the micro dress, but the maxi one didn't do much to hide her. She didn't move, not like you would expect. When she turned to face me, there was something lethal about her, something unhuman. I shivered in the memory of what she'd done and his hazy explanation of it. Her 'gifts' were a bit of a stretch, even if he'd been raised from the dead.

"Thank you." I stuttered.

She smiled. "You do not have to thank me, Maryanne. I only ask that you take his caution into consideration. He is worried you will find nowhere to go but your past."

"No." I said it like she'd punched me in the gut. "No – I mean – I can't. I'm not going to. I just – need a minute. Not a minute, you know, just time. To figure it out. I don't know what to do after – after this." I wasn't sure what 'this' was.

"He only needs to know you are safe." She purred.

"That makes two of us then." I muttered to myself more than her. She dipped her head once, before stepping out of view.

◆

He looked over his shoulder, staring at the empty hallway. We were hovering at the entrance to the apartment – my apartment, as I had to keep repeating in my head. It had been mine for the last eighteen hours, ever since he had handed me the keys to a place in a part of the city I didn't think either of us could afford. My stuttering protest was met with her permanent silence and his passive dismissal that what I had done for him what felt like a century before meant more than

165

even this. But still, something was off, yet every time I got close to thinking I figured it out, nothing clicked. He wasn't telling the truth – not the truth that mattered. He was dodging the only question I still wanted answered, why all of the secrecy and the never ending vague answers, why I felt like the obvious solution was staring me in the face and I couldn't see it, why they were leaving so soon, and why he had said to never tell anyone how I got the place or what she'd done. And most importantly, if he would be coming back.

We could handle ourselves. She couldn't, which was all too obvious, but I had agreed to stay to see to it she would have a decent start. I had made it that long clinging to the responses I knew she would want, making my expression change when I recognized a shift in hers, reminding my hands to fidget so I wouldn't be too still, I even made myself eat every time she did. I had no misconceptions that the charade could last another day without a potentially catastrophic outcome. Sticking around only put her at even greater risk, be it a risk of her figuring it out or of someone getting wind that we were there, it did not matter.

Standing in front of her, knowing all of her questions still were unanswered, I knew I would have to do this again. Not soon. There were too many threats. But she would not let us go without some promise of a blank check she could cash.

"I know you're scared," beyond the raised heartbeat, epinephrine in her blood, and enlargement of her eyes, she was wringing her hands, so stating that as obviously as I had could be explained as normal human insight if she thought to question how I could still see through her now that her masks were also thickened by time's unforgiving nature. "But you are safe here, but not with us. I am still going to tell you everything, as soon as I can."

"And until then my silence it bought with plush carpets and granite counters."

"Exactly."

166

"You just expect me to let you go – just like that – without any real proof that you're even telling the truth?" The wringing hand went to her hip.

"Yes."

She looked behind me, at Stargazer. She had not spoken to Mary directly that I had ever witnessed, her behavior raising one of the warning sirens ringing through my head. Neither of them heard it, Mary was working up the courage to speak, and Star met her stare from behind her shades without wavering.

"You know how much I…much I can't take something happening, again. I don't know how to thank you, I won't ever be able to, but I know you can keep him out of trouble, right? Everything that you did – however you did it – I don't care who you are or what he's hiding, as long as you both survive it. I need to know, somehow, that he's okay, that you both are. I mean, I'm not expecting post cards, but…" She sighed, looking back at me.

I knew that had been coming, and even with the risk, the gold disk I handed her may implicate her to us if the time ever came when someone who knew what it was found her with it, but it was still safer than a burner cell. The gold was hollow, but it weighed nearly ten ounces, the core of it linked directly to Stargazer. There were only four others like it, owned by the Lieutenant, a midlevel FBI agent we trusted, the group that ran a large rehabilitation home we funded, and one high society/crime 'fixer' who passed us tips, out of a debt to her healing him of a terminal cancer.

"What the heck is that?"

"It's like a walkie-talkie. Just hold it in both hands, and say whatever you need to, and we will hear you."

She stared at me, bewildered.

"So you're not going to disappear into thin air again?"

"No."

The lines around her eyes lessened, the blood that had pooled under the skin of her face dissipating.

167

"Then I'll see you soon then." It was an obvious question.

"You will."

◆

It had been of unspoken consent we had not gone straight back to our home. His steps had not paused, keeping the same tune as his swiftly moving thoughts. I had followed him through the streets, focused on him alone so that the deluge of consciousness around me would be kept at bay. The poured-hard-sand beneath me gave way to brick and then to grass.

The tall-windowed buildings caused a premature twilight amid the large-ancient-wide-girthed-oaks and sweet-syrup-producing-maples. Falling-leaves made the ground a mirage of shifting-gold-red-amber-plum colors. The sounds of rustling-pre-hibernation animals filled the air around us. The scents-sounds-and energies of the city were lost there.

"Let us stop here." I spoke, laying against the ground, contented at the peace this place offered amid the chaos around us. The earth sighed, wrapping me in a cool-living blanket of its power. He laid next to me, his body causing a sizable dip in the grass' blade like forms. His pale, angled face was half hidden, though that mask did nothing to shield my sight from what was behind it.

I let my mind softly sweep against his, brushing aside all that pulled and whispered without end.

"Thank you." He turned towards me.

"What is truly troubling you?"

He exhaled, blades of the grass seized between his fingers.

"Someone made me like this – That's what I had to believe, what I had to hold onto – that someone deliberately took what I hope was decent person, a kid, and made him hate,

168

myself, the world, everything. I had to believe that I didn't do this to myself, that the lines I have to force myself not to cross were ones I put there to reign in something I couldn't control.

I didn't want to believe that deep down, somewhere, there was something they didn't touch – because that would make me responsible, for all of it, but there has to be, or why would I even try to tame it? I had to hold onto that idea that every time I want to take someone's life rather than turn them over, never mind if it would save other people, that darkness couldn't possibly be mine. It had to be what they made, the monster, the machine. But if she could change so much…in the face of darkness…then I can't not take responsibility for it. It is me-"

He stopped my interjection before I could make it with a raise of his hand.

"I'm not saying it's all I am. I get it now. There's no division, it is in all of me, but I can *choose*. I won't fail – I won't give in, but if she can go so *deep* into that darkness…"

"I promised to see you overcome it, Dagger, and as the shadows of her past were pulled from her, so too will you be freed. She is herself now, she has been restored to the way you knew her. She recognized the shift in your behavior, a threat you heeded, but you never once gave into the instincts you fight against. As I do, Maryanne knows you to be good, and recognizes your change still."

"Like what?"

"Nothing that I was not able to muddle her conclusions over…" I trailed off.

So many things weighed-dragged my mind, anchors on my soul. The way he had held her – I nearly dared to look into her mind then.

"And?"

"Nothing more than what she voiced to you over her curiosities of our lives and her questions that remained from years past. And, it seems, us... She was inquisitive as to how we had met and how we were 'labeled'. Your response was lacking to her interests."

"I didn't know what say to that."

"Magnetic. I am drawn to you. No matter how much I would once have liked to think otherwise, and so in turn are you to I." She explained and smiled. "Or am I being a charlatan for labeling something neither of us grasp as if it were written into the atoms of the universe until it collapses upon itself?"

I let my eyes trace her face, how different she suddenly looked. She'd every right to be curious, but it wasn't curiosity, it was uncertainty. She looked rather human.

"Permanently, you mean."

She smiled slightly, turning her head, staring up at the sky that to anyone else was only a yellowy blur. She watched the stars, expression saying more than she ever could, her smoldering eyes brooding, a small line between her dark brows forming as she studied what I could not see. I didn't tense, despite the whisper that her severity could mean a threat, because no matter what was coming, I would face it with her.

"What are you thinking?"

"I should apologize, for behaving as I did. I overstepped in revealing the lengths of my prowess when I healed her. I did not act with the conscious desire of her to be wary of me, yet I know now it was without any other reason but that."

The meaning of what she said, how she'd acted, hit me a long second later. She never 'showed off' – or took any kind of liking in overpowering someone – even those I had trouble not tearing to pieces. If anything, she was the most controlled in the presence of those she despised, leaving only one variable, her own form of trigger, for her to have felt with Mary.

"Are you *afraid* of her?"

"Of course."

She said it so simply I couldn't tell if she was practicing her new found sarcasm.

"How – what could possibly make you afraid of her? You said you were able to keep her from connecting the dots, and even if she knew, she wouldn't turn us in. Or are you jealous?" I wasn't entirely sure what I was basing that on, but every observation I had made seemed to support it unconsciously.

"*That*, I am *not*." She turned her head away from me, hiding her guilt stricken face behind the shadows of the grass.

"Why would *you* be jealous?"

She tried to ignore me.

"She *is* able to see you, for who you were then, and even who you are now. She got unnervingly close to guessing our vocation, your identity, so much that I..." She paused, pulling her hands against her. The faintest of glows that always surrounded her faltered, leaving both of us lost for a moment in the darkness of our thoughts. "...She is human, Dagger."

"And...?"

She blinked, the only sign of her surprise.

"Nothing of consequence."

"You don't allow me to not talk –"

"I don't permit you to keep things buried that need to be unearthed, for in this world you would say that bad seeds yield poisoned fruit as I would say an altered perception of reality clouds a consciousness. What I ponder is not a seed nor is it a faulted perception, it is a perfectly clear one, and it is the lack of rose hued vision that ails me, not the shaded view of pain or anger. So distract me, tell me what you were thinking a moment ago. Tell me why your energy blazed white. Tell me why everything about you – all I have memorized for these months had changed entirely, for you were overcome in fury-defiance-joy-victory. I was too lost in the skies to notice until it was too late, and you spoke before I could."

"I was happy that we're here, together." I said, confused to the near desperate note in her voice.

"You're telling the truth." She looked at me then.

"Why wouldn't I be?"

"Even after seeing her that way? How can you, you who struggle within yourself, in a battle I find myself unable to help you defeat?" She was genuinely confused. I moved closer to her, taking her hand in mine, raising it between us.

"This isn't a part of that war."

Her eyes went a shade darker.

"…You are not the same man I first saw."

"Maybe not. He wouldn't have asked you this, do you believe in fate?"

"…What do *you* trust in?" She asked quietly. "For in that response is where your question truly lies. Do you believe in what is called by your own as 'fate' or is life just a gathering of an unsystematic series of happen-stance? Is there a destiny for all of us or only pure likelihoods? Are there multiple 'superior powers' or a single God or nothing at all but our own existence and then its ending with nothing more to it?

Is your life your own to live and end for yourself, or are you held to accountability much higher? Do you trust in the fact that decisions you make today determines your tomorrow or will nothing you do change your life because it has been predefined? Or do you know that each action is significant and leads towards how your existence is destined to be?"

Her voice was still soft, but unwavering.

"Only luck, which I do *not* have, or some kind fate, or God could have brought you here."

She looked up at me, her eyes gold and glowing.

"I doubt God would approve of my actions when I left my former home." She said, and I believed she was serious.

"But you did come, and you saved me."

"If it were only that simple, Dagger." She wistfully whispered, nuzzling into the grass. "You have asked the same question as another had of me years ago. My answer has yet to change. I believe that we are given a form of 'purpose'; you could call it a 'divine calling' if you wish, before we even have come to exist. Once we have fulfilled it we then are, well...we move on to another type of existence, one where our degree of fulfilling of our purpose will decide our path and life forever after. Not necessarily a reincarnation, but similar to a 'heaven' or 'hell' as they are most commonly named." She faintly smiled again and rolled her eyes. "But one can only have faith in such things." She said with a half laugh.

"Faith is all humanity has going for them."

"I consider that is a multi-universal trait."

"So you do believe in God then?" In the year I had been with her, I had never asked her, because there was never a time I could remember when I cared to ask myself the same.

She smiled, allowing her skin to boil with light beneath its surface as she spoke, despite the risk of someone seeing. "Only months ago you were mindless to powers such as I, of our definite presence and seemingly impossible nature, the thought of energy gaining its own awareness and bending space to shorten time, coming here from galaxies millions years of what inanimate light would take to reach, of such a being having the will to mold the vastness of their consciousness to a physical human scale, of having the desire to walk amid and love humanity, was madness, and those who believed in 'aliens' were and are considered radicals or lunatics. Despite the evidence for us, or against us, we are real, I am real. I would be a fool to not think an even greater power unknown to my kind as well exists, and as I can look upon you as I do, could not that being be great enough to look at all humanity in such love. There rests more evidence to a greater knowledge than even I or my teacher could fathom, more than graspable by your kind. I dare not disregard such things, nor do I claim to be able to *prove* my beliefs, only that I believe them.

If such is true, if there is a Maker and a purpose for all, then I accept it, so in that, I believe it."

"What's your purpose then?"

"Your purpose is what you are willing to die for ...or greater still, live for." She sounded far off even if she never looked away. "I wouldn't have agreed to exist if I hadn't somehow known that *we* would be as now."

"You had a lot longer of a wait time than I did."

"Are you still at harmony over that, not knowing who you were, before?" A slight scowl creased her forehead. She had long before offered to help me, to discover some clue to what had been lost either by picking apart every memory I did have or looking for someone in the world who had known me before. I had refused. I had to live with my past, even the parts of it I didn't remember.

"I can't change it. I am not who I was. You saw that. I am probably nothing more than a giant black hole underneath all this."

She saw the humor behind the words.

"Dagger, if that's true, then light cannot escape their reach."

"And what if it is?" I grabbed her wrist, holding it to her side, even as her skin beneath my hands rose another few dozen degrees.

"Then I would know from many years before now that I lack the strength to deny such a pull." She laughed, pulling her hands from mine, placing them on the sides of my face, her warmth instantly flowing through me. That same peace, fulfillment, and subtle ecstasy had only multiplied, leaving me longing to hold her longer. When I was with her this way, I was not a man at war with himself, I was just a man, desperately, impossibly in love with someone he might never know all the secrets or answers to, and I cherished her all the more because of that.

...If You are by chance listening, thank you.

Shredded Reality

The tension of his body-power-energy increased as his mind flicking back through the last night, replaying the scenes of violence-horrors-pain we stopped only an hour before. The confines of our city around us lost their comfort in the wake of what we each faced in the aftermath of our visit to the port. Each of the dirt-grime smeared faces of the children in that rancid-metal-box-crate were forever burned into my forever replaying consciousness. Their thoughts, their emotions, their fears, and their memories, they were as nothing I had wished still existed in this time, in a society claiming enlightenment to the majority of its inhabitants blinded to or in utter ignorance of the primordial evil hidden behind peeling-paint-doors.

To be stolen, or worse, handed over by your own blood, and brought to a strange land, forced into things I dared not ponder. So many were promised safe haven, while others were handed over by families believing there the be a better existence on the other side of the world. The false pretenses were stolen with the same depravity they had come to expect from all around them. Their passage here alone had been minutes away from taking the lives of more than a few, and had we been any later, all the power I used to heal them would have instead been manifest in retribution for their deaths.

I had wanted nothing more than to deliver them into a safety only I could provide, one where they were in a place without contact with the world, without fear, and in an equally unmet desire, I had come near to allowing the dark need to end the lives of those who had done those things to them become an action.

I did something else instead, the action the first like such that I had made. With his aid, and his mind as my haven, I had entered those we had been able to find responsible and took away their ability to ever hurt someone in such a manner again. Hours it took, each new face and name bringing us to a different place, until the trail ended with the last of them falling limp at my feet. He had not resisted my tactics, in his equal rage agreeing that even though the possibly immoral tactics of altering a mind were great, the pain they had caused was greater still. They would remain fully aware of their actions, with an irresistible urge to confess them for the remainder of their lives to any and all near them, but they would never be able to repeat such sins again.

While he gathered them, I healed the rest of the children, who both cowered from my touch and still sought it out as the first kindness they had been shown in months. Soothing as many of their memories as I could, I sat among them for nearly two hours before we brought them to the people we trusted, leaving those who had been responsible for their abductions and transport across the ocean in the same crate we had pulled their victims from. Dagger's contact with this countries governing police would have his colleagues arriving there shortly.

As if in tune with my thoughts, I felt the pressure of another's consciousness against my own. I recognized it as the agent and allowed it access.

They got them all in custody. I don't want answers on how you did it, it'll just complicate things if they find out I was the one who sourced the tip. I assume those are everyone you could find in connection to it?

Yes. That is all of them.

They won't shut up – half of the personnel who know about it so far think they're possessed. Where are the trafficking victims?

Safe.

We need to-

The time it would take for you to grant them haven here is too great.

That is not ho-

Do you believe you will succeed in this argument? I will see to them.

...Have him get in touch. Forty-eight hours.

I severed the connection.

"It is taken care of, Dagger." I said, turning to see him sitting next to me, his knees drawn in as if to make a wall around him.

"Is it?" He stared at his hands, studying the sinews of muscle beneath his skin. His gaze caught on a fleck of dried blood on his wrist.

"What do you mean?"

"It's not over. It will never be over." He shook his head, his jaw clenched in indignation. "I want them dead. Screw whatever they did to me. This isn't just programmed bloodlust – *I* want them dead. Right now my bones could be on fire and it wouldn't make it any harder to keep still."

"You are not alone in that."

He paused, nodding in recognition that what I had done was merely the alternative to what I too had wished to do. It was the first time we had gone to such measures, but it would be far from the last.

"Those kids... you made them forget – they'll never have to remember any of what happened to them? Tell me that somehow we stopped more from...from ending up like that. Tell me we can stop it all."

"Dagger...there are as many as thirty mill-"

"Dammit, I know that! I don't want to hear the numbers. I want to kill everyone who is creating them! I want to know the last fourteen months have meant something – that we're somehow closer to stopping it!" He growled, fists clasped against his sides, mirroring the contraction of grey-hued power surrounding him. The roof around us disappeared as I looked within him, to know what it is he needed, to find a way to soothe him.

"You did not let me finish…there are as many as thirty million people who are now slaves, as those children had been, but in a single handful of hours, we saved nearly two hundred, and I saw to it that the three dozen responsible for facilitating that evil would never be able to physically harm another in such a way again, and you saw to it that every one of them will be placed in prisons and face the justice of your kind. And should that fail, we will find a way to see to their imprisonment again. In this, we have stopped hundreds more from being taken at their hands…

I did all I could for those children, I took away the pains of their bodies, and spoke to them about the pains of their souls, but I cannot make them forget, not entirely. As cruel as it may be, they will never be as they were once, and they will need to know why, and when they come to understand it, they will have to be able to call upon their memories to make sense of things. They will grow older, and they will come to know who it was that saved them, and who are their enemies, and in time they will follow what you have done and choose to fight back, and we will have allies then. Perhaps we will see the end of this brutality… but even if we fail to eradicate it, is it not enough that we did all we could? As we will again soon?"

He look away, remembering the cold metal in his hands, the doors he had bent open, the faces staring up at him in terror. I knew it from another perspective, the victim's own. I could bear no more of it that night.

I struggled to rise before going to the ledge, looking down at the false-orange-red-white lit streets below us. It took me a moment to remember this was not our city, and the displacement I felt was justified and not a product of my exhaustion.

"…All I could do, I did." I had done something I had sworn to never do, alter the functions of a human for my own will, but I felt not guilt. I felt only rage that that had been all I

178

brought myself to do, and sadness, because the moment I had left the children with enough silken-paper for them to be cared for until they were older than I, with the only group of people I trusted to tend to them, ones who had been doing this for longer than I had existed, I had been able to do no more. With a brush of my being against the inner turmoil of their own, and a few words of comfort whispered in their own languages, we had to leave them, to finish what we had started with their captors. Their fate lied in their own hands then, even as his and my own were grasping at some shred of hope for the collective of humanity that seemed to have been compromised by the actions of those directly responsible and those who chose to thoughtlessly take no notice of the darkness or partake in it.

He pushed himself upright, letting his mind's-eye fall to the present, sensing my own distress. He came to stand behind me, his head resting against the back of my own.

"It is enough..." He consented to my original question, his arm latching around my shoulders as we stared out at the buildings around us. "Why would you choose to come here? To have to see all of this madness?"

"For the same reason you chose to accept my help, Dagger...I could not live knowing there were those who were dying. Now that I have seen it, my resolve, and my gratitude to you, have only grown in their depth."

He held me tighter, the word's that followed heavy with his breath.

"Tell me we can stop it."

I raised my hand, resting it on his forearm that pressed against my chest.

"I cannot lie to you, no matter how greatly I wish it were true that there is a cure to this disease of apathy and evil, but there is not, yet there is hope. We aren't alone, Dagger. We are the voice of those who have fought in anonymity for decades in hopes of changing this shredded reality. We are the combined force of their prowess, and we are the only ones who can do what they cannot. We are merely the ones fueled by the declarations of centuries of martyrs for the same cause we fight. Whether we can end it, I do not know, for there are countless battles in the war for the souls of this planet, a war that seems as endless as the universe."

"Be we will fight." He swore, his power taking on the fierce-sharp-edges of his resolve.

"Indeed, we will."

What's Up? I'm Jonathan

"What is it?" She stood at the door to my apartment, holding one of her communication disks. We had been going the last ninety-seven hours, nonstop, only breaking long enough before then for a meal and a shower, so for her to break her own rule of forcing me to sleep the threat I sensed had to be valid.

"It is Maryanne." She hurriedly had handed me disk and pushed the energy connecting it to her to me.

"Mary-"

Despite the energy tie that allowed me to hear her, I spoke aloud, but heard her internally.

"Brad! You have to help me-he's gone! He's gone!"

"Who?"

"Jonathan! My brother! He's gone!" She yelled *frantically. "He went missing last week! My parents put out a report and- and- he didn't show up anywhere and they and they didn't get any calls!"*

"Did he run?"

"He wouldn't run away! That's why I'm scared! He wouldn't do that!"

"Calm down."

It took her a minute, but when she did talk she was oddly level.

"...Brad I don't know what you do, I don't know who you are, or who she is, and I don't care. I didn't fight her. I trusted you way back and I trust you then and I still trust you

181

now. Whatever, whoever you are, maybe you or someone you know can find him...Please. I know he can't make it alone. I couldn't, and ...he wouldn't run away! He didn't have a reason to! He was happy!" She lost her cool halfway through.

"Where was he last seen?"

"Umm, my father said that he started to miss school a month back, but he would text to check in on me almost every day until he just stopped. He vanished from the house-no note-no call! ... Well, until today."

"He called you?"

"This morning, he said to not tell anyone, but Brad he said that 'they' were after him and that he had to do something to stop them! He said something about waking up and he didn't know where he was! Doesn't that mean someone kidnapped him?! I knew he wouldn't have just run off! He said he was hiding out in New Jersey — and like he was changed, like something was really wrong with him and he didn't know how to explain it. He said he was someone else, but Brad he was nuts! He was scared and I think he's in trouble and I don't know what to do! He's just a kid!"

"I will find him. If he calls you again ask him-No. Just tell me."

"I know you will...Thank you."

The connection terminated.

The room had already started spinning a few moments before, by then I could barely see the walls in front of me. The dust in the air even seemed to sway back and forth, like the world's axis now went east to west and gravity had doubled, anchoring me to the realization that I had struggled to not be drowned by. *They did it to a kid! Those (...) did it again!*

"Dagger, what did she mean? If he has contacted her then *he* knows where *she* is and there are ways for him to reach her."

It was only then that I noticed Star was still standing next to me, her smooth fingers on mine, prying the disk out of my hand to keep me from crushing it.

"They did it again."

"Who has done what?" I asked anxiously. His stone-cold eyes slowly met mine. I knew the answer without the need to look into his thoughts, for the pain behind his stare could have but one source. "It could not be so. He might have only ran. 'They' may only be a similarity, a mere coincidence." I tried to counteract it for his sanity's sake.

"There are no coincidences."

"Do not leap to hasty conclusions just yet. We will go to him, and he will be all right."

"No, he won't. They – they did it *again*."

"Let me help you."

"*No*, this is something I should have done a long time ago, before *this* happened to anyone else." He pointed vaguely to his chest then hit himself, the echoing boom of the contact shaking my soul loose.

"Do not dwell on what you or anyone else cannot change." I cautioned.

"I could have. I could have changed it." He growled, throwing his hand to the side to ward off the invisible enemies within him. He fell against the wall and slid to the floor in a single motion, as if his strength was broken in tune with his peace. His head rested between his palms, his eyes closed as a scowl played its dangerous game across his face. I bent down in front of him, resting my forehead to the back of his hands, even as my mind slowly encompassed his, holding him, trying to understand what the ever changing yet unmoving energy in him meant and how to comfort him, yet his fury was met in equal measure by my confusion.

I was not fond of this feeling, this helplessness.

"...If the child has called his sister, then he isn't their captive, he *remembers* her, and he wishes to *leave* them. Your fears are grounded, but they are not needed. Do not allow false guilt to overpower you. I am here. I will help you find him. We will return him to his family, and if the chance arises and we are able, we will ensure this does not take place again by whatever means required of us. I will see to it that we resolve this, permanently."

"I should have never ra-"

"Black Dagger" I warned.

He clenched his jaw and nodded, accepting my rebuff.

I took the negative energies in him and pulled them from his being. I could not ward off his demons forever, but I could cause them to cease their manic screaming, temporarily. It worked to some minute degree, for he held my hands in return as I pulled him to his feet.

"How will you find him?"

"The same way I found her."

"Which is?" He pressed, desperate for a semblance of sanity and logic amid all the chaos he feared to secretly be brewing around us.

"I know of him from her mind and her power, and I will use that knowing to locate him, for his essence will mimic hers. I will have his location by morning."

"We need to go now."

"I cannot rush this." I refrained from telling him just how difficult it would be. Even if my being functioned at speeds true to the light that made me, so much that my actions and speaking had once been forced to change to a pace this race could comprehend, even if I was able to narrow the minds I must search by the age of their aura's, even if I had Mary's energy to compare him to, it would not be an easy task.

"I don't have time to-"

"We will have to have it. You are in no state to go now, and even if you were, I would not assist in a blind search of

184

one among seven billion. It will take less time for me to find him than for us to pick up on his path."

"I have to find him."

"*We* shall."

When he met my stare, there was a need behind his own, begging for consolation, comfort. As if by instinct I had not known my kind to possess, my form was against his, my arms wrapping around his shoulders, his cool skin sending shockwaves through the metal-gold-flesh of mine. I caught myself again testing the boundaries of how much closer we could get, how close I could stand to be near him without forgoing myself completely, ceasing only when he turned aside so that he might breathe. He buried his face in my hair, holding me differently then, as if he feared I might evaporate under his hold.

"It's happening, Star." He whispered, his ominous confession an horrified warning. "I can't – I can't fight it." He held me tighter before leaving me swaying where I stood. The agony in his eyes brought unshed tears to mine. I started to speak, my voice ceased by the sudden reoccurrence and rise of his own. "I don't want you to see this." Without a pause, he slipped into the shutting door.

I stayed there for only a handful of moments before becoming light. I went through the walls, finding him in the windowless-sound-guarded room where he slept. His vacant eyes glared at the ceiling, as if the white expanse was the source of all his amassed anarchy, churning inside of him like the most violent of storms . His hands were in fists at his sides, seizing the bed's dark linens, anchoring him to its surface to keep the forces driving him at bay.

The harsh, pale streak of his jaw and the lines of angst carved into his features were barely visible, his complete lack of radiance and the room's darkness leaving me to see with my sight and not my eyes. I looked over the room, realizing with a shock I had never been in here before, only seen glimpses of it in his mind. There was nothing, save the bed, and for a brief moment, I thought about how neither of us held any physical ties to our present.

He stirred when I materialized next to him. I rested my head next to his, laying on my side so I could see him. He turned his sights towards mine, their dimming soul fire a blatant reminder to the battle he fought. My hand intertwined with his, swearing in a single touch to not leave his side, even as the other stroked the tightness of his brow, the heavy angle of his cheeks, the cold lines around his eyes, taking from him what little of the pain I could. It was not of his body, but his mind, his fight to remain in control over the orders screamed in the shadows by voices that could not be heard nor silenced.

He nodded to my unsaid words, not trusting himself to speak.

◆

He was perfectly-deathly still next to me. His eyes never left the clearing-of-grass in front of us. I had tracked the human-boy here, after getting nearly a hundred other locations over the last hours. We had gone to a few of them, only to be met with a random assortment of "middle of nowhere" as Dagger had put it. He had grown increasingly agitated each time our hunting left us empty-handed. The moment the boy's power had entered into this place we had departed as fast as I dared to fly with him, and though he had yet to see it for himself, I knew the boy to be nearby, for then at the very least. How I had gotten it wrong so many times before, I had no explanation to offer him, for there had been no way to mistake one's life-light for another's, but I did not believe he would have accepted one either.

"Stay hidden."

"I would not let you venture alone."

His energy changed, spiking abruptly in yellow tinted hues.

"We have no idea what this kid is now. If he is like me…if he is one of them…I know how he will think, and I know what I thought when I first saw you. I won't be a threat to him, we would be equals, but you will be, and we are made to subdue threats. Just like I fought against the idea then, he won't know to deny the instinct. It took me months to even want to try to fight it. If something were to happen to you I couldn't-"

"I will do as you have requested, only as long as I am unneeded. What is it you are planning to do?"

"If he's still human?" The question was weighted, the scales tipping upon the fulcrum of his sanity. He was not seeking a reply or my aid, he was at war, and that was his battle cry, not a plea for surrender. Had I fought him on it then I would have found myself not on the sidelines-of-battle, but on the opposing front. Thus, I titled the mask of my face in response, unable to speak the agreement. "Bring him home. If he's not… you'll have to put him under, because there won't be a way to reason with him to go with us."

I was acutely aware of another desire welling up within him, one much darker.

"You wish to kill the ones who did this to him, to you." I whispered. He nodded; it was more of an affirming shudder as his body struggled to contain the grey-coated-red-cored-boiling rage within him. "Dagger, they may be 'evil' and they deserve much, but would you want to be the one to decide his or their fate? Could you bring yourself to be both prosecutor and judge and executioner? You know what it means to take a life, and I ask you, could you do it, knowing what you know now, who you are, what we are. You speak of your humanity as if it was stolen from you, but if you do this you are surrendering it willingly at the altar of your hatred. You would be exactly what they wanted."

He didn't answer.

"We may be greater in power and stronger in mind, but we are only to *protect* them, we do not control them or end their right to life, no matter what they may be capable of doing or have done. *Please* do not do this." I pleaded.

He looked to me, the planes of his expression void of any thought, and then without a word disappeared between the needle-leafed-trees.

-BD- SG S//5- [What's up...?]

Mary has to be freaking out. I can't let her get crazy again...I should probably call her again. No, if they are watching her place then they'll know I talked to her. They could use her like bait or something. But she's fine, now. But what if they do take her? Ugh what the heck can I do!? What am I going to do now!? I should just go home – no they'll find me there. I'm in this alone. I guess that's safer. But I don't know what to do! Where do I go-WHO do I become!?

I heard the faintest crack from behind, the only warning before the avalanche smashed into me, driving me head on a few feet before I struck something hard. I landed in a heap up against a splintering tree trunk. I was too stunned to shift out and in too much pain to fight back. I just sat there, unable to breathe or think, looking as stunned as if I had just been shot with a cannon. For all I knew I had been.

"Stop! He isn't who he appears to be!" How I heard the shouting voice over the ringing in my ears, I had no idea.

A woman suddenly stood in front of me, a blurry outline against the dark trees behind her. She looked familiar, but I thought I was just pain drunk. I wanted to scream for help, but no air came through my mouth when I opened it, and when it finally did, my lungs howled louder than I did in pain.

The woman feel to her knees, putting her hand on me. It was as hot as asphalt in July, and more painful against my skin than the lovely set of broken ribs the tree had given me.

I gritted my teeth, an involuntary moan the first real sound I made as I felt my bones snap back into place, my skin crawling as the bruise dissipated under her touch.

"You are healed Jonathan." She whispered and stood, the pain leaving the moment her hand left my side.

She knows who I am!

I wanted to run, to shift, but something held me still. My brain seemed to be in a stall, possibly because I had just been slammed into a tree. Possibly because I had gotten who knows what done to me over the last however-many-days I'd been in captivity. Possibly because I had just gotten miraculously healed. And I hadn't let myself sleep in three days. And I was pretty sure I was insane. And she was hot.

"Sorry kid…You look a lot different than I expected." The mountain looming off to the side tried to apologize for practically killing me. I just glared, debating on whether or not to shift out and pretend I had never been there, or try and return his favor. I was pretty sure I could take him, even if he did make rugby players look like yoga gurus.

Not worth it. I visualized the hill they used as old school computer backgrounds. Not the most imaginative destination, but one I had seen plenty of times to know I could focus hard and long enough to end up there.

"Do not try to move, you will only hit a barrier." The woman advised me.

I tried to shift, but couldn't.

I tried again. It had only been tricky the first few days. I had ended up in some hut in the middle of Nepal trying to get to Niceville, but this wasn't a slip out. I couldn't do it, at all, I couldn't even move to the other side of them.

"Jonathan, please do not leave. You do not understand, I am afraid we have given you the wrong impression on who we are. You see we are here to protect you." She said evenly, standing a few feet from me, him further back.

It hit me about as hard as he had. *They're the* Protectors*! Holy- this isn't real! ...I think he's Black Dagger. I got knocked out by Black Dagger!* I was almost giddy about that for some reason. It's not that fun. And the memory of my first beat down is a lousy souvenir.

"Do you remember Mary?" He asked suddenly, before I was given time to outwardly freak out.

"How do you know *her*!?" I shouted, and then got another question. "Umm... Why wouldn't I remember my sister?" I was getting scared, and I didn't think it was unjustified. They were the Protectors for crying out loud. They only showed up when the you-know-what hits the fan. *I* was the one who'd woken up on an R rated remake of Dexter's Laboratory, so what the heck did my sister have to do with it? *Is she hurt? How do they know her or about me?!* "Is she okay?!"

"Dagger, your fears were unnecessary and your plan futile, for he knows not where they had kept him, neither is he altered as you were." She looked at me after her strange little rant; her eyes were actually *glowing*. "I will allow you to change back into your natural form, but you will not be able to leave, should you attempt it again."

I stared like a dog waiting to see which ball pouring from the bucket hit the ground first.

"She means shape-shift kid." He muttered, his voice flat.

Oh.

I did as I was told.

She smiled, glancing to him.

"Do you see now?" She explained, before turning back to me, her hands folded in front of her. "Mary will be pleased to know you are well, and though we are left without any leads and your experience with those people was unpleasant, I do not foresee it being too great a burden. You are well, are you not Jonathan?"

190

"Are they after you too?!"

"No, they are not after me, however you will have to be protected. I promise you that we will see to that."

"But why do you care?" It wasn't the most pleasant experience I'd ever had, the machine had been like a supped up MRI and I don't even know how long I had been inside of it, but between that and the dozens of IV's that made me feel literally fuzzy, I had woken up one day, shockingly not drugged up out of my mind, and had thought that I wanted to leave. Next thing I knew, I was sitting at a Chinese buffet. A few panic attacks later I had realized I needed to hide, and I hadn't been able to stop moving since.

"We were sent to find you." He said point-blank.

By who?! The psycho with the bad highlights...?

"Your sister." I soothed his fears.

"Whoa...Wait...Did they find her?!"

"No. She's safe kid. The men who had you, did they say anything?" Dagger was trying to learn something, anything from the young-science-gifted-matter-moving-human, despite my fears against it when the boy was still reeling from his experiences even I didn't fully understand. I had not been able to enter Dagger's mind to discuss these things, for his walls were impenetrable in his angst.

"Well, uh, Black Dagger." he tried to appear calm, the surging blushing shades of light around him betraying his superficial façade, "...They didn't talk to me, I mean I don't know who they are. I don't even know where I was. Someone said he how he was going 'to make it again,' but I have no idea. They made me able to shift, but I don't really know how. I don't remember, I mean, I was stoned on something. I didn't want to figure it out I just wanted out. I was freaked, okay? I got out there as soon as the meds started to wear off." He looked at me and then to Dagger. "I just wanted to leave, and suddenly I was somewhere else. And I just kept jumping –

shifting – until you showed up." Their combined energies-minds had both been trying to both comprehend it all, the boy's leaping from one thought to the next with the same impossible speed and unexplainable directions as he was physically capable of doing.

"That's *it*?" Dagger demanded, taking a step forward.

"Well it's not like I stuck around for coffee and donuts!" The boy snapped, his sunset-hued-energies rising as he sensed he was being 'cornered.'

"Enough, both of you, there is no need for such animosity. I will answer these questions and the ramifications of them can be dealt with another time. Now, Jonathan, Mary wants us to bring you to her, but I can see transportation isn't a problem for you." The boy smiled at the complement.

"Not really." He lifted his shoulders. I did not take the time to ponder at the meaning behind his carelessness, desiring only to get them both out of the open and to a place I knew.

"Do you wish to race?"

"Star, watch it." Black Dagger's voice was about as sweet as the red tide. I kid you not, I was *freaked out,* and I hate to admit now about as much as I did way back then. Picture the biggest, baddest MMA fighter you've ever seen, sprinkle it with a smidge of "goth" a dash of "I can kill you with one finger" attitude, and add about fifty pounds of muscle.

Yeah. That's him.

"Twenty bucks says I can beat you." I scoffed, taking an up and down glance at her. I'd seen her fly – that's pretty much all the last year had been, videos of them two, so I was still kind of shocked at how long it took me to recognize them. Anyway, I knew she was fast, but she had no idea what she was getting into.

"I will not take your bet, but if you do succeed to win I shall do one thing you ask of me."

"Anything?"

Black Dagger's head shot up. His eyes were all black, blacker than even his hair. I didn't let it show, but I was ready to ditch them. I didn't think I could, and I didn't want her to still somehow be keeping me there and know I tried to.

"Within reason." She assured him.

"To my sis's place?" I asked.

Apparently, they knew where that was because she'd nodded.

"What about you?" I looked to him, attempting to pretend the last fifteen seconds of silent stare-hate hadn't happened. "You going with her?"

"I'm afraid if I am to race you, I cannot bring him."

"No worries, I got him." I could carry some things with me. I had figured that out an hour before when I was leaning against a tree, thought to shift out since some people with camera phones were walking through the park, and ended up in the middle of a Walmart parking lot... with the tree.

He loved that, you could tell by the gleam in his eyes. Or those were the sparks of the fire he wanted to light under me. Either way, I hesitantly touched his shoulder.

(Two seconds later.)

"Beat ya' *While* I was carrying him too." I jabbed a finger towards Black Dagger. The hallway made him seem bigger, which didn't make my attempt at pretending he didn't intimidate the you-know-what out of me any easier to keep up.

"That you did." She said lightly.

He didn't say anything, which I would learn was a bad habit of his.

Marathon

"So ya'll coming in?" We were outside of her door and had been standing there for longer than I thought was normal. I mean, I wasn't entirely sure if they were coming in. But they were still there, so it didn't seem like I was getting dropped up. But if they did, that meant they and my sis were even cooler than what I thought. *Where* they could have met her, I had no idea. *Why* they had agreed to run her errands, I suspected but had no real idea. And *what* business they had with me, I knew I'd likely learn pretty soon. But I was certain that despite everything, was the most awesome thing ever.

"Soon. She and I need to talk. Go ahead." I said, trying to keep my cool. He nodded, and I watched in muted shock when he disappeared.

Star entered my mind.

He went to 'freshen up' before he met her. He knows his disappearance frightened her and did not desire to cause her any further distress at the state of his disheveled appearance. He will be back in a few moments.

Is he sane?

He is perfectly fine.

He won't be for long if he keeps this up. She didn't mention his eyes are bigger than his self-control. *I catch him gawking at you again I am going to throw him into another tree.*

Her immediate soft, song like laughter made it worse.

It is fine Dagger. For if your thoughts were not driven in single directions, they too would wander without your consent if given the opportunity, and his are, to both of our reliefs, unchanged by anything they did. Do not forget that.

...Still.

It is all right. He understands now. You can 'lighten up'. Although I cannot say I am not amused... However, there is something greater we need to address. I cannot cloud her understanding if there is proof set before her; you do recognize she will know of us now.

Yeah. Once it was all out in the open, she couldn't block the obvious any longer.

Then that is not that all which is disturbing you?

He's not changed.

I told you, I cannot find any evidence that they tampered with his cognitive abilities, beyond a heightened sense of direction. His body is something else entirely, but as for his mind, he is sound. That is a good thing, is it not?

Then what did they do different to him?

Are you asking because you are in envy?

No! But, if they came so close to making 'the perfect killing machine' with me, why would they change it? They did it even! Look at me! I- She cut me off.

I do see you. Do not think I do not. I have seen you from the hour I met you. I have seen more of you than I believe even you have. I will tell you what I do not see, I do not see a machine – I see a man, I see a heart capable of caring, a soul capable of feeling, and a spirit capable of grieving. Show me a man-made instrument with those. Show me something that 'isn't real' that has these things. You cannot, because you are not 'the perfect killing machine.' You are not your title - You are what you make of yourself.

She waited for me to counter, and when I couldn't she waited for me to speak anyway.

...Why – What could they be planning, Star? Think. They made me...Brawns, lack of morality, obedience. They made him, covert ops and transportation... If they made him different on purpose – what is next? Something – someone like you? The only loose end is intelligence. Power. It fits too well. There's no weakness now, no chance of getting cornered. What could they be doing? If they try again – what could they possibly make? But if they don't then that means they could know what you are, what you can do, and we could play right into their hands. If it's not just random, it can't be, so what is the plan behind it?

She couldn't hide her fear.

It is possible, isn't it? For them to know – to be planning something?

I do not know, Dagger. I have not revealed the extent of my essence to anyone, not even you. If they contain a knowledge of me, then it is of my kind, of which I am not truly a part of and surpass in many things, so even if this is true, that they have grasped at some shred of knowledge, all hope is not lost. Do not think of it too much, there is slight we can do to anticipate the future. We only hope to find them and end them before another is taken. Right now, however, we are needed more in the present than in our ponderings.

He had returned, smelling like gym soap and wearing something straight out of one of a poorly lit and overly perfumed store, with a Starbucks that was more sugar than coffee in one hand and a slice of pizza in the other.

"Oh good, ya'll didn't bail. We okay to stay out here a minute? I'm going to finish this before we go in. Mary totally guilt trips me for drinking these." He laughed, shoving a quarter of the pizza into his mouth the next moment.

Star smiled, nodding in agreement.

He has real feeling. I added, *that* I might have envied.

As do you.

You know what I mean. I have to fight, every second I have to fight. I have to fight against wanting to tear the heads off of child abusers and fight to talk to the kid afterwards. He cares that his sister hates his coffee. He hasn't had his head tripped up. 'Dr. Evil' made it sound like that was what the serum did to whoever had it, that when our DNA is screwed with our heads get wiped too, so what did they do to him!?

I cannot say now. Please, be at peace.

I got some stupid, clueless kid with freaking superpowers to deal with – the entire U.S. government breathing down our spines, and a mad genius with a knack for literally making *problems just created one who already thinks this is a game.*

"Hey, BD come on!"

You also have me, and I will be here to help you. We shall talk at a later tense. Please think on what I said.

"What you call me?" I demanded. He shrunk.

"Uh, BD, you know, Black Dagger."

I noticed that Stargazer had moved behind me,.

I tried to meet her eyes. She wouldn't let me.

Here we go again.

The kid opened the door, taking two steps in before Mary tackled him.

"Jonathan Alexander if you ever, ever, *ever* pull a stupid stunt like that again I swear I will lock you in the closet!" Her tone was a sad-happy as she locked her arms around him, the flares of her power taking on magenta shades in the wake of her passing worry and rising relief. Jonathan took the rebuke without any protest, attempting to comfort her without giving fully into her embrace, wary of appearing too childish before Dagger.

"I won't, I promise." He was self-conscious at our presence and her reaction, his tone revealing such to them that his energy had already spoken of to me.

Maryanne released her hold and turned to address Black Dagger and I. "Thank you so much Brad, Cel –"

"Did you just say *'Brad'?!*" Jonathan asked incredulously, his energy splaying a variety of shades like the pulsars that dotted the many galaxies I had passed to come here.

"Yes?"

"The guy who disappeared? That *Brad*?!" He pointed to Dagger, who had not as much as exhaled since the first signs of understanding had appeared on Jonathan.

"Yes…?" She answered again, her eyes widening as the glow around her fluttered in losing strength.

"Okay fine. Well, are you going to tell her or do you want me to?" He asked, standing back with one brow raised.

I looked between the three humans in front of me. Dagger was a perfect-faultless-unmoving statue, untouched by the madness-unrest around him; Mary, slightly fearful-unsure as she cowered under the weight of her doubt; and Jonathan, bearing nothing but a look of pure shock-disbelief across his young-sun-tinted-face.

"Tell me *what* Jonathan?!" The room's energy went to yellow and paler grays, nervousness-fear. He grabbed my hand, his touch littered with the sharp hooks of uncertainty, bedding themselves deeper into his flesh at her startled expression. "Okay, *fine*, have it your way. I'll freaking beg if I have to. Please – *someone* talk – someone *tell* me what is going on?"

I kept my silence.

"We are …" His mind searched for the right words.

"They're the Protectors!" Jonathan shouted, throwing his arms towards us.

"*What?*" She whispered, shaking her head as I pulled out the last of the barricades around her thoughts.

"He's telling the truth. We're the Protectors." Dagger told her, for once taking on the name we had been given without mockery.

"How? – *What*?! Wait – So that means that you're Black Dagger-" he nodded. "And then that means that you're…" Her gaze drifted to mine, I kept my own downward.

"Yeah." He told her, his grasp holding mine tighter, his power pulsing in slow- deliberate surges as he fought to maintain absolute-unfaltering control.

"It makes sense, all of it!" She said breathlessly, the tumbling-blocks-of-reason falling into their designated places without hindrance. Her memories flashed behind her eyes as she connected each to the moment that stood in front of her then. "How you disappeared, how she healed me, all of it. How you found him! I never thought…Why didn't you tell me!?"

He paused. The question hung in the nitrogen based atmosphere, suspended by their turmoil and Dagger's silence.

"You had no idea?" Jonathan scoffed, his scowl deepening.

"No." Mary shook her head, once again turning to Dagger for answers. "Brad, what happened? Really – tell me everything."

It was a long stance of time before he was able to make himself speak, for I refused in this to aid him. If he was to voice it, it would have to be of his own will and resolution.

"When I vanished for that week, I was taken by some biological warfare or whatever it is, company. I have no idea what or who they are, but they made me into something I wasn't before. Something inhuman." His tone was as flat and solid as the walls that surrounded his mind. Her face then became the mask, her energy fearful, not of him, but for him. Her brother's eyes widened. "They made me…The perfect weapon. And they wanted to use me. So I ran. I thought they would leave you alone. You did not know anything, and I did not give them a reason to use you as bait to lead me back. I ran to our city and hid, hoping to never have to see them, or you, again, that they would give up trying to find me, and I would be left alone. And then, Stargazer came here and we became what we are today. But they kept trying... I'm so sorry Mary, Jonathan, I never thought that-" She cut him off.

"What are you sorry for? You found him." She mumbled, bewilderedly shaking her head, the orb of her dark hair shaking along with her aura.

"I'm the reason they took him."

"*Who* took *who* Brad?!" She shrilled, her energy taking flight to the wind his produced.

"No way. *You're* it! He meant *you*! That is why he said to *recreate* it...*You* already existed!" Jonathan's power grew jumpy.

"They took him to try to reinvent what they did to *me*. *That* is why he went *missing*! I should have done something and I didn't and they *took* him! When you called I knew – they didn't leave you alone – they knew you'd find a way to me and there's still *nothing* I-"

"We will return in a moment." I pulled him away before he could protest. They stared after us until the door closed behind us, the same we had entered through what felt, even to me, like an eternity before.

"Dagger–"

"No – I can't right now." He growled, turning away as he raised his arms above his head, resting his brow against them as he leaned into the wall. His breaths were strained, his power nearly non-existent. The faint sound of his teeth grating against each other and the fast thudding of his heart echoed within the gap between the wall and his face.

"Then I will not speak." I whispered, standing beside him. I raised my hand to his neck, running my mineral-form similar to fingers through his hair. The other went around him, holding him until his walls crumbled beneath my grasp.

It was the first time I had seen her in longer than a while, and in the back of my head I had been dreading what I might find, but she looked perfectly normal. Better than normal actually. *At least one of us is...* In the midst of everything I was glad for that.

She was worried sick though, and at some point during his scarily angry outburst she had collapsed on the couch, holding a pillow in her lap. She looked up at me, holding the pillow tighter.

"Did they Jonny...are you like him, whatever he does?"

"Not really. I'm not, as far as I know. I can do this though." I bragged. Mary wasn't the type to be called 'rational,' not in the couple years anyway, but I hoped that had changed too. I shifted into a guy in one of the new action movies and moved to the other side of the room almost instantly.

She jumped. "What the- *How*?!"

"No idea, just can. I picture who I want to look like, to be, and where I want to be and it just happens, though I get really tired after doing it a whole lot." I had never been good at writing essays or presenting to the class. Explaining this wasn't any different. "It comes naturally. Sort of like running. I can walk anytime I wanted and when I want to run I just decided to go faster."

Actually, it's nothing like that, but as I said, it was hard to understand at first. It's more like I was given two extra senses, where to me they were as natural as touch or smell is to most people. If I wanted to change my face, I could do more than smile, I could change its shape. I had to have a mental picture of it, same as babies learn from other people what a smile means and how to make themselves mirror it. As for the shifting, well, it was like I was conscious of my whole body, every cell in it, and I told it to move, same as someone standing up or dodging a ball. There wasn't a delay in the thought that said "get out of the way" and "shift" because shifting would be as natural to me as flinching is to someone else.

"This is *nuts*."

"Agreed, but no sense freaking out."

"He said that he was the *perfect weapon* and her I don't know, now you are a *shape-shifter?*"

She tried to laugh, but it sounded more hysterical than we would have both preferred. I wasn't looking for her to have a panic attack. I wasn't entirely sure if I shouldn't be having one, but I'd spent a lot of my life wishing I had a way out of things and a new start, and even if the way I'd gotten them wasn't all rainbows and fairy wishes, it was still awesome.

"Hey, I didn't believe it at first either, but yeah. I guess so. And I don't know anything he was talking about or about her either…You said she'd healed you?"

She sighed and hugged a pillow tightly. "Um…a few months ago, they just showed up."

"When you flipped back into reality." I commented. She smirked again, pleased to see I didn't hold her to it. "The phone call - you said everything was 'fine now'?"

"Yes. She and Brad were only here a few days. He was different, but I never would have guessed they were the Protectors, CIA yes, psychotic freaks maybe, but not *them* two."

"That is why you wanted him to help find me." She'd personally hired two superheroes as personal investigators. How cool is that? Seriously. …*She has to see that as cool too.* It was a marathon of awesome and no one else seemed to be running in it.

"I didn't know what else to do. You just disappeared. Did they, the people who took you, did they *hurt* you …like I know they did him?" Her voice got softer.

"If they did hurt me, Stargazer would have healed me from it when she fixed me up. I don't think *anything* could hurt *that* guy, he actually *broke my ribs* just by *hitting* me -*once*, but no, at least I don't think so." I was originally trying to tell on him. It back fired.

"He hit you?! Why? *What did you do?*"

"*I do?* Really?! The guy practically turns me into a pancake and it's my fault?"

She glowered.

"Okay, well kind of, I guess he thought I was one of the bad guys."

"He-well, I know he could have done a lot worse, so you're lucky she was there…" She had her thinking face on. I shifted back next to her on the couch; she jumped, trying to hide it from me. I put my arm around her, laughing at her reactions. Nothing should have surprised her at that point. She glanced over. "You got huge, kid." She complimented, eyeing me over. I smiled proudly. That wasn't all me. I had gotten bigger after the abduction thing, from whatever HGH, steroid and testosterone cocktail they'd jacked me up with, but *she* didn't know that.

"Yeah, another perk I guess."

"This in all insane." She muttered to herself and leaned against me. I remembered the last time I saw her, telling me she just had to leave and I had to cover for her as long as I could. Against every fiber of common sense I had, I did what she'd asked, the pain and lifelessness of her face burned forever into my all too visual mind.

"I don't know what to think Jonny." She shook her head. I held her a bit tighter. *Whatever you've been through sis, you got me, and apparently the Protectors. Or if this goes well, three of them.*

"That makes two of us."

"What are you going to do?"

I shrugged, for a moment wondering where they were and if they had ditched me forever. It wasn't like they could hide forever, but I didn't feel like shifting any more that night. I was exhausted, and still hungry, but I wasn't passing out without a fight.

"Are you going to go back home with mom and dad or do you want to stay here with me? I'm starting my school soon, but I could get a bigger place and you could stay. We'd figure out a way to get them to agree and you could go to school here and everything would be okay."

I shrugged again. I hadn't thought farther ahead than the next ten minutes.

"I'm sorry. I know, I know. Who cares about that with all this going on, I get it. I'm just so glad you're safe. I don't...I don't want that again." She whispered.

"Want what?" I asked guardedly. She buried her face in my shoulder, sighing.

"To have someone run away."

She means him. *Huh...Were they a thing or just friends? This is so confusing when I only get half the story.*

"I'm not going anywhere, at least if I do I'm coming back."

"Not funny kid. I don't want to freak out like that again...I know I'm supposed to be the sane one. But things don't always work out that way." She tried to laugh it off. Getting her to talk was something I could do really well, but I honestly hadn't wanted to. I was still her kid brother. Whatever *it* was, it wasn't good and she didn't plan on helping me out with details. I wasn't entirely positive I wanted the blanks to be filled.

"Whatever happens, it isn't like I can't be here whenever I want-" I cut off my words as they reentered the apartment.

26 Arguing is Pretty Much Useless

"You want to join us." He said. It wasn't a question. "You're sure kid?" That was the *big* question. One I knew the answer to.

"Yeah man, totally... Besides, what if whoever decided screwing with someone's genetics wants their science project back? I can make a quick getaway but I know y'all will have eyes on me anyway so at least now you can watch me closer. And she said she can't take you everywhere going as fast as we did so that means you need me, right? So why not? Arguing with me about it won't help. I've made up my mind. How else am I going to use this, the ultimate travel guide or stuntman or body double?"

"It's less bloody." I muttered.

"No, I want in on *this*." He motioned towards the TV screen, which happened to be muted on a major news channel, the news that we practically wrote running along the bottom of the screen. It highlighted the multi-million dollar cocaine bust we had orchestrated the week prior. We had sunk the cargo ship and the drugs, leaving only enough evidence to convict those we had been able to track down. We hadn't made it higher than the number three on it, the trial dying at the doorstep of a large import company, a fact that irritated me. We needed a way to see what was coming – this track and bolt way of operating took too long.

Glancing outside of my thoughts, I saw Mary's mouth drop open as she looked at her brother and then to me. Her heart raced violently in justified panic. The smell of cortisol overpowered her flowery scented oil burner in the corner.

Star had brought me back to level, and we'd known this was coming. My suspicions that his altering was deliberate meant we needed to keep him close, so we weren't in a position to refuse. He knew too much and was too oblivious to not get himself killed or captured, and lead to the same for us. I wasn't looking for anything else to be over my head.

"Before I say yes, you need to know you can't go back. You can't just up and quit. It sucks you in deep, and even if you wanted and found a way to get back to some form of normal, you can't; you've seen too much of what is behind the curtain to ever be on the other side again. The rose glasses won't fit anymore. There is no off button or rewind. I don't care how you word it, it can't be done.

I can't promise you'll be able to handle it. The news won't show you some things, just like we are good at what we do, so are other people, and they want us dead. Not just machine gun gangs, I'm talking about countries, governments, even our own, with their own agendas, with their own gun running, drug and people trading, and terrorist training agendas. There are companies that run politics and politics that run crime and crime that runs people. Nothing is sacred. This is their playing field we've intruded on and we have to learn to master it every day or be beaten by the evil outside of us, and worse, the evil we can be infected with by even for a second thinking we are above it. This world isn't the one you know, it's our world, and it has a dark side."

I wasn't going to sugar coat. He should know what he was getting himself into.

"Sci-fi, horror, conspiracy theories, whatever, it doesn't exist in the tight little boxes we've seen them as – *reality* does – and reality is everything thrown together in a mess of endless fighting. If you choose to accept it, to take it on, you will be giving up every false hope or pretense, every optimistic lie you have ever been told. You'll see the rotted bones beneath the masquerading pretenses of society and you'll have to be strong enough to break them. There won't be any more innocence, kid."

He rolled his eyes.

"For one, quit calling me a 'kid', second, I don't care. I'm not going to sit around and play video games or whatever you think is the 'normal' I'll be giving up, when I can live them. No way am I going to go back to school-"

"Jonny, please." Mary softly pleaded. Her eyes begged me, but I was not in charge of the kid, he was in it for himself. He wanted that life. I had let him have it. And when he decided it was too much, I had let him leave – maybe without the 'I told you so'. I gave him three weeks before he figured out that what we did wasn't what you see in the summer blockbuster movies. They don't show you the kids who are so broken and messed up from years of every kind of use and abuse imaginable and unimaginable that even Star can't heal them completely. They don't show you the women who are treated like disposable property or the men who are worked worse than animals and broken until they consider themselves to actually be animals. They don't show you the desperation, the utter emptiness in a little girl's eyes who was sold at five years old and has never known a touch to be capable of kindness. They don't tell you about the boys forced to act in evil, handed machine guns and drugs and told to kill or be killed. Or the plea of a soldier forced into battle against his own family. Or countries told their leaders are gods and to suffer is worship. They can't show you these things. They don't want their ratings to go down.

But we see it every day.

And he was about to.

"Mary, I am doing this." He told her flatly.

"But what about Mom and Dad?"

"No." I said, and felt Star's hand on my back. Mary blinked, stunned.

"I'm with BD. They'll lose it, and we know how they get. Not right now."

"Where will you sleep? What will you do? You can't just up and-"

"We have an apartment."

"See? They have an apartment." He smirked. "But seriously, it's not like I can't be here every time I'm not off kicking butt. I'll bring the take out, you rent the movie, same as ever. You're not going to win, okay? I don't care what you think or what BD said, I want to do this. I can take it. If I wanted to goof off I would, but I want to help them, and they don't get to kick me out. I'll just keep showing up. And when I'm not there I'll be here and it will be fine. So don't freak out, but this is it." He attempted to put his foot down.

"...It was worth a shot." She whispered. He smirked. She rolled her eyes back. *So now it is settled, he got big sis's approval.* "Brad-um- Black Dagger, Stargazer, keep him safe for me. He is a pretty stupid kid."

"I appreciate your concern." He said sarcastically, even though he hugged her around her shoulders. "You kept me out of trouble a lot, but I can get out now!" He shifted a foot back to prove his point.

"We will." I told her.

"...Stargazer, you have two people who are more important to me than anything with you. Make sure they're safe."

She nodded, offering Mary her first real acknowledgement.

[Scratch that- I'm Shift]

You make your own life…live and love the life you make…

S//5

I had just purchased the boy, Jonathan, a place of stacked-man-built residence a few hours prior, ignoring Dagger's assumption he would forgo his choice soon. We then possessed almost the complete 'story' of the city-centered-tall-metal-glass-construction, an excess I believed, but something they desired for privacies sake. We were then in its hallway.

"So your name is seriously Black Dagger?"

Dagger nodded, opening the door. By the time we walked through he was already in the food-containing-portion of the dwelling.

"I mean I'm all for the dark grungy thing you have going on, but that's still weird. SG kind of works, you know. Is it like I mandate, so I get a cool name too right?" He asked hopefully. In his mind he was going to 'milk' the 'superhero gig' as his hand closed around a petrol-derived-container full of actual milk.

"Don't care kid."

"I'm not a kid!" The boy was defensive. I would have had to look into his mind to have seen why, for he *was* a child, even by the terms shorter-lived human race.

My mind flashed to Black Dagger, he unlike his fellow beings, did not change that much. He would die, eventually, but I could not bear to think of that.

"Whatever." He muttered, his voice bringing me back into what was called the present.

"You have named yourself already, human. What is it you call when you do your abilities?"

Jonathan's expression had momentarily blanked.

"Uh…shifting, I guess. Oh cool! That's it! Okay from now on my name isn't 'kid' or Jonathan or Jonny…It's Shift." He said surely.

We nodded in approval. Dagger had been simply happy he would "shut up."

Shift's ever joyous and curious energies changed to confusion and surprise as he slowly lowered the cup in his hand.

"*Hey*, how come you called me a 'human', like you're not one? What are you like an alien or something?" His tone was one of a teasing nature, mindless to the insight in his words. I smiled, allowing my eyes to glow brighter, the stars reaching past the light of my soul. My surface emitted the light from my inner being, as I watched the thousands of colors dancing through the room change as it shone through them. The cup he had been holding hit the smoothed-compressed-mineral-stone counter as he forgot his grip. "You're kidding."

"I am afraid jokes escape me more often than I care to admit."

"…I'm so telling Mary." He said and huffed. His energy showed he was not surprised too much as he slowly constructed together the many pieces of me he had observed over our short time together. My appearance helped to convince him the truth more than my abilities. By his own justified reasoning, it was evident that anyone could be made 'awesome.'

"She isn't an a jo-" Dagger began to retort.

"I will return shortly."

You need to talk to him.

About what?

Anything.

Why? He talks enough for the both of us, combined.

Please?

What would we even say-'wow you see the weather today?' Or better yet, 'that bust yesterday was tough. Did you know that some gangs use kids as young as five to be ferries between turfs? I sure didn't! Want to go see for yourself?'

That is not amusing.

...Fine...what would you want me to say that isn't obvious?

Dagger please, let him see you and not what you let others believe.

Don't get your hopes up.

"Uh…I think she ditched us." I mumbled, going back to making my sandwich. I can't say her revelation had been the most mind blowing thing in the world. I woke up one morning to find I could shape shift. The idea one of my 'mentors' for lack of a better word was an alien didn't quite top that. Though it had gotten close, I'll give her that.

Oddly enough, it was him that made me more nervous than her. He remained on the other side of the counter, hands in fists at his sides, glaring at the mayo splatter on the granite. *I am so shifting into him the next time someone wants to fight me. They'll just run! ...Can I shift to being as big as him? Huh...I'll try later-if they'll ever leave me alone. I signed up to be a superhero, not to be babysat every second by 'Goth superman'.*

"She thinks we need to talk." He muttered under his breath.

"Eh...Uh-Do we?" I asked as I licked the mustard off the spoon, grateful that she'd given me some cash to stock the fridge and every available counter, since I wasn't always allowed or up to going for 'take out.' I feel no shame in admitting that Lucky Charms and I were in a serious relationship at the time.

"You tell me. You have questions?" He was being forced to talk, you could tell by the way he grimaced. Never mind. Bad example. He always looked like that.

"Well, I mean, it's not like I hadn't googled everything about ya'll before all this... And there's some stuff I'm not sure I want to know."

"There's not much you can't guess."

"Okay... Then what are we supposed to do until she comes back?" I looked around, knowing I could go anywhere, but they always demanded to know where I planned on going and rare was the day I actually had a plan. "Fine, twenty questions it is then, I'll go first."

He didn't answer me.

Fine. I'll appease her by myself.

"Can I tell the press who I am, like you and her did?"

(Nod.)

(Bite of sandwich.)

"Cool. They seem to like us this week. That's good, hit 'em while they're being nice."

(Nod.)

(Bite of sandwich.)

"And you're not going to throw me into another tree if I do something to show off? I get to make a big entrance too, right?"

(Nod.)

(Bite of sandwich.)

(Half a glass of milk.)

"Sweet. And I can start going with soon?"

"Training first."

"...Fine." He'd hinted at that, as much as five words can be a hint. We started the next day, a promising morning full of target practice and I didn't know what else.

(Bite of sandwich.)

"Before it gets nuts, can I get some cash? I want to get some stuff to stock my room."

He took a folded up wad of bills from his pocket, tossing it in my direction with barely enough time for me to let go of one half of my dinner to catch it.

"Where do you guys get this?" *Somehow I doubt we have cooperate sponsors.*

"Gold."

"From some kind of bank thing you busted?"

"Stargazer."

"Wait, like she's actually made of gold?"

(Nod.)

"And you and her are…together?" *Does he even realize how weird that is for me to try to understand?*

(Nod.)

"So no 'dibs' to call on the hot alien right?" I promise I meant it as a joke. Apparently he didn't get jokes either, because the fists at his sides raised just slightly and my sandwich decided it wasn't happy in my stomach anymore as it tried to crawl up my throat.

"Don't make me hurt you." He gave me a quick glower.

"Chill I was joking. Sorry." I was, not for him but for myself that I had ticked him off, but I couldn't drop the subject. It was the only thing that I hadn't pieced together, and I wasn't about to miss the chance to straighten it all out. Despite his attitude. Yes, I was that stupid. "So…Gold. That's pretty handy I bet. Okay fine, I don't get it. You I get, but first she's alien, then she's literally made of gold, but she acts like us. Other than the flying and the healing and the crazy stuff with the brain reading, but she *looks* normal… But if you're together she's, like *human* human-like right?"

Don't judge me. I know. Stupidest. Thing. Ever. I get it. Got it. Got it about the time I said it. Haven't forgot it. Shutting up. I know.

213

"I'm shoving bar of soap shoved down your throat if you don't shut up." He growled, and the granite counter between us could have been a paper wall for all the protection it gave me. I jumped, or in my case shifted, away. I had a foot in my mouth instantly, praying it wouldn't be replaced with soap.

"...Sorry. Maybe they did screw with my head." I said rapidly, trying to change the subject as quickly as possible.

"I can crack it open and find out if it makes you feel any better."

I stared at him, waiting to see just how serious he was before I decided whether or not to run or answer. "...I'm good. Sorry. I get it." I said, ready to get the heck out of dodge. His glare was replaced with an apathetic mask. *At least I'm alive... nope, no plus side to this...All I need is to be on his bad side, or his worse side since.* Stargazer couldn't have shown up at a better time. I shifted out, hoping to hide out at my sister's until he simmered down. I had already bought and brought enough stuff there to live on without feeling like a tourist. Doing the same to my own part of the apartment would give me something to do to stay away from him the following day.

-BD-SG S//5

"Did you speak with him?" She asked, with me following her into the main part of the apartment. I hadn't even seen all of it, and I didn't care to make that night an exception. But the roof was closed for construction, leaving us trapped.

The last thing I wanted were walls around me.

"Yeah."

"You have not stopped to consume for nearly a day and a half." She lifted her hand towards the kitchen, glancing back to make sure I got the message, which wasn't a suggestion. "Though, I do not understand how much of what is sold as edible is seen as such, but I assume I am the least qualified to judge. Shift has devoured all that you kept here before, so I hope this will sustain you both for some time."

"Thank you."

"What are your thoughts over him thus far?"

"Infuriatingly enthusiastic."

"Was I not also overly zealous in your sight on a night not long past?" She laughed, the soft light around her getting brighter. "His heart is in the right, but we shall know more with time."

"You like him?" I tried to get her to admit or disagree.

"Whether I *like* it or not does not matter, he has made his choice. I am fond of the fact that he has chosen our side, against what you had formally feared. He may become a helpful ally, when he learns how to use his gifts fully, and begins to completely comprehend what our responsibilities are to each other and to the world, and where our lines must be drawn."

"What does he do?" I said quickly, should she wonder at my silence and glance at my head.

"I have no clearer answer to give you than that which I have said before, what I managed to understand within the first hours. He moves his matter where he wants it to appear to others. It is actually easier than it may sound, for him at least. The same way you tell your body to go from one place to another, or tell your face to smile, so does he tell himself where to go and what appearance to give."

"How did they do that to him?"

"His molecules are unbounded, how they accomplished that escapes me. ...Bonding I can understand, un-bonding, no." She stared out the windows, her starry eyes glowing faintly. "They made it where his molecular make up isn't connected by individual bonds but it is merged as one entity so he has ultimate control over every aspect of his body."

Except his mouth.

"His mind and heart are untouched, but his form, it is, it is in a method of conveyance. That is why his few abilities come to him with a mere thought. It is the near same as my transferring of states."

"Great- now we're a perfect weapon, a banished alien princess and a science experiment?"

"However much I appreciate the attempt at humor," she laughed, "that is as true as we will come to deciphering us *materially*, but you are more than the perfect weapon and I in a form of words banished myself, remember, and princess is only a translation of a title not my own or desired by me. Things such as these Shift will come to understand, when he sees the extent of the new person he is becoming."

She paused, expecting a reply I wasn't paying enough attention to give.

"Hunger is not what, as is said, eating at you, is it Dagger?"

"It's nothing."

"Yours and mine judgements of that word's significance vary a great deal. If it was Shift, he is still coming to terms with who we are, and what he is. It would be unfair to him, and unbecoming to your peace, to let whatever judgement he made be taken as fact."

"He didn't judge. He's a prying little punk, that's all." *Just a stupid kid with stupid questions.* I sat down at a dining table I had never even noticed before, not wanting to face her directly.

"What did he want to know?" She frowned, her eyes darkening with concern. She glided into the seat across from me, noticing my odd pattern of behavior paired with every other unseen tell I had no control over.

"Nothing important." I glared at the iron works underneath the glass top. I knew the concentration strengthened the walls around my mind, and hoped it would keep my energy from betraying anything further than I already had.

The degree of light she gave lessened for a moment, the same time her lips opened.

"Oh." Her breath escaped like someone had just punched her in the chest. She wore an expression to match.

"You didn't."

"I do not see how you could expect anything different." She said in meek defense, her eyes dropping from mine. She traced a design in the glass, the perfectly clear surface becoming muddled where her fingers touched.

"Why would you *look*?" I stopped myself from throwing my fist against the table, and in turn shattering it, by sheer force. I knew she had seen what he meant by it, leaving out any 'misunderstanding' argument I could have argued.

"Why would you feel the need to hide it from me? Is that not what you want?" She stared at me, her auric eyes burning.

"*Not* because he said that."

She appeared in front of me, her eyes levels with mine, her legs folded at her knees, floating a few inches above the ground. Her fingers closed around my fist, prying it open.

"And regardless of what he said? Or what Maryanne had?"

"Star-"

"Do not try to muddle this, I am not ignorant. I know these things, I have before I even came here. I have seen into thousands of minds, I know what his words entailed, and I know why it caused you angst, but what I do not know is why you sought to conceal it, and more still, I do not know what you desire." Her pause was weighted. "I recognize it is our own doing that has led to this. I do not shun the blame, for I have kept such at a distance because Shift was just in his doubts, even though they are not justified. It is not that I do not...I do not *want* you-"

"I know, Star." There was no greater tell to her uncertainty than when she became awkwardly human like. "I didn't tell you because I don't want to have this conversation." There were only a two reasons I hadn't brought it up, but they were very big reasons. She had never once invited more between us and I didn't need more.

She slowly nodded, her analyzing expression becoming more pronounced. I sensed the flickering gold of her mind and struggled to not let her in.

"You speak even when you are silent, so let me speak, before you attempt to stop me, for there are things you have to understand." She let her eyes fall, her hands loose at her sides, the colors of her power underneath her skin moving in waves. "Do you recall our first night, when I attempted to explain this form, what it means, what I am? There is more to this – to what you see. I call it a shell because that is all I know the word to be, that this is the outside of what your kind would call sentient light, what I am, who I am, but even in its undistinguishable mirror of human form it is not separate from the core of my being. It is bound to my power, and to any who share it with me. If we, if you w-"

"I want you to shut up and give me permission to break a few more of his ribs." I said before she tried something other than civil discussion.

"If it were as simple as he thinks it-"

"Enough." She gave me all I needed in simply being near me, in somehow – in some way – seeing me as the one person on earth who deserved her. The last thing I wanted was for her to think otherwise.

She brought her hands together, looking up at me.

"You were not hiding from this because you feared my abjuration?"

"No, I'm avoiding it because I don't want that punk to have any kind of hand in it." I corrected, and nearly smiled as she rolled her eyes, the first sign of surrender.

"There will come a time when he is not the catalyst."

"Then we'll talk."

Anonymous

"Are we ever gonna take a day off?" I complained, with good reason, as I tried to find a comfortable position for the twelfth time that minute. I had slept about six hours in the last two days, and was ready for an all-you-can-eat buffet and a dirt nap. I didn't even care if it was on actual dirt, I just wanted sleep.

BD had other plans. Ones I found myself involved in.

"No."

"We've been 'protecting' for *months*, don't you get tired – *ever...?*" *He goes and goes, and where I go nobody knows. Except the mind reader.* I think, with years of experience behind me now, that if I had been given a bit more credit for what I did I would have taken the down sides to this 'gig,' which I had been shocked to learn were a great many, a bit more gracefully. Think about it, to the newspapers we were headlines that moved copies, to the TV stations, we were ratings, to the government, from the CIA and FBI to the DOD to the NSA, all the way down to the ATM machine camera's, we were targets, but I was still me.

And I needed a day off.

I think shifting a few thousand people off a sinking cruise ship deserves that. They had been forced to give me time to recoup from that one, considering I had slept for three days afterwards I don't think I'd given them a chance to not. If there was ever a prime example of being 'shifted out,' that would have been it. No one would hold still, no one wanted to trust me to not make them disappear, no one even knew we were who we were the first few minutes, making the anarchy

219

all the more chaotic. I don't even know how Stargazer had gotten wind of it, all I know is that BD had broken into my room, grabbed me out of bed by the back of my shirt, and shoved me out the door, all the while yelling that I hurry up shift him out to some random GPS coordinate.

We'd arrived at a modern day Titanic, without the classical music playing in the background. It was a big ship, lots of flags, waterslides, the kind of thing my father would have taken Mary and I on during our middle school days. People were running around us, screaming, crying, holding cell phones aimlessly in the air. Smoke had nearly clouded out the massive array of stars above us, thick enough to blind me if I was caught downwind. BD had taken all of a second to stop and take things in before running off, turning back long enough to shout, "Get them out of here!" before going right into the smoke pillar at the back of the ship.

Ship is such a small word for how big that thing was. I took one glance and knew it would have been easier just to shift the entire thing to shore than trying to take all the people three or four at a time. The problem was, I had never done something that big, and I wasn't about to start experimenting with so many lives at stake. One screw up and we'd all drown.

So I did what I had to, grabbing the collars of the two closest to me, a couple with wide eyes and shaking hands, and shifted them to one of my few predetermined drop points for trauma situations like this, a courtyard in front of a large hospital in the Northeast. I came back and grabbed another few, repeating the process for minutes that felt like days, not stopping even when my head swam, like I knew they'd end up doing soon if I didn't push myself to go faster. Water had already started pooling in from the blowout in the hull, reminding me of my time limit.

SG had helped as best as she could, but so many people had needed healing from the engine explosion she had been completely slammed. The power was out on the ship, and like moths, if people are trapped in the dark they will look for the light, so that's what she had done, made herself a giant spotlight. Soon there were crowds, then hordes, and then a mosh pit I had the joy of throwing myself into so I could touch as many people as possible in order to shift them out to another hospital's parking lot. BD had been nowhere to be found. I later learned he had been digging people out of the debris for SG to heal, leaving me and a couple of Coast Guard copters to be the only transport.

That had been less than two weeks before then. There were no casualties, thanks to SG whatever critical condition wounds had been taken care of, and I had managed, incoherent with exhaustion after nearly an hour of constant long-distance shifting of over five-thousand people, all the while in a panic to get everyone out.

Except us.

I had collapsed on deck the moment I got back from bringing the final group of nearly a dozen. The last thing I remembered from that night was the sound of blood rushing through my head and helicopter blades spinning. I would later be told that BD, the only one of us not entirely spent, had loaded me and an equally unconscious Stargazer into the departing Coast Guard helicopter just as the ship began to tilt. The pilot and crew were thankfully on our side, so no feds got called. I'm pretty sure the reward SG gave them once she came to helped encourage other emergency people to help us, because in the weeks since, the smaller levels of government aid had been noticeably more compliant.

I was still mad I had left them hanging like that. I didn't know if Black Dagger had held it against me, even if he had said 'Good job, kid,' when I had woken up in my room three long days later. Stargazer had been sitting next to me, a glowing hand on my head and another on my chest. BD had been looming behind her. I only exhaled when I saw they hadn't called Mary.

"He's up. That's enough." He'd said, and she smiled, lifting her hands.

"I am afraid that's all I can do now, Shift. You will still need to rest."

"So do you." BD ordered.

I wasn't awake enough to do more than stare when he picked her up. And when he had finally said his own version of thanks, I'd barely nodded.

Well, even if most don't like us, we know what we do. I guess I am okay with anonymity.

I crossed my legs and uncrossed them again.

I was getting antsy.

"BD, seriously, after this we need to call it a night. Or week."

He wasn't listening to me. I didn't take it personally, I didn't listen to him much either. I got my 'perks' when I was able to find the time to sneak off, even if he didn't approve. He'd cut me some sort of slack recently, but I had a hunch that was SG's influence more than his understanding of my arguments.

"I told you not to join if you would get tired of it, kid." He stated. *Okay, he is listening, for once.*

"I'm not sick of the work, I know why we are doing it. I believe in it. I can handle it, but I can't take the hours. I haven't slept longer than a nap since Monday."

"I don't know what day it is.".

"Thursday." *Bunny hopping over six different time zones every night does not count as time management.*

"Then go to Mary's tomorrow if you can't deal."

"I can deal." I defended myself, resided to the fact it was now a challenge.

He laughed under his breath, rolling his eyes slightly from what I could tell, since he had his mask on. So glad I didn't have to wear one of those.

"What's so funny?" He ignored me. "BD." I warned. I had recently found out I might have a shot at taking him...and he'd never see me coming. It gave me more confidence in messing with him, which had been my only normal entertainment in those days.

"It's Stargazer." He 'explained.'

"What about her?"

"She says you sleep 'longer than a lion' and that your life is hard, talking as much as you do will take a lot out of any human." He smirked and crossed his arms over his chest as he spoke. He was staring straight ahead of him, focusing as hard as any Hawk Eye sniper. I glanced to where he looked to make sure there wasn't something there and smirked at the graffiti'd cement. I had always known he was crazy.

"How long does a lion sleep?" SG made the strangest comparisons, and whenever I got them, they were pretty funny in her own odd way.

He lifted his shoulder in an indifferent shrug. They had taken away my phone, so a quick google was out of the question. I'd already started looking for techies or members of Anonymous who were supporters of us, hoping a few of them would help me get an untraceable network, or at least a single computer, set up. As of that week, the only taker was a twelve year old in Albania, who was pretty good in his own right, but then again, "Shift" was still earning street credit. If I wanted to be taken seriously I knew it would take time.

"How does Stargazer know what we're talking about? We're in an entirely different *state* than she is. And I don't talk that much..." I mumbled in defense. *Well I kind of do, compared to them at least.*

"She can still be in your head from this far. She can enter your consciousness. It's surreal. It is like you've been touched by an angel." He *murmured.*

I scowled.

He's got to be on something. It explains the wall staring issue. And no sleeping. And his haircut. Or lack of. We did confiscate a lot of cocaine yesterday... Yeah, he's a roid and coke junkie, SG's on shrooms, and I'm hooked on speed. I thought sarcastically, even if I was pretty sure his head wasn't screwed on completely right.

"Uh-huh…She's an alien, not angel." I stated, trying to not laugh. He didn't dig comedy. He glanced at me in a 'suit yourself' kind of way, except it came across as 'I don't care what you think, so shut up.' "Can she do that to everyone?"

Would you like me to try it on you? Stargazer said. I looked behind me out of instinct, except she wasn't there. He closed his eyes and leaned against the other wall creating the crevice we hid in, at perfect peace in the midst of my flipping out.

It was as if I had been living my life through rabbit ears and suddenly the Boss with the universal remote had flipped on the IMAX 4-D HD channel, as my 'receiver' struggled with the rush of new sensations. It had been too much to take in at first, but as the pain set in, I realized just how much I was suddenly feeling, and seeing. I felt like I had a fever, every part of my body twitched in preparation to shift away from the massive amount of energy coursing through me, and everything I felt became intense. The cold air burned in my lungs, the concrete I leaned against felt like a treadmill with a belt made of sandpaper, and even the small pebbles under my hands were like glass shards. I could hear everything; my blood pumping through my veins, my bones in my joints moving against each other, my skull expanding and compressing to pump spinal fluid down my backbone. I felt every cell in my body and knew those that were splitting, those that were dying, and those that were still connected to me. All of them through my own heightened ability of control were always ready to move at a stray order, but it was a different kind of awareness I was forced into, one that rightfully scared the heck out of me.

Then I paid attention to everything else, and nearly blacked out at the intensity of the lights and colors that suddenly surrounded everything around me, leaving me with a migraine capable of killing. The whole world had been thrown in a blender, myself and every color and lightning bolt with it, and someone had hit "pulse" at a speed even I couldn't comprehend.

Then it all stopped with the same sudden violence it had come with.

I'm so sorry. You are much different than he is... Forgive me, Shift. I am adapted to dulling my perceptions of time and matter for Dagger's sake, but I forgot the greater degree to which they must be muted to avoid causing your mind to be overwhelmed.

That was you?!

It took you long enough to figure it out kid.

BD! What is this, like a three way conference call with our minds? *I'm the one in the middle?*

It is similar, but I cannot reach you from this far away, the only thing connecting us is Dagger, for he is the center of this. It was both of our perceptions of the world you experienced, a side effect, if you will, of his own consciousness bridging ours.

Why can you reach him but not me?

We are magnetic.

How does a magnet have anything to do with our heads?

Nice. He muttered.

What? Seriously?

There is no magnet Shift, do not fret over this. Be safe, the both of you. I will join you if I am needed.

You won't be.

She might be? I added.

The weird feeling vanished and I opened my eyes. I glanced to him, he still looked like she was in his head, but his eyes were open too.

"That was…terrifying. And cool. Did it make you go crazy at first? I thought I was dying." However true the description, as it turns out I really was taking on a 4D signal with 3D hardware, or so SG has since explained better. He didn't seem phased at all though.

"No. Not like that."

"Will I get used to it then or what? When did she first do that to you?"

"The first night." He trailed off. I hated it when he did that.

"And?"

"What you felt is what I feel. What you saw is what she sees. When she first did it we were both not paying attention to the outside, so I didn't see what you saw. We – she – was looking through my memories, everything at once."

That makes me the only one out of the loop.

"When did you meet her? After or before, you know 'them'?"

"After."

"How long after?" I tried to do a time line but I figure it took a while for the internet and the press to catch on.

"Time didn't exist."

Well, that's a record for him, a dozen or so sentences. Normally he's not much of a chatter box. I don't think they *were as, uh – nice? – to him as me. He certainly doesn't ever talk about it.*

"Huh..." I nodded, not really sure what that meant. I decided to follow all routes of common sense and not ask about them, not directly. "And ya'll did what exactly?"

"Same thing as now."

"That's it?"

"Give or take."

"And I take it you don't plan on giving me details?"

He smirked, shaking his head.

I wasn't allowed to disappear, no sir, that was a definite no-go in his book, but they managed to do it every few days. I had a few ideas about what they were up to, but the only one I had a chance of asking and living to tell about it was if it was 'gig related,' which meant they were ditching me because I would be a risk, not a third-wheel.

"Anyway, what's the plan?" I leaned over the edge of the building, watching a few guys unload one of those big metal shipping crates, every box an identical size. To an outsider, it looked positively legit, despite the fact it was near three in the morning. It was an inside job, of that BD was sure, and from what he had said it had been around for a while, and the merchandise wasn't always inanimate. We'd be picking off this particular "shipping, transport, and security" operation for months until the last of it was gone.

"You go in as a guard and tell me what the security is like, take the stuff out," (stolen cars, electronics, art, jewelry, counterfeit cash, heroin, cocaine, random other drugs, fake meds, whoever was shipping their stuff that night and whatever fit the box…) "Before getting caught. I will deal with them."

The 'stuff' would go to Port Security, along with the thugs, an arrangement SG had made earlier that week with the officers who she had made sure didn't deal dirty.

"Stargazer will do what?" *No comment obviously.* "So no cops coming here?"

He shook his head. I needed to know if I was shifting it *all* or if there would be a rare partnership with the local fuzz. When I say 'rare' I mean it. That had only happened once outside of our home city and it was only because the cops were the one that needed our 'protecting'.

"Where's SG anyway? Why'd she bail out?"

"She's not coming."

"Why? We didn't do that much yesterday…robbery and storage bunker break-in down in Fort Knox right?" I had to agree with BD. The days were beginning to run together. (The second one had been interesting – *we* ended up being the ones they wanted.) "But nothing too hard...I mean it's not like she sleeps." *Course I've never witnessed him sleep either, now that I think about it.*

"She isn't invincible kid. The ship?"

"Um…Yeah?"

"Fighting doesn't exhaust her, healing does."

Oh. Right. He doesn't like to leave her, that's why he's all Mr. Happy Rainbows tonight.

"You could've stayed with her. I can handle myself." I hinted.

He adjusted his stance, setting his arms over his knees as he peered down, always looking like he was ready to jump somebody.

"Yeah right, I'm leaving you alone with eight guards with M-15's. That is genius." He muttered, glancing at me. His black eyes were mocking.

"Not fair! You were solo for a while. I can do this. You've seen it, so don't act like I'm helpless." I defended my ego, fighting to keep my voice at a ticked off whisper.

"Being *able* to do something is different than knowing how to use it and when to do it. You don't know your own limits. You aren't good to anyone if you drive yourself into the ground again trying to prove something."

"You and her go off without me all the time."

"We know our weaknesses."

"She's the one laid up."

"And you're the one that can die from a bullet. You're stuck with us, like it or not."

"Well I don't like it."

"You don't want to be solo. There's no one there to help you when you need it."

"I don't need help." *I can do this without a stupid babysitter all the time!*

"We do. Whether you want to admit it or not is up to you. You might get it if you ever grow up."

I decided to shut up. I was still figuring out how to show them that I could handle myself and do my own gigs, but that night didn't look like the best one to do it.

"Whatever." I growled, taking on the flat appearance of their uniforms.

"Let's get this over with." He said and stood, flexing his hands.

(He's just one big ray of sunshine ain't he?)

◆

Universal Truths

I studied the silvery-twinkling-starred-old-home-black-blue-yellow skies, past lives I had once called mine running through my thoughts. Colors beyond compare to what eyes can see lit the skies in pulsing forces of light and power, moving at speeds only I could grasp and taking forms only I knew. It was one of the greatest beauties I had ever beheld, and for a single moment, it was solely mine to appreciate.

"You all right Miss?"

I jumped inside, instantly reaching for my diminished power, if I should need it. I had not noticed the approaching force from behind me, and the unknowing left me paranoid at what I might find. I turned around to see a male human over the age of seventy-earth-years, judging by his sun-thinned surface and dimming light.

"I am." *What is he doing at this place, especially at this late hour of the darkness?* I had very little trust to give when I was alone.

"You should back up from the ledge, Miss. You could fall if you aren't careful." His energy was curious, worried, possibly for me.

"Thank you." I complied solely for his peace-of-mind, taking a new place a few steps from the edge.

"So, you are a star gazer as well?"

It took a moment of panic-alarm-shock to pass before I understood his meaning, reaching my consciousness towards his to soothe my suspicions and confirm his harmlessness. "I couldn't help but notice the way you looked up at them." He explained and pointed to the sky, his finger oddly shaped against the invisible light above.

"I have watched them from my beginning. They are a constant, a comfort." I told the gentleman in absolute truth. I was no longer afraid, he was no threat and he seemed to want my company, and I found I mimicked his desire. Rare was the time when I was able to simply speak with someone.

"Ah...Yes, they are beautiful. What secrets could they hold I wonder?"

"More than many are blessed to know, but with knowledge comes a burden as well."

"All too true, young lady. I never miss a chance to look at them. They are absolutely exquisite. There aren't many clear nights in this city."

I smiled. Few but those who made it their profession ever studied my home, and it was an odd satisfaction to know I wasn't alone in my study of the powers above.

"That there is not. I am Celeste, what do they call you?" The man had a pleasant sense of peace-quiet-calm, something I did not encounter much. It floated like a mild breeze-of-the-spring-time, gently enfolding my being within it. I shivered in delight, instantly taking to such a pleasing energy.

"The one who is of the heavens or is heavenly.... I'm Dan, Dan Haledon."

"The morning star." I softly commented on the meaning of his name. His face lit up at my words.

"I wouldn't have pegged someone so young to know any of that, but yes, you are a star gazer. What do you see Celeste, when you look up at them?" He stared at my once home, unknowing that he was in the presence of a living star. I could feel her power, her brilliance and her light, the very essence of Vivimerea in my memories. I had not sought to recall such, and in my inner battle I did not answer him.

"Well, I see life, they are life. Bright, shining, glorious life...and love, always, it lights up even the largest of the blackness... Hate because it can last for long, burning brighter than this sun, but can just as easily be over looked. Hope, faith, because no matter how small it may seem to you, you know there is more than you see, and though you cannot prove it you trust in it nevertheless. Courage, since everybody should know by the time that they're as old as me that no matter where we stand, the stars are the same, and in that where we stand is as high, no of this other nonsense people preach. And peace...peace because they rarely change, they will always be waiting for us, even after we are gone."

"You speak with great wisdom." I smiled at his eloquent speech. My slightly differing-to-the-human appearance did not worry me, it was dark and he was losing his vision just enough not to notice my eyes if I refrained from letting them emit my soul's light-radiance, which I found difficult in my happiness.

"When you've lived as long as I have dear, you know the only thing that sticks around is your mind, till you lose that too." He laughed, looking back to me. "If I may ask, do you live here? I noticed you are alone on this quite fine night."

"Yes, my brother owns the floor beneath us. He and his friends shall be returning shortly." Dagger had wanted to stay with me, but I would not let my promise to the human Maryanne be broken. Shift was too new to his abilities to be trusted to himself.

"I see. Well then, would you like some company Celeste?" His tired face beamed, the lines that had formed showing the many times he smiled in his life, the roads all leading up or down from the grin. He had lived an enjoyable life, for that I was thankful.

"Of course, please sit with me." I placed my hand against the cold-sand-rock-roof's surface. He moved cautiously, his body creaking with the strain. That was more difficult for me to witness than much of what I had seen in this world. Age was a concept I had only recently come to even know of, much less to be such an intimate observer of its slowly overpowering nature. It seemed cruel, to grant one with the wisdom, courage, and strength of a lifetime, only to steal from them the body and some, the mind, they needed to enjoy all they had fought for in their youth. The price for life was death, but death nearly seemed kinder than the measured descent so many endured. The only comfort I had was knowing there is a part of people beyond the minds I entered and the bodies I healed, that never changed, a part I could not grasp or name, that remained just beyond my reach, never altering, always present no matter the age or state of the person it was within.

I gently grabbed his arm and helped him down. His papery skin was a-warm-soft-cool. I healed him in that small-contact-moment, though I could not do much, for I had done more than I could already within hours of then. The ease of his pain would be only moderate, the drop in my strength afterwards was too great for me to have done any more that night.

"Thank you... As much as I abhor admitting it, I guess I need more help these days."

"To age in the flesh isn't something to be ashamed of. It shows that you have lived fully." I gently admonished him. He roughly chuckled.

"You're quite the little philosopher aren't you?"

I resisted the urge to shine forth my happiness-soul-lit-fire-light.

"You are wedded?" I looked at the faded-light-gilded-ring on his finger. I saw the shining radiance coming from within it was over half a century in its mined-formed-worn existence.

"Fifty-six years, next month." He told me proudly, grinning as he had before. "We grew up on the same street, but I didn't meet her till I was twenty-four years old, back when color TV was still new huh? Funny how that works. We've never been apart since...well since now. Do you have someone, or still waiting?" It was too dark for him to have seen my appeared human age, though I guessed that it wouldn't have mattered, he was not the manner of man to judge by age of years in the life. He was similar to my kind in that, more specifically he was similar to *me*.

Dagger.

"Yes." .

"That is good. Everyone always needs someone."

"We all do…" I had included myself in his analogy. *We are not much different you and I. Both of us have watched the skies and asked 'is there something more to this existence' and have both found the one that is on our side no matter what may come. Though you and I are diverse in every aspect of the flesh, of our life, and even so much in the mind of each other, our basic beliefs have yet to differ themselves apart.*

"Hmm…Well, my wife is in the hospital again. Silly, sweet thing sent me back here. We're only here in the city with our oldest grandson right now to be closer to her doctors. He is a good boy, he is with her tonight. She knows I need to rest, as if I can find any right now. I thought I'd come up here to think. She isn't doing too well…and I don't sleep alone too good either." He looked to my concerned stare, slapping his hands on his knees. "But this isn't the subject to speak of tonight. We are star gazers, melancholy does not become of us! We must tarry onward to see daybreak and smile when the stars fade because we know they will return, and in that we know we have completed another day!" He said indisputably.

"As you have said, so it shall be for all of time."

"But...I am rambling...old man boring you?" He smiled faintly, seeing if I had only spoken to him out of sympathy.

"Unquestionably not. You have not the need to control your tongue, I enjoy your rambling, as you say."

"Well that's very sweet of you young lady." His heavy eyes glinted in joy.

◆

"Star, you okay?" He knocked on her door, one arm raised so his forehead rested on his arm and his arm on the doorway. Even then he was hunched over to reach that low. I sighed and shook my head. Even I wasn't that stupid.

"She's not here." I muttered impatiently. He spun around; I instinctively shifted back. I saw him do too much damage that night to not have the reflex. Unless you want to be reading my thoughts of "ohmygosh!" over and over again, just know good cop/bad cop works best when the bad cop doesn't knock out the guys before the good cop could work his magic.

"Then where is she?" He asked flatly.

"The roof, dummy." That guy would be so clueless sometimes.

He pushed past me and went to the stairs.

"Hey, wait!" *Oh, duh...*

Star.

You are back safely?

He's being melodramatic. Another than that, he's fine. I managed to get out with few scratches, nothing serious. And no, you don't have permission to heal them.

I did not propose to ask your permission.

I invulnerably rolled my eyes when her energy, like molted gold, covered my mind and body, drinking in every impurity she could find, the dark flecks lost in her consciousness.

If I say thank you that doesn't mean I approve.

Of course. I saw something about another operation you learned of...?

It is a meeting next month. Juarez. Cartel trade route coming through there – these guys were part of a group going to ship it north to Canada. Tunnels underground near the border in need of collapsing, into California and the Midwest.

235

Cops in the area are extinct, corrupt, or too afraid to do much. Government I would bet is in on it, so we move in soon — before the blood bath gets any worse. Don't tell Shift. We should be in and out before Mary can lose his attention.

This is an entire city infested? Let us start at the source, Dagger.

Two cities. The border does little to keep it contained. Their influence reaches across most of the states. There's an Army base nearby — you'll need to black out their communication somehow unless we want fighter pilots on our tails.

Hmm...that will take time. My power is not suited to that of man's. At best I may be able to flood their sensors.

We have time. We're not leaving until your better, so don't get any ideas.

I know.

What feds do we turn them over to?

Who said anything about letting some 'elected' spokesperson choose their so-called justice in this case? I most certainly would not expect someone who could be influenced by their power choose their fate. I say we let their own people decide. Once those at fault are detained, we release their former victims upon them. I do not believe in mercy for things of this matter, but it is their choice. I just might just have to remind those people that their fear of the supernatural is a warranted one.

Heaven forbid you try to keep a low cover.

Well, my form of heaven already forbids that, yet here I stand.

...Who's with you?

Come meet him for yourself. He is less terrifying than he looks.

"And if you look very closely Celeste, you can see one of my favorite of the constellations."

She replied, saying how there are many stars 'we' can't see that are behind it, before turning and alerting him to my presence. The lighting was poor, and I had already known from the sound of his heart beat that recognizing us at close distance was a slim to none chance.

"Daniel, I would like to introduce you to my 'someone', this is Darrell, Darrell this is Dan."

"Dan." I said to him. My mind was on what Star had referred to me as *hers*. Not on the '*The Outsiders*' themed name she gave me. I normally didn't get names. No one ever asked. "And this is my brother, Alexander." Star motioned towards Shift. He had sensed his queue coming and took on the cover model for some surf brand. He didn't even come close to his target of mirroring her.

"Hey, nice to meet you." Shift said, taking his time to walk up to us.

"Forgive me if I don't get up, I think I'm stuck fast to this roof." The man smiled self-consciously. I held out my hand and easily pulled him up. "Youth…it is an amazing, wonderful thing."

I battled a grimace. What he thought was an innocent youth's strength was the product of something made to be the definitive evil.

His eyes ran me over and he whispered something to Star, who had stood up next to him. Only I noticed it had been hard for her too. She and he looked at me and smiled. I didn't hear what he said, due to the tug a war that had still been going on in my head, but she was apparently pleased by it, whatever *it* was.

"I must be off to bed, it is past my curfew." He joked. "Good night to all of you. May the heavens be good in their will for you star gazer."

I froze.

My mind was automatically weighing every immediate option. Shift tensed, the edges of his body growing fuzzy as he prepared for, well, whatever we thought might happen.

"You as well." She said calmly. He turned and left down the stairs, a bit gawkily. "What he called me is a 'star gazer' not *Stargazer* …He is one as well." She laughed the explanation, as if Shift and I had been the funniest things ever.

I didn't answer.

You are sure you are alright?

Not right now, Shift is mad that we talk like this…he is touchy about not being 'included'.

"So…our cover is still good right?" He asked, going back to normal.

"Of course, there is no need for any apprehension. He moved in to the dwelling only a short while ago. He wished to also look at the stars."

"And I wish to sleep till noon… so consider that my lion's share." He pouted.

"Of course. Thank you, for aiding Dagger this evening. I will be fit to accompany once more soon, but I am grateful to know you were with him in my absence."

He smirked, her praise winning him over faster than food could.

"No sweat. But seriously, only get me if something awesome pops up." He disappeared.

"I truly am grateful." She whispered, her eyes glowing brighter.

"What did he tell you? What didn't he want me know?"

Does he know or am I just overeating? Not that I don't have a reason to - I don't need them right now. Shift is nowhere near ready.

"Nothing of consequence. How is Shift? I fear I forgot to check on him, beyond looking for any physical pain."

I shrugged. I knew we'd put him through a lot, but as long as he was eating and sleeping, how bad could it be?

"Have you asked him, Dagger?"

"I guess."

"He will not answer directly unless asked in the same manner."

"Then you do it. It's hard to talk when you barely care enough to want answers, never mind ask for them."

"The more you dwell on that, the more real it will become for you. If you care for me, which I know you do, then you can learn to care for others as well. Do not think of him as a child or element of our assembly, but as a member of a rather...unusual...family. He is a real, living, young, heroic person who seeks your approval more than you have yet to realize."

"I don't just choose to care." I defended.

"I know, for it isn't something done consciously. Did you not care for Mary, even after your change? You ran for her safety as much as your own, it was not sole selfishness, and you cared enough to go against your artificial internal indoctrination to shun all that occurred prior to your change, and helped her reclaim her life as it was."

"You helped me, and I had to, I didn't get an alternative. It was practically life or death."

"So too could this be." She stepped towards me, resting her head against my chest. She sighed, taking a moment before continuing. "If we are to continue in this, we need to be careful that Shift does not grow calloused by what he will come to experience. His mind is much to childish to be at risk now, but promise me, if the time comes where his perspective has become acrimonious toward the world, you will seek to right him. To know its evils is to no longer be blinded by one's own denial; in the same manner, to be void of any faith is to lose the anchor to which sanity is secured. He cannot lose his hold, Dagger. We are capable of facing the darkness, but Shift is not, and I cannot let his eagerness to take hold of his self-chosen calling for his abilities lead him into that which we fight against. You have experienced what it is to be jaded within your own mind, and unless I were to overstep human means, you alone can speak to him…And I still will aid you, no matter what. You forget you have broken this before, even now. You can do it yet again."

Her mind brushed against mine with the same slow deliberateness as her arms wrapped around me. The undeniable otherworldly feeling of her made everything beyond her blurred. I breathed her in, dissolving into the tranquility of her hold.

"You're amazing, you know that?"

She smiled. I watched the light behind her eyes flicker, like candle nearly blown out. I took her against me, holding her upright, knowing the support she offered me was still greater even then.

"You're still weak."

"It is nothing but my own making. I healed him of some of his pains…though he won't notice right away." She made that seem easier for her than I knew it had been.

"Star."

"I do not understand why you would continue to expect anything else from me. I cannot bear to let others suffer, you have chastised me for it before this, I did not stop then, I will not now, so to waste breath is pointless."

"You can't cure everything, you can't cure old age and eventually you are going to try to cure death and-"

"I am not ignorant to the rules of existence." She interjected, resting her head into the curve of my shoulder. Her breath was hot and terribly off-putting. My thoughts became a void for a brief moment before she consumed every corner of them. She knew that, and had been going for it.

"You need to be more careful."

"I shall, for you, but I am never not cautious. You should not bear such a purposeless burden. Unlike Shift, I indeed know my limits, as you recognize, so something else is weighing on you...what is it?"

"You can look."

"And you can speak."

"...What you called me."

She lifted her head, looking up at me. "He and I were speaking of many things before you came, and he asked me a question your presence answered. You are the 'someone' I want to be with, for as long as I can. That is what I meant. He has been with his 'one' for over fifty of your years."

"You know you are mine." I ventured. Rare was my surrender met with hers, not to each other, but to ourselves. The death of the perceived threat of Dan had quieted the constant demands of my artificial instincts, leaving me capable of existing without the endless need to interrogate the source of thought or urge that came over me.

She smiled brightly, the glow of her eyes expanding to the rest of her body.

[Just a Girl]

"Celeste! Oh, I am so glad I caught you. I wanted to thank you for our delightful conversation the other night. I woke up the next morning feeling fifteen years younger! What a morning it's been!"

Dan run into the lobby to catch up with us. I didn't think someone his age *could* run. I realized he was the reason BD had us actually take the elevator to the ground floor that day, rather than shifting out. Thankfully, I looked like 'Alexander' – not my favorite of my normal go-to's, but the best one for our cover stories.

"You are welcome. It was my pleasure. Perhaps the next time we are able to speak, you may find yourself even better rested." Stargazer beamed, not literally but she might as well have.

"Well, I certainly think you are my good luck charm."

"A charm of luck I am not, but if you wish to trust that then you may not be far off." She said lightly.

Why don't you just go ahead and tell *the guy who we are? That might be faster than the whole hit dropping. Maybe we should just make a vine video for every secret* - During my mental rant I missed something because this was the next thing I heard:

"She's going into another surgery today. Tough thing she is, but I want to be there before it."

"You want to split the cab with us?"

I looked at BD, struggling to keep the complete cluelessness of my shock from showing up on my face. They

242

never drove in a cab, if flying was out of the question, I shifted him, (but I was planning to do something about our civilian transportation.) And, more scary than his sudden change of pace, he'd talked *pleasantly*.

"I wouldn't mind that." He agreed.

"Shotgun!" I yelled. No way was I sitting in the back seat with 'Mr. Alien's new BFF/with a story for everything' and the alien herself. I wanted to live. Boredom kills, I promise it does, or I am just highly allergic to it.

-BD-SG S//5

"What do you do Darrell?"

"Uh, security… for a bank." It was the best I could come up with. I had stopped memorizing my cover stories when I realized no one ever asked and I had never planned on getting in a situation that called for one.

"I did security once. But that was for a circus. The stories I could tell you kids… Back then a quarter could buy you a whole day of fun and people weren't in such a hurry. I went to a fair with my daughter last year and everyone was pushing and running around like chickens."

She replied, keeping him talking, distracted, even as I focused on every time she'd "accidentally" touch him.

"And you Alexander?"

"I work with a travel agency." Shift said from the front of the cab, smirking in the rear view mirror.

"I hope you get to travel too. When I was your age me and my wife went on this trip in Europe, we were there nearly a month – her parents were from Italy – Nice I think. I'm afraid I don't remember. Oh, wait, please pull over here." Dan told the driver suddenly. I made a quick mental note of which hospital we had pulled in front of.

"Please, allow me." Star told him. She handed the driver a few bills before the man had a chance to protest.

"Thank you. I will see you tonight star gazer?"

Shift jumped, but kept his mouth shut for once. I would have had to figure out a way to slug him into silence had he not.

She told him something along the lines of 'possibly'. He nodded before shutting the door and walking into the courtyard in front of the large building. A parking garage loomed to our right, a camera on its corner aimed directly in our direction. Even behind the black sunglasses, I pulled the hood on my jacket up, turning away.

"...You two want to tell me why we are in cab?" Shift asked, miffed. The fact we were still *in* the cab, with the driver, had apparently escaped him.

"We shall discuss this later."

"Whatever. Not like I can't be clued in." He mumbled.

"Pull over at the next light."

The driver nodded.

We got out of the car and I handed him double what we owed him. He thanked us, smiled widely, and drove off. Shift tapped his foot, his heart rate increasing with his impatience.

"Can you tell me why *now*?" I hated being left out of his loop.

"I had to find out what hospital his wife was staying at and why she was there."

Stargazer's face lit up and she hugged him. It was the first time I had ever seen the two of them show some PDA, even if it was just a hug.

"Eh-hem, why is that? No head digging today SG?" *You want to heal her too right? Or maybe send flowers like a normal person?* She let go of him and looked at me, or I thought looked at me since her shades were mirrored.

"I do not force my presence on those who do not seek it, not unless lives are at risk. But before I pursue his wife, you must show me what you do for fun. We are taking that day of respite that you have been asking for."

"Oh." I hadn't gotten that vibe. BD had dragged me out of bed at nine. I figured it was another twenty-four hour stretch before I could breathe easy again.

"It was Dagger's idea."

He smirked, dropping the hood of the black sweatshirt he wore under his equally dark leather jacket. *That guy wants to go have 'fun'. He sees what we do every night as 'fun'. ...What exactly are we supposed to do? I wanted a day off, not to play tour guide. I don't think he'd go for half of what I normally get into. This is still so weird. I am so going to write a tell-all book about this in fifteen years.* (As it turns out, we *did*! Ha!)

"Cool, uh, well, the mall is a pretty safe bet."

"Security cameras." He said minimally.

"What is this mall?" She asked, taking my attention off the Goth Superman.

"Just keep your shades on, Top Gun."

"And if something happens we're putting hundreds of civilians at risk."

"Come on, she's never seen a mall! You're going to deny her that because you're paranoid? If something happens, whatever you're worried about, we'll just bolt."

"I don't like running."

"Good thing you have practice in it then." I snipped, more teasing than serious, but he still couldn't take a joke even if you spoon fed it to him. In fact, he nearly growled. *Well this is off to a good start.*

"We will accomplish nothing by standing her without action." SG intervened.

◆

I looked around the artificially-lit-stale-aired space. Large-multicolored-neon-signs hung overhead and the

245

combined energy of hundreds of living beings surrounded me. It was similar to the 'club', though I had expected as much from the brief descriptions Shift had given and remained focused on Dagger's energy alone.

"So, how do like it?" He seemed to be self-satisfied, his gaze roaming from specific items in the windows to certain people before taking in the whole expanse and then once more finding a single thing to focus on.

"It is surreal." I told him as I too scanned the area, both with my humanoid form and my naturally-occurring-precise-ways-of-analyzing. It seemed barbaric in a modern-consumer-steel-and-glass society for so many to have the mindset of a hunt, but then again, so did we when the streets were ours.

"BD...?" Shift sought feedback to his choice of 'day off'. His reasoning behind the desire for a semi-normal human existence was not something to judge, he gave it up to become a part of us, but I sensed and saw that he was not as easily entertained as he'd originally proclaimed to be. Even this had already begun to bore him, for he was quick to keep us moving over the cold tiles beneath their feet.

"Just keep a low profile kid.".

BD looked like should have been hiding in the back of Spencer's, what with the fact he was wearing almost all black, except for his t-shirt, barely visible beneath the two unzipped jackets, and he had on his sun glasses, *inside*. I mean I know the guy was paranoid and I guess I could figure out why, but still, I was being sarcastic when I had suggested it before. He got more looks and attention than "Alexander" got walking through a teen pop concert.

I was shifted into just me that day, but I had changed a few things, just in case. I'd lost the Ken doll look as soon as Dan was out of the picture. I could get in anywhere and had made full use of that perk whenever I wasn't being baby sat. Stargazer knew about my 'top secret gigs', but for my own safety she didn't tell Black Dagger. Although *she* gave me a pretty scary warning over if I didn't stop doing all of that sooner or later. ...I picked later.

By habit I looked around, scanning more than the merchandise in the windows. There was this curly haired blonde that I had seen when we'd first walked in, and hadn't taken eyes off of since, but apparently she'd caught Stargazer's as well.

"Ya'll know her or something?"

"No. She's just a girl." She said quickly.

"Is she single?"

She didn't answer me, but held on to BD a lot tighter, like she was going to fall. He kept his arms around her, one at her waist and one around her shoulders, standing behind her. He looked huge. She looked scared. The mom pushing the stroller past us looked irritated that we were standing in the middle of the balcony.

"...You ok?"

"I am fine."

"You don't really look it." I commented dryly.

"I have yet to be exposed to this energy before." She explained.

I filed it under 'alien issues' and dismissed her weirdness with no more than a second thought because we'd yet to hit the food court. *That* was a big deal.

You sure you're alright?

I just did not realize the ramifications of our last outing are still with me.

We'd done a big operation a few nights before, the one prior to Shift and my first outing without her. Dozens of hostages had been involved, and as you can guess, she couldn't live without healing them, down to the last scratch. Her insistence on helping Dan had only exacerbated the issue.

We aren't going to his wife today.

I am getting stronger by the moment Dagger, simply because my body hides the molecular fusion within me does not mean it is not happening. You are worried for not, my one.

That's debatable. I caught what she said.

I looked up. Shift stared with an abnormally serious expression.

"You two were doing it again."

"Doing what?"

He didn't move, but he did cock an eyebrow at us and huffed.

"Don't even act like you don't *know* -" he lowered his voice and leaned across the table. He had lead us to the food court ten minutes back. "Ya'll were talking – I can tell. We're not even on the job and I'm still out of the loop. I hate it, and you guys make me feel like a sidekick."

"I am sorry that copious numbers of our discussions are not voiced aloud, but much of that which we speak of isn't for unknowing ears to heed. If you would like, I can include you in our link."

"Can't you just *whisper* or something? It's freaky to have you in my head. Like I'm being *abducted*..." He made a very animated shiver. I stayed out of that conversation. I might have said something she would try to get me to regret later.

"Of course. I will make sure we refrain from speaking of anything you might desire to partake in. As it stands, that was nothing of consequence. What is it that you wish to do next?"

His wheels were turning. He smiled and wrote something down on a napkin, folded it once, and passed it to her flat across the table, his way of proving there were more inclusive, even if conspicuous, ways of communication in front of civilians.

She picked it up, opening it so we both could see.

"ICE-SKATING?"

This is why you don't let the kid be in charge.

248

I skeptically looked at the shiny-scratched floor beneath me. Small-white waves of energy escaped from its frozen surface, hindered by the cold-slow-moving nature of the matter below. I felt the radiance of my energy mix and blend with it. I knew what would come next and stepped back, breaking the unseen contact.

"I cannot do this..." I whispered, knowing it to be the first time those words had ever been spoken by me in such a context. Shift's head had shot up from the laced-wide-solid-mineral-bladed shoes he was pulling on. I, even though preferred to not wear such things, had similar on as well.

"It's not like I can't catch you if you do slip up." He had a mocking tone that never quite left his voice.

Dagger stood right behind me, his soft-pressure-applying hands resting at the curve where my torso ended. His energy rippled around me in subtle breakers of soothing-burning-magnetism, none making that which I was trying to *not* do any easier. He drew me against him, his cool breath running across my shoulder. His lips brushed against my ear as he whispered, "I won't let you fall."

"I'll melt it..." I shook my head to clear myself from his fog more than to supplement what I had said. I could control my own temperature, but not the energy I gave off—not around him.

"Come on SG, don't be such a kill joy, even BD is doing this and he can break it just by *catching* himself. You aren't *that* hot you know. You will go down as the..." he lowered his voice "*alien* that was completely *terrified* of *ice*..."

I could tell Dagger already knew I would break from my softened stance, a stance he alone had supported. *If it will get him to stop his constant badgering.*

"All right." I consented, my eyes still on the glassy surface I could destroy with the slightest raise in my radiation.

"You *sure*?" He joked. I nodded. "Good, now get your butt out there!" He yelled and took off, circling the other humans with ever-increasing-inertia.

I stayed where I was, inches from the edge. I never let my eyes off the surface, even when I sensed him letting me go.

"Star?"

He was a few feet ahead of me by then, already on the ice.

I briefly wondered if he'd ever done that in the life he could not recall, for he was quite fine at it.

[Aliens on Ice-Skates and Other Anomalies]

"What were you so worried about?" I found myself questioning her seemingly effortless gliding.

"They could fall and get harmed if I were to soften it, even slightly."

I stopped, she stopped with me.

"There's more to it." I stated, not giving her the luxury of wording it as a question she might try to dodge. She sighed, grabbed my hand, and pulled me over to a bench built into the rink. She sat down, her arms around herself. To anyone looking, and I saw out of the corner of my always scanning vision that quite a few were, she appeared cold. I knew it was something much more dangerous.

"I saw the girl who I healed." She whispered.

"Which one?"

"The one that I felt I could not." She murmured.

"Is she okay?"

"I could not tell. That is what frightens me. I did not recognize her Dagger, as if she is not the same child. It was *she* who remembered *me*, somehow her very essence seemed to flare when I laid eyes on her."

"So...?"

"No one has done that before. Every person I have healed, their bodies take on the energy and the strength I give them as if it were merely a surplus of their own abilities. Hers recognized me as her source. They are fine, but her, I simply do not know…" She trialed off and put her arms tighter around her, trembling. "If anything is erroneous, if she is somehow

251

damaged from me, then it only proves others were right and I was mistaken for coming here, for believing I could save them. I cannot be mistaken."

"Is she still here?"

"Yes. I have been fighting the urge to go to her, for fear of what I will find. Dagger, I cannot be wrong, I am telling you this so that you will find a way to be my anchor here, that if my fears are true then I…then I do not know what I will do. What I can do, even. I am terrified, but I can't be *wrong*." She hissed, her eyes flashing brown.

"Stargazer…" I whispered soothingly.

I put my hand against the side of her face, leaning into her. Her lips parted against mine as my arm wrapped around her waist, pulling towards me. To say the least we'd forgotten that we were in the middle of a crowd.

"Guys, we have a problem!"

Star pulled away at Shift's outburst. I saw him standing next to us, clinging to the bench, his expression one of shock and laughter. Everyone else in the rink was on the ground sprawled out in hazardous stances. Stargazer bent down and put her hands against the, what I realized, was partially melted ice. It froze instantly, and the skaters slowly began to rise back to their feet. *She wasn't even touching it before.* Whatever I was about to think was lost in another one of Shift's suddenly increasing rants.

"Nice going SG, you *melted* it. How the heck did you manage that?!" I had yet to register what she'd just done with BD. It hit me short instant later. *Oh. …Ewe, actually. I think I preferred the mystery to the reality. FYI: Never kiss an alien! They might melt you!*

"I forgot." She said in a small voice.

I rolled my eyes.

It's not like it's that hard. "Hey, the ground is frozen, maybe I should hold off making out with Goth Superman till we get home and Shift's not in the audience." Seriously. And I'm supposed to be the clueless one.

"Let's go." BD said flatly. For once we were thinking the exact same thing. "Can you carry me?"

No. Thanks to your lack of having 'let's call it a night' in your vocabulary and the fact you only let me sleep five hours, I am totally and completely 'shifted' out... A nap sounds good though.

"Can't we just slip out? I'm tired from last night." *That's completely an understatement. We need superhero curfews. Badly. I-* Only then did I notice the crowd around us. Someone had noticed what Stargazer had done.

"We wouldn't make it to an exit the feds get wind of this... They will lock the whole mall down." He said, not caring if everyone heard him, and they had. *Not a problem for us, but I see your point, the 'citizen endangerment' and stuff like that. Crap. He was right. Again. At least I'm not the one that blew cover.*

"Great..."

"I *could* crack the ice. It would be easy enough. Might give us thirty seconds at best." He sounded like he actually meant it.

"No." I looked at Star; she was focused intently on the growing, gawking mob. Her eyes were glowing, her skin looked like a lava lamp was beneath it, and her hands looked like they were feeling the air. It was the most bizarre thing I had ever seen. And it killed whatever chance we had of pleading the fifth.

"She okay?" I whispered to BD. He nodded once. Stargazer walked up to the crowd, most of them took three steps back for every one of hers forward. The only ones in the front who were mindless to it was a group of little kids, who shuffled between SG and the crowd, their eyes on their feet. She seemed to not see them, going straight up to a group of girls that were packed together on the side. I couldn't see much where I was so I grabbed BD's arm and shifted us outside of the rink, not far enough to cause me any major exhaustion, but enough that I knew I had maybe four shifts left in me before I passed out.

Only one of them saw her walk up, a red-headed girl wearing a plaid scarf. She tapped her friend franticly on the shoulder. She turned around and instantly paled. She had green, I mean like *seriously* green eyes, and really curly blonde hair, the same girl I had seen earlier near the food court, which still didn't explain much. She gawped at what she saw: a gold woman, a huge, scary looking man, and an average looking teen guy who was about as stunned as she was, for different reason.

I watched as Stargazer reached out and opened her palm to the girl. A small piece of paper was in it. *Where did she get that?* She took the girl lightly by the wrist and placed the folded paper in her small pink tinted hand. The chick was too scared to pull back, but her friend's weren't. She was deserted, standing alone in front of us with about two dozen witnesses scattered about.

"If you wish to know." Stargazer told her quietly. I doubted anyone else had heard her. The girl's hand closed around the paper.

SG smiled and disappeared.

Get yourself and Dagger out of here now. She ordered just as a spark shot down my spine, forcing me to move. I grabbed BD just before the world around me changed.

"Okay, you officially have topped the scales of all universal weirdness. I could handle the PDA and the ice, but what the heck was *that*?!" Shift tossed his hands in the air, the rushed expansion of ginger-fear-confused power around him striking my own with similar force.

"Peace. I shall explain all in due time."

"You better."

"*You* better watch it kid." Dagger warned, his aggression fed by Shift's mistrust.

"Stop, both of you. I will explain, so there is no need for your hostilities."

Dagger, you need to be at peace as well.

He is acting like-

He is young and his emotions rule him. You do not have the same excuse.

"Anytime now SG."

...Although he is a bit annoying at times.

Told you.

I proceeded to tell him how we had come to know that girl, though not in full-all-encompassing detail, some things of that gilded dawn were not for his knowing.

◆

"What was all that about Cynthia?" My friend pulled at my shoulder. I felt her hand and heard her voice, but they seemed to be coming from far away. I was *seeing* something that wasn't there, something about them ...and something about *me*. I knew it wasn't real, at least it wasn't really happening right then, but it felt like it, it felt as close as Katie's hand on my arm and Keisha's voice ringing in my head.

"I don't know." I held the paper tightly in my clenched fist. The crowd had dissipated after they left. Those who remained were yelling into their cell phones or hovering around us. Someone took a picture, I could feel the light of the camera hit my skin.

"Don't you girls see?! Those were the Protectors! That is how they disappeared like that! They *talked* to you and-" Hannah's voice was lost in my roaring head.

"Cynth, what did she give you?" Katie's awe didn't compare to my terror, and somehow they were all still able to

255

think, to breathe even. My heart felt like I had one of those shock boxes attached to my chest.

I looked down at my hand. My nails were cutting into my palm, but I didn't loosen my grip, it could disappear *too*. Slivers of pure white paper showed in between my fingers and the stark contrast of blood from my palm brilliantly stained it's surface, but I didn't realize that I was hurting myself. I wasn't feeling or seeing the present time.

That wasn't a dream last night. ...It really happened, just now. Just like the others. I thought it was just...just déjà vu. I didn't really think it could – how would I even know that? I saw them here and it...it was real. I didn't have any ideas on how I had known, but I had. Just like everything else I mysteriously woke up knowing in the last eight months.

"*Cynth*? ...Your hand?"

I barely heard her.

"I have to go." *I need to go home.*

I ran out of there. My mind was focused on one thing: *forward*. I ran straight to my mom's apartment. I didn't know I could run that fast. Or that far. It had been two bus rides to get to that mall from our block, the forty minutes somehow cut down to barely over fifteen. I crashed through the wooden door. Panting, I slammed it shut behind me. The subdued sounds of the building's hallway terminated. The air-conditioned atmosphere hit my hot face and filled my burning lungs.

The colors returned to normal, at least for then. They said it was stress that made my vision go hazy, but I was beginning to realize otherwise.

"Honey, you're home early! How was the mall?"

I shot a quick glance at my mom. She was stirring something on the stove. I saw a half-hidden phone in her ear behind her hair. She instantly looked worried after seeing how winded and pink I was.

"I'll call you back – You ok sweetheart?" She set the phone and spoon down, wiped her hands on a stained kitchen rag, and took a step towards me. Her sage green eyes were worried.

"Oh yeah, I'm great, I just forgot Katie has my phone. I have to let her know to bring it tomorrow. I'll be in my room!" I felt her watching me as I raced up the stairs, two or three at a time, and locked the door behind me.

I opened my cramped hand and placed the paper on my bed. The cuts were not bleeding anymore. There were only slightly pink crescents where they had once been, the only evidence left were the stains on the paper. I stared and the crinkled, folded mass for over ten minutes. If I took my eyes off it, it would vanish. It gave me a mocking lack of movement as if it was teasing me, subtly calling me to open it just so it could evaporate the second my hand touched it again. I paced around the room, finally sitting next to it on my bed. I stared at it, trying to solve whether to burn it or read the insultingly unmoving paper.

I took a meant to be calming breath and opened it.

It didn't vaporize.

~~Cynthia,~~

*If you wish to know why you recognize things beyond your understanding, do not be troubled, for I have some of the answers you seek. Why you are alive today is one of them. I would have told you sooner, but you vanished before I could have found you, and I had not known then what I do now. Do not be frightened of that which you don't know. You see things that you can't explain; you know things you have never learned. And you feel things, though they are not happening to you. **You need not fear us;** we are here to protect you. You are more than you know, and you must only find out who and what you are to understand this. I will explain tomorrow, under the pavilion at your school.*

Answers wait, but you must seek them first.

I have them.

My mind swirled around the curling hand-written words. It was in gold lettering and seemed to shine against the white paper. It felt heavier than it should have, as if more than just ink weighted it down.

How can she know about all of this? I didn't even tell my mom! What do I do? I'll pretend to be sick! Mom won't make me go and they'll just leave me alone when I don't show...What if they don't? What if they follow me, stalk me or something?! What if they come here?! What do I tell mom?! My heart raced, my head pounded, and I broke out in a cold sweat. *They'll say I'm crazy! But if they come here and she finds out then it's even worse. I can't be crazy! Crazy people don't know their crazy and I know this is nuts!*

IF I do go to school tomorrow, maybe *talk to her, see if any of this is actually real or- I go live with dad. OR- I forget everything that ever happened, start a new life, change my name, dye my hair, learn Portuguese and move to Argentina.*

I didn't like any of my choices; all of them were equally hard for me to do.

Awareness

I didn't know what to think about Shift's reaction. He had been waiting for us to get back from the hospital where Dan's wife was, and once we had, before we could say anything, he'd shouted, "It's the *same!*" and just left, disappearing to whatever corner of the globe he thought he could hide in. Star told me he would be back, and that he was safe, but she wouldn't say where he went.

Testing the boundaries of my patience, she had refused to answer anything I asked, but I looked to her again for answers. She was seamlessly still, her face blank and her hands delicately folded in her lap. The only giveaway to her apparent peaceful state was her eyes, tense, dark.

"You are confused?" She asked quietly, keeping her head down. I knew she had not been in my mind, due to my lack of peace. I wouldn't have thought confused was the right word, but it was close enough.

"Shift's a big headed punk, but he had never blown up like that." *And over absolutely nothing...That's more like, well,* me. *If there is a valid risk he picked up on and that I'm missing, then we could have a potential problem. He could put us in lines of sight we need to be out of – I need to reign him in. Now.*

"He knows that I healed his sister, he believes that whatever has occurred to that girl, because of *me*, will happen to Maryanne. That perhaps something was wrong – That I was wrong. I could not reason with him. He thought that I-" She was forced to stop, her quaking voice threatening to break.

"We both know that isn't how this works."

She nodded, the jolting motion betraying her struggle.

I can't believe he thought that she could do that again. He knows it nearly killed her. What was worse than his idiotic reasoning was the fact that it had gotten to her. And things rarely did.

"He has a right to know some of these things, if his family is concerned."

"You know it's not your fault. You healed her, you saved her life, she won't be mad at you no matter what the side effects are." Star had tried to explain everything she saw about that girl, but even she didn't understand. The chick was not wholly human. My genes may have be altered, but this girl's were entirely rearranged. Star gave her part of her energy when she'd healed her, which had not been unusual, but apparently, some of it had *stayed* in the girl.

"...She does not know why she is the way she is. I fear what will happen if I tell, for even you would have wished not known the genesis of your abilities. What if she is the same?" She begged as she looked back to me, her only sign of weakness the line between her eyes.

"If she shows tomorrow, then she does want to know, besides, side effect is a lot better than perfect weapon, no matter how you want to look at it. What they did to me was meant to cause suffering, you saved her from hers. There is nothing about that that is similar. You know it. She will know it when she comes."

"And if she does, then what will she choose to do? How can I mend what I have done, if I do not even know what she is, what *I* did?" She asked in an enormously small voice.

"We will find out tomorrow." I said simply. There wasn't much else we could do given the fact *we* couldn't see the future.

She turned away, her skin cooling.

"If I were her, I would run from such an ultimatum."

"No you wouldn't."

"Yes, Dagger, I would. I would flee as far and as fast as I could. I would be terrified of such unknown power and the thought that someone else sought to control it that I would escape anything and everyone, until I could learn what it was and what to do, and even then, it would take an act of divine serendipity for me to return."

"Why?" I wasn't so shut off from the world and those in it that I couldn't understand a bit of what that girl was facing, but even my logic driven analysis produced nothing to support Stargazer's theory. A teen girl being told there was something about her that made her special wasn't a fight or flight sympathetic response. It was inevitable. She would show up.

She did not answer. Her eyes were amber; her skin dark, lit by only the faint moon above her, her reddish gold hair the only thing reflecting its light. I ran my hand down her cheek.

"She will be there, and you will figure this out. You didn't ruin her life, you gave it back. No matter how many minds you read you will never be able to understand just how easily most people can overcome what seems impossible. A part of her will be freaked out, but another part knows the truth, same as I do."

"Thank you." She whispered. "Shift has returned. He is looking for us. We should not delay his search."

I got up and helped Stargazer to her feet, a product of her exhaustion from healing both Dan and his wife. Shift appeared a second later. She smiled and welcomed him as if nothing had happened.

"Sorry, about before. I wasn't thinking." He mumbled. "... I thought that, well Mary said you healed her too, so I didn't know if-but she's fine and is mad at me for getting mad at you and I feel like a dirt bag for being such a jerk. I mean it, I overreacted because you said the chick wasn't normal and I just thought that Mary could have side effects too and I freaked." He said quickly. He paced back and forth and rubbed his hands together. Star felt badly enough already, without having to talk about it to him too. Not that he was trying to make her feel worse – he was *trying* to apologize.

"She sounds just like your dad right?" I asked him.

"Uh…Yeah, she does." He said, confused. "How'd *you* know?"

"They've both chewed me out before."

"I will return in a moment." Star said slowly. She faintly smiled, her one acceptance to Shift and her gratefulness to me for distracting him, and walked down to the roof's entrance. I looked at her direction long after she'd disappeared until I noticed Shift had one eye-brow cocked.

"What?"

"Nothing." He tried to hide a snicker. I ignored him. He got his breath back a second later and continued. "Mary has gotten mad at *you*? Why?" he shifted to where he was sat cross-legged on the cement, pure curiosity on his face.

"I did something stupid when she told me not to."

"*You* did something *stupid*? *What*?" He asked unbelievingly. He would have been on the edge of his seat if he was sitting on one.

"Nothing worth the details. I got even for her with someone." The taste of metal burned my tongue. *Again true enough.*

His heart stopped racing.

"*Sam*?" He asked quietly.

"How do *you* know about *him*?" Fury rushed through me at even his name, but I pushed it back before I did anything I would not like myself for next time I saw Star. I felt the constrictions of the walls as they began to rise and fought them, knowing that if they rose, my control would be lost in their shadow, and Shift would see that what had been hidden behind cold indifference for so many months wasn't jaded apathy. It was rage.

"...Oh, uh, well. I, uh, I guessed. I knew that Mary had a (freaking dirt) bag of a boyfriend back then. I first thought it was *you*, believe it or not." I found myself believing it. "But after, I realized it was him, not you. I knew you two had gotten into it, and it was tied to her. I might have read a little of her diary, after she left I mean, so, well, yeah." He added guiltily.

I was just glad he didn't look like he knew *why* I had gotten even with the SOB.

"Her diary?"

He shrugged. "Yeah...I was *just* fourteen, cut me a break BD. There wasn't much in it anyway." He face fell. "I don't think she was very sane then..." He answered the unasked matter. "His name and yours, but that was pretty much all the recent stuff in it and something like 'Safe is an illusion and life is fleet-'" He saw my expression, whatever it had been, and stopped talking for a minute. "...It scared me a little actually." He whispered. "I didn't know what happened to her."

"Didn't know *what*?" I asked bitingly. There was a lot he could have not known.

He was instantly uncomfortable, the hairs on his body standing tall as he instinctively prepared to shift. *She won't tell her parents and didn't tell the doctors but she'll tell her kid brother.*

"What he did...to her... I didn't know before, but after I joined you guys she told me about... about what happened." He mumbled, his slurred voice attempting to hide the way his eyes flashed and his hands went into fists. "I owe you big time for taking care of her... and *him*." The last word caught my full attention, the way he said it, how his expression had changed from anger to twisted satisfaction.

"What did she tell you?" I asked in a guarded tone.

"About what?" He looked like he didn't know what I was talking about. He made his voice as light as possible. He was a bad liar.

"Sam." I hissed. My hands flexed.

"Oh…" He fidgeted with his white sleeves, pretending to try to get them even. He wore all white, in order to get his clothes to mimic whatever he looked like.

"*What did she tell you Shift?*" I forced my voice to stay somewhat level. He quit his moving, shifted to where he was standing, his arms folded across his chest. He stared right at me.

"I don't know what you want me to say BD. I know everything so you don't have to pretend anymore. You killed that guy, that's why Mary thought you were dead and went ballistic. You hit him and he went down, dead on impact, and then everyone said you tried to run from the scene, went through a red light, and was..." He trailed off.

My eyes were open, but I was watching what had happened at that college campus in faultless detail. My first memory as the Perfect Weapon. I saw what I had done. What I had originally *planned* to do once I got there, the minor offense it had been of painting something starting with an f and ending in u on his car. And knew what I had always, deep down, wanted to do.

I killed him.

"BD…? Hey, you okay, man?"

"I didn't know that."

"What?" He seemed confused.

"That I killed him."

I was almost happy that the serum was numbing whatever I was feeling, because I have no idea what it would have been. *I killed him.* I knew that was *exactly* what I was *designed* to do. I had wanted him dead more than I had wanted anything else at the time.

I killed him.

"But…I thought that's why Mary and y-"

264

"Don't." I growled. I had let the walls rise unhindered around what little bit of humanity I had, leaving what was left unchained. I couldn't face it otherwise.

He stopped, pausing long enough to see the struggle I was facing was whether or not to hit myself in the gut, not him.

"Well it saved me from having to do it." He smiled, though it was forced.

"I guess." I had to change the discussion, to distract myself from jump to the roof three buildings over and leaving him there alone. "What do think about the girl?"

His oxytocin levels rose slightly as his epinephrine ones gradually fell towards half-life, his outward recognition of my dismissing the topic only visible by the fall of his shoulders.

"Stargazer seems off about it. So there's that. But she's off about a lot of things, you know? Not in a bad way but in an alienish one. Don't get snippy, it's just how I have to label it. But the girl, I don't even know what the chick does, but she's gorgeous, so I'm not going to complain." I grinned, happy that he'd changed the theme to someone I'd much rather be reminded about. I didn't want to talk about his and my sister's blacklist any more than he did.

It had been at the pit of my stomach for a few weeks. I had stayed with Mary for a few days uninterrupted when BD and SG had raided a North Korean prison. They hadn't called me for transport until the end, leaving me and Mary to ourselves. It was the second day that I had finally managed to ask her how she and BD had a history, and what had caused her to leave, and the morning of the third that she had answered.

He nodded, but didn't say anything about her, the girl, more than: "Well that is good for you huh?"

I said, "Yeah, *really* good. And I know I'm a (butt) for flipping out earlier but, I still need to know if has she ever done this to anyone else. I don't think I have any side effects." *Not that they'd show up much with all the craziness.*

"What happened that day was a fluke. She gave too much energy and it almost killed her. It took her weeks to get all of her strength back."

"Was it bad?" I had no doubt that he would put up the 'no comment' face, but he didn't and *that* was stranger than even the girl.

"Not entirely."

Okay, now I am confused. She almost died, you sounded mad, and you're saying that was a good day? Are you really that weird? And you're talking to me, even after I told you...that?

He took a deep, almost shaking breath.

"That was the day I first told her that I loved her."

Uh...Well that kind of explains it.

"Took her almost dying for you to say that?" I had personally never seen him tell her that he loved her. But then again, I hadn't ever doubted that he did.

"Yeah."

"Look at us! We're actually bonding, kind of. I'm *so* proud!"

He grimaced.

"Ok, fine, we'll mark this down for good progress." I smirked, before shifting out.

How could I have done that? I wanted to...I would still want to —

But I actually did it.

He's dead.

My head felt like it was a giant rock, same as my stomach. I flexed my hands a few times, trying to get some feeling back. I had forced the walls down, digging through the rubble for pieces of some type of sentiment. I didn't find any. I couldn't even begin to look. I couldn't reach the surface. I couldn't breathe.

She was there as soon as I had stood to go find her, standing in front of me. The weight of what I had done kept me from having the strength to lift my head, to speak, but I didn't have to. She knew.

It wasn't merely weakness, it was surrender.

I couldn't fight it.

I didn't want to.

Her arms were around me, catching me as my legs gave out.

When I had taken upon the weight of his body, so too did his mind and power crash into my own, their pain pouring from wounds once believed to be scars. Even as I sought-struggled to understand it all, I pulled him upright, so that his legs were folded below him, his head falling against his chest despondent-submission-despair. I rose to my knees, closing my arm around the curve of his jaw, drawing him against me. I whispered his name, my hand enwrapping at the curve of his shoulder, the other resting against the side of his head farthest from me, my power seeking to draw out the darkness he had disappeared into.

"You had no notion of what you were capable of doing ." I whispered, one of the dozens of comforts I had tried to offer him in the minutes that had passed, holding him tighter against me at the memory that this was not the first shadow of death my light had been unable to destroy. I refused to be as helpless as I had once been, for I knew I could help, more importantly I knew I had to before the unseen-in-this-race effect took its place.

Listen to me, I said above the incomprehensible roars of his thoughts, *I am right here, Dagger. I am with you. I need you to come back from this, come back to me.*

His chest shook as he struggled to inhale.

"I killed him." He forced the cold words from his lips, his breath broken. He pulled back from me, turning away.

"I can't. I didn't-I don't want to be a *weapon.*" He said as if he knew that to be the only truth.

"You are not, and you know it. You did not strike him with the conscious mind to end his life, and you could not have known what it was that drove you to such an extent and ability." I ran my fingers through his hair and leaned towards him, feeling his abnormally fast heartbeat, his panic raging through his body even as his mind remained in the fog of his abjuration of reality. I drew his sight with my own, forcing him to look upon me. His expression was drawn with agony, but I did not give into its demands.

Dagger speak to me. Do not lose yourself in this - "No matter what, *nothing* ever will make you what you fear yourself to be. You are not a weapon against your kind. I saw your memories, I know what you were thinking. You did not know what you were doing." I seized his wrists, bringing his submitting grasp to my sides. I wanted his hands on me, no matter what they had once done, because in that I said more than I knew to in words, more than he would understand if I even attempted to. He had not fought me, not when I arrested his stare or when I made him to hold me, but he did not answer what hadn't been spoken.

"Yes – I did." I no longer held his eyes, but they did not fall from mine. He was not hiding from it, but I feared for man who ran into the light with no rightful fear of being blinded.

"If you had known a single strike could have taken his breath, you would not have fought him." I took his hand and raised it to my lips, holding it there. He did not wrench himself from my grip, though I could sense the trembling of his muscles below his skin. "I have wanted to end many lives Dagger…of my own kind and of this world. Had I not been taught to control myself from before I even grasped at the magnitude of my strength, then there would have been many no longer in existence. Do you see? From the moment you learned what your false nature was, you vowed to overcome it, and until this hour, you believed you had, but you cannot condemn your own life forfeit to what you did before you understood, before you took control.

...I cannot save you from your own guilt, just as I cannot fight this battle for you. I can only tell you that I seek to cause none of it. What is done cannot be changed, and it has changed nothing in how I or Shift see you. You cannot let it change your own self view. You cannot lose yourself to this."

"I ki-"

"*No.*" I said and pressed my lips to his, despising the detachment of his touch. Defeated, I turned my head slightly, his cool-pale cheek to mine. "I know what you will say. And you know what I have." I buried my face in his neck, tightening my arms around him, my hands knotting in his hair, at a helpless loss for anything more I could possibly do. "You cannot dwell on it my one. It will *destroy* you. I will not let it, even if I must hold you under the stars cease to expand. I am with you, in this as I am in all things. You cannot lose yourself. " I didn't know how many times I tried to tell him that promise before, and I didn't care. I would say it as many times as it took for him to believe it.

I came too late then. I will not fail for Dagger. I will never let his soul go. My mind was racing-frantic, contradicting my tone-of-voice. The fear I had of the possibility of that phenomenon was overwhelming-consuming me from the inside out.

I brushed against his thoughts, whispering at the base of the walls so that the part of him trapped behind them might hear.

If you let this beat you Dagger, the darkness wins. What you did – to let it consume you now, to let it destroy you, there is no redemption there. I am not afraid – you are not the monster that they wanted you to be, you are mine, and I will not see you taken from me by this, but I cannot fight with you if you surrender now. I am right here with you, I will be here come the dawn, and every night that follows.

I held him, letting the pure truth of what I said become evidence in my embrace, and delighted beyond description when he let me behind his self-named-walls, though he still had not the might or will to speak. His energy's color-shade-tone had lightened, though he was highly affected by his 'biological-mental modifications', leaving his conscious mind numb, but he, in a sense of words, had needed to be.

It was nearly dawn when he sighed, the first movement either of us had made in some hours. I released my hold around his neck, falling back against my feet so that our faces might be level. His eyes met mine once more and I saw their blackened-soul-fire-spirit light growing in intensity. My own eyes glossed over in my ease, light shining from beneath my skin just as the sun was breaking at the farthest edge of the Earth. Our cities chaotic sounds were lost in both of our minds as his once more opened to mine.

I'm not surrendering. He lifted his hand, resting it against the curve of my cheek. I fell into him as if we were one, his raised breath blending with mine, the soft whisper of his skin lulling my thoughts away from fears. I only broke away from him when I could no longer trust that my desire to see him whole would not bind him beyond his desire.

"Thank you." He whispered before falling into sleep that I had helped lead him into, his hand in my own, his other holding me near him, resting on the trough of my body's wave. I curled against him, lending him my warmth as I watched him, listening to his steady-slow heart and softened breath, feeling the cool fog of his power grow in vastness and lighten as the sun rose higher.

This dawn, and all to come.

Side Effects

Seconds chances should be treated as if it's the first and the last shot we have. – Love Shads

"Hey! What's going on, Cynth? What's *up*? ...*Cynthia*!" I jumped at the unexpected locker slamming shut next to me.

Will no one leave me alone?!

"Nothing." I stammered, shutting my locker, holding my books against my chest and wishing it was an invisibility cloak made of Kevlar. Or whatever could protect me from both my friends and...and them.

I kept my eyes on the ground. I made my feet continue moving, slowly, I didn't trust myself not to run if I were to stop or change pace. I tried to ignore my friends who had been closely following me. Their eyes were wide with speculation, and when I had turned off my phone the night before, I knew it would only heighten their demand today.

"Is this about the Protectors!?" One of them yelled. It didn't matter; everyone heard. I was officially popular, which made things even worse. I had done really well to become invisible, at least so that no one found me interesting after the first few times they saw me. Suddenly there was no hope for that.

"They are the good guys you know. They aren't going to kidnap you or something." Keisha told me, waving her dusky hand in the air carelessly, her tight curls bouncing as she laughed at my panic stricken face.

They might!

271

"Yeah, Cynthia-some of us missed it! What is your deal already? Just tell us what they wanted! What'd you see? Was it scary? You've said like two words all day." Marcia interrupted my thoughts, bumping my shoulder with hers. Her brightly made-up faced pulled into a lovingly mocking smile. Her spotless bronze skin was a reminder of how terribly pale I was in the face of the constant panic I had been in for hours.

Katie stepped in, seeing that my terror wasn't from being star struck.

"Okay girls – she'll tell us when she's ready – won't you?" She raised one red eyebrow.

I tried to smile, nodding.

I let them follow me for protection from the Protectors (even in my freaking out state I could appreciate how ironic that sounded). They followed me outside, asking why we were going to walk through the grass instead of the indoor hallway to get to the bus ramp. I ignored them and carefully rounded the corner of the school, overlooking the small PE field. Sure enough, they were there, under the pavilion. Just like she said.

They were all dressed normally; no one else could tell what, who they were. But the papers hadn't given them much credit. The biggest of them, the one who had disappeared with the kid, was standing perfectly straight, his arms crossed. He in particular was scary. I only let myself briefly think on who the guy was... The other one, the youngest, was leaning up against one of the metal picnic tables. I could tell that he was smiling. I thought that was kind of rude, considering I was scared to death. Faded, torn up jeans and tight light blue Hollister t-shirt made him seem like a glitch in the Matrix next to the other one's towering, darkly terrifying stature.

But they were not the focus of my terror, however much the big guy demanded me to be aware of him out of my, and everyone else's, hereditary life preservation instinct. The woman stood in front of them, her eyes threatening to lock with mine if I dared to meet them. The intensity of her stare was enough to halt my last ditch effort to forget all this and make a break for the bus.

"...Girls, um, I'll catch up with you later." I said suddenly. I was too far in to turn around. *At least I hope I can see you later...if I'm even still alive.*

"Where you going?" They said together. I turned and walked away. I knew they were all wondering why I left them, but that wasn't why my heart was racing too fast to be real, nearly breaking through my chest. Or why my head felt like I was floating. Or why I felt like my stomach was being pushed into my throat. Or why my skin felt like it was melting into my clothes. Or why my hands were ice cold and slowly going numb.

My sight went reddish, becoming fuzzier every second. I couldn't even walk straight.

I made it to about two and a half feet from them before I couldn't go any further. The woman held out her hand. I noticed that her skin was gold, not tan, but perfectly gold. I took it, not caring what or who she was as long I wasn't about to fall flat on my face. She pulled me to seat before I collapsed from a 'post-accident' habit of fainting. I sat down, my hands on my knees, my head down, barely able to keep from falling over as I panted, trying to catch my breath. *What is wrong with me?!* I *almost* forgot who I was with, or tried to so I could focus on getting back to normal.

Sadly, that never happened.

"How was school?"

I jumped and looked at the most regular looking of the three, the kind of cute one. He was sitting above me, on top of the metal mesh table. I could barely get enough air to breathe, much less talk.

The woman stepped forward, her perfectly proportioned hand on my forearm, burning against my skin. And as much as I knew to pull away, I couldn't. My heart beat slowed back down to my version of normal. I took a few deep breaths and waited for my head to stop spinning.

"Hello Cynthia." Her voice was as smooth as honey and even sweeter, and I don't even like honey. I could only stare at her. I couldn't understand exactly how she'd gotten me to calm down or why seeing her seemed to trip out my brain, because the colors were back, and they were everywhere. Strips running through the air, clouds of them around them, even my hands had a weird yellow tint around them.

"Star, we need to go before citizens get more involved in this than they *already* are." The man stated. He looked at me and then tilted his head towards a group of kids that were about a dozen feet from us. I noticed some of my friends within it. I would have said something in their defense, if I could have even been able to speak...especially to *him*.

"Shift, get the car." No sooner had he said that did the guy who was on the table jump down, step behind a pole, and disappear. I gasped. I wanted to run, but I couldn't do that either.

"If you still want to know, you may come with us Cynthia." Her voice was meant to be soothing, but every time I heard it I felt like I knew her, and the fact I didn't scared me even more.

I do right?

I didn't get a chance to answer my own question. She grabbed my hand and pulled me up to my feet, letting go only to lead me to the back of the main gym building. I would have fallen a few times - okay I would have fallen a lot, if the man hadn't caught me. He'd practically carried me the whole way there. I hadn't protested. I couldn't. I was petrified. I hadn't even turned pink I had been so out of it. When we stopped walking, well they stopped walking and he'd set me down, I stared vacantly at the empty soccer field in front of us. I blinked and in that second, a slick, black, darkly tinted, sports car was less than two feet in front of me. Chrome lining and a sleek, foreign design screamed its suggestive appeal. The driver door opened *up wards* and the boy stepped out, a huge grin on his face. He moved the driver's seat up so I could get in.

"Thanks." I said, barely. He grinned even wider. His eyes were a really pretty hazel, but I had only enough guts to look into them for a split second.

"My pleasure. Hey!" the man slapped him on the back of the head. I would not think on his name. He rubbed his head, wearing a hurt expression. "That *hurt* BD!" his voice said that it hadn't, but I wouldn't have put it past the man to *have* made it hurt him. I nonetheless had stifled a giggle. The guy noticed and winked. Then I turned pink.

I still refused to admit who they were so I wouldn't faint.

"Don't push it." He muttered before getting into the driver's seat. The women got into the back with me. Either she was glowing a little bit or my eyes had yet to adjust to the surreal darkness inside the car's heavily tinted interior. When the door shut I realized I was trapped.

"W-what is going on?" I whispered. *Now I want to go home... I feel different.*

"Be with peace..." She placed her hand against my face, it burned the same way it had done on my arm, and I again was instantly calmed when I should have been officially freaked out. "I have much to tell you. When you were injured last year Cynthia, I healed you. That is how you are in the life now.." Her eyes were glowing softly and they changed color to a light brown. I saw the man driving look into the rear-view mirror, checking on her.

"But-"

Basically the 'movie' started about then, the scenes jumping out from the faint rainbow in the back of my mind.

Her... Him... Me... I'm lying on a bed. It is white. Cold. We are scared. Death.

Its smell left?

No more pain. But it is different now.

-Not pain – numbness.

She's on the ground. He is in the doorway.

Healed. Can't breathe. Tubes. Something wrong.

-Looked around the hallway-. 'She's hurt!'– Escape. Stairs. Window. Rain. Racing.

-Confusion.

-Peace. Roof top. Sunrise.

I came back to reality with a burst of light and another dizzy spell.

"What have you seen child?" She whispered. Her face was worried.

"I saw *you*..." I whispered.

"Did you show her that Star?" His eyes were black in the rectangular mirror, the kind of black that makes you think if you looked into it long enough, you'd get lost, only matched by his hair. The boy next to him had turned around, staring at us.

The woman shook her head at his strange question.

"What she has seen, she has shown herself. She is feeling what I felt when I could not stop, for her panic is constant, I am continuing to drain it."

What does that mean? I felt her eyes on me like they were seeing my very soul.

"What happened to me? Why are you here now?" *And why am I losing my mind?*

I looked at the human girl, though I saw I could not lump her with the rest of her kind. She'd been feeling what I *and* Black Dagger had felt, though to a lesser, more controlled degree. How she had done that, I was unsure and not taught, which worried me to no end. Not only did *I* not know of it, but also the best of my race would not either.

"When I healed you Cynthia, something happened...That is why you saw us, why you see things and occurrences. It is because of me...It is because of what I did.

276

You were left with more than intended, a part of me and what I am remains within you, blending into your own nature where you are a part of it, same as it's a part of you. It has never happened before, and I fear there is nothing I can do to reverse what my healing left you with."

"It's a *side effect*?" She shrilly demanded.

"I'm a science experiment. It could be worse, you could be an alien." Shift said proudly.

"Watch it." Dagger muttered, as he stopped the car, exiting it and pulling the barrier of his seat forward so that we might follow. He did not like the way Shift would say that, though it was true. I am an 'alien', I am different than his race, there is nothing to deny in that, yet Dagger saw it differently.

"Sorry." Shift mumbled, before being overcome in blanket of energy that propelled him outside the metal door.

The girl squealed, her power spiking into multihued fuscia.

"How is all this real?" Her coloring-of-energy showed her fear and panic. She did not want that, and I did not know how to take it back, I didn't know how I gave it.

"You get used to it eventually." Shift indifferently told her, offering her assistance out of the vehicle in the same manner Dagger had just done for me. I grabbed his hand for comfort-consoling. His mind was still, calming me.

"Cynthia, you have come to point where a path of your life must be chosen. I can't take back my gift to you. There will always be a part of you that you do not understand, and though I do not fully know what to expect, I would offer you my help in any way I can. Any questions you have, when you are of the right mind to think of them, you will be given the answers to. I do not know what gifts you possess in their entirety, but I will help you learn them, and if you choose to use it, then I will teach you to the best of my ability, and if you chose to join us after, you would never be alone. Whatever you choose to do with this knowledge, choose wisely, there are burdens to all sides. It is your decision alone, but no matter what you choose,

I will be as close as a thought for you, for what I have done I will take responsibility for, and so your life will forever be guarded by mine. I do not ask for your forgiveness for what I did to you, because I do not deserve it, I can only offer you all I have to give. To accept, you need only say."

"...Can I please just go home? I'll think about it alright? I'm just fifteen, I can't be a – uh – protector, I can't even pass driver's ed!" She searched frantically for an answer to her frightened questions.

"I'm sixteen, what is so wrong with it?" I knew Shift was giving her a 'hard time', but she did not, her gaze-power widening.

"You're different than me then. I don't know what I want to do, okay?! I was blaming it on hormones and fried brain cells or just plain going nuts and you just expect me to somehow accept all this in ten minutes? What am I *supposed* to do?"

Black Dagger squeezed my hand tightly and then released it. As he reached into his second covering, the girl tensed. He pulled out a polymer-eletronic.

"If you happen to change your mind and *do* want to talk... Believe me, I know how this is. Don't do anything because you think that it is your only option."

The girl nodded and took the electronic card, her surprise at his speaking and her remaining fear surrounding her in a russet vapor.

"Thanks...Sorry. I'm just freaking out, it's not you all. Okay it is but.. I'm sorry. I just can't figure this out. It's too much. Thank you Stargazer, for saving me. I really like what happened, what I can do. It's scary. It's really scary. But I don't know what you guys want from me. I can't control it, I don't even know what it is I'm seeing most of the time. I can't figure this out – and I-I just don't know if I want *that* life. ...I'm not grown up enough."

"I understand." I said soothingly. I smiled at her, her energy splaying out in response.

"But you'll still help me." It was not a question, she had seen without seeing what was to come that there would be many an hour between us.

"Of course, the moment you seek me." I assured her, though I feared what I could offer her without being near her when the visions she saw came.

"So, I guess I'll see ya'll around?" She asked us lightly.

"Up to you." Shift said in a defeated tone. "I'll take you home."

The girl shot a glance at me, much like that of an asking child would look to a parent. The gesture surprised me and was reassuring of her lack of a hardened position. I smiled and tilted my head to indicate that all was well.

"Okay." She said after. "It's on June and 11th."

He took her by her shoulder and disappeared, returning less than three seconds later to the front of the vehicle, crossing his arms over his chest as he leaned back into the seat. "This sucks." He grumbled, "We *driving* the car or am I the express shipping?"

"You're the express shipping." Dagger said, still staring at me, as I was him. Soul-fire was all I saw. He placed his hand on the metal-paint-roof of the car, going with Shift as I too departed. The next moment we were in the parking garage below our building. I had known Shift's desire to be home, and had followed them here, waiting patiently for them to exit the metal machine I leaned against.

"We freaked her out. I said it was too much for her all at once." He fussed, throwing the door open and stepping out into the well secured-lit-concrete space. We had disabled the cameras in our private "spot" – allowing them the freedom to speak without hesitation.

"She will be back." Dagger told him smoothly, coming to stand next to me.

"How do you know?"

"Would you have accepted right away if circumstances weren't like they were?" I asked, following Dagger's reasoning.

"Yes." He relented a moment later. "No, probably not… Right away anyway." He smirked. "I'd have had a bit of fun with it first."

"I give her a week - two tops."

I cooled at the thought that I had trapped her into this existence, my decrease in self-assurance made clear at the cold touch of my body to his.

Are you ok?

Yes. I am now.

Thank you for…for it all. He said once more. His mind fruitlessly fought to suppress the vivid memories.

I had simply nodded, I refused to address it any further.

"Y'all done?" Shift was tapping his fingers on his opposite arm in impatience. I smiled, accepting his rebuff. "Don't wait up. I'm going to go check in with our contacts and run some deliveries."

"If you need our assistance-"

"Yeah, I know." He lifted his own gold-energy-connector from his pocket. "I'll be back by midnight."

-BD- SG S//5

I'm crazy. I can't do this! What will I tell mom!? '…HI, uh, I'm going to join a group of crazy superheroes. Don't worry though, I can see the freaking future! So nothing can happen to me, because I know it's coming! And those ten years of gymnastics – you were right! They will do me some good! I bet my old leotard would make a killer costume!'… Yeah, that will get her to let me slide. Do or die-Wait! I don't want to die! …AH! I'm losing my mind!!

I paced outside the building.

I can't do it. I can't.

I have to.

No. I don't. I want to. Right? I mean seriously, they are superheroes. I could be one. That would be awesome. I would totally rock it. How hard can it be? ... Hard. Very hard. Like trying to flat iron my hair hard. Like trying to shop with dad hard.

My stomach hurts.

I need a hot shower.

And chocolate.

What if I get hurt?

What if we get caught or if I'm no good?

I'm not cut out for this. This doesn't even feel real. They don't seem real at all.

I thought about when the boy, trying to understand what part he played, because he hadn't been in any of the pictures, then went back to thinking about my mom. She'd gotten a call from a girl at my school saying that I had 'run off in some fancy car with a bunch of older kids and disappeared.' My mom completely flipped. I had been grounded for a month. Like seriously grounded, to the point where I wondered if it wouldn't have been easier to tell her the truth, because even it seemed less likely to warrant a punishment capable of giving me cabin fever. Still, I had submitted, knowing that she had a right to freak, since I refused to say who I had been with. She'd just lifted my sentencing the week before then. It took me that long to come up with the guts to show up. And I was still deliberating on running home.

I don't think I can do this.

What am I going to do?

"Who are you looking for?"

I jumped at the unexpected male voice. I turned and saw a man in his mid-thirties standing behind me. He was the blonde hot shot type, perfect suit, slicked back hair, a touch of Botox. I can read people pretty well. I could before my 'side effect' condition and even better after. I tried to not show my surprise and relief at whoever the guy was, or was*n't*.

"Oh, uh. My friends live here."

He wasn't convinced. My sweatshirt didn't help.

"Um, a woman, really pretty, tall, tanned..."

He frowned. I wasn't making it clear enough because that covered half the girls I had passed on the street and most of the ones he likely dated.

"She has gold skin, really long hair, gorgeous, like hazardously *hot* as all get out?" He smiled. I just needed to speak his language. "She would be with this really big guy, black hair, pale. There's a kid too, they live here?"

"I don't know about the kid, but the girl definitely lives here, with her brother. But that's all you need to know. You probably want to take whatever you're selling somewhere else. This is a private high rise." He wasn't as easy to convince as he looked. (Had I looked older it might have gone a bit better.)

"Here." I handed him the card that the guy had given me, digging it out of my old Hollister with about as much grace as clipped-wing duck in a pool of swans. I had kept it hidden under the floorboard in my room so my mom wouldn't have found it. I had lived the last weeks in panic. The fact I was still breathing was a miracle.

He looked over it for a second then handed it back to me, smiling again.

"...Are you a relative?"

"Why?"

"So no then. If I let anyone inside who is not my personal guest or specifically invited then I could get in trouble. Even if you have the card, since you could have stolen it."

"I didn't."

"Oh I know. Thieves tend to not be memorable, but I still will have to invite you in, that is if you will introduce me to your friend upstairs." He winked.

"I don't see why not."

"Alright then." He put his own little hotel key sort of card in the door and it opened automatically. A security guard with shoulders as wide as a bus seat and hands wider than my whole body looked up from his post, dismissing us the second he recognized the man. He let me walk in before him. I consciously kept myself from blushing. It wasn't something I did intentionally, it just happened and I completely *hated* it.

"You know what apartment they're in?" He asked.

That had been left out. I had figured he'd known, just by his wanting 'to get to know' the woman who had given me my life back. I could have lied and said yes and snuck off to find them myself, but I needed a witness. You know, just in case I was kidnapped by deranged superheroes or something. But I was confused too. I speculated what he would do if he also knew that she, the girl he was so desperately trying to get introduced to was *Stargazer*. He might think twice, if only for the reason he'd have Black Dagger to deal with.

I focused, sensing the indescribable colors around her directly above us, at the highest point before the building's colder and more harshly edged colors ended.

"The loft." I said coolly.

He raised one brushed eyebrow.

After another round of the key-card, the metal doors to the elevator opened and we stepped in. I looked around the mirrored walls, sighing at my reflection. I hadn't slept in days, leaving me looking like a mess, and the faded jeans and thin sweat shirt paled – no – disappeared in comparison to Hot Shot's Rolex and Armani.

I didn't even want to look at my hair.

It was going to be a long ride.

"How do you know her?"

This guy just won't quit.

"Met her a month ago at some, uh, women's convention."

"You're going to have to get better at lying."

"What?"

"Babydoll, no one gets into buildings like this unless they are an actor, who is paid to lie, some high end political shaker who covers up for other people's lies, or someone who gets paid extremely large amounts of money to see to it that the people who make it aren't caught out in the open without a cover story and an alibi. You're in the wrong neighborhood to be caught telling a story."

"What does that make you?"

He smirked, checking his watch.

"I'm the one who keeps the liars from burning down the world."

"Right."

I turned away, not needing any more drama. It took *hours* to reach the top.

The door opened.

I laughed at the guy next to me's face when *she* was waiting there. Her hands were folded in front of her. Her emerald green halter top was held onto her by four barely there strings, tying behind her neck and at her back. Her long skirt was touching the ground.

I saw all of those things, but the only things I could pay attention to were the firecracker like sparks that seemed to be jumping between us every time I blinked, even though I didn't feel anything, and she didn't seem to notice. She simply smiled. I was too shocked to return it. She winked, closing one gold eye for a split second.

"Good afternoon Cynthia, Trent." Her voice sent a chill up my spine. She stood perfect and still, staring at me with an intensity that could light a fire. *Oh my...this gets weirder doesn't it?*

I glanced over to him, only to find him more terrified than I was. He looked like a deer caught in head lights

"Uh…I came. Like he said I could." I said timidly. I expected the door to shut. We'd been standing there a while.

"As we knew you would." She softly replied. She took a step back and motioned for me to follow her with a slight, graceful dip of her head. I saw Trent try to come with us, but the elevator door slammed shut in his face.

She laughed softly.

"Did *you* do that?!" I asked, looking back towards the elevator, which had been heading to the bottom floor.

"Yes. He has a surprisingly confident mentality towards the females of your kind, and he believes that I am one of them." She purred while she pranced, barefoot. I wondered how normal *I* was when I considered how that the most offsetting thing she'd done so far.

"You're *not?*" *She is a girl…there is* no *denying that…so that means the only other variable would be 'your kind.' The guy mentioned something about aliens… She isn't a human?!*

"Your confusion is understandable…for I am not." She answered for my thoughts.

I didn't stop walking, not until the large metal lined doors were in front of us. Somewhere in the whirlwind of panic and disbelief I had realized I'd assumed that all along. Then again, I could have known it and not even known I knew it. Which was weird.

And it was indeed getting weirder.

-BD-SG S//5 ▓S▓

Shadow

I looked around the window lined apartment. Everything was soft, subdued, and clean edged, as if you expected Vera Wang to burst in at any moment with a few throw pillows and a speech on a blank canvas and room ambiance. There was a large round table in the first part of the open room, the top of it made a glass that was at least four inches thick, the bottom made of very modern style minimalistic metal beams made to look like they were piled at random. It was surrounded by four molded,. The boy was replaced with a tanned, blonde guy who looked like he belonged on the cover of a magazine, with shining eyes, perfect teeth, and body proportions that nearly mirrored Stargazer's.

"Hi." I said. My voice was even higher than normal. The guy waved to me. Stargazer pulled me to the table, since my feet refused to move past the first few adrenaline fueled steps. I fell into the chair the man pulled out for me. I didn't have the strength to think his name. *I am going to start hyperventilating. ...Don't faint! Whatever you do- Don't faint!*

Black Dagger leaned towards me, his hands in constant fists on the table's surface, his eyes flicking as they calculated the movements of all my individual cells. I feel sorry for the frog I had dissected in eighth grade. I knew how it felt now, only my skin remained attached to me, even as I dreamed of melting into the ultra-plush carpet that my Toms are surely leaving tread marks on.

"You showed." Black Dagger's voice was even. It was bizarre...it was a voice that could be as scary and menacing as its speaker, and yet it was almost sympathetic.

"Yeah, but, I don't know how any of this works...My mom thinks that I am at my dad's... I've got less than a few hours before she calls to check that the bus made it there safely, and he thinks that I decided to not come. He won't call her, but she always makes sure she talks to him within a few hours. I'm supposed to be there a week for Thanksgiving break but, I don't know." I was trying to understand how it would all go down. I knew people disappeared easy enough. I hoped they'd exclude my mom from the likely 'no contact' rule.

"I can handle that. Got a picture? And a voicemail?" I looked at the guy and gasped. He sounded the same, but he looked like the boy who had been at my school with them.

"You get used to *him* too." Black Dagger muttered.

"Uh...A...voicemail?" I stuttered.

"Of your dad, and a picture, it doesn't have to be any good, I just need to see his face. A few pictures should keep your mom at bay for now." He flashed me a beaming smile. *He's kind of cute.*

"Oh-" I unlocked my phone and passed it to him, before I pulled a wallet out of my oversized purse and grabbed one of the few pictures in existence of my parents together with me. I kept it with me all the time, as proof it once happened. "Here, it's old, but he looks about the same now."

The guy looked at it for a few seconds and then I was sitting across from my dad.

"A shape-shifter...that's *very* cool."

He smiled wider at the complement. I admit it. I was flirting. Badly. (Hey, it is an art, art takes practice, of which I had zip in.)

"It is *very* cool." He agreed, rolling his shoulders underneath the full length white shirt he wore before he spoke again. "So, what do you actually do? Stargazer and BD have a way of keeping secrets from me."

I saw Black Dagger shoot him a look. The kid just stuck his tongue out.

287

"I guess I see the future, sometimes it's the past, but I have no idea how I do it, it just happens." I couldn't really explain. I had spent the last few months trying to convince myself I hadn't gone clinically insane. I had barely bought my own argument, much less graduated to the 'Show and Tell' stage. But even with that taken into consideration, I was at ease. I didn't know why, I had every reason in the world to be having a panic attack, but I just felt at home. I hadn't felt like that since my parents had split. All my freakiness was considered normal here. I didn't have to hide. I didn't have to paint on the apathetic, care free bubble gum teen smile that was expected of the miracle girl. I could babble about my latest vision and the colors that floated on air and not end up in a padded room. I could. Not that I would, yet, but I *could* and they'd not even blink.

He laughed, smiling in approval.

"*Awesome*! Don't worry, we will get you prepped. I can help you with the public if you want. We can do it online, they stuck to old school, but I've found internet cafés in Amsterdam to be handy. Oh, speaking of, what's your name?" He smirked at Black Dagger, who just rolled his eyes. Stargazer remained perfectly striking, her lips in a small smile.

"I'm Cynthia." *I thought you knew that Big Shot.*

He snorted, not even trying to hide the fact he wanted to roll out of his chair with laughter. *What is so dang funny?*

"Not that one-I mean your other one-" he chuckled, shaking his head, hair swooshing. "I'm Jonathan, if you ask my sister, it is Jonathan Alexander or *Jonny*. But Shift is *who* and *what* I am now." His eyes were shining, not glowing, but in the sunlight they looked more blue-green than hazel. I looked away but still felt the heat rush to my face when I blushed.

"Just as I am Stargazer." Her voice made me mentally tremble again, not from fear, but like I knew exactly what I was hearing. Her, an alien, someone who had power, someone who gave me my power, and someone who I had instinctively known was stronger than she let on to with the others.

I hope that's going to wear off soon.

"Black Dagger." He said as one word.

There was an awkward pause. I realized they were all waiting for *me* to talk.

"Oh. I have no idea...I told you I am completely clueless. I mean, I don't even know how much help I can be or why you'd want me at all... I didn't know I had the guts to show up until I was standing outside and I couldn't even walk in alone. I'm not exactly hardcore." I nervously rambled. "I don't even know how to do this small stuff, I didn't think that far. I could ask my cousin though. He is a real fantasy buff-"

"This isn't fantasy... It's real whether you like it or not, and it's take it or leave it deal Cynthia. We want you to see it, while we are here to help you understand what it is you will be seeing. Unlike most people you don't have the option to ignore it and pretend the world is fine. So if you choose to join us, you're accepting the fact we won't let you hide from it, but we will face it with you. If you choose otherwise then that is your decision, but no matter what, we can't protect you from this reality." Black Dagger's eyes locked with mine. They seemed to be looking for *something.*

"I know... I have seen a lot, but I don't understand it. That's why I'm here. There's got to be more than what I'm seeing."

"There is, and it's not pretty." He stated.

Shift rolled his eyes.

"Could you not freak her out before she's even picked a name? Gosh. You always have to make everything so morbid."

Morbid seems to describe a lot of what I've seen with him though.

"Oh, right, I don't know-umm...Stargazer, what are you exactly?" I instantly regretted asking it the way I had when I saw the kid raise an eyebrow. I guiltily glanced over to her. She showed no signs of offense, though I knew she wouldn't even if I had tripped a wire.

"Light. It is the simplest way I can put this, except I am conscious of my existence, as pure energy in this realm fails to be. Think of your sun, it is made of self-sustaining energy, as am I." She explained calmly.

"And I am what?"

She tensed at *that* particular question, her eyes tightening. The rainbows in the air held still, and for a moment I freaked out a bit because I thought that it was my sight that had frozen, until they resumed their always making me think I'm losing my mind spirals just as she gave the appearance of an exhale. I blinked in surprise, realizing it was her that had held all the colors in the room at a momentary standstill.

"I do not have an answer for you, Cynthia, neither do I believe my people nor the one to have taught me to know it, as there has never before been one such as you. You have my ability to see the powers that move this world, but beyond me, you are also tied to the powers without organic origin, powers that drive the machines and are within the signals coursing through the atmosphere. This alone has left me without answer, not addressing your ability to follow the trails where the energies will go or have been. As for how such came to be, I do not know. You are a part of me, for just as I am energy, you read it as if it is planned to your mind. You do not feel the power or have it make you, but you decipher it when you come into contact with it as if it written in a language you can only understand, a language I fear I do not speak."

I didn't let her ignorance of what I was freak me out, at least not outwardly. I hadn't come into this expecting it to be easy. I didn't know what I expected actually.

Shift had been making his finger go in a circle around the side of his head until Black Dagger silenced him with a quick glare. He pouted, but it was a cute sulk.

"You called yourself the sun." I recalled aloud.

Black Dagger stared at me, waiting to see where I went with that. I wasn't even sure where I was going. She had not looked away from me either, and I assumed from the tightly bound, sharp edged gold light around her that she too was taken off guard.

"In a sense of words, yes. Others have called us the people of the sun, though we are neither the sun, stars, nor even to be called *people* by definition."

Black Dagger shot Shift another glare. Shift had his hands up in an innocent motion. Stargazer acted like she had not noticed. It was another silent discussion, or accusation.

"My name means 'goddess of the moon'…I did a report on it last year in literature." I thought aloud, again. "The moon has light because of the sun…I have life because of you… What about Reflect?"

"Seriously, *Reflect?* I mean-it's nice, but *Reflect?*" Shift seemed to be holding back another laugh, biting his bottom lip.

"Hey I wasn't exactly prepared for any of this." I muttered. I was *this* close to kicking him from under the table, (yes, I know it was a glass table.) I knew it was dumb, for all the oddness of their alter egos, or in all I knew, Black Dagger and Stargazer only had one name and at least their names fit. It seemed ridiculous for it to be such a big deal, but it was, and it was more important than I realized at the time to have a label for my part in this that I literally had to put a name to.

"You are a shadow of her. Not a reflection." Black Dagger said, still staring at me.

"So Shadow?" *A cat aimlessly wandering around, trying to find home. Well there's some symbolism for you.*

"There you go Blondie." Shift happily approved.

"It is your choice, all of this is, and if you choose it, Cynthia, you will not be alone." Stargazer comforted me, her hand taking mine. I hadn't realized I had been running my nails up my jeans so forcefully that the denim was actually tufting. The nervousness I hadn't wanted to admit existed stopped when the colors were lost in a gold haze.

"I know…"

"And?" Shift pressed, leaning forward, elbows on the table.

"When's the first training?" I asked, half laughing, half exhaling in relief when they all smiled, even Black Dagger.

"Yes!" Shift jumped up from the table, throwing his hands in the air.

Stunned, I could only laugh.

36 Rocks and Hard Places

How do I manage this?

Maybe I should tell her…No, she'll put me on meds for being a nut.

I can't just disappear… But I want to run away!!!

Following a few hours of the general "no telling, sharing, or hinting" rules being said in a thousand different ways, Shift had taken us downtown, and left Black Dagger and I there, alone. He had walked me all the way to my mom's apartment. I didn't know why Shift hadn't taken me, or why we were downtown, because it was quite a long way, nearly an hour, but I wasn't going to say anything about it. I wasn't planning on saying anything at all really, but he did.

"You can't just leave." He had said clearly.

"Huh?"

"I have done that, just up and left. Someone got themselves into a big mess because of it, because of me. You can't just quit your life like that, it's not right. I didn't have a choice, I couldn't stay there, but *you* do." He glanced down to me, walking on the edge of the sidewalk to keep me away from the road.

"Oh…Okay. Why did *you* leave?" I asked quietly. As far as I had known, he was the original 'Protector'. No one was there to recruit him.

"I had to. There was no other option."

"When?"

"Three years ago, I think, since I'm somewhere around nineteen."

I gaped. I couldn't believe it. Twenty-five, *maybe*.

"I could just go missing. Except for my mom." I hinted.

"Hell no"

I jumped. He noticed and lowered he voice, instantly calmer.

"...Sorry." I nodded. "That is what I did, went missing. I have no idea about before." I was trying to figure out what he meant by 'before' but he didn't give me time to. "Even if it didn't stay that way. Someone else faked my death for me, Shadow."

"Who?"

He kept walking *through* the crowd. For every one of his steps, I had to take two or three. He'd slowed down when he noticed me struggling to find a balance between walking and sprinting.

"The people who started this mess. You don't think I was born like this do you?"

"Um, I hadn't thought about that yet." I mumbled. I hadn't seen him do anything other than be big and scary, and as far as I was concerned if that was all he did then I would be perfectly okay with it.

"You'll learn. When the time comes. Not before. There's too much darkness in this world, and even if I can't stop you from seeing it, I won't add to it. Training starts tomorrow. Deal with your mother tonight. If you don't, we will. I'm not letting you hide from any aspect of this."

Deal with your mother...I rolled over on my bed, replaying the last thing he had said again. The faded blue walls spun. I didn't know *what* to do. I was a future seeing fifteen year old who had only been assured she wasn't insane quite recently. Cut me some slack. *What did he mean by 'no other option'? I have tons, but I don't like any of them very much.* Too many questions, not enough answers.

I'm going to tell her. I forced myself off my overly soft, seventh grade paisley obsession phase bedspread and walked down the narrow staircase to my mom's room. *At least this is going to be a lot easier than telling her I have a boyfriend.*

"...Mom?" I pushed open the would-be white door.

"Come in honey!" My mom had papers laid out on her bed in small piles, organizing receipts from the look of things. Her face changed. "What's wrong Cynth, you look stressed out." I shrugged and she took it as 'no I'm not ok'. "Is it school, or a boy?"

"It's not school, or a boy." *It is a boy, a man, and I guess a female alien to be specific. So there is a boy involved.* I put the papers carefully on the ground before I flopped down onto the bed. The ceiling fan I stared at gave me no answers; though it reminded me I was slacking on my chores since it needed dusting.

"That fire..." I stated, no more words needed. Her eyes glossed over instantly.

It was a car accident, at least that's the only way to describe it.

Both of my parents had been inside the courthouse. I had left them in there, sick of it all, deciding to wait in the car in passive aggressive protest to the paperwork and the arguing. I was sitting in the passenger seat, oblivious to anything outside of my headphones. Someone had spun around the corner, drifting over two whole lanes, before finally slamming into me at a lethal speed. I don't remember much of it, but I know by the time I came to, the car seemed to have exploded around me, and I couldn't get out. I had never felt such a debilitating terror before. It hurt – more than words can describe. I had screamed for help, fruitlessly fighting to unpin myself from the caved in, melting dashboard. Someone had been there, trying to get me out, but it felt like years before he was even able to get to me. By a miracle, he did though. He'd broken the windshield, I remember because the glass had cut my burning hands when I had reached for him, screaming that my legs were stuck. How, I will never know, but he'd pulled me out and managed to stop the fire on me too, giving me CPR, keeping me alive.

I remember his voice, screaming at me to stay awake, his face covered in soot, hiding his identity. To this day I don't know who he is.

Whether they had heard the explosion that came soon after or my screaming that had been leading up to it, both of my parents ran outside, along with the rest of the courthouse staff. The last memory I had seen through bloody eyes was my mom crying and racing towards me, the sooty miracle man shaking my shoulders just slightly, trying to keep my conscious. The next thing I knew I was in what sounded like hospital, I could hear people saying I wouldn't make it more than a few more hours. I just wanted to go *home*.

Then I would subconsciously realize I didn't know where that was anymore, leaving me desperate for any escape.

The light came, then it had all been over.

I found out why over half a year later.

"The Protectors-" She frowned. "Stargazer healed me when I was in the hospital."

"I know..." She whispered. "I was there sweetie." She looked surprised that *I* knew, but not at *what* I knew.

"You knew?!" I demanded, flying upright to face her. The delicate lines in her expression gave way to the muddled tincture of shock and guilt playing out underneath her skin.

"Yes."

"And you didn't tell me?!" *Stem-cell trial my butt!*

"I thought you would be afraid." She confessed, grabbing my hand. "It was so scary, even the doctors didn't know what to think of it. I wanted to tell you but it was...I was scared of what you would think."

I smiled to make her feel better and she smiled back, eyes still watery.

"You were there?" I asked. She nodded.

296

"And your father. He was chasing down the head of the burn unit when it happened… I was right outside." The quake in her voice only proceeded the tears in her eyes by a moment. "We thought we had lost you…had they not come…"

"What'd you see?"

"You wouldn't believe me." She said, shaking her head in past tense awe.

I might.

"If I told you there were side effects?"

She looked scared then. Her eyes widened and she sucked in a shallow breath.

"What kind Cynthia? Do we need to go to the ER?!" She was halfway up off the bed. I held up my hands and shook my head to show her I was fine, or close to it.

"No, calm down ok? You remember why you grounded me?" She nodded. "That was their car I got in."

"*Who's?*"

"The Protectors'." Her mouth dropped open and she paled. "Mom, I know this is going to sound crazy to you, it sounds nuts to me, but Stargazer, because she healed me, something happened, something that wasn't really supposed to happen. She doesn't really know everything, but we are going to find out. It's not bad – but there is more to it than the hair. I ran into them and she told me what I've been seeing. I didn't tell you, I thought I was crazy, I mean I really thought I was losing it, but I'm not! I can see the future, and the past and I don't know if I can do other stuff yet."

I waited for her to freak out, but she sat there, like one of those Madam what's-her-name's wax figures. A badly designed, spaced out one.

"*Mom?*"

Her shaky hand rose, tremblingly pointing behind me.

I turned around and *she* was sitting in my mom's never-used sewing chair, hands crossed in her lap. She rose to her feet when we noticed her.

How can I convince her, a mother of a child to trust me...? I fled all I knew, all I could trust or see, all who had cared for me, I am breaking vows made in power and blood, and even now I desire nothing more than to forage a vow that would be treason, is treason, even to consider. To any who knew these things, the unavoidable-unchangeable truth of my inability to...to be with such beings would seem just So how can I convince-pursued her mother otherwise, to trust me with Shadow?

"What she says is true Noel. We, I, have sought to explain all that has come. You have a daughter who has much to learn and even more to give to this world, should she choose it." The air-color-scent of the older human's fear washed over me. She had witnessed what I had done, though I did not remember her. I had only seen it in Dagger's mind, and even so, his memories of that time were spacey-riled-lacking detail in his terror-determination over me. I had yet to look upon hers. I was not entirely sure I desired to do such a thing.

"Mom, this is Stargazer." She explained calmly. I sensed the young-shadow-of-mine's acceptance to my arrival.

"Nice to- m-meet you." Her mind stuttered.

"It is an honor of mine. Shadow has much to tell you, and I have come to help her elucidate what is to come."

"Shadow?" She asked in fear.

"Your daughter has chosen to join us."

The woman's energy dropped spectacularly, nanoseconds before her mind lost its grip of her body. I caught her before she could have fallen, though I had been on the other side of the room, a fact she was sure-positive to notice. I put a small amount of my power into her, sparks jumping from my form to hers. She woke with a start, the muscles around her eyes contracting in quick bursts when she saw I was holding her. She must have felt my above average surface temperature as well, for her body recoiled against mine.

298

I set her down and took a step back. I avoided humans for the plain reason that I am not one. If they will shut one of their own out because of mere appearance or beliefs, then they would do far more to me. I was not of them or their world, but I was trespassing on their soil, committing betrayal to my own kind by waging a war against the intangible past. Yet I planned to do so much more.

"No – You – Cynthia, you can't! You'll get hurt…you can't! I won't let you! Something is wrong! You can't!" The woman yelled frantically. She held her daughter tightly against her, her wary, accusing eyes on me.

"Mom, calm down…I'm okay." She said from her human confines.

"What're you thinking? How-"

"Currently, I am thinking on how in twenty minutes the rest of the Protectors will be here, you'll be completely chill and I would have joined them, *with* your permission."

The woman stared dumbstruck at her daughter.

"I see the future. I can't explain it well yet. But I can. So I know this will all be okay, I promise."

"Is this true?" She looked at me.

"I know not the future, Noel, nor can I offer much more insight into this present than what your daughter will, but yes, Shift will be bringing Black Dagger here, but in not twenty, but if only ten of your minutes."

"Close enough." She muttered under her breath. The woman's head shot towards me. Her face was too emotionally expressive for me to have read it well. I looked into her mind; my curiosity was greater than knowing I had no right to 'peek', but the screaming-frantic questions I was met with were as solar winds against me. I pulled away as fast as was possible.

"Shadow…if you can, show your mother your thoughts. Show her nothing has been done to harm you, that I would never harm you, and what I did I will do all in my power to help you grasp and control." My words barely hid my hurting.

"*What?*" They said in union.

"Perhaps that was not given to you. I shall then." I gently pushed my consciousness into the woman's, facing the questions she had rights to ask, showing what I saw of her daughter's abilities. I showed her how the change she had seen in Cynthia and the ones that had been hidden from her had come to pass, how Cynthia had already chosen to join us, and was only there for her mother's sake. I revealed to her how we were able to protect our own, and how much Cynthia was willing to risk to keep the purely human part of her active

I promise you, Noel, by the every star in the universe and by the Star that watched over me as a child, I will take care of her with the same unwavering strength and diligence as he, and as you have done. If ever a time comes where her life is in peril, I will defend it, even at the cost of my own. I will never let her be harmed beyond that which I can once more heal, and I will never see her put into a place where she is at risk to herself, or at a risk greater than we can overcome. I do not ask you to let her go, but to allow her to follow this path that she has chosen to follow. I did not force it upon her, as I fear my healing her forced these abilities. Her forgiveness has been granted, in time I hope to have yours, as she learns the gifts hidden within her.

In my last moments I offered her the one piece of union I might give as proof to my loyalty, a glimpse of the light that made me burning in what appeared to be an abyss, and its smaller, fainter shadow shining in Shadow's multi-colored hued consciousness.

If anything happens to her-

I seek to see her with the same joy as you have wished over her since birth, and I will fight for her, and defend her, from anything that seeks to take it from her.

The woman looked at me for a long-contemplating moment and then turned to her offspring.

"So that's it then…I have a superhero for a kid." She smiled slightly. The girl-that-was-made-from-the-woman-and-

me hugged her tightly. "One condition, you're going to school, no matter what, you're not dropping out. And you stay here every other weekend, and under no circumstances are to ever be out of her sight." She turned to me, I nodded to the probing of her gaze. I had already recognized within Shadow the same energy that created the communication between my consciousness and others, and in that, we would never be without a way to reach the other.

"Oh my gosh – yes - Deal! Thank you Mom!"

Undoubtedly, there would be many more qualifications I must meet and rules Shadow was to fulfill, but Noel was prepared to bring up in the presence of her daughter's overbidding joy-elation.

I felt his approaching calming-settling-alluring-energy, its signal the same as they would have heard the doorbell, since they aimed to use it for Noel's comfort alone. I was soothed instantaneously, knowing I would not be alone any longer. I went to it before it had been rung. They stood to the front of the hallway. I let Shift in the structure without a word, his eager thoughts lit like newborn-stars at the realization she was indeed "sticking around" by the laughs coming from the center room.

I blocked him from following. His onyx eyes narrowed as he titled his head, judging my reactions. In all of a second I had absorbed his perfection and pulled him into a tight embrace, concealing my being in his, not a distinction between us but what there had to be. He embraced me even tighter, the fleeting minutes melting as I wished to do. I sighed, breathing in the air around him. Every nagging-fearful-unsure thought vanished, dissolving into oblivion.

"Thank you…" I whispered, releasing him when I realized the minutes were ever lengthening. Time had never held significance, more then than ever before.

"I don't sense any threats. I take it everything is set?" His eyes had the black-soul-fire burning within them that made my entire being crawl with anticipation.

"Yes. Her mother has not been given much of a choice, at least that Shadow presented. She is merely grateful that Shadow desired her to be a part of this."

"Any big conditions?"

"She must attend school, and may not be with us for the last days of your week on alternating times. I am to oversee her, at all times. I am not confident these will be the last of her terms, however, neither would I expect less."

"We are basically going to have another kid?" He flicked his eyes towards the room they were in. His cool hand was still on my back, urging me forward.

"As it would seem."

We rounded the doorway that led to the main room of the dwelling. Shift was sitting on the short-brown-chair, across from the longer one Shadow and her mother rested on. They spoke in animated tones, each of their powers leaping and changing with the chords of their voices.

"I am telling the truth! They really did! He just-" He stopped when we entered.

"Mom, that's Black Dagger. He's the leader." She whispered.

I felt his slight pride, though he would never admit it.

"Shift, come on." I told him, holding Star's hand tighter as I titled my head towards the door we wouldn't use. Her mom was on the verge of collapse. He grunted in obligated acceptance, getting up off the loveseat. "We'll see you tomorrow, Shadow."

"Why don't you stay?" Shadow asked politely. I looked directly at her and then flicked my eyes towards her mom.

"Busy night."

"I can't come?" Her eyes turned the size of plastic poker chips, and were just as worthless for all the good begging would get her.

Her mom made a squeaking sound, air freezing halfway out her throat. Shadow's adrenaline laced the air, as did her mother's fear.

"Not until you're ready." Star would have her hands full teaching her what little we understood at that time, and I had to see what she was capable of before letting her out. *If I let her out at all... She doesn't look like she can take a hit, much less a bullet.*

"I'll pick you up from school tomorrow though." Shift offered. I saw exactly where he was going with that, but it wasn't that bad of an idea, especially for him to have come up with it, even if his reasons for doing it were different than why it was a good plan.

"Okay-but *don't* bring the Porsche *please*. I have to be invisible remember?"

Her mom looked at us differently after the car was mentioned. In his eyes, Star literally *made* money, so 'why settle for anything less' was Shift's idea. I didn't care, couldn't care, so he'd gone out and bought it without telling us.

"Whatever. It's not like *I* need a car to get around." He reminded her. She laughed, so did her mom. He grabbed his jacket and hung it over his shoulder. "Bye Shads." He said right before he put his hand on us.

"*Shads*?"

"I have no idea. He has the guts to call Black Dagger 'BD'- but I don't think he minds that much. Or he just puts up with it really well." I didn't understand the calm, I only knew that since Stargazer had appeared I hadn't been worried anymore, and even after they had left, everything still felt like it was going to work out. My mother, however, wasn't there yet.

Her eyes widened, a response to everything.

"I know. It's crazy. Shift is the most normal one so he tries to make a joke out of everything, I think." I said that to my mom in a 'please excuse it tone' that she had not taken.

"I think he likes you." She said happily, desperately clinging to whatever miniscule shred of normal was sewn into this jumbled mess. Much like my first attempts at sewing, there was no point.

"*MOM*! Since when do *you* even try to notice when guys hit on me?!"

"I guess this is different sweetie. You are growing up, that doesn't mean you can date him you hear? I think he feels out of place... I can only imagine what it is like being alone in this. You said that she is an alien, so no chance there-"

"She and Black Dagger are together." *They are* always *together*. I'd made a point to do as much "seeing" of them as I possibly could, even if my attempts were nothing more than blind casts in the wind. I had been able to track them better than I saw them, simply following the energy paths rather than trying to decipher them, and I had yet to find anything greater than a handful of three hour stretches when they weren't within a hundred feet of each other.

"Oh... Well that only emphasizes my point." She stated for sure

"Which is?"

She winked. . Leave it to my mother to look for a romantic comedy in a sci-fi thriller.

"At least you're not freaking out still." I rolled my eyes.

"Oh no, I am. But I'm not going to go paralyzed with it. You need me more than I need sanity. No other mom, well okay, three other moms, can say their *kid* is a real superhero, and since no one invited me to the support group, what happens now?" She was really milking it...but it was better than hating it, so I went with it a little bit, even though I was pretty positive her cherry topped outlook had to be a stage of shock. (Spoiler: It was. The next morning started with her sitting at the foot of my bed with an entire hand written list of questions she wanted to have answered, in written detail, and given to her by dinner, that way in case I tried to play something down there would be written proof of my fallacy.)

"Oh. I don't know, actually, I think you're the only one. Remember Shift says only his sister knows about him... and that she'd known Black Dagger, like before he was Black Dagger." *Can't picture that one. Or see it.*

"What about his parents?" Her worry was comforting, considering it wasn't directed at me. I had seen Stargazer's energy come over my mom when she had showed her whatever it was she needed to see, and I suspected I wasn't the only one with a list of questions to answer.

"Shift's?" *I think I just said this?*

"No, Black Dagger's? Is that really his name? Jonathan at least was kind enough to share his, not that I really mind but, really, *Black Dagger*?"

"No idea. He hasn't told me anything." I shrugged. *He is like school teachers. They just materialize, no parents, no sibling stories, just them. ... I seriously think I'm crazy. I just compared him to a teacher. Of what? How to look bad, sound bad, but beat the bad?*

"Stargazer's?" She asked. I knew she was curious about her more than them.

"I only see earth."

"Oh. I see." My mom avoided the alien aspect of it, wanting things to stay as sane as possible, so when she just went right along with the conversation, I let it drop. "What about the costume then?"

"*Tonight*? I have to train first and I don't even know if I'm ever going in public."

"I know. I don't even want you to, but I can't just let you show up in jeans. I want in on this." She smirked. She had her heart set on being the 'cool mom' since in her mind she had just set out to adopt every single one of them. "We could go

305

through all your competition costumes! I bet there is something in there we can work with!" She smiled from ear to ear, like a kid who just got a new doll to dress up.

We were up until two a.m., one of the many long nights I would come to know well. She went through different stages, from excitement to veiled terror, laughing and teasing over long boxed up leotards to staring at me nearly in tears, making me promise to never take too big a risk, to always come home. I did. It was a long night, but it was a good one.

Victor

I ran out of my last class, making a beeline for the exit, hoping to hit home for a nap before my second life started. I was on five hours of sleep a night, if I was lucky. They got me home by one in the morning most nights, allowing for a few precious hours of sleep before mom called me down for breakfast. The average day was waking up to my mom in the kitchen, patiently waiting for the run down on the night before, then school, followed by enough physical training to leave me sore all over, lasting until well after dark, and ending with a few hours of would-be meditation. Stargazer made me sit with my legs crossed, focusing on small flashes of light at the back of my mind, which I learned was me picking up on the energies around me, ones that I could actually read if I opened myself up to them, letting all other thoughts and sensations go in the process. I would sit for what felt like days, trying to see Shift, then my Mom, then the janitor at my school, and so on. A few Migraines was a small price to pay for being a psychic, so to speak, but it wasn't exactly what I thought I had signed up for. Even if it was just 'training,' they didn't allow any time outs.

Black Dagger always had his turn first, making me read him, see if he was lying, guess what he was thinking, see where he'd been a few hours before. I might as well have been trying to explain a Mark Rothko piece to the three year old I used to babysit, for all the good that did the first few weeks. Then Shift would take me to a building literally in the middle of nowhere, which he had converted into an Olympic style gym.

With the promise of dinner anywhere in the world if I played along, I got trapped into whatever scheme he had planned to leave me pink faced and physically beat. It had started slowly at first – with seemingly random tasks that he directed and BD watched. They began with "how long can you hold a plank?" to "how fast can you go if your life depended on it?" to "how long can you sit at the bottom of the pool?" and then "let's see if you can hold a forty pound dummy on your back while dodging tennis balls flying at you at however fast BD can hurl them!" Which, in fact, was fast.

It went without saying that by the end of the first few weeks I was exhausted. Stargazer would heal me from whatever bruises hadn't cleared before Shift brought me home, but even with that I'd come to appreciate the blessing of Study Hall – a fleeting forty-five minutes of silence in the hectic frenzy of my life. The only disruption in the schedule was every few days when Shift and I would be left alone. From what I was able to see, it was as much for him to watch me as it was for me to watch him when they did the kinds of things too risky for either of us. Most of the time was spent with him breaking down what I knew from gymnastics into what I would need to know if I ever found myself alone and being followed or in pursuit of someone. After a few sessions, I was pretty sure I had learned enough Parkour to become a Youtube sensation. The one time he wasn't acting out was when he was teaching me. He wasn't the most patient of coaches, but he didn't let me give up, even if I would have given him the satisfaction of letting him know he'd made me throw in the towel, something I refused to do.

Then there was my solo day with Black Dagger.

I had been alone with Stargazer, with Shift, and then with he and Shift, but never just him. Shift had brought me to an abandoned city eerily similar to a video I had seen Chernobyl. *Or for that matter, Detroit.* I didn't ask where it was, all I knew was that the energies around it were completely void of human contact, except my own and Black Dagger's. The walls of the buildings around us crumbled, with paint peeling off the concrete and windows stood like the violent edges of anarchy, shattered in their panes. Tuffs of brown, dried grass broke through the dirt covered sidewalks. A piece of crumpled paper rolled in the slight breeze.

Black Dagger was standing in front of us, braced in the middle of the abandoned street.

Shift was gone by the time I turned around.

"Why are we here?"

"This is what we're fighting for." He looked up, the buildings above us casting us in long afternoon shadows. I could appreciate ominous atmosphere it gave to the situation, but my amusement faded when I realized the seriousness of what he was saying. "This is our city, every city. This is what society will become if its left to tear itself apart, if darkness wins. This is what happens when light leaves, when people turn on each other, when people don't stand up for what they are supposed to. If you are really in, you have to be able to face this, and the people who are blindly causing it to come."

I grimly nodded, dropping my back pack at my side.

"What do you want me to do?"

"Stop being afraid."

"I'm not." I scowled. I had seen some scary stuff, something he was aware of quite well. A few of those meditation sessions with Stargazer had ended in panic attacks, but I had gotten better. I wasn't afraid, not then, at least.

He raised his hand. He was holding a gun.

My head pounded with the sound of my heart.

"We aren't playing target practice..." My weight shifted to the balls of my feet.

"No. You're never going to carry one of these – unless you choose to – but this is what they have. This is the sound that is going to ring in your ears when you try to fall asleep at night. This is what you are going to see pointed at you, at the heads of the people you are trying to protect, and at the people who defend you, and at us, and you are going to have to fight your fear of survival. If you fear it, it controls you. If you freeze, you're dead. You are going to deny the instinct of fear and learn to move, learn that facing the threat and intentionally taking a bullet in the shoulder when you go to disarm them is better than accidentally taking one in the heart when you turn to run."

"...I don't understand."

"You're going to see this aimed at the heads of people who have never known violence in the hands of those who had it forced on them. There will be times when you can stop it, and times when you can't. There will come times when you won't know who to save, the one holding it or the one at its end. But no matter who is holding it, you cannot be afraid of it. Fearing something gives it power over you. Don't. You have three choices right now Shadow. You can ask to go home, you can take the bullet, or you can take the gun and shoot yourself in the leg."

"*What*?!"

I stumbled back, taking in his granite expression even as the ground under me moved on its own will.

"Are you kidding? What the heck is this?! Is this some type of test?"

He nodded.

"Is there even a right answer? What the heck BD!? This isn't okay!"

"You're afraid. Before you saw the gun you were fine. The destruction around you did not faze you. The decay, the solitude, my presence, your uncertainty – none of it made a noticeable change in your mental or physical state. Your heart beat did not rise, and your adrenaline and cortisol levels were below a state of panic. But somewhere in the last three minutes, that changed. Right now, you are terrified. You do not think I am going to kill you – it is not death you fear. It is this gun. You've been raised your whole life to fear pain, thinking it is the epitome of evil. The fire you lived through disregarded much of that for you, yet you are still horrified at what I said, you still fear what your choices will be. Why? Didn't the fire hurt you worse than a single bullet will? Were you not healed of that, same as you will be of this? If you have lived through worse, the only fear you are experiencing now is a lie. You are going to get shot, at some point, be it next week or a year from now, from a gun I do not hold with an intent darker than mine. When that happens, you have to know you'll survive. You can't panic then, because that is what is going to get you killed."

I wanted to scream that he was insane, that everything he had said was a bunch of philosophical BS and that I was leaving with or without Shift's assistance or his permission.

But I didn't. I stayed there, standing.

Waiting.

"Cops get sprayed with pepper spray, military gets drilled and pushed past their breaking point, astronauts are put in simulators, Coast Guard are nearly drowned, they are all given a glimpse of what they face. You have the ability to take it directly. This won't be the last test. And it won't be the last bullet. Choose Shadow." He hadn't moved since raising the gun into view, but everything in me said he was about to attack. The hair on the back of my neck stood up, my skin grew cool as blood rushed into my chest, my hands sweated, my heart nearly vibrated it beat so quickly, and then my mouth opened, my tongue taking it upon itself to be the only brave muscle in my body.

"Did Shift do this?" I panted, wanting to throw up and/or start crying. Shift had tased me a couple of times, and even if I had wanted to throw him out of a window, I knew it was relevant to training, and SG was always there.

This, however, seemed like insanity.

He nodded.

"How?"

"To himself, eventually. His survival instinct beat him, and he got careless and didn't go all the way through with it.

311

He shifted out just before it'd hit. Nearly cut his aorta. Had Stargazer not kept him from shifting farther than a few feet, he would have bled out. His panic nearly cost him, Shadow. It was a week before he tried again, but by the end of it he was able to take four without pausing."

"*How?*"

"He learned to trust we would protect him. Fear and pain didn't control him anymore."

I gulped.

"We are not going to let you die. If it ever became a choice between your life or mine, yours would come first, but we won't let it get that far. You have to trust us, and trust that you can live through more than what they will think you can. Shadow, the only power people have over you is the power you give them. The only power fear has over you is the eagerness that you believe it with. You are stronger than your fear, but I cannot tell you this. You have to learn it."

"And this helps?"

"It's a start."

"...Do it."

I registered four things in that moment. Two were conscious, two were not. The first was that he had raised his other arm, both hands clasped around the weapon, his eyes seeming to become impossibly darker as they became the only things I looked at. The second was that I locked my jaw, to keep myself from saying anything else. The unconscious were the most important, since they were the observations made much faster and much more inclusive than the ones more prominent in my thoughts, even if I didn't realize I had done them right then. The first of those was the way I found myself standing, my feet apart, braced against the ground. I wasn't flinching, I was doing what he had said, facing. The second tied into the first. I had not seen this afternoon coming, a fact I would hate myself for missing later, but I could feel the spark in the barrel, and saw the vibrations of energy radiating around it, watched them hit me milliseconds before the bullet would, and turned my torso just enough that when it did make contact, it would hit my shoulder. I would learn that in those fractions of a second, I could dodge it entirely, but in that instant the bullet was as inevitable as the nightmare I would have that night over it.

When those four things had passed, there was only a loud pop and a hole in my shoulder lined with fire like pain.

I heard myself scream over the ringing in my ears. I felt the ground slam into my knees and my hand clasp the warm, wet wound.

My breathing became sporadic. My eyes were closed.

"Don't try to block it out. Your brain associates this gun with every movie, every story you have ever heard. It sees this and believes that it is the source of pain. It is lying to you."

"It freaking *hurts*."

"No. It doesn't."

"Yes it *does*!" I shouted, feeling my stomach in my throat as the realization that Stargazer hadn't healed me yet sank in.

"Your brain is telling you you're in peril, that your life is at risk. It is sending signals to get you to run from anything like this again, fear, the memory of pain. Your mind is convincing you are in mortal danger – but you have to fight what you believe. Do you honestly think I am going to let you bleed to death? Do you think I would let you die? Think, don't feel. Think. Fight your instincts. Overcome."

"No! It hurts!" I growled, clutching my shoulder while forcing myself onto my feet, feeling my shoes catch in a crack of the asphalt. I lurched at him, only stopping when he laughed. It wasn't the shock of seeing him show any type of expression, it was my furiousness at him that made me scream "Give me the damn gun and we'll see who is laughing!"

He smirked. I wanted to punch his face.

Then Stargazer appeared next to him, her expression less than joyful.

"You were meant to wait for me."

"She didn't need you." He said, and I dared to hope it sounded like pride in his voice.

She reached out for me, and I caught myself stepping away.

Something clicked.

"Wait."

She paused.

I inhaled, forcing air into my lungs. I thought of a swinging pendulum, going from one side to the another in a constant, slow pace that never changed, the mental entrainment making my heart rate slowly begin to resume its normal, at least by my standards, pace. Only when I felt my energy's balance return back to neutral did I nod to her, releasing my grip. I made myself look, and didn't shun away at the red stains pooling down my shirt and onto my jeans. *Dang, I really liked these...*

Her gold hand replaced where mine had been.

Shift appeared, looking first to Black Dagger and then to me. SG still had her hand on me, the fire beneath it bearable to the searing hole she was healing.

"So how'd it go?"

"He shot me." I said flatly, still ticked that he had laughed.

"She passed." He didn't laugh then, but he did smirk, sort of.

Shift did laugh, however, and clapped his hands together once. "I knew it! See! I told you she was hard core under it all. Ha! I win. Pay up."

BD scowled.

"I never said she wouldn't. You're the one who nearly-"

"Hey! She doesn't need to know all that – don't rain on her parade here."

"It's fine, I'm just glad it's over with."

"You are all carbon-based fools." Stargazer muttered, but when we all stared at her in shock, she was smiling. "I will never understand the eagerness to take unneeded risk, yet I too have danced along the edges of the mass you deem a black hole only to be flung from its grasp by one greater than I."

"And you had to go and one up us. Really SG? Can't ya'll just go on out, I got it from here."

"Very well. Take her back to our dwelling before bringing her home Shift. Shadow, I will try to visit you and your mother this evening." Stargazer stared at me longer than I thought she should have, considering I thought I had done pretty well under the circumstances and wasn't freaking out anymore.

"Okay, no worries if you can't. I don't plan on telling her about this yet."

"That is your choice, however I will be obligated to when I see her."

"Oh…right." I hated that. The full disclosure policy had more cons than pros, but it kept my mother happy, terrified, but happy.

She and BD flew off.

"So, babydoll's got grit." He smirked, smacking the shoulder that had had a bullet go through it minutes before.

"Isn't the first rule of superhero club that we don't talk about superhero club?"

"Ha, true. But still, congrats. Believe it or not, BD shooting you was the more gutsy choice, because you didn't know what was coming. I mean, I shot myself like five times, once I got the hang of it, so I still beat you, but I'm surprised. He bet you'd bail the first time out here but I didn't expect you to get it on your first try."

"He laughed at me though."

"*When*?" He seemed as shocked as I was.

"After he shot me I tried to hit him and —"

"He wasn't laughing at you Shads." He cut me off.

"What?"

He smiled his biggest, most deceitful 'there's no way this face could ever make you want to scream in frustration' smile.

"That was the point. He wanted you to want something more than just escape. I was begging for SG the first time. You didn't even know if she was going to show up here. You just wanted to slap him. That's what he wanted, I mean, not to slap him, but for you to fight back. That's the whole point."

"Oh, right."

"Yeah."

"What the heck happened to your clothes?"

"Well you're one to talk." He smiled, but he didn't look anywhere but my face. For all his bravado, I don't think he cared much for the sight of blood.

"Yeah well I'm changing soon. You're covered in rice. And you smell like bananas."

"Oh, that." He shrugged. "Delivery."

"Of rice and *bananas*?"

"Today, yeah. It sort of hangs on what I have access to. I've done chickens, seeds, and water filters, and about four semi-trucks full of canned stuff this month. Today was rice, I had to pretty much throw myself against the bags to get them all there faster."

"Where is there?"

I remembered I had no idea where "here" was too, but I didn't feel the need to rush home, even if I was exhausted, and I didn't feel the need to fight for answers, I was done fighting. I'd already won.

"East Africa, North Korea, rural Siberia, Tennessee, a few other places." He said simply. I raised an eye brow, picking a piece of brown rice off of the top of his shoulder. "What?"

"I didn't know you did stuff like this." I hadn't paid much attention to what he did, except when he was forcing me to vault myself over a twelve foot wall, or putting saran wrap around doorways for me to face plant into. Most of the time was too tired to think about anything but what was in front of me or what I was seeing, and I did my best never to look too far into him.

"I do a lot when I'm not babysitting you, blondie. Whenever I'm not shifted out, I try to get as much stuff moved as I can."

"You buy it all?"

"For the most part, yeah." He shrugged again, raising his hands like it was nothing. "Come on, I don't want to be out here. This place gives me the creeps." He mock shivered and took me by my arm.

He shifted us out, and I found myself at their apartment, standing in the bathroom, alone with a six by five foot steam shower beckoning me to it.

◆

Another day in the life of a superhero. Today's episode? How to overdose on caffeine in three easy steps. Step one: Coffee and Black Tea will slowly begin to replace the hemoglobin in your blood. Step two: Your brain may feel like it is going to explode at the slightest hint of withdrawal, but this can easily be solved with another cup. Step three: Invest in a suitcase to carry your coffee and supplies in wherever you go.

I smirked at my own humor. Keurig cups and tea bags were sitting on a magnetic shelf in my locker, my notes from Health Science leaning up against them. It was as close to studying as I could hope to get.

"Cynthia, wait for us!" I heard a high pitch yell.

I slammed the door shut, closing the lock as I squeaked out a hurried, "Hi!"

I had been avoiding them, something Shift had said I should not do, since it would only raise more questions as to why I disappeared so often, but I hadn't listened. If he could get away with half the stupid stunts he did then I could get away with avoiding awkward conversations. Or, that had been the plan. The hype of the Protectors showing up at the mall had passed in the time that had passed since, and thank goodness they hadn't recognized them at the school.

"Where have you been?! We haven't seen you in weeks."

"Oh uh, I've started Gymnastics again – at the Academy."

"Really? They let you back in?! I thought you missed trials?!" No one at school knew about the accident, since it had happened at the beginning of summer. The story was that I had gone to live with my dad for a couple months, months I'd spent convinced I was insane, back when my absurd curls and deepened eye color were "stem cell generated burn repair side effects." Or a perm and contacts to my friends. They believed it had to with money issues that I had stopped going to gymnastics before, not because I had begged my mother to let me out of it, since it was hard to balance on a high beam with the room is covered in moving colors. She'd consented, and if I could help it, my friends would keep believing all of it.

"I did. They, uh, found a loophole...I've been training like crazy. Sorry I keep bailing on you all, but there's a pretty big event coming up and I can't risk missing it again." *I need to get better at lying if they are going to keep this up.*

"So you get to go to regionals?!"

"Oh I doubt it...it's pretty hard after being on break for so long."

"But you were so good!"

"Yeah! They have to let you back in, right?" Kelly begged.

"Oh, well, I guess we will see. If they don't, I guess that's just life. I don't really care, it's just something to do after school, you know?" *Someone save me.*

I could have screamed in surprise when a hand suddenly rested on my shoulder, but I should have recognized it.

"Hey girls." He said casually, his voice taking on an even more prominent flirty tone than it normally had. I saw the surprised faces of my friends and their curiosity as to who the insanely cute, 'cut' boy next to me was, and why I was letting him touch me. The last guy to sneak up behind me that week had gotten elbowed in the gut. (*Shadow* had been the one to hit him, *Cynthia* kept her mouth shut, and got sent to the councilor.)

"Hi!" they said together.

Shift smiled in his most confident, make you melt, sort of way, leaving them like play-doh. He could have said anything and they'd devoured it like calorie-free chocolate, which is all the more reason I had to hate him for what that smirk let out next.

"You're the reason Cynthia is late for our date?"

I was going to have to kick his butt now too. I figured out how after he had put baby powder in my hair dryer. That had been unforgiveable. You set out a little food and he'll show up eventually.

"Date? You're her *boyfriend*? You have a boyfriend?!" Repeated by everyone there. It was all I could do to keep from rolling my eyes. I was trying to dig myself out of social holes, not bury myself in one.

With a shade of skin my art teacher would have called 'Royal Ruby,' I muttered "Yeah. Girls, this is Jonathan. He, uh, picks me up after school, and uh, takes me to practice…That's why I'm not on the bus." If this was it, my one saving grace, I was going to cover *everything*.

"Nice to meet ya'll." He purred, leaning on my shoulder. I suppressed a growl.

They squeaked similar.

"I'll bring up the car." He nudged me in the side, winking.

You didn't?! Oh you are so dead*!* He said bye to my friends and left down the hall, disappearing with all the other freedom searching kids.

"Wow."

"Girl, he's *hot*." Keisha summed up.

In hot water, yep.

"Thanks." I muttered, thinking on how to get him back. His immaturity had overridden his cuteness by week three. And it was only getting worse. He had his moments, like the rice incident, but they were overshadowed by things like waking me up by shifting a pile of snow into my bed. Or, telling a bunch of teenage girls with too much time on their hands that their "no boys no drama no life outside of lunch" friend had in fact been keeping a secret boyfriend with bathtubs full of drama to spare.

"I wanna see the car!" Someone yelled.

"I guess if you want to." I was trying to make it sound like no big deal so they would drop it...problem was, they *didn't*. I cut through the parking lot, snarling under my breath.

"Which one is it?"

"That one." *The one that is surrounded by a supermodel, a professional boxer, and a very smug punk who's about to be murdered.*

"Oh. My. Gosh! That is awesome!" Keisha shouted. Don't even ask me what kind of car it was, or why they had it with them that day. I stopped asking questions when I realized no one ever had a straight answer, leaving me to "see" it myself.

Then they noticed we weren't alone. Keisha smoothed back her charcoal hair, looking down. Marcia and Abigail followed suit, each of them ducking their eyes. Kelly fiddled with her reddish braid, turning back to me for an explanation.

"...*Who* are *they*?" She shrilly whispered.

Anyone could guess who they were if they thought hard enough. No girl alive looks like Stargazer and Black Dagger is hard to forget. Shift was the only variable. But then again, no one could think hard enough, a fact I realized was a credit to Stargazer. When anyone who they wanted to hide from was in direct contact with them, she clouded things up just enough to make it difficult.

"The girl's his big sister." He wasn't shifted to look like her, but I doubted my friends would notice. "The guy is her boyfriend." It was close enough to make me not flush at the lie.

"Dang! Why didn't you tell us about him?"

"I guess she forgot, didn't you Cynth?" Kelly intervened.

"Yeah." I said. She tossed her cherry braid in satisfaction. She was pretty sure she'd earned brownie points she'd trade for secrets later.

'Celeste' noticed my stress and met us a few feet from the car. She was wearing a simple, golden bronze colored dress that nearly matched her skin tone. Even if it wasn't meant to be flashy, she made it so.

"How was your day Cynthia?" She asked lightly. She wore sunglasses to hide her eyes, so she wasn't *too* obvious.

"Good. These are my friends." I recited each of their names, pointing, laughing, basically just trying my hardest to not turn red.

She smiled and nodded to them. They didn't even try not to stare, each flicking her eyes around to pick who deserved most of their combined attention. Black Dagger had *loomed* – there is no better word – behind Stargazer, monitoring the entire situation behind the protection of his own mirrored shades. Shift leaned against the roof, standing on the other side of the car, making sure there was a ton of metal between us. If you can even call *that* a 'car'...Car implies a minivan or Volvo, or Ford. Not that Batmobile knock off.

"You are going to be late to practice, Cynthia. Say goodbye and let's get going." She pulled off her persona with attitude to spare. Wider eyes ensued. She noticed, smiled slightly, and motioned for me to get in the car. When she turned one of the girls tried to not gasp. Her hair couldn't cover everything. The "simple" dress was open from the base of her spine up.

I smiled and went pink when I noticed Black Dagger. He had been watching her too, even if I couldn't see his eyes with all the "practice" they'd forced on me, he wasn't *that* unreadable.

"Oh ok, well I'll see you girls later! Text me!" I dashed for the door and slammed it shut behind me. Shift was already crammed in the back seat, a fact I knew he wasn't too pleased about, since I'd "seen" him call shotgun earlier. I hit him as hard as I could.

"Shads! What was that for?!"

"Don't play that game with me *boyfriend*! Do you know how many texts I'm going to have to send tonight? *Hundreds*! They'll never let it go! They'll think I've got something to hide because I didn't tell them and I'll have to find a way to lie to cover up this mess! Do you understand that there's nothing I can say to fix this! They think I hid you from them! Hid you! That means you're interesting! That's not okay – they'll start wondering and this school sentence will be even worse!" I frantically accused him.

"Drama queen." He rolled his eyes.

"Why did you say *date*? Why not study group or something?! Anything?!"

"It was all that I thought of, okay? Maybe I want a bit of normal too, and if things were normal then maybe, well, I just want normal, you're not the only one with a hard time splitting between everything." He didn't snap at me, but he might as well have, considering the guilt trip that followed.

"Sorry." I mumbled.

"It's okay…that *was* pretty stupid." He admitted with a smirk.

"*You think*?" I cynically demanded. I briefly noticed that Black Dagger and Stargazer had yet to join us in the car. They were either letting me kill him or making us work it out before either of them offered themselves as a buffer.

"I want to ask you something though." *Oh boy.* "I talked to your mom." *Oh gosh no.* "And to BD and SG," *Okay?* "-and they said it would be fine, but I wanted your opinion. I think want to go to school too."

Thank goodness…What!?

"You *want* to go to school?!" *I'm being held to a blood contract and you want to go to school?!*

"Yeah, it'll be fun."

"You're kidding."

He smiled and shook his head. His fluffy hair swung slightly. I forced the 'cute' comment out of my hormone/alien/algebra addled brain and thought about how much junk he had me in with my friends and how much of a big shot he was and how annoying he could be... I wished it'd worked, but it hadn't.

"I'm not. I want to go to school with you."

You want to go to school 'with me'. Oh boy…

"You complain all the time about not getting enough freedom from them. This isn't going to help that."

"I know, but even they agreed that it would be good for me, to have some type of routine. And you won't have to deal alone. BD's been paranoid about you getting found out, so I thought this would be a good safety net, you know?"

Stargazer got in *then*, Black Dagger a second or so later. He looked at us through the rear view mirror, having removed his shades. His eyes were even blacker without his mask on. I shivered down my spine. It was involuntarily, the last time I'd been in close proximity to him I'd gotten shot, and I knew that wasn't the reason but I instantly felt guilty, because I didn't have an excuse.

Stargazer turned and looked at me. I unsurely smiled as a sorry; it wasn't the first time I had gotten that basic reaction from him. Barely a day went by when I didn't jump when he spoke, dogged his stare, or felt my stomach tighten whenever he moved too fast. I didn't mean to do any of it, but no matter what I believed, it didn't stop.

Her face was soft and sympathetic. She knew my thoughts and nodded.

"Shift starts this week." He said, just said, no adjectives to give.

I still felt the need to ask "*Why*?!"

"He can keep an eye on you, and you on him."

"So he's babysitting me." I growled, crossing my arms. *The backseat is too small.*

"We have already given it thought, Shadow. It allows Dagger and I the chance to tend to matters out of your present abilities, provides a sense of normalcy and stability for you both, guarantees you will be under each other's watch in our absence, and ensures your mother's agreement is managed that one of us be within proximity to you at all times. Dagger and I have been bound to this continent whenever you are not with your mother, and though I would never place your or Shift's wellbeing second, there are things we must attend to on other land masses without the worry that one of you would be unaided should anything ever go amiss. I trust that whatever disagreements you may have against your mother for insisting you remain within the school will be set aside, and you will understand Shift's reasons for joining you." She so eloquently explained with enough decisiveness to make the debate team cry.

"You're all *serious*?"

"If you're in, he's in." He finalized.

...*Why me?*

Eternal

"Shads! You're making us late! Let's go!" I yelled for the third time to the shut door. She appeared from her room a moment later. Her hair was a half dried mass of yellow frizz around her face. She hand a hanger in one hand and a brush in the other. *Clearing out your closet or battling a bad hair day?* I forced myself not to laugh.

"...Lock yourself out of the car?" She said sarcastically.

"Hilarious." *You forget you have superpowers for five minutes and they hold it over you for life.* "But no. We're leaving."

She seemed to take that in longer than she should have. *It's not like you can't see it coming...* "What is up? You scared or something?" *This is an easy enough gig tonight... Highway confrontation. California. No cops. She saw it go down already.*

"No! Just give me a sec." She said and hurriedly shut the door.

Stargazer and BD had already left. I'd been doing *homework*, of all things. We had report cards they expected us to keep at least a B in, state tests we had to pass to remain under the radar, and to make matters worse, instead of parents, we got mind readers as guardians. The grass is exactly the same color on this side of the (very, very, unconventional) culture fence.

You're the one who wanted *to go to school! VERY DUMB MOVE! Boring for the most part -BD said no power using at all-and I can't keep* anything *from Stargazer. Now I can't even go out until I finish homework! I haven't even gotten anywhere with Shads - and we're in separate classes!* No amount of computer hacking I had mastered that far into it did me any good in altering that.

"Come on Shadow! You're the one who saw this one. It's your first real gig and you're making us late! Get your butt out here!"

...Four whole months of training and she is late! And me! Late! ...Me!

"Okay! I'm coming!" She ran out of her personal mini apartment.

My mouth fell open. She was wearing a full length, silver and grey swirled body suit, a shiny mask covering from her cheeks to the top of her forehead, and her hair was set with so much hair spray it didn't dare move. Or super glue. I don't ask questions.

"What?" She asked.

"Where'd you get *that*?" I vaguely pointed to her 'apparel'.

She blushed, but I had already made the mistake of making fun of that once. "Well you're the one who said they don't care what we wear...Are we going or what?"

You sure you don't want to go to a movie? Or anywhere where there isn't a mind reader? Please...?

◆

The energies moved by hazardously-uncontrollably. I pulled the life force from those who held the most potentially damaging of the humans' weapons. They fell to the floor, rendered helpless. I did not care if I hurt them. I almost wished I had. I seized the faint traces of energy within the metal of the guns, tearing the molecular bonds within them apart so that there was nothing tangible left but dust.

Dagger grabbed the edged of the crate's mangled-bent door. It yelled in shrilling protest, he exposed the inside in only a second later. The driver of the large engine-truck that had been hauling it was slumped unconscious at the front of the vehicle-I-had-crushed when it struck me as I had materialized in front of it. A young human girl tried to crawl from the crumpled remains. He lifted her from it, only to have more follow her. She had a small cut on her arm, but was not gravely harmed by the crash. My assistance was unneeded, but I allowed my consciousness to brush against each of theirs, soothing their frayed thoughts.

Many of them were stunned by that which their captors –*sellers* had forced them to take. It was far from the first time he and I had intervened into such a practice, but it was the first time we had been aided by Shift and Shadow.

I was once again reminded of the evil that permeates this world, the pure disregard for the value of life, the very insolence of their existence. My power blazed – an inferno eager to destroy the darkness. The only thing keeping me from ending them was the one imbedded rule-in-my-race that if they did not threaten me, I could not kill them.

I clamped my hands shut, not trusting myself to turn the black expanse of road into a gust of wind carrying the dust of what had once been bodies. I watched as even more appeared from the approaching vehicles rendered immobile by Shadow. All nonliving-non-biological energies were terminating their operation once they had crossed into a power-ceasing-barrier she had set around us, a gift of hers we had spent nearly an entire timed-month practicing.

I looked to Dagger, dipping my head in confirmation. He and I faced them, a wall between them and the remainder of their victims Shadow and Shift were evacuating.

I opened my hands towards them, the tendrils of my power seeking out theirs, closing my fists the moment they were within my grasp. They buckled, bowing before me in surrender that still failed to sate my anger. Dagger took hold of my wrist, I as much of his reminder as he was mine to the limits we must hold over our actions.

"Secure them." I consented. Within a minute of our combined efforts, there were no others for us to 'take care of'.

Dagger gave Shift the 'go ahead'. Shadow went with him to deliver the last few victims to a previously arranged place of safe holding, a hospital I aided in the funding of, with a specific group of medicine-practitioners we trusted awaiting their arrival. They returned a moment later.

"That was different than I saw before. I didn't know there were so many." Shadow said quietly, crossing her arms, holding herself in comfort. Shift was too light in his heart and head for it to affect him longer than a day or even an hour, but on that evening she began to see what monster the world was 'underneath the day time talk show exterior,' as Shift had tried to explain, as Dagger had done to him nearly a year before. That night was the first of many to follow what would leave her shaken.

"It does get easier to see to a certain degree." I assured her, knowing the shock-revulsion from my own experiences. *You have much to learn, but I should not have allowed you to come with us tonight. I sensed your distress, yet I thought little of it…Why must I see what* is *and not what* you *see?*

She sighed heavily. I hugged her lightly around her silver coated bodice.

"We will not leave you to face it alone. This very thing took Dagger and I many nights to come to terms with, and even then there are times when we are faced with more than we wish to see, but knowing your place and purpose to end it, and accepting that even the smallest of victories is worth more than inaction eases the distress. Nevertheless, *you* will never and should never grow *used* to it, child."

"Yeah, when that day comes, I'll know that I'm a Protector because I'll think it's more fun than even Black Dagger does." She said with an unsure laugh.

I kept my comment for his defense to myself. He did not like the fact that he liked it, but that did little to counter her statement meant-to-lighten the ambiance.

His energy turned towards our direction at Shadow's mention of his name.

"This *wasn't* fun." He said from across the wide expanse of black-yellow-stripped-roadway. The people we had detained were being loaded into our own version of their animalistic crates, their delivery to the local police impending. "You've heard about these things Shadow, about modern slavery or whatever else CNN calls it, but it isn't just in other countries." He stated.

"It's in our backyard." Shift sullenly nodded, shaking his head with disbelief as he rubbed his palm against the back of her neck. "Freaking kids too." He muttered.

"Shift, take Shadow home." I said hurriedly, before her mind become any less sound.

"*Why?*" Her voice was that of a child.

"You have done more than I could have ever expected of you tonight, without your aid there would have been many more variables to see to. But Dagger and I can tend to things from here. Go before the daylight turns, your mother would like such, rather than having her wait for you all the night, and it is best to appease her wishes while we have the time to. There will be days and nights where you are needed without end. Tonight is not one of these. If you see anything, inform me."

She relented, nodding in understanding.

"Fine...come on Big Shot." From over her shoulder, Shift winked at Dagger. They departed. I knew he would not return for another half of an hour at the earliest. He rarely left her side without being kicked out by her mother late into the next morning.

The scorching magnet of his approaching energy brushed against mine. I turned and gave him a small smile; my eyes traced his face, stalling on his eyes.

"You really shouldn't let him be alone with her, for *his* sake. She'll hurt him if he messes with her enough and he will." He said in complete truth.

"I would rather her teach him a lesson than you or I."

I had gotten close to knocking his lights out on more than a small number of occasions, but in my defense it was always for good reasons.

"We should leave before the feds show." *They'll be all over us tomorrow for not asking for their 'permission' to do this.*

"I would presume they already have Dagger."

I grimly nodded. It didn't matter. The victims were safe, the criminals were in custody, and if they got out by some loophole in the paperwork, Shadow and Star would have very little issues tracking them down again. We'd simply tip off the local PD, if it came to that, and have a legit raid, with us overseeing if needed.

She fly us out, back to the edges of our city before I told her to land. I wanted to walk, stating that if any drones were nearby we should stay ground level, preferably below the radar. Shadow's site had offered me some degree of comfort that we couldn't be snuck up on, and that if someone – they – found us, we would have a warning, but I was still suspicious. She hadn't argued.

"What you said to Shadow, does it still get to you?" I asked, once we were far enough away from the last few people on the street to not draw attention to ourselves.

"Yes." She relented and grabbed my hand, her fingers tangled with mine. "I am neither their god nor their counsel, nor do I seek to be, but if I were to exert my power as influence I would not stand for it. The world is tainted. To hide from that fact would be futile. I have long ago realized the effects it has on me will always have to be monitored, lest I begin a war to cleanse what can never be purified completely."

"When it gets me to react, well, you know what happens." I reminded her she wasn't alone in her battle to hold back. Her hand held mine tighter.

"You might dislike me for saying this." She whispered.

"Impossible."

"Perhaps there is some good in your...your, shall we say detachment? To these people- to what they do, because of what you can do. If everything affected you, like it does me, not only would you need to work on patience, but self-restraint. The only fact holding me back is I am not human, and by all laws of nature I should take very little part in their punishment, but you have no such moderation, and in that it would be easy for you to justify final retribution. For in that aspect at least, perhaps there is a blessing, not for the notion that you do not dwell on anger, but because you are able to overcome it."

I was shocked at where I found myself. I knew not whether he'd recognized the long-forgotten-storehouse, or if he had taken that route deliberately. He grabbed the door, over twenty-five paces high and another twenty wide, forcing its rusted hinges to swing, before offering his hand to me, taking us inside. His lack of surprise resonated with a sense of confidence in stark contrast to my own questioning. A small smile was on his shadowed-black-framed-angled expression. His eyes were again the black-soul-fire; I felt his power seeping into me like the softly-searching light just-before-the-dawn. I sighed against him, no longer astonished at how human he made me feel, how human I desired to be.

"Will you make me one more promise?"

"Whatever it is it you seek from me, you already possess it. Ask."

"To love me."

This I do...where are you going with this Dagger? It isn't like you. What is it that is making you act this way... nervous?

"I *do* love you, more than anything of this world, or outside of it."

He smiled wider. He let me go and grasped my hands in his, holding them in his own between the both of our bodies. He was no longer nervous, but *I* was. The walls of his mind were down, yet the power around him seemed to nearly stand still – not out of forced control, but *peace*.

"Then marry me, Stargazer."

The stand still became a flood, as if a thousand super novas had exploded around me, sending me crashing into him. I knew only that the ground was no longer beneath me and that I held him.

"I promise." I breathed in his ear. "I promise, with all I am, I promise you this." I was overwhelmed and knew I was glowing brightly. I don't recall my thoughts, I had not any to remember.

He held me even tighter. I pressed my soul into his, a sense of relief and ecstasy unlike anything I thought possible consuming me. *I promise. I promise. I promise.* I thought a thousand times, holding him all the tighter at each, heeding the equally covetous tenor of his touch, my damp eyes like flashlights against his pale skin.

I made myself release him a long-perfect-lifetime later. He wrapped his arms around my waist, a living, breathing statue-of-stone curling me into an eternal embrace, urging me closer, but not nearly as close as I so desperately-suddenly wanted to be.

"What is it?" I asked softly, having sensed a change in his energy. I feared he had recalled the last time we had spoken over things such as this, and I chose then to never say what I had sought to speak then, for it was no longer worth the air I used to voice it. He was worth more than anything, even that.

"I don't have a ring." He admitted. "It isn't easy to keep anything from you... I was distracting you earlier." He said with a half laugh. I smiled and grasped his left hand in my right, reaching within the deepest parts to my tangibility to mold around him. I let go a moment later. On his finger was a three-dimensional black-and-gold-set-ring. Designs made of an unearthly form of gold, my own, in encircled it, surrounding a small, perfectly formed black dagger in the ring's center. Faultless-new-made-enlightened-gold was set behind this.

"Beautiful." He said.

"Thank you."

"I wasn't talking about the ring." He smiled.

Whatever silence that had once been in my mind was gone as I smiled in return, feeling my power shine brighter and seeing the shadows of his face disappear in my glow.

"What do you wear?"

I hesitated, realizing that this was now mine to choose. I placed my fingers together, the ends of my power meeting in a multi-leveled triangular shape. I pushed the energy and substance from within my body between them, a circle of pure gold forming at the synapse between the pathways of my light. I raised it above my head, pausing when his hands overlaid mine as it rested atop it. I felt him gently kissing my forehead.

"I love you Stargazer." He promised. I may have flown above the ground, but I am unsure if that was why I felt as if I was floating. I had never been as happy as I was; I had not known such euphoria to exist. It was all I could do to not blind him when he kissed me again. I felt him smile, laughing at my inability to control my light.

I found him, and kissed him back, forgoing any self-made-control for this perfect moment. His fingers caught against the slight ridges of my back, casting me to his icy-inflexible-mold.

His cool lips were too yielding, softly wandering against mine, his hold a caressing pressure along my back and arms. My hands were suddenly in his hair, drawing him closer. Every second I held him I lost ties to any thought he had not been the one to build. As if knowing I would belong to him had already changed things, just by him promising me through this pledge, this so human-of-earth act, my power searched for his, seeking to draw it in. It was all him. His touch, his breath, his heart thudding in tune with my power, his skin a mixture of fire and ice that left me mindlessly surrendering.

I found the strength to turn away, noting how easily I managed to forget his human needs for air when we were this close. I buried my face in his chest, letting him surround me in a strong-holding wall that kept the world and all its doubts at bay.

A group of uncounted minutes later I pulled back from him and sighed in my lack of care to what I knew. It took me a moment to inhale enough air to speak.

"I truly *hate* to say this...but Shift is going into a state of ...of pure panic at our absence. I can't ...reach him from here."

He rolled his eyes, his arms tightening. "He'll get over it." He whispered, returning to his power-flare inducing actions. I lost thought, which I realized is what he wanted.

[...YOU DID?!]

"Have they called *you* yet?" I tapped the wall impatiently, holding the phone with my shoulder. I was too tired and freaked out to shift and was shamefully reduced to cell phones. Which irritated me even more than I already was.

"Jonny? What time is it? Who- Wait, what?" She sounded like I had just woke her up. In her defense it was about four a.m. but I hadn't thought about it. I had woken up to an empty apartment and no note explaining their absence, and no sign they had even come home.

"Uh seriously...? Who else? *Brad* and *Celeste* ditched me after I took Shads to her moms. I haven't heard anything from them in nearly eight hours."

"Oh. What's wrong then?"

"The you-know-who's weren't far off our trail. I went back and they were all over the place. They weren't there – and I couldn't pick up anything. They haven't called m-"

"Get Cynthia. You both need to come here, just to be safe. I'm sure that they're fine. We'll wait for them to show up. It isn't like they can't take care of themselves. Chill out okay?" She said smoothly. *How are you so calm?! They're missing! FBI, CIA, NSA, uh, OSS, DOD, MI-6, the freaky company-Area 51-any of that is ringing a bell?*

"Fine." I hung up the phone. BD hadn't been in the lightest mood before we left, he'd been off for days actually. I was scared for whoever ticked him off. Okay *was* a *little* scared for them too.

"Shift." I heard her say calmly.

I spun around. *Hey-she's wearing a headband, that's new- focus! You are* really *mad at them!*

"Where the have you *been!*? Why didn't you call me?! What happened?! I thought you guys got abducted or something!" I continued to rant until Stargazer *materialized* right in front of me. Her eyes locked with mine. I couldn't look away. *Get out SG! My head, my rules!*

If you don't calm yourself you will cause your own harm. We are here, we are in excellent health, and there is no call for your fears. I am sorry that we'd disappeared without allowing you to know our intended return time. I promise to you we shall not do that again.

Get out! I hate this! You feel like sticky! *Why are you in my head?!*

I am here because you will not listen to me otherwise (True). *Tonight isn't a night for this.*

Fine. Where were you? You owe me that answer at least. I've been freaking out for a while in case you care. Did you guys get to 'interrogate' someone? He looks happy enough for it. Maybe throw a few cars?

Stop. ...Please Shift. Her voice sounded hurt. I tried to understand how she could be the one upset. *I* was the one who had been ditched and was being brain seized by an alien. *I will not let him be seen that way. He does not like the constant struggling, he likes feeling that comes with the presence violence and self-endangerment, he does not enjoy the chaos itself.* Her tone changed significantly at this: *If you tell him I have told you any of this I will shock you so that you won't be able to move more than your eyes for days.*

Okay I won't. Yeesh...you are the one who needs to take a chill pill okay? ...Then why is *he happy?*

We are happy and if you promise to remain calm we'll tell you.

I already said I would 'freeze'.

If I were the one to freeze you know you are in danger.

What? She always said half of whatever she thought, even when talking to you with her thoughts. Alien issues.

Good then. Do not forget my warning.

The strange feeling of 'honey-glazed brain' left.

I hate it when she does that!

"I'm going to get Shads. Meet us at Mary's. She knows we are on our way." I muttered, even though I knew it wasn't called for anymore, I needed to vent to someone, and Mary was expecting us. I didn't have an explanation for either of them, but it was better than standing there trying to not yell at them again.

...I stood at the doorway. *This isn't going to be easy to explain. 'Hi Ms. Noel, can I borrow Shads for a few hours...yes I know it's this early in the morning and her day off.'* I was about to knock on the door when it burst open. Shadow stood there, decked out in loose sweat pants and a tank top, not at all surprised. She was actually annoyed.

"Yeah?"

"You knew I was coming?" I managed to say, trying to not grin at the fluffiness of her hair. I was still ticked. *Otherwise she'd be asleep-like I want to be..*

"I see the future-*duh*. I didn't see anything else happening tonight. You can stop checking on me Big Shot. I fine." She was whispering, her mom was still asleep. *A very lucky woman.*

"We have to go see Mary."

"Your sister?" She yawned, ruining the judgmental tone she'd been aiming for.

"She thinks BD and SG are missing." I wasn't allowed to say names anywhere others could hear it. That hadn't been a huge problem *before* Shads, but she couldn't change how she looked, wasn't an alien who didn't have any known earthly threats, or a Goth superman who didn't have an identity other than *being* Goth superman. With Snowden's big reveal, I had been forced to nearly cease most of my internet life, even with the help of hackers on our side.

"Are they?!"

I heard her mom move around in room behind her. She stepped out into the hallway and quietly shut the door behind her.

"No, they were earlier, but they're back."

'Hey Shift-we're leaving you. Go to Italy for some pizza.' How hard is that to say- I mean seriously?

"They do that *all* the time. They *always* show up." She emphasized it like was *my* fault.

"I *know* that. You think I'd go through all this trouble if I thought there wasn't something wrong?"

"Okay, fine, I'll see what I got." She sighed, closing her eyes in one of her 'focus on the energy' modes she'd been attempting to perfect.

"You don't have to-"

"No. I'm coming. Our future has changed and I want to see why." She slipped back into her apartment, leaving me waiting like a pre-paid cab driver/teleport machine in the hallway.

Why. Is. My. Life. So. Complicated? I whined, quite depressed. *I'm stuck with two people who have a habit a vanishing, a sister who thinks she knows everything and that has to be in the loop, and a girl who is totally not in to me…no matter* what *I do.*

She was back in less than a minute, in her mega hot get up. A massive backpack full of supplies ranging from Cliff bars to Saline IV's hung at her side. Somehow having enough food and med supplies to run a small army made sense to her, despite the all-healing alien and instant delivery boy.

"I get it. It's overkill, but I want to be ready. I didn't see anything, which doesn't help. My mom isn't thrilled, but we should go before she changes her mind. You know where they went off to?" She sounded less annoyed, more curious.

"Nope…she said they *would* tell us. They might be meeting us at Mary's. "

"Then let's go." She said and put her backpack on.

"Well? Have you found them?" I jumped up as soon as he had appeared in the living room. I knew I sounded a little irritated. I had a right to be. He was exasperated, or made a point to look like he was the moment I opened my mouth. Shadow was half-asleep, fighting to look formidable. *...Poor thing... She needs a serious break. I need a break. College and superheroes and little brothers and being just me don't mix.*

"Yeah, they showed up." He said as if he didn't care. "But it wasn't nothing. I didn't overreact, so you both know." I turned up the radio. The neighbors would complain, but it was better than catching a word or two that would land us in actual trouble.

"What happened then?"

"No clue…they said they'll be here soon. I'm going to shower." He stated. The large three-bedroom condo they'd gotten me allowed Jonathan to have, what he called, "a sanctuary from the mind reader." Shadow was also on human time-share, though I doubted she liked hers as much as he enjoyed popping in on me at the most inconvenient times.

"Hey Mary, can I ask you something?" Shadow peeped up, her voice enormously tiny.

"Yeah, I guess." I had only hung out with her on a few occasions, and had the most elementary of understandings as to what she was, most of my insight coming from the ranting, hormone laced therapy sessions with Jonny. What I did know was that she was about as out of place in that world as I felt in the real one, and with that, I could sympathize. Plus, she'd managed to make my kid brother go love-struck nuts, which was winning *tons* of points in my book, so I owed her.

"I think we have some time to kill, I don't feel her near here anyway, and I was just wondering – well I haven't seen it so I was curious."

"About?"

"How do you know Black Dagger?"

"No one told you?" I felt my brows rise beneath my bangs.

"Nope, Shift said that you had known him *before* and I just can't picture *that* – and can't see it. I don't know how it would be *possible*, like Black Dagger *not* being Black Dagger. Shift – Jonny said I'd have to ask you if I ever wanted details and I kind of do, I can't see it is all." She smiled uneasily, setting a massive backpack down next to the dining table before coming to the living room.

She curled up with a pillow on the sofa, folding in half so that she looked like a Broadway Cat peering over it. Her bright emerald eyes were wide with expectation. She looked like she was waiting for a bed time story, which wasn't what I was going to give.

"I couldn't either, if I hadn't seen it, lived it I mean. He, uh, rode my bus." She tried to not laugh. It couldn't get more normal. "We became close, I guess. At least, we felt safe enough around each other to talk about things…He had already been changed from, well normal, then, but we didn't know that. It wasn't the same as what you see."

"What do you mean, not the same?"

"He…He was softer, I guess?" I tried to laugh it off, but the differences between the boy sitting on top of the table and the man who often appeared but never seemed present were too many to try to describe. I didn't even want to try. "That's not the point though. He and I were friends, or sounding boards for each others issues more so at first. But it's a lot more than that now. He has saved me, twice."

Her eyes went to being worried.

"*How?*"

341

"Stargazer was here for the second. She healed me from…some stuff." By habit my eyes fell to my now spotless arms before looking back at her. She nodded like she saw that. *Wonderful.* "The first was well…I threw a party and my-" I shuddered and pushed it back. "I was being stupid. You better know better. If anyone wants something from you first – they don't freaking 'love you'." I hissed, ready to explode in hatred, and combust in regret and grief.

She nodded again, seeing the wolves behind my eyes fighting over the scraps of my fragile sanity. "I saw that…I didn't mean to."

"No. I get it." I stammered, not sure how much I could hold over her. Jonny said she rarely had any control over what she saw, especially in those first weeks.

"I didn't know he was there, though."

He was. He…he saved me…But as soon as he did, he disappeared for a week, taken by the people that changed him before. Next thing I knew he was showing back up on my doorstep. I helped him get out of town, he needed cash and I was the only one he trusted." I explained.

"And you trusted him?"

I blinked. That'd never even been a question in my thoughts. "Of course. He said he would tell me everything, when he could. He eventually explained why he had to leave and what had happened, and why he seemed so different, but it took him over a year."

"Were you the one who got hurt from his running away?" She whispered. I stared at her, dumbstruck. I told Jonny *some* of what had happened, but he wouldn't and hadn't told her. I had been hurt by a lot of things, for as long as I could remember, mostly myself. And I had attached to the first thing, the first person, who wasn't hurting me, and it had been *him,* both times he'd showed up in my life. When that was taken from me, I hadn't thought I had the strength to stand on my own two feet.

"Did you see that, Shads?" I asked cautiously.

"No...Black Dagger told me I couldn't run away because someone would get hurt. He made me promise to keep Cynthia in the works, at least for now. I know I'm not much help yet, I have a lot to learn but I just think there has to be more to it, because I can hold my own, even if I need backup. I have even started to see mechanical and electrical energy now like I see people's energy and SG says it's only a matter of time before I figure out how to influence it too. Earlier tonight I was even able to make a dead zone, so I know they need me fulltime, but BD is adamant on stalling it by making me stick to the double life."

It's bad enough Stargazer reads minds...and likely tells him everything. I didn't want him to think - That was all my fault. I chose the (aftermath) *and I should've never let it get that far, but I didn't feel like I had any control.*

"From what I have seen you had to be the one." She pressed, the first time I had known her to let her curiosity get the better of her. Her expecting face said she wanted to know what I thought about that.

Honesty was my only way out of that one...that or not saying anything.

"He knows what happens when ends aren't tied and are left to fray. It got to where being alone wasn't an option. I had to find a way to become numb – I had tried guilt, pain, hatred for myself and all things – and nothing that helped. It seemed the only way out was to go deeper, to lose whatever was left, so nothing hurt anymore. Needless to say, it didn't work, not like I believed should have. I have to live with it and I wish more than anything that I hadn't done any of it … Don't go digging into it, for your own sake."

"I know...I just wanted to make sure you're okay. I really didn't try to see you that far back but-"

"Hard to look away from a wreck?"

"No, but I was worried. Shift said something once when I told him one of my friends was throwing a party and it just kind of connected something in my head to you. I won't let it happen again though …What do you think of Shift?" The question caught me off guard. Her subject changing ways were appreciated, if not subtle.

"He is my little brother, so I might be a little biased, *both* ways." She nodded and laughed. "He likes you though; even if he purposely tries to annoy you …It's his own strange way of flirting."

"That was obvious from the start. BD hit him on the back of his head the first time I met them, so he saw right through it." She laughed. "It was funny."

"I don't doubt it. Whatever pranks he has pulled, I should probably apologize since I was his first mentor and victim."

"No worries, I get him back."

I smirked. I didn't doubt it.

I listened to a particularly catching song and before I knew it, she was sound asleep, halfway curled up on top of a few large pillows. *No chance of me carrying you to bed. You're bigger than I am!*

Jonathan was suddenly in front of me, like changing a channel to find the next station at the exact same scene, plus an added character. He was smiling, like always. I jumped backwards and gasped. He had simply laughed, feigning innocence.

"I *hate* it when you do *that*!"

"Easy," he laughed, raising his hands in mock surrender.

You were listening weren't you?

He looked down at Shadow, his face different instantly, almost thoughtful. *He actually likes her. This isn't some kiddy crush. Wow. I never thought I would see the day. You-*

"You want me to bring her to bed?" He asked. His strength was well above average, not close to what Brad's had

344

been, but significant. I'd found out when he'd ripped my door frame out of the wall when trying to set up a pull-up bar. Joy.

"Like I can control what you do."

He carefully picked her up before he disappeared. I heard him in my room. He was back five seconds later.

"Thanks."

He smiled wider. *Your pleasure, I know.*

"You going to bed?"

"Nah, I'm waiting for *this* explanation from 'em. It is getting old, really old, Mary." He rolled his eyes. It wasn't the first time he'd been ditched. He would normally hit my place and go check their roof after he had enjoyed an old cartoon marathon and a nap, and they'd be there, as if it was no big deal.

"Maybe they try to get away from you. Ditching you is their only escape."

"He might. He *would* actually." He grimaced. "But I don't think they would be gone that long-it was two hours! They just left! And there were feds! What was I supposed to think – that they up and decided to visit Fiji for some sunbathing?"

He ranted for another minute before he sighed, knowing it was pointless, and shifted out to come back with food from whatever country he'd come up with first. I wasn't hungry, but he was, like always. My apartment often reeked with the scent of take-out in the truest sense of the term.

"They should at least have given me a heads up." He muttered between bites of the massive and oddly topped pasta.

"It isn't the first time he has left and she left her *planet* …might be a habit or something." I was still adjusting to the fact that Stargazer was a real, actual alien. She was not easy to get used to seeing either. Besides total gorgeousness, she seemed to be either looking *through* or at something else *while* she looked at *you*. Sometimes she wouldn't talk, or even move much for that matter. She would just stand behind him, her eyes down to the ground and her hands behind her back, but I knew that was the most obvious sign of how powerful she was, if she felt the need to feign passivity on that high a level, and I could remember clearer than anything else in my entire life the feeling of her ripping out pieces of me I never wanted back, so whatever her reasoning behind it, it had backfired. It just freaked me out more.

I asked Brad why that was, tired of guessing. He had said in a very even and controlled voice, "She doesn't know how to not scare you." It had taken some will power to not go off on how that part was obvious, it was the *why* I wanted to know. Jonny had told me to get over the awkward stage and just ask her, but he'd also said she would get in his head to make him understand things she didn't know how or didn't want to talk about aloud, so to be prepared for that if the question required it. *"Honey-glazed-brain" is what he called it.*

I exhaled, hoping the air that left my body would take some of my insecurities with it.

"Mary*anne*!" I shook her out of pesky brother habits. Her eyes opened.

"I fell asleep?" She asked, after pushing me off in a half drugged daze.

"You went out hard. Snored and everything."

"Did not." She muttered.

"And you know that how?" I questioned, to receive an eye roll for an answer. "You're getting her up. I want to live to hear this." I told her, my tone showing the meaning behind it. Shadow had a habit of knocking out whoever tried to wake her up – claiming no memory of it once fully conscious. I'd gotten an elbow to the face one too many times to try my luck again. Even BD quietly avoided it.

"You scared of your girlfriend?" She teased.

"She isn't my girlfriend!" *She's a physic! You would be too!!*

"But you wish."

I was about to jump her when the hall light flicked on. *She is up! NOW HOW AM I GOING TO TAKE MARY TO CUBA AND LEAVE HER THERE?!*

"What's with the yelling?" Shads asked us, rubbing her eyes as she stumbled back into the living room, drunk on sleep.

"Jonny has denial issues." Mary said coolly.

"I do not!" I yelled.

"See?" She asked Shads. My mouth fell open. *She got me at my own game!*

"Oh... Are they here?" She looked around the room, wide, expectant eyes looking at everything but what we were able to see. "Wait…One, two...three." She snapped her fingers towards the door. It opened.

"You're getting good Shads." I smiled when she flushed at the compliment. I wasn't exactly hoping for her to hit SG's level of selective-omnipresence (if that makes any sense) but it was exciting to see her make progress. She had come a long way from the girl who was afraid of our sparring matches.

"Eh, good teachers help. I may just surprise you one day."

I felt my ears go hot and shifted my skin tone to hide it, knowing Mary would have something to say about it the moment she noticed.

"Did you get to rest before our arrival?" I questioned. The energy of the room was a yellow tinted suspicious-shocked. Mary, though silent, noticed of my unusual voicing was profound in her surprise. She was just as enquiring and even more worried than Shift had been, thought he was still incensed at our prolonged stalling of telling him the 'full story'. Dagger was as concerned-unsure as I was with their oddly placed reactions. He listened to their raised heartbeats,

347

his eyes focused on the tension in Shift's palms, the miniscule flexion betraying his remaining agitation.

"Where were you?" Shadow asked evenly, her tone-power void of confusion or questioning. She had just *seen* why we were gone, and in turn, learned what had happened, and was simply asking us for the others' sake. She was glowing beyond measure, though they could not see hers as mine was visible. She was the same as other humans, who were only capable of making their energy viewable when they were with child, because they were carrying another power entirely. Hers however invisible was different in the sheer intensity of it, flaring as it sensed my presence near her.

"We were at a warehouse outside the city." My answer, though true, didn't satisfy their confusion.

"Can I ask *why*?" He sniffed.

"I am regretful we 'ditched you' Shift, and even sorrier that you brought Shadow and Maryanne in all of this. There was no danger for us."

Shift rolled his eyes at Dagger and I.

"And I was supposed to just *figure* that out?"

I smiled at what I knew he would say, at what it meant, at all of it. *Fiancée...hmm...this is a new heading-label for me...* I got a soul-jumping-light-giving sensation at the next title to come. I had not even known the word to exist, before him, and without him it would have held no meaning for me.

"I asked Stargazer to marry me."

I let my power brush his, our elated minds in brief contact amid the crashing chaos around us. I watched with attentiveness as the room's energies became a shifting-rainbow-deluge of sensations, the sheer amount of the rotating-life-light-powers was a pool of pure-mind-washing force.

"You did?! You *did*!" He stammered, looking between us and then to his sister.

"He did." Shadow smiled, crossing her arms at her wrists and interlocking her hands together, her laughter-energy as that of a child's.

"Wow... I'm happy for you both." Mary said calmly, unlike her brother, taking without shock what had left the rest of us without words.

"Thank you...I do not have the means to express my own joy without blinding you all." Mary looked at me-pure-uncontained-shock on her face. I wondered at it but did not look in her mind to see its source.

"BD, I – well I tell you later." Shift smiled at *me*, winking. I refrained from looking into his thoughts, unsure if I truly sought to know them.

I felt my form crushed, looking down to see Shadow holding me tightly.

"I can't believe it. Well I can, but...wow. Yay!" She squealed. She released me. Her smile was true and wide. I caught the pause in her energy as it stalled in its following of another's course, as she was seeing something.

"What have you seen?" I whispered to her alone.

"Oh my gosh, oh my goodness, wow... No looking in my head! I'll tell you when it happens- ok?!" He eyes shone brightly and their gloss was greater, thought I nodded in agreement and forbid myself from looking further. If she had reacted with anything less than joy, I knew my control would have faltered, but her happiness was my assurance that all was well. As if, I realized, it could ever be anything but perfect in these hours.

"Easy SG! Ow!" Shift exclaimed and put his hand up to his eyes, shielding them.

"Star." He said softly and knotted his fingers around mine. I severed off the flow of energy to my surface, guilty-ashamed that I had not given mind to its existence before. I felt the eyes of everyone laying on me, the black-light-absorbing-circumference of their pupils expanding back into proper form.

"There are little words and many lights within me tonight." I explained, taking their mid-expanded yawns as passive acceptance.

"No harm done." Mary smiled to us, before calling out, "Time for bed!" She clapped her hands loudly. No one objected, for it had been nearly four nights since Dagger had allowed himself rest, and the others bore an exhaustion equal to his own. I followed Dagger to the room he would share with Shift. He paused outside of it, turning to face me before leaned against the wall, his hand in mine and the other around my waist, drawing me towards him.

"I suppose this is where I wish you sweet dreams." I rarely spoke aloud to him in this moments, watching him in all ways that I could as he fell to unconscious surrender was my greatest peace-giver, and even when he slept I remained near him. If this night was to be different, I would not fight it.

He cocked one of his brows, something he had 'picked up' from Shift.

"I don't have to worry about that with *you* here." I smiled as he kissed me. His hand moved up my back, the cool touch of his power rendering me with only a need to be closer.

"No...you will on no occasion have to endure trepidation." I murmured, tearing away from him. His mind-stalling-soul-seeing gaze flashed behind me for a brief second. Shift was waiting behind us, his presence aimed to be a reminder to Dagger of the apology he believe we owed him. "Go on... I will be here in the morning." He tightened his mind-stalling grip on me before he went into the darkened room.

"What is it that you seek, Shift?" I asked, hearing the metallic tone of my voice return as my thoughts were lethally distracted from my ever conscious efforts to soften my nature.

"Oh, me? Nothing at all...Can't say I thought this was your alibi though. Congrats, seriously SG."

"Thank you. Now go rest."

He thought *'you are not in charge of me'* as he rolled his eyes and entered the room.

"You don't want to go to bed? There's a pull-out under where Shads is. I have another pair of sheets I think." I hadn't exactly planned on having them all stick around, but Jonny was, in his own words, shifted out, and I doubted they would have all given into my saving grace suggestion of a nap if they hadn't really needed one. Brad and Shads especially.

She smiled and practically *floated* above the chair on the opposite side of the room. Her feet never fully touched to ground, something that I was surprised to find was more noticeable than you'd think.

"No, although I thank you for your kindness, but I do not sleep." She said delicately. I stared in shock, not trusting myself to answer in anything but a poorly thought through vampire joke. "I know what you believe, 'how does she not need sleep?' but it is true. I regenerate my strength by doing just that, generating it from within my own body. It is similar to the functioning of stars, in such, there is no need for my form to appear to be at rest during this process, unless I lack the power to animate my body, which right now I do not."

"Oh, uh, well you're welcome to turn on TV." I would fuss at myself for that awkward comment later, but it was all I managed to come up with at the time.

"You may, if you desire to wait for their rising, but I am content to wait for the sunrise. " She smiled, her ultra-white teeth a stark contrast to her deep gold skin. I couldn't help but smile back. The hazy memory of the first time I had met her filled my mind. I silently laughed at how shocked I was that Brad had been with a girl. Out of everything else - *that* was what I had taken out of it.

"You really love him, don't you?" I wanted to hear her say it. A vice of mine was that I do not believe something until I saw it or heard it for myself. I think I am supposed to be from the "show me state" and not the "sunshine state." But still, I had to hear it. Alien or not, capable of miracles or not, I had to hear her profess it the same way any human could, because it was a human she was with, and even if my brother seemed to be able to dismiss the fact she was not one by throwing everything weird into a box at the back of his head, never to be opened, I couldn't. The idea that someone who was capable of knowing everything there was to a person and could still be able to say that they love them, much less actually, truly, love them, was beyond me, no matter how jadedly noble Brad was or how forgiving she claimed to be.

Her countenance softened.

"Yes. I do, more so anything." Her eyes *lightened* into a bright, shiny gold. "...I have not looked into your thoughts, but it is not a far leap of judgment for me to assume why it is you ask this, Maryanne, and although I owe you not the answer to this matter, for the kindness you have shown him you shall receive one. I am not of this earth – this I hold no disillusions over. As you stare at me and I appear to look back at you, I am also watching the air that leaves your brother's lungs and returns back into them, the dreams that flicker through the level of existence humans would call Dagger's subconscious, and the energies Shadow is emitting, should any of them alter with a reading she may glean in her sleep. I am watching the memories of yours and Shift's trip to a character-featured-theme park mix in with his memory of taking Shadow there only weeks ago.

I can feel the earth's core beneath me, the vibrations of the molten metals and rock rolling over each other miles below us, the tremors of the solid layers at the surface slowly smashing into one another, the faint sway of this building in relation to the spin of the planet verses its gravity. I can feel the sun's radiation through the window gaining power as we turn towards it. I can even feel this planet, and this galaxy, flying through this universe in endless spirals. I feel all of this, and even as I speak these things, you do not doubt them. Yet you question how could I, who knows not what it is to be human, claim to feel love for one?"

I blinked. Her words had been woven with more accuracy than my great grandmother's embroidery, and the needle that drove them had been just as sharp, if not accusing.

"Yes." I didn't back down, though, and even if it wasn't the most eloquent of answers, it stood its ground.

She smiled tenderly, looking to the wall his room hid behind.

"If you were to behold one of the stained glass windows your kind creates, say one with its expanse over fifty paces in any direction, as far as you could see without turning your head, and you were able to look upon it as a whole, to take in the magnitude of its beauty and its greatness, and also its fragile delicateness, would you cast it to be destroyed for the fact there was a crack in a single pane of its glass? If one color had begun to bleed into another, would it destroy its splendor? Or would these things pale in comparison to the whole that they have created?

Or what of the woven tapestry, if a single threat has frayed, what then of the great masterpiece it belonged to? Is it fodder to a fire, or thrown to the ground to be trampled by blind crowds? If you saw these things, the worth of that to which they belonged would not diminish in your eyes, because in the first few moments you beheld it, Maryanne, you knew its magnificence, its story, its light and its dark, and in those moments you chose whether or not you gave it worth, if you loved it, so when those moments pass and the cracks and frays are seen, you do not care.

It is your glass casting colors across the fabric hanging from your wall, and your ownership and the worth you chose to give these things is greater than any assumed imperfection they might bear.

Thus is this love.

So that night when I looked upon Dagger, I loved him, not with the consciousness that comes from understanding, but with the awe of beholding. And each day that has passed since, no matter what we have faced or what has been revealed, I have not forgotten what I saw that night, and now I believe the man I have promised more to than I would have thought I could promise to another is even greater than the one who first drew me to this continent. And it is by his side I will remain, at any cost, and without any hesitation.

Does this help you understand?"

"Yes..." I vacantly nodded.

I had forgotten it was dark outside, with the light she gave.

"Why do you glow?" I asked suddenly, too curious to mind my manners.

"That," she smiled, "Is a much easier question to answer. I am *happy*. My soul will darken when I am angry or troubled, thus my eyes show that. The stars in them expand and my skin appears to glow when I am joyous. I have yet to be able to manage it without a margin of error, as you all had just seen. I am not in any danger, so I can be, for lack of a better word, 'me', and in doing so I release power, which is what you see as light and even a form of heat. My kind do not speak in words in the sense yours does, and it is our souls and our powers that relay our thoughts. This is the last evidence of that I bear."

"...What do you think about *me*?"

She looked back to me, her movements slow and precise. Her eyes were slightly narrowed, she was as caught off guard by the question as I was unsure over why I was asking it.

"You are who you are. No one can say 'what they think of you,' since it is irrelevant to the truth. *What* you are, *who* you are *now*, who you *will* become, *why* you are the way you are, can only be determined by you by yourself. No one but you controls that. Nothing anyone will think or do will ever mean anything if you trust in the belief that you know whether what they state is true or false, and that your view of your past and present is your own reality. ...But, to answer your question, I think you are 'human'. It is an obvious statement, but that does not make it any less true, and I do not say it simply because I am not one, as you feared before. I say it since it is true and it is right."

"Human." It wasn't a question, but it sounded like one.

"You have made mistakes, given a second chance, forgiven the past offenses and the offenders are no more, learned from the history, looked for your future, lived in the present as best as you can, and changed for the better. Despite what you may believe of me, we are all 'human' in some way."

"Jonny was right. You are pretty good to talk to." I unsteadily smiled.

"I recognize your curiosity of my previous silence, I also know that he considers he has previously articulated to you why that was." She had not moved, but I felt like she should have. She seemed to get closer, until I realized I was the one leaning towards her.

"You *aren't* scary." I told her with a tone to show how extraordinarily stupid I thought that excuse was. She was bizarrely hypnotic, but not *scary*. Brad was actually scarier than her (well not to me but in general.)

"Perhaps not now, nevertheless, I can be. Every instance I have become close enough to a human for the them to grasp at my nature has been at the risk of their fear. Jonathan was too sure of himself, excited, and rather distracted by my exterior to have been apprehensive to any great degree. Shadow was, terrified, not of me in particular, but of her situation, and I was unsure if I were to allow you to know me if you would be unsure as well. I do not judge you now for your questions, because I know no matter how true my words, even if I do not owe you the answers, you do deserve them, at least those I can give." She glanced over, the thin black void around her bronze star eyes shining with the faint light she gave. "Before Shadow, you were the only female of this race I knew closely, and it took me coming to know her, with what of me is within her as an aid in the understanding we have come to know of each other, before I could face you."

"Face me?" I caught myself before I laughed.

"In so many words of this language, yes."

"You could have just told me. I didn't know what to think of you either-course you knew that. You read minds." I said, mainly to myself. She shook her head, frowning.

"I do not look into the minds of those who do not wish it. By nature and instruction, I can know what you are feeling. I do not know what you hold in your consciousness unless I was to look. They have given me permission to observe them, as one might stand at a window above the skyline and attempt to watch all below at once. Never in detail, but enough to ensure their wellbeing. As I told you, even now in dreams I watch them, and on occasion I offer my redirection, should dreams become a nightmare."

"Where the heck were you last year?" I muttered to myself. She stared *at* me, *through* me, and at something else. .

"I have been on this world for nearly three earth-sun-rotations and I would have helped you both sooner had I been able."

"You have?" I asked in disbelief. She nodded, swiping away her hair from her face with one hand, her fingers stalling on her new headband, the oddly human gesture sticking out against her previous stillness. "Oh-I thought you met him at what would be like the earth's customs or something." I honestly had never thought about her being here without him.

"No. I was close to fourteen of your sun's years of age when I left my home. The space you would call distance took me time to cross to come here, even with the aid of the bridges of power between the galaxies. When I arrived, I spent even greater time learning to slow my outward gestures, and mimic them to those of the many cultures here. I did not meet him until my sixteenth year of existence. I have been within his presence for just over twenty of your moon's cycles, though it seems I forget more of my time before him." She was seeing something other than me up until that point. Then she looked at me.

"Wow." I whistled lowly. "We all have a past."

"Since the concept of time came, nothing has been created or destroyed, and no new thing has come to be, Maryanne."

I thought over *all* of it, the memories and guilt reproducing a rate I couldn't hope to combat against. I felt my throat get tighter, the spaces behind my eyes filling with the images I didn't want to see. I couldn't believe I was breaking down; our first real conversation and I just started bawling.

Her hand suddenly grabbed mine.

"Let me help you." She whispered and held my hand tighter.

I felt my mind go gold. Everything I was reliving or thinking about or beating myself up over was gone, all the horrors I was feeling again, the pain I had been forced to endure and the pain I had brought on myself.

Have you learned better? She asked. I nodded, holding back another sob, my shoulders barely able to keep from shaking. *Can you change anything that was done or that you did?* I didn't answer. I couldn't answer. I did want to change it, more than I wanted anything I wanted to redo that one stupid night and every single night that had followed for over a year.

"I wish." I whispered unsteadily. "...I *can't* get over it. I've *tried.* I did what he said – I went back to school and got straight. I got nice friends. I'm even going to church again for goodness sake. And now Jonny is here and it is better but I – I still remember. I still remember abandoning him, getting hooked on all that stuff – just because I can't see the scars anymore... they're still there, they still *hurt.*"

"Even the man this world believes to be its savior bears scars, Maryanne, as do we all." Her warm fingers ran along my forehead. "I did all I knew to do for you, the rest will heal in time, but your wounds are gone, there is no denying that. The demons you face lie within you now, only *you* have the power to overcome them. You are strong enough to win. You can conquer this."

"I can't do it alone." I stared at my wrist, knowing exactly how deep my giving up had gone once.

"You are not alone."

41 Reality?

I rolled out of bed, careful not to trip over Shift. I had heard Star's and Mary's voices from the main room, and the instant the realization came that they were talking, I was conscious. Despite my intentions to learn what had drawn Star out of her silence, my interest on wanting to hear was significantly weaker than my wanting to see her. I silently opened the door, pausing in awe to find her waiting for me. A soft luminescence surrounded her in a layer of pure light. I took her against me, sharing her smile when she flew up to meet me.

"You have no notion to how close I was to asking you similar." She said when my fingers traced the gold band around her head. "I knew not how to even voice it." She shook her head, smiling.

"That's comforting." I hadn't held in full sureness that she would say yes, that her presence was true to the forever she once promised, that it would be spent with me. For once, that unknowing hadn't driven me into madness, but my own sense of desperation, a need to have a right to her that no one, regardless of if they knew us or not, could claim wasn't true. But that had only come after I saw that if everything she had said to me, every hour I had spent struggling to hold onto my humanity with her right there with me, ever touch, was as real as I knew it to be, then there would be proof, not to justify us – but to know that when I looked to her and knew she was mine, and I was hers, nothing inside of me, chosen or forced, my humanity or artificial reason, could argue against it.

It seems I need not the words, after all. For you have them. She laughed, the light coming off her skin increasing, blinding me to everything surrounding us.

"Y-a-awn...Ouch." I pulled my numb hand out from under my head. It felt like I had a million needles stuck in it. I huffed. Supposedly, SG had told me I might have the ability to have conscious control over *every* cell in my body, but that theory hadn't panned out. Even if I had played around with changing race, height, and to some degree, size, even gender (at the very rare and mentally scarring occasion,) fixing a numb hand was beyond me.

Annoying, *mean* light came in through the window. I pulled the blanket over my head. *It's still dark in California...I might-Nah. I have to wake up sometime. ...What...is... that smell? Bacon ... and cinnamon rolls. Who's cooking? Mary? She cooks now? Or is it Shads? I know her mom does but I've never seen her... Stargazer? Does she? No way is it BD. IS IT? Dang it, I gotta' get up now...*

I shifted to a hot spring, then a desert, and finally back to my room. I pulled on a pair of jeans and a clean shirt from the pile on the dresser and pushed my hair back and to the side. It was about as much "primping" as I went for. I walked down the hallway, forgetting for the hundredth time, despite my morning routine, I was above such measly ways of transportation. A really bright light was at the end, as was the source of the smell. I was utterly, completely shocked at what I saw...and instantly less hungry. Well not really, but it wasn't the main thing on my mind.

They're all *cooking!? What did I miss last night!? ...Wow that smells good.*

BD wasn't, obviously, *thankfully*. That would be completely un-Goth superman, but they were still all huddled in the kitchen like some freaky team building exercise with edible rewards. I stumbled in the room. I couldn't decide

360

whether to wake myself up or let this dream go on until I had cleared the table and, well never mind. Shadow might kill me.

"Look who finally decided to wake up." Shads joked. She had a giant bowl of *icing* in her hands. Half my mind was on the food, the hungry part of my brain, and the other half was on Shadow, the teenage boy part. She wasn't in her super crazy, silvery swirled get up, but she made faded jeans and sweater look as sweet as the icing.

"You think you've got enough?"

"She better. I'm out of sugar." Mary was pulling something out of the cabinet. She was holding a plate in one hand that was *full of cinnamon rolls...I might just take one...I wonder if they would notice if I shifted a few of them?*

"I do not have to look into your thoughts. Wait, Shift." Stargazer ordered. I turned behind me. She was sitting on top of the counter, due to lack of space in the kitchen, wearing a red hued dress that hung around her shoulders like a shawl before getting tighter as it went down. *Where does she get all these strange clothes???*

Weirder part- A pan of uncooked eggs was sitting in her lap. She passed her hand above the metal pan. The air *shimmered.* The eggs *moved.* The pan turned to a bright reddish pink. The whole 'I'm dreaming thing' was reinforced.

Well that is a new one. Huh...she can read minds and cook breakfast. I think the cooking part will come in handy more often...and it is a heck of a lot less annoying. What if she's reading me right now? Or when I walked in? OH. MY. GOSH...I'm toast. She'll fry me up the same way she did the eggs! SHUT UP before you kill yourself!

"All is completed." She said a second later. She put the eggs on a large plate and with his *bare* hand, Black Dagger put the pan in the water filled sink. A mountain of steam erupted into the air. Stargazer rolled her eyes for our benefit, putting her hand on his shoulder.

How the heck *did BD do that?! I wonder if I can...I'll try when I don't need both hands to eat...of course Stargazer could heal me.*

"Can I try?"

"Try what?" I had caught him at a rare moment of passiveness, where the question didn't come with enough attitude to make you forget what you asked.

"You just picked up a *red hot* pan with your *bare* hand. *Duh.* I want to see if I can too." Mary's head shot up and her eyes widened, but she didn't interject. He took a while to answer, and when he did I knew I wasn't getting anywhere.

"... You didn't end up anything like me."

"I know, but I *could* do that too."

Your fiancée may be a little bit less of a kill joy.

"*Please* Stargazer." I knew saying please would get her attention. Her smoky gold eyes narrowed. "If you don't help me I'll do it by myself. *Unsupervised.*" (The humanitarian who wasn't a human wouldn't let that happen of course.) Mary looked at both of us, twice. Stargazer looked at Black Dagger. He scowled, before consenting in a nod.

"As you wish, Shift," she said slowly, "but it would be wise to head his warning-"

"Nope." I hadn't heard what she said after saying yes. She sighed, exasperated. I noticed Shadow having a hard time keeping a straight face. *Well that can't be a good thing can it? Or is it?*

Stargazer held her hand out, palm upwards.

I stared, unsure.

"Do you desire to be in pain?"

I took it and I felt her surprising hot, gold skin on mine. It wasn't what else I would have expected, except that it was actually getting *hotter. She's going to test me...on* her! *BD, you have got some serious issues with- Hey- what the-* Her temperature continued to rise. I kept my hand on hers until I couldn't bear the intense, searing pain. I shifted back in a yell.

My palm was bright red. I felt my blood rush to it and that only made the pain worse. *That has to be the most stupid thing I have ever done! I wish Shads didn't see that...Oh my poor hand.*

Mary and Shads were concerned, SG looked guilty for the first time ever, and BD was *amused*. Stargazer grabbed my hand again and although she'd done it tenderly, it still hurt like heck. Her skin felt like *ice* for once and she'd healed me in less than a second.

"I should not have done that." She apologized.

"I asked for it...literally. It looks like I'm really not a whole lot like you, BD. That flipping hurt."

"You should be glad about that." He said under his breath.

I let it pass due to my newly rediscovered focus on the food.

"Need help?"

My eyes were torn. I could watch them cook, watch the food that they cooked, or watch Shads struggle with the last batch of bacon. I know it's hard to believe, but the food won. My hunger was bigger than my humor or my hormones.

I shifted to the table, next to BD. *He* wasn't letting the food win his attention. His eyes never left her. I saw the ring on his hand. I have to admit it was *really* cool. The black part looked like it was moving. *Mercury does that. But isn't it silver?* The dagger was a nice touch too. *Did she make that? It looks alien-ish.*

I came back to full attention when there was suddenly a plate of piping hot food in front of me. I think ate myself into a coma because I don't remember anything after that.

I carefully slid the plate into the dishwasher, noticing that even if she continued to hand the rinsed dishes to me in one of the most seamless, naturally human acts I had ever seen her do, Stargazer wasn't paying attention to anything but Black

Dagger. I don't blame her, I mean she was his fiancée and all, but this guy kind of demanded your attention if you were within a hundred yards of him. It was like what Shift said, 'Goth superman'...sort of.

I would say 'why get married' since I didn't have great experience with the whole marriage thing, but BD and SG were different. In *every* way. One, they were both actually in love, and two; well...neither of them could ever be called average, over everything. Not to mention what I saw – I had to keep it from her at all costs.

"You shouldn't put that there- it will fall on your foot the next time you open the door."

Mary looked up, taken off guard by the sudden break in the silence.

"You come in handy don't you?" Mary decided to put the can of unused frozen juice in the drawer instead of on the shelf.

"She does. Shadow does much more than simply see the future though." Stargazer hummed happily, handing me the last bowl.

I felt myself start to blush at the continuing compliments.

"You do? Like what?!" Mary asked curiously.

"Uh...I can sometimes see the past and other stuff too, but it is kind of random and it doesn't always work... I could be trying to make a black out and actually fry a system, not just shut it down. I am still working out how different energies look and interact, but sometimes I get lucky." I laughed, trying to play it off. The most impressive thing I'd done to date was create a dead zone, meaning no electrical signal that I hadn't personally allowed access to could get in or out, so not satellites, microphones, or even SG's energy radiation could be picked up by outsiders.

"You do a heck of a lot more than that." I jumped at his voice, looking up to find he had gotten up from the table.

He'd his arms wrapped around her and his head on her shoulder. He smiled. I don't think I had ever seen him smile like *that* before.

"She does." She agreed. She kissed the side of his face. I looked at my feet, hiding my instantly flushed cheeks. The tanned Mary was not disturbed in the slightest; my cream skin showed *everything* I thought.

I saw them talking to each other, their faces were blurred against a backdrop of equally hazed, glowing lights of a hundred different colors. It wasn't the first time, so I didn't question why I was seeing it, only what I was seeing. *I'm going to have to ask her about that some time. And what my other power is supposed to be...*

"So...what do you guys want to do until Shift wakes up?" I think he ate five cinnamon rolls all by himself. *He is such a Big Shot, but you feed him and then he is dead for hours. Sad. I wish I didn't kind of... like... him. Eww I thought it!*

"Well, before we take you both back home for school, we have an early birthday present for you Shadow." I looked at Stargazer. BD was still holding her, but she was anything but minding. I was instantly curious. My birthday wasn't for a couple weeks, but I wasn't about to question their timing.

"What is it?!"

She looked up at Black Dagger; he let go of her, pulling something out of his pocket. He handed me a small package.

"It was Shift's idea."

Shift's idea? I opened the box. A bed of small, silver moons/suns were in it. I recognized them as the symbol I had drawn on the corner of my mask.

"Wow...they're beautiful."

"The real gift is what's under them...but you might want to wait."

"Why?"

"Shift wants to be *alive* when you open it." He muttered.

Mary had succeeded in waking him up a second later and he appeared right next to me.

"Go! Open it!" He looked like a kid at Christmas too, a very excited, cute kid.

"Okay! I am!" I pushed the moons out of the way and pulled out a sheer, silver bag. I opened it.

A key! A key to a CAR!!!!

Her energy expanded greatly, filling the room with bright-new-shimmering-essence. "Thank you! Thank you!!! Thank you!" She yelled gleefully.

Shift told us the week before that he wanted us to get that for her, and that her mother was in agreement, at least in theory to his suggestion of it, but that he needed our help to keep it from her. Shift had suffered fairly at keeping the surprise for as long as he did, but his wish to surprise her was strong enough to subdue his expressions and tongue.

She ran up and hugged him before embracing all of us, even Dagger. His energy expanded as well, their mirrored reactions drawing a similar one from my own.

Inferno

I felt the future forming itself from random strands of power. I watched the energy of the 'present' as it melded and formed patterns in my mind. Of the patterns, I discerned groups. Whether the groups formed themselves into families of individuals, situations, actions, or a collection of people, were completely up to them. Each individual strand of energy wrapped around another in unique ways that I had no control over. Of the self-made groups, I managed to see the imprecise pairings of events and places. Of the pairings of places and events and finally people, I made out the timing. All that equaled the *future*.

(Cool huh?)

"What's the game plan Shads?" He was hanging upside down from the roof of our training gym. He had shifted himself onto the massive *ceiling fan* about sixteen feet above me. I was surprised it could hold his weight, and I had debated turning it on, but didn't. Unfortunately, I liked him a little too much to do that and you have no idea how glad I was that he wasn't the mind reader...But Stargazer wasn't much better. *She* knew that *I* knew that *she* knew, which just made it that much more complicated.

"Well, the usual stuff." The 'usual stuff' was a new term for me. Not long ago I didn't see any of it as 'usual'. "But after that everything seems to go up in flames." I didn't give much thought to it, I could never be sure how accurate my visions were. There had been nights where I had woken up from my dreams believing they had been real, and I had even been forced to have Stargazer sort reality from my subconscious more than once, so against better knowing, I didn't put as much thought into the last moments of the vision as I should have.

"Maybe we get the rest of the night off. Go watch that firefighter movie – or a bonfire! I could take us to some random island and we could make the biggest one ever!" He was still upside down; acting like it was natural.

"If you want to go get eaten alive by bugs, that's on you. I just want to get this done. Are you coming down?" I had already got in my 'get up' as Shift called it. I was going to make the most out of my job, including the excuse to wear something that I wouldn't dream of wearing anywhere outside of my old competitions.

"My mind is at a pleasant state of head-rush, so yeah."

He dropped from the ceiling; he'd done a somersault in the air as he did so, showing off. *Impressive- wait! That is what he wants you to think! ...Cut it out!*

"Are we meeting them or...?"

"No. They'll be here in a minute." They'd been gone for a whole day and night before, leaving us to keep busy. *So we could train and study for finals... but I don't mind really...he is nice to hang out with. What am I saying?!*

In my distraction, I had missed the queues leading up to their entrance. I had taken the hike in my heart rate to be from irritation at myself, not from Stargazer being near me.

I jumped when the door shut behind me.

"Let's go!" Shift yelled, already up and ready.

What was that I saw after...maybe we're going out for hibachi...or worse, Shift was right about the bonfire! I'll smell like smoke for days. Ok. Stay focused. Tonight's no big deal...in-out...bad guys in cops' hands, drugs and stuff in evidence locker, and we're done. BD and SG take over a hostage situation in Paris. Shift and I bring a bunch of supplies to the refuges over in the Middle East. I get home for a bath by two. In bed at two forty-five. Piece of cake...if you like cake that could possibly kill you. Killer Cake.

"Shadow..." She looked like she was worried. "I will not allow you to be hurt or taken from us. You should not poison your mind." She put her hand on my shoulder. I *felt* her pulling the negative energy from my body.

"It's nothing. Let's go." I said happily. She looked slightly reassured and allowed me to lead the way up to the roof. Shift would bring BD and I close to the site and Stargazer would follow us, always careful to arrive split second after us. You could just *see* Shift's chest swell and I kid you not his head actually got a little bigger.

-BD-SG S//5▦S▦

The reverberating waves of power bounced off of the outer edges of my own, their vibrations reaching into my conscious mind. I turned my head, searching for their source with my eyes as well as my own inner sight. Dagger had also taken heed, though his was born of the scents in the air, and was manifested by the walls of his mind rising and the muscles of his body tightening in preparation to the threat.

"What is it?" Shift noticed our change, our attentions torn from the last stages of "clean-up" from our previous venture.

Shadow looked to him, and then to us, waiting for my explanation. I felt the release of large amounts of energy in the direction of Dagger's intent-searching-stare. I sensed the *dying* of energy as well. The amount being given off could only be described as *me, my kind...*or for the only type on Earth...

"Fire." He said simply.

"*Up in flames...*" She said to herself. I felt Shadow's sudden tension. Her mind filled with what she was seeing, the visions and sensations tumbling within her in an uncontrolled-unstoppable landslide. She began to shake.

369

His mind was completely level, contradicting theirs.

"Get Shads home. Stay with her. We got this." He ordered, taking only a few seconds to look to Shift to see if it would be heeded, before turning his sights back in the direction of the soot filled wind. He had already calculated the chance of their injury if they were accompanying us, a number-percent that did not weigh in their favor. We had faced such things before, and though they could *help*, the risk of their harm was too great, and I could not shield so many.

Her eyes widened in horror.

"But you can't g-"

"Shadow, we will be all right." I soothed, falsely-believing her terror to be of her own past experience with fire. The illuminations of the ether around them were fluctuating, spiraling into violent shades of red-orange-pain-fear, their magnificent but lethal display distracting me from her pleas. She gave me a pained-fearful expression, pulling away from Shift's reach as he took her by the arm before their bodies were consumed in a burst of spontaneous energy so great it propelled them through space at speeds near rival to my own.

"This blaze is greater in might than anything we have done before." I told him quietly, pressing my mind against the barricades around his own so that I might glean the thoughts hidden with it. "Fire isn't of this world, Dagger." I knew he understood my meaning. *Fire* was the closest thing on the earth that matched my own being, and it, as any release of pure power, was the one thing I could not control completely, for it fed off of the release of other beings and objects, the opposite of where my own originated. It was because of this my teacher had never thought to show me how to manipulate its forces, for in what you call space, fire in the sense it lives on Earth does not exist.

If we were one, this would not hold his life above him. I silently cursed letting my unknowing of how to breach certain-but-inevitable-actions put him in danger.

He nodded and looked at me, the soul-blaze-black-light in his eyes for a brief second before they turned to the stone-hard-iced-black. For like me, his soul seemed to change with his emotion, and so it was that we faced a threat we knew ourselves to be equally yoked with.

◆

The air left bits of burnt substance in my throat that made it hard to call out for the survivors, and at each inhale I could feel the ash settling in my lungs as it had on my skin. The firefighters had been forced to give up nearly ten minutes before, and in that time the blaze had only grown all the more volatile. The inferno was too intense for them to even enter the building by the time we'd arrived. By then, the air itself shimmered. The smoke stung at my eyes, nearly blinding me. I felt the consuming heat of the fire and was uncomfortably reminded of a memory/dream I once had. It was another reminder of what I still had yet to do, something I wasn't looking forward to.

Through half closed eyes I could see her ahead of me, staying close enough that the barrier she had placed around me would remain intact. She spun around when I did my best to call to her. In her hands, she was holding a small, smoke blackened child. Her ash covered face was blank, her fire lit eyes frantic at the impossibility of saving everyone still stranded above us.

"Can you take two more?!" I yelled once I had half a breath. We had given up on our unseen communication, my thoughts were far too scattered to communicate, and it took nearly all of her concentration to keep the flames at bay. She nodded and I gave her the others from the many half engulfed rooms we'd just cleared.

She left and returned in only a few, long heat filled moments.

My mind spun as I calculated the likely location of others by the variations of the fire's path, the sound of their muffled heart beats beneath the continuous roar of the ever growing blaze, and how to reach them the fastest way possible without getting fried. It only took a few seconds for me to know there was very little time left, for any of us, if we remained there. Their heartbeats were too slow, stalled by the loss of oxygen as the fire consumed much of what was in the building. It would only been another few minutes before their unconsciousness became permanent, if the flames didn't reach them first.

I motioned above us; she nodded to confirm. We ran, racing against the fire that chased upwards from the third floor. I heard their struggled breathing underneath the deafening roar of the flames before we reached them. The apartment was nearly consumed, the path to the closet they were hiding in blocked by a toppled shelf, it's entire structure engulfed by the fire. The walls themselves were on fire to my left, and to the right the couch was hell's throne. I was keenly aware of their sudden silence, and the small window of time I had left. There was no way to reach them without walking through it all. I ignored the small amount of self-preservation instinct I still had and went to throw the shelf out of my way, stopping when her icy hand closed around my wrist. She placed the other into the flames, lifting the bookcase and pushing it to our side. The door was thankfully still intact when I opened it. I pulled them out as fast and as pain free for them as I could. One, a woman around thirty, was burnt, not nearly as badly as Shadow had been, but enough to put her in the most danger.

"Star – heal her! I'll take the other one!"

"You cannot go down! The fire is too strong for me to shield you from it if I heal her now! It is at a flash point-I cannot help you!" She yelled desperately amidst the red hot haze, her hands overlapping mine, taking them from me. "We go together!"

I shook my head, my mind pushing the limits of 'being able to solve any problem'. There was over a hundred and seventy feet between me and the ground, the oxygen in the room was forty-two seconds away from being burned up, and

Stargazer's warning of flashpoint meant I had less than a minute to get them out before we all ignited. It would take her longer than that to get us all out.

"No – go now! I'll jump!"

I had never jumped down that far before. Nine stories was my known and tested max, and even then, it hadn't been a pleasant landing. Fifteen was a significantly greater risk, but the state the people were in didn't allow for all of us to fly out together.

"I will not leave you!" She fiercely screamed. She slashed her hand into a bed of flames. Her skin glowed brighter than I thought it should have, as if it was reflecting the fire's light.

"They can't breathe! Go!"

She stepped to me, kissed me harshly, her fraught touch desperate, her skin still shockingly cold against mine.

"I will return for you." She said as she raised her hand, her palm facing a wall that crumbled within seconds of her invisible touch, with her leaving just as quickly as the new, oxygen rich air flooded the room as the fire roared to greater life with it.

I begged that she would not come back.

I stepped towards the opening. Acid air burned my eyes, my throat caught with the ashes. My head was filling with the smoke surrounding us in a wall that blinded me where I could barely see more than a few inches in any direction. The air gleamed, creating walls of mirages that surrounded me in a suffocating vacuum of searing heat, hiding the only escape left. Glass *melted* down the blue and white inferno engulfed wall. The temperature, though never causing me true pain, brought me to my knees. And in suddenly hysterical epiphany, I realized the shield she had given me had broken against the forces around me. Everything became blurred. My thoughts were clumsy from lack of oxygen. My fingers did not bend properly where they had been burned nearly to the bone.

The ground shook and trembled under me, foretelling of the coming cave in.

I made a break for the blazing hole in the side of the building as the floor fell out beneath me in a stomach lurching crash. I held out my hands and caught myself before I slammed into the rising, flame covered ground. The edge of the carpet I clung to was covered in ash and singed at the edges. I pulled my body up to the surface, heeding without caring the burns covering my arms, hands, and stomach, and the increasingly large cinders landing on my back, searing through my clothing into my skin.

There was nowhere to go. Flames engulfed the walls around me, closing in faster and faster as they stole the air from my lungs. I clung to the floor, panting as I struggled to form a thought. If I couldn't get to the opening I had to make it to a window. Even if the glass was melting – I could jump over it and out. I had to get out. I didn't feel it, the fire catching on my clothes, I couldn't, but even that did not give me the ability to rise again.

Get up. Dammit – get up.

I heard the roof cracking before I found the presence of mind to turn towards the sound, its magnitude loud enough to pierce the thunder of the fire, and saw its source crashing down towards me as the walls once holding the roof in place seemed to disintegrate. Everything was in slow motion, a red, yellow, and blue haze of heat and sparks flying down from a hellish sky, giving me bitter time to realize I wasn't cheating death any longer.

STAY AWAY! I shouted. I closed my eyes before the crushing impact and threw my arms around my head. The walls fell with a fury to rival Jericho, the intense heat followed by the cool embrace of nothingness plugging me into perfect darkness. All the horrifying sounds – the boiling air – the suddenness of my fear – the reconciled acceptance – were gone.

I was at *peace*, for reasons I didn't know, and I didn't care to. There was nothing, nothing to influence me, nothing to keep me from being influenced, nothing to even put a name or a thought or an emotion to, and nothing to give me the desire to do any of those things. I did not feel. I did not remember. There was only me, in the truest sense that can be stated, floating through stages of what was surely emptiness; my mind flew freely in and out of my own thoughts. It was as if everything had ceased to matter. I was free, free from the fear that the guilt humanity had tried to put on me, a guilt I had shunned, made me inhuman. Free from the thought that such inhumanity made me a monster. Free from the reality that my only ties were once I fought to keep the darker side of myself from cutting.

There was nothing there anymore. No fear, no shame for being unafraid. There was only a single flaw to the blank slated paradise. I knew something was wrong, that there had been something I was trying to do, someone I had been thinking of before I came to this place, but it was just outside of my reach, at the edge of the allusion. It was shady, this paradise, but light surrounded the darkness, threatening to take it over, a light so bright and alluring that even the instinct it might blind me could not make me turn away.

It was beautiful.

◆

"We have to go back!" She screamed, attempting to pull out of my grip with a frantic dive to the ground. Her hands flew upwards, against me, back down again, failing to make contact with me hard enough to let her go.

"What you see?" I held her arm, struggling more with keeping my head level than keeping her still.

"Nothing... Nothing! There isn't anything to see! She didn't listen! There's nothing to see! Shift, we have to go back!" She pulled against my grip, twisting away and repeating again her hysterical demand. Her cheeks were flushed, her hair tousled, and her eyes wide with what I thought was some remaining fear of her own. I had never seen her lose it. I hadn't

375

even thought she was capable of something so hysterical. I was normally the nutty one.

"They said to stay here." I reminded guardedly. I thought she might have been losing it. SG had told me Shads had a thing against fire, even if she would never admit it. I had gotten her the car to help her overcome a source of it. She and I had even helped evacuate a small store fire once when the babysitters were off doing their own thing and, conceding she'd been a little jumpy, we'd done well. I had never seen her act like *that* before. "I'm sure they're fine, Shads. They know what they're doing without us."

She hung her head, her confusing, multiplying tears leaving me helpless and freaked out. When she finally talked, it wasn't the agreement I had been hoping for. "I can't...I can't see...I can't *feel* her. Shift I can't..." Her voice broke about the same time my faith in them always coming home did. I realized there may be something to this, the bone chilling idea sitting in the pit of my stomach as heat muddled my head.

We have to find them.

I made her look at me by putting my hands on either side of her face. She surprisingly didn't pull away.

"Shads, I need you to breath, okay? Stay sane. Tell me, what did you see? You saw the fire earlier?"

She weakly nodded.

"What did you see after it?"

"Nothing...that's what is wrong. We have to go — now." Her glassy eyes pleaded with me, her hands closing around my wrists.

"Nothing? What do you mean nothing?"

"I can't see them, I can't see. It's *gone*." She held back a sob, her knees shaking. I realized I was the only thing keeping her upright, hugging her as soon as I had. She didn't stop crying, if anything it got worse, but she hugged me back.

"I need you to see, Shads."

376

"I can't feel her…" She whimpered. "We *have* to go. We have to go back."

"We'll go, but you need to calm down. They are going to be fine." My voice struggled to hide my own doubts. I shifted us to the area where we left them.

My jaw went slack.

The mountain of literal mayhem emitted the black smoke, choking us instantly. What once was a burning building was a crumpled, charred void of ruble the size of marbles, standing nearly eight feet high, piles upon piles of soot settling all around it, and …*glitter?* Except it wasn't glitter. Itty bitty pieces of actual *light* shone within the ashes, their radiance like billions of tiny suns buried within the crushed debris. The rising sun hadn't outshone them yet, making the scene all the more unbelievable.

Fire trucks and ambulances circled the perimeter. Some of the vehicles were speeding away, others coming from the sound of the approaching sirens. Unmoving bodies were scattered on the edge of the disaster zone, all at random intervals, even . EMT's were checking their vitals, too busy to notice us. Their constant rush meant the people were still alive, something I found comfort in even if I could feel every hair on my body standing upright with electricity. I wasn't ready to shift, not right then, so I wasn't the source of the buzz.

Shadow fell against me, her eyes rolling in the back of her head. I caught her, shifting us out of the smoke filled dead zone to the other side of the block. Her eyes shot open the moment the air cleared.

"Shift!" She pushed away from me and pointed to a black van that was speeding from us. "S.W.A.T." was painted in big white letters on its side. It wasn't a part of the Emergency Relief. SWAT was notoriously for terrorists, murdering/hostage taking psychos, or one of *us*.

"They've handled them before." I had even been there once, but even more so, I had heard the stories of the governments they had dealt with, and that's not even including the unofficial groups they'd faced in other countries. SWAT was never a good sign for *us* though, not without backup. Those guys were hard core and they worked differently than the cops, which was pretty much all *we* had experience with. I had about a dozen shifts left in me, so I knew we would be fine, but I wasn't letting her out of my sight in case we had to bolt.

She shook her head and pointed to two other vehicles. Their lack of identification spoke more than any big white letter ever could. The *entire* government was in on it. (Unluckily for us, we're the only thing in modern history that all of Washington has ever been able to agree on.)

"They aren't here...*something* is wrong!"

"If they were picked up by the feds, she'll bust them out when it doesn't threaten civilians. She's done it before." It had never been that long, but I wasn't letting panic turn me helpless, yet. She spun in a circle, her feet nearly tripping over each other as she struggled to take in all of our surroundings and the things in them I couldn't see. "Don't go nutty on me. They'll be fine."

"No. No. No. No! We need to find them! I can't feel her!" She screamed, her hands clutched against her stomach.

"Shads – Hey! – Shut up!" Someone was walking towards us, *gun raised*. Eight others followed behind him. One of the SWAT teams hadn't packed up yet, and her get up might as well have been a spotlight on our wanted poster.

I grabbed her arm and took us away, landing back in the living room we had left only two minutes before, even if it felt like hours.

"We ha-!"

"No! I'm not letting you get taken too! We can't be out in the open. We're laying low, understand? No direct contact. We stick to their rules. We stay safe. We're not going back there. Find them Shads, just see if they're all right."

"I ca-"

"You *have* to."

She broke, falling to her knees, her head in her hands. I was too stunned to have caught her. I had stumbled back, her surrender as terrifying as if it was my own. I hadn't let it sink in, not entirely, that her panic attack was justified. They'd dealt with some serious situations before, but if she was that petrified that she couldn't even stand up... *What if it really is this bad? If they're –*

"I can't – I can't – I *can't*!" Each sentence grew more desperate, her fingers lodging deeper into her curls with frustration. "She's not there...not there...I can't. I...I can't *see*!" She shouted into the carpet, her scream only partially muted by her sobbing. I stared, unsure of what to do, and it didn't seem temporary. I couldn't think to move, my head was going so fast over everything we had seen that the world was put in slow motion. I finally sat down next to her, putting an arm over her, but it was another five minutes of helplessly watching her cry before I managed to swallow my own fears enough to speak.

"Listen to me Shads. You're a kickass alien side effect who can shut down freaking satellites. You don't get to freak out now. If they're in trouble, we are all they have, and heaven help whoever has them when we come for them. I mean it, if I have to search every single square mile of the planet – I will. We are going to find them."

"*How*?" She sat up, my pep talk failing to convince her.

"Can you see the number for their FBI guy?"

She looked up, her puffy eyes blinking in surprise before closing again. I waited. Gold disks were useless to us, but if I could get a number or an address, we would have an in. After a few minutes she opened her hand. I passed her my burner.

I entered the numbers, handing it back to him. I couldn't breathe deep enough to talk, not even to ask what he was planning. If I did I would break down again. I had to stay strong – like he was – we had to find them. I had to be able to feel her again. I had to see her. I had to be able to find him. I had to know they were okay. I had to bring them home. I had to be able to see. I had to be able to find her.

His voice cut through my panic filled mantra. I didn't know what I hadn't heard, only that what I did wasn't promising. My heart vibrated when I saw the colors around him a deeper red than I thought he could ever possibly be surrounded by.

"*No.* You listen to me. Don't give me that crap. – I don't care if you don't know, find out. Now. – No. – I'm not giving you a choice. – *Clearance*!? – If I have to go in front of every news station as the freaking president and publicly demand that they be released then I will. – No I don't believe you, why would I? — Yes. –Then find the (freak) out and do it now! – Oh you caught on? Yes, I'm threatening you! I will threaten the whole damned government if I have to! I will reveal you've been our contact. I'll call out every underground op we have evidence on. I will make (flipping) George Washington come out of the grave to tell everyone you've taken them! – If not the FBI then the CIA. SOMEONE has them then! *Find out*!"

He paused when he saw me staring.

"What? No! If I have to call the director or the freaking anchor of CNN I will. I'll go live right now. You think I won't? – I know you have them! – FIND OUT! They trusted you and you're telling me your hands are tied! They saved your life dammit and you're just going to sit there and (freaking) tell me you can't find out if the biggest (freaking) capture of the millennia was made today! Call someone! – Who?! How the (freak) do I know! – You're the one they trusted! They – I will find them on my own – YES I will go public. Try to stop me, go ahead! If you can't freaking tell me who has them I will drag it out into the daylight. –Yes that is a (freaking) threat!"

The shouting escalated, ending only when the phone was a pile of broken glass and bent metal imbedded in the wall across the room. Shift glared at it, before falling into the couch, staring at the ceiling. I couldn't find the strength to get up again, as if moving was going to help me see her, feel her.

"You didn't need to hear that." His voice was level, but I knew I wasn't the only one struggling to breathe. The color around him was nearly that of a bruise. I forced myself upright, even if that only meant crawling the foot between the couch and I and pulling myself up to sit next to him. It was emptiness that I saw, that I felt, that consumed me from my stomach out until I wasn't even sure I was really sitting next to him. The last thing I remember I was standing a few feet in front of us. I could have still been there, begging him to take me back there, for all the good my brain could see reality.

I shuddered, leaning back until the ceiling was the only thing blocking both of us from leaping off the edge of insanity.

"I can't...I can't see him. Or her. I can't feel – I always feel her, she's inside of me – but I can't. Shift...I'm scar-"

"Don't. Don't say it."

He looked to me, his hand opening against his knee in invitation.

"Don't say it Shads. We're going to find them."

Insurgence

Another jolt was sent through me, starting at the holds they bound me with, with flashes of pain-heat-light entering through my hands and scorching through to the edges of my tangible form. I closed my eyes, focusing all my sight on what they could not see, gritting what appeared to be my teeth as I fought to make the energy mine so it could not hurt me, altering its currents to mirror my own in a frantic attempt to sway its destructive course.

Far more times than I remember or care to ever think of again, I could not do it fast enough, leaving the energy free to plow through me, unencumbered, unstopped by any feeble resistance I had to effect its path, and I was far too weak to fight back. It had taken all I had to destroy the fire, and in the expanse of time since, my influence over the power within me had barely begun to recover. If they had given me more than a few moments of respite, I could have become light and left, but in the mere microseconds that would pass since my thoughts cleared, I was already facing the next sequence, where each pulse of ever increasing power lit into me like lightning, surging in a relentless torrent until my very essence was scorched with the foreign energy forcing its way in.

Whatever vitality of body and presence of mind I managed to spare from their pulsating-rapid-spark-agony, I poured into Dagger, in the hope to heal him before he became conscious, knowing the injuries he had endured were too great for the artificial barriers in his mind to block the pain much longer. I longed to touch him, for it would mend his wounds much faster than my unseen contact allowed, as much as a trickle of water left dripping from an unclosed screw-tunnel faucet is to a waterfall falling over mile high cliffs, but even at such a painstakingly dawdling pace, and even if it made them question and understand his nature or my own to greater depths, I had to heal him.

What could have been hours passed this way, each torturous second drowning me under a sea of delusion, every minute leaving me further separated from reality as I fought the power-that-was-not-natural threatening to 'short circuit' my own. My one sanity was the faint presence of his mind, untouched by the chaos consuming us both. It was all that gave me the will and strength to endure, no matter how long this hades went on.

"Stop." A low, controlled voice commanded.

I tried to lift my head, and found I did not have the strength. I could not even become light, for so great were my wounds they could not see that to let my power pulse through me and return me to light would be to let it go without paths to follow, for their torturous-shocks had shattered the paths within me as a crashing of tectonic plates beneath the ground crumbles what lies above.

"Let her down."

I thought it was only a test, so when the power-fielded-man-made-metal shackles around my wrists and ankles released and the ground-incapable-of-conducting-power swiftly rushed up to meet me, I could not catch myself.

Tangibility was a foolish thing to want. I cursed as my body shuddered in exhaustion and quivered with what I can only describe as absolute pain, not that which warns you of incoming permanent harm, but that which begs you to surrender because of it.

I poured as much power as I could spare into Dagger, knowing this respite to be short lived. He was gaining awareness, and his wounds were too great to survive if he knew them to exist. His mind, however altered, would sense a danger so great his body would increase its chemical-epinephrine levels so great that his heart would be overwhelmed. I had held them at bay from touching him until then, but I knew that too, was going to be short in its life. I dropped the barrier that had kept their bodies from coming near his, using the power that had made it to urge his body to heal, even as my mind reached for his, easing his rise into awareness once more.

I slowly pushed my hands beneath my chest, attempting to close the course of my own energy by placing my palms together, knowing that simple motion would give me the might to flee. Pressure suddenly crushed me, keeping my physical body close to the floor. I realized it was a strong magnet holding me down, the remaining clamps around my waist, legs, and forearms pulled into its electronic force.

I will not be made to bow before such insolence!

"Stargazer, I am apologetic of the way you've been treated. I had hoped you would not have been so violent in your resistance. Surely, you understand the precautions we have taken. You pose quite a threat, and until that threat is neutralized, I'm afraid civility is out of reach."

You certainly will be remorseful as soon as I can stand, you mindless-sack-of-carbon.

"However, I would very much like to speak with you, in a more polite manner."

I held my tongue. The weakness of my state and the unknowing of Dagger's full situation meant I must to humor them. My mind was barely clear enough to think its own thoughts, so breaking into his was far out of my grasp.

"...Is this how you treat your protectors?" I lifted my head, straining to see whom I spoke to through the clear, enhanced-glass-like-but-not-glass case I was surrounded by.

"We only want to speak with you Stargazer. We had to make sure you wouldn't attack us first. The threat you pose isn't something we can allow. We seek only your answers and cooperation at this time." His grey tinted hair, dark skin, and yellow power molded into the other colors of the room as my vision flickered.

384

"I do not *submit* to you."

"It would be in both our best interests, and his, for you to listen to us, Stargazer. I have been sent by the President to speak to you on behalf of the entire United States Government and certain countries within the UN. Your existence has become an international concern, one that we hope to solve today, with your assistance, of course."

"Your standing is meaningless." I growled, growing tired of such words-terms-titles that they were petty enough to believe gave them power. "I am not a citizen of this world and I refuse to bow to you!" The magnet increased, as did the shock waves when they mistook my vow for a threat. I fought it, recognizing the slipping away of time as my mind searching frantically for Shadow's. The tendrils of her energy were greater than ever before, reaching out far beyond what I had known her to be capable of, for her desire to find me equal as mine to hers. *Tell Shift. Get him. He's* here. *Tell Shift. Get him now.* I spoke, hoping that despite her panic, she recognized my voice.

"Stargazer, you of all people – or should I say – beings – understand just how hypocritical that statement is. We have been aware for quite some time now your history here, so let's not pretend this is not necessary measures."

"No - It is *you* who bow. You *chose* to make false gods." I spat, feeling my reason slipping in the bolts that lit through every course of my power. "I did not…choose that. You did. You crave to be overcome, you elect those in power … you believe a system is the only way to survive, that ranks are made to keep you safe…in line. Y-You speak of liberty, yet seek out idols among your own to prostrate yourself before. …You shout equality – B…but exalt those of petty qualities to places of adulation, and crucify any who question who is the mass that you follow blindly. Jus…Justice – you preach justice but justice is nothing…nothing more than your own tainted perceptions. You let your young live in want but pay the way for the transgressors, you beg…g for integrity but shun anyone

...who speaks against the will of the common, you let your old die of negligence while pretending...to be immortal. Your short lives are spent serving beneath the gods you anointed, ones you claim to be evil... but offer your bodies and minds to each choice you make, greed...lust...*murder*."

"Be rational Stargazer."

If you wanted me to be rational, you should have thought twice about taking him from me. Somewhere in the endlessness of their cruelty, I had learned they had already discovered the proof of Dagger's human-yet-completely-organic nature long before, and for months had been studying the internal codes hid body ran on from the samples of the protein-spun-cells that made his body, and I could feel their minds edging closer to seeking its source, a process that could only end in his death. They would not give him up so easily, no more than they would ever let us go. They would end him before they let him leave, even if it meant reducing their chances of replication of him.

I struggled to regain my strength before the next jolt came. I was inside of it – this machine-chamber – denied any escape, and the reality of the volatile nature of that situation sunk through the faltering walls of my consciousness. The massive force whirring behind me sparked and snapped just before it came, like a star narrowed down to a needle point, cutting into me with the force of a Supernova.

Would it not have given them the satisfaction of my pain, I would have screamed.

His voice became sharper, to be heard over the hiss.

"We are not the one responsible for more bloodshed than any war we have created among ourselves, all wars combined even, and that blood is on *your* hands. We're neither blind nor ignorant to myths based on truths. *You* are the threat to humanity, us, and we are to see to it that it is neutralized. You are the greatest threat. You – not us."

"I am not!" I exclaimed, shaking my head.

"Explain that then." He pointed to a screen on the wall furthest from me, in a room I had not noticed before, for my existence was so consumed with the false light overpowering my own. Then I saw what it's flat expanse held. The building-once-burning lay in ruins. Bodies, alive or dead I could not tell, were scattered across the ground. Ash fell like black rain. I knew what it was, and I did not find the reasons to deny it, for in those moments I knew not the extent of my actions, and if that was their result...

"They cannot be dead..." I whispered, hiding my face in the floor, overcome with life-draining guilt. They image stirred my memories, a billion other views eating away at me as acid-to-flesh. Their blood red eyes and mangled bodies, sacrificed on alters made from the very substance that created my own physical existence, displayed as an erubescent canvas of chaos, uncovered by centuries of time, brought me to the edge of collapse. I had given my life to write the wrongs of my people's past, and yet I was writing myself into it.

My determination to escape fading with the last of my ability to fight against the pull on me, I let the power-not-mine burn through me, surrendering as it burned like hell-fire. In mindless submission, I whimpered a silent apology to Dagger for being as weak as to let them do this to me, for not keeping us safe, but I was so tired, tired of fighting, tired of the constant battle to prove myself and my motives, tired of living in the shadow of the dead, tired of fighting to belong – tired of fighting to prove someone wrong. Shift would take him home – they would be safe – that was enough. All I wanted was to disappear, to melt into that cold not-metal-magnet floor, to never have to face another judgment.

"They cannot be dead..." I whispered.

"You are to remain in our custody until the manner of your incarceration is decided upon. There are crimes you must answer for, and if you refuse to cooperate, then he will suffer the consequences." More than a dozen eyes rested on me, waiting for me to move.

Dagger.

My hands flexed with the pulsing currents they shot through me.

The dark satisfaction at the bitterly hostile epiphany their words and his name had given me carved across my face, my lips rising in a sneer at the lethal mistake they had made, one I finally recognized. They had given me the excuse; they had hurt me – They threatened the same for he who I loved. For many years, I had yearned with a determined-resolved-hatred to show them what I was – what power I welded. The desire had been buried beneath the arguments of right-to-power, of lack of provocation, of my own resolve to not be feared. Each of these things were no more, burned by their false power and false sense of it. They were going to know who, what, manner of being they had attempted-dared to tame-detain, and they would suffer greatly for it. And not even my vows could stop me.

I reached out to Dagger, knowing the moments were few until the first battle began.

I pushed myself up to my hands and knees, fighting against the pull to earth and the shocks of their synthetic energy, searching for the vitality I needed within, feeding off of my anger at the deepest parts of me. I tore out of the magnet's pull, locking my hands together, feeling the seared edges of my being connect once again. Light poured into me from within the hidden alcoves of my being, every piece of who and what I was brought into the front of the war I faced.

Slowly, I rose to my feet, floating a foot above the cement-ground.

Their expressions became pale underneath their lead-plated coverings.

I lifted my head, moving my gaze slowly across the room. Every speck of inorganic matter my gaze met broke into individual molecules, torn from their forms until they fell as piles of microscopic dust lying where objects once stood. The air around me ceased to exist, a burning void filling wherever my power reached. Those who had stood beside the machines they believed capable of taming me were thrown to the ground, their bodies held to it as mine had been, bowing as they had forced me to bow.

◆

STARGAZER! I opened my eyes to white surgical lights above me. I looked down and saw I was restrained with metal bars.

You've got to be kidding.

I wasn't being held by the company, of that I was sure and immensely thankful for. Had I been, they would have known better than to leave me like this, considering it was far from the first time I had bested such restraints. But that left a variable unanswered. If it wasn't the people responsible for me, then it was someone else who wanted to control me, and of that list there were many, and none of them were less formidable than the others.

...Stargazer! Where is she?! Did she stay out of there?! Is she hurt?! Is she okay?!

...Peace.

Star! Thank God. What happened?!

Be still. ...You are under observation.

Where are you? What happened? ...You came back?! Where am I? Another unwanted déjà vu. *I told you to stay away from me! You could have gotten hurt!*

You would have perished. ...Do not cause a reason...for them to drug you again.

What happened?

Are...Are you in pain?

No. I realized then how soft her presence was, even compared to my prior version of panic. *What's wrong? Are you hurt?* The weakness of her *mind* was unlike anything I had

389

known could happen to her. Her ever-present gold had faded, and her question was one she could have found the answer to herself in fractions of a second by simply looking at what laid behind my thoughts.

I had to destroy the... fire's life...It would have killed you. I would not leave you... What you saw was my mind...I held you there. It was the only way to protect you from what I did to the fire... I couldn't hold it...we were buried by that which had fallen... ...Keeping you within me was the only way to heal you from afar. I was helpless to those who found us. I couldn't deny the shade her mind has darkened. *I could not fight them Dagger. Watching you be taken from me was extremely...trying.*

Thank you – What is going on, are you safe?

They will face their consequences. A flash of her mind slipped, a brief moment of strange blue light and crashing sound echoed in my head, before she hid it again.

What was that?

They are testing me. Her mind took on a motion I can only describe as panting, expanding and decreasing much too fast.

Who are 'they'? I fumed.

The United States Government. And others. They will not dare to try this once more.

What are we going to do? Star? I asked, sensing the sharp edge her mind took.

No – they are mine.

You c-

Do not come for me.

Then she was gone.

I opened my eyes again, having only a few seconds to take in the blinding white light above me before a whisper of air from behind gave him away.

"Take me t-"

He reeled away from Shift, his eyes livid.

"Where are we?!" He demanded, his jaw clenched.

Shift stepped back, in front of me. I had no idea where we were, actually, but we were safe, and SG had told me to get them safe, so that's all I knew. It was all I was able to think about once I had stopped shaking.

Shift had chosen the spot. It looked like it was in a condemned building, void of any surveillance. And secluded enough that if BD flipped, the damage wouldn't stick out, I realized with a gulp. The surprising clean room was void of everything but a bed. A small kitchen and bathroom were off to the side. I realized it was one of Shift's safe zones we would use to hide people who helped us before setting them up somewhere new by the lingering energies and the pasts that went to them.

"She doesn't want us there. She told Shads where you were and for me to get you – so I did. That's all I know." He tried to explain, pushing me farther away from BD's rage.

Black Dagger cursed and threatened him, vowing that if Shift didn't take him back he'd be sorry, in a manner of words. I don't remember exactly what they were but in the efforts to keep this book PG-13 we'll just say he was absolutely livid. I did all I could to softened the edges of the power flying off of him like a firecracker held too long before being thrown, and right then he just as dangerous as one.

"I can't!" Shift looked to me, finding my expression unmoved by BD's threats. There was only one thing I was afraid of, and it was not him.

"I swear to you if you don't I will-"

"She needs to know you're safe." I whispered. He paused, glaring black eyes then on me. "Yell at us all you want, but she told me to and Shift to keep you safe, so we did."

"That works both ways." He stated, flexing his hands. "Listen –

"If she wanted us there she would h-"

"I am not asking you, Shadow. I am telling you I am not going to freaking sit here while they do whatever they want to her! They were *hurting* her! Don't you get it?! She could be trapped! Something is wrong – she wasn't thinking straight. We are not *leaving* her there!" He was desperate now.

I touched Shift's shoulder.

"He's telling the truth." I whispered. I hadn't tried to see, I never could see their conversations between their minds, but it was the first time the colors around him were as steep in contrast as mine or Shift's and I could feel his fear just like I could feel Shift's.

BD's furious eyes narrowed.

"Shift..." Black Dagger rivaled her threatening with his own.

He sighed, rubbing his hand over his face.

"She's gonna to fry me..." He moaned.

*Star...*I raced down the hallway. Alarms continued to sound and I heard people following me. *Where are you?* No answer.

Someone attempted to shoot me again. I was certain that ducking and running was the best option, but I do not lie when I say that almost every part of me revolted at the idea, causing me actually physical pain at each step I made.

A group of soldiers gathered to block me off.

"We have orders," one of them said loudly, "to shoot you if you don't cooperate with us. You are now under my custody."

I turned partially. That whole 'cooperate' thing had done in my barely existent patience. I remembered hearing it echo in Star's mind, and it was that word she had tied to the flash of blue light that had caused her what I then knew to be pain.

"Who -ah keep your hands up where I can see them!" The men and women around him raised their weapons a little higher. Their franticly beating hearts hummed. "I will not ask you again."

I glared at him, more worried about the threats whispering inside my head than the loud mouthed one outside of it.

I looked at the multiple personnel next to him.

"We're still on the same side."

Some of the younger ones smirked and one even nodded in what I took to be permission. I dropped the small container I had pulled from my belt, military grade tear gas, released its contents, and kept going, immune to the agony they had been caught in.

I looked to the side, feeling the slight displacements of air hit my skin every handful of seconds. Shift was moving in order to keep up.

"Get out of here." I growled, still livid at him.

"That wasn't my idea to take you out okay? I didn't want solo – We are *not* doing that again. We're a team. No more ditching."

"You know where she is?"

"You aren't talking to her?" He asked, surprised.

"Can't." I muttered. He grimaced, not liking that any more than I did.

"Keep an eye out for Shads up ahead. She's working on shutting down the system. I'm going to look for SG."

"Thanks."

He nodded and disappeared.

I saw her waiting. She could keep up with me, or I could keep up with her.

"Seven minutes to eclipse."

I nodded. Eclipse was her own code for a black out – not in the sense that the power would be cut, but that she would stop it from connecting to anything within range. Any waves of information would come to a halt, leaving them completely powerless. She had been working on it for the last half an hour, ever since Star had told them where we were being kept. I didn't trust her time estimate, but it would help us, whenever it happened.

Then we saw the wall – a giant, metal door closing ahead of us, and I could hear the ones behind us. We were trapped. I wasn't surprised they had this kind of security, only that it had taken them that long to get it in place. Shadow would render it worthless soon enough, we only had to buy time.

A new future formed itself; the power I had been following was consumed by what looked to be an explosion. I didn't try to figure out why. I stopped asking why when things I saw scared me, and I was terrified.

BD stared at me, waiting for an explanation as to why I had stopped breathing.

"Up! We need to go up NOW!"

Shift appeared a moment later. His panicked face dripped with sweat, terror burning behind his altered eyes.

"We have to get out of here!" He grabbed us and the next moment we were at 'ground level'. BD spun away, eyes darting for danger. Shift stumbled back, his gaze spacey and glazed. "Don't – don't try to – f-find her." He panted, as he leaned against the wall for support.

"Why are we up here?!" He demanded, oblivious to Shift's sudden and complete exhaustion. I grabbed his arm, holding him upright. I forced my influence over the signals in the air out even further, in hopes to shut things down sooner.

"She's changed the whole thing – all of it – I couldn't get back, I was *stuck*. …I was *stuck*. I don't even know – I couldn't land – I was falling and I was stuck – somehow – between here and there… Something's *wrong*. …We need to get out. *Now.* Shads, please. Tell him." Shift looked at me, begging me to support him in this.

Then I saw what he was talking about and felt the blood drain from my face. I turned to BD, ready to beg that he come with us. Right as I did so, the ground shook beneath us. I braced Shift, nearly falling to the ground when he was too weak to hold his own anymore. Even Black Dagger had to catch himself from the after-shock. The lights flickered before going out, and it wasn't from my planned black out. I could feel the waves of power in the air still, radio, Bluetooth, cell phone signals. I had spent nearly forty minutes locking in on their sources to shut them down, but I hadn't finished yet. So it wasn't me.

I turned behind me, looking for the source of the newly blaring beam. Stargazer walked up to us, the form of a white-hot orb of light that expanded nearly three inches around her. Her eyes were empty, sucking in the light around them like a black hole. Her face was a cold slate, her empty glare burning hot enough to melt metal, which, I would later find out, it had.

I closed every open end of my power, knowing if it came into contact with hers I would be rendered helpless.

BD looked *scared*...something he *never* once done. He hadn't moved, and his stillness was terrifying. He had no idea what to do either.

"Star..." He said soothingly. Her eyes lightened, returning to a shape we could see, but she did not cool off. I glanced at all three of them, in the process realizing we were at some nuke plant that apparently was the cover for the feds' superhero torture chamber. I know you are like 'how can *you* not know where you are? You're the one who got everyone there!' but I had only gotten to there by Shadow telling me the latitude and longitude of the place. I didn't like geography even if it had somehow been formatted in my head. (Science Experiment props.)

"We're ok...I'm safe, we're all safe." He smiled slightly. He didn't look as scared anymore. Shadow did though. Same as I had leaned on her only moments before, she then leaned on me, standing between SG and I in what I was shocked to see as a shield.

Stargazer shook her head.

"No. It is not. They are not going to be granted my grace any longer. I, we, have put up with enough of their tricks. You have suffered in fear of being captured, you all have, but no further. They will not, cannot do what they wished to and not answer for it. Leave me to this. Thiers is the evil worst of all, for it believes itself righteous, even the blood on their palms is seen as a seal of their justification. If it is my submission they seek, they will find they are not the only ones with the power of the stars." Her icy voice rang.

"Star, you told me we aren't their judge, that it isn't up to us, or you. Let's just go home."

She didn't move, her calm more unnerving than if she'd raised her fist or shook her head or even yelled at him. "No, Dagger. They seek to make themselves gods of war, of death, of power. If I must become one of the beasts they grovel at the base of the altar of darkness to become, if only to end them, I shall. I will no longer pretend to be something I am not, for I am not under their control. I came here to save them and if it is from themselves so be it."

He stepped closer to her, reaching out.

She floated back.

"They will not get away with this! They want us as marionettes in their games. They want you to build their army, and I to destroy any who stand against them. They wish *death*, Dagger. I will not let that happen!" She growled, the light around her expanding another few inches, preventing him from touching her.

What did they do to her...? Despite the fact I was so tired even breathing hurt, I knew I should take us all out of there, before she or anyone else did something stupid, but

396

knowing that and having the ability to make myself do it are different. I wasn't even sure I could. My shifting uses power, and had I come in contact with hers again that day, I doubted I would survive. I had barely made it out the first time.

"Stargazer, listen to me, listen to yourself. Come home – stay with me, don't do this."

"They cannot get away with this." She whispered in what sounded like defense.

"Don't. For me. Don't."

"For you is why I do this." She turned and ran down a wide hallway, disappearing into her light a second later.

"Where is she going?"

"The Pentagon. Go. Now." He stated flatly.

I did. Don't ask me how he knew, or how I managed it, or why he'd known, or who the guy really was that you'll meet next paragraph, but I did.

◆

"W-what do you want?! What's going on?!" He quaked. I smiled, despite the growing-ever-darker mass within me. The country who had ordered our 'abduction' would forever more fear one from me.

"An invasion, if it pleases you." I told him, raising him slightly higher.

"An in...in –invasion?" His voice quavered.

"Do not push me *human*." I threatened, tossing him back in his chair with a wall of unseen power – my power – power he had no right to control or dominate. His face paled. "I have shown you my supremacy over the place you deemed capable of holding me, the chains you attempted to bind me with now lay in ruins at the altar you once believed to be a throne."

I let my energy flow to my surface, causing me to glow brightly, though my eyes were blackening by the moment. I felt his energy weaken, but I did not take pity on him, he should know what, who was against him, and what his actions would cost.

"You thought you could break me, force me into your weapon, your servant, and at the cost of his life you deemed I treasured more than my own. You believed I would have obeyed every whim of your petty concerns, if only to spare him your wrath. But first, you wanted to know what breed of beast you had on your leash. You wanted to see the extent of my power? Who am I not to oblige, but, I will offer you a greater gift; I will let you experience it."

His skin turned red with the radiation I emitted.

"You don't know who-what you are t-talking about!" He screamed.

"I will *not* be taken from his side nor he from mine again. No matter the implications for me or *you*. If it costs me my very soul I will end you before any of the plans you deemed to force upon us can be completed. Do I not speak clearly enough? Have you not heard me? I will not submit to *you*."

Even as I spoke, I felt him reaching for a button that would send for help for him and for forces to overpower me. I saw in his mind the devices he held for us, the orders and tests and things of this world so dark I dare not speak of...Of torture and of pain, of things of Dagger and of I, of Shift and Shadow, of things he had done to others in the past who posed a 'threat' to him. Of the plans he had when he discovered the 'source of our abilities' and the ways they could be corrupted or manipulated. The darkness of his mind and the minds of those he had once interacted with was not like anything else. It did not try to seep into my power – it attacked it. What made it so dangerous was that he believed such things for the good, his reasoning found to be meaningless the blackness of his actions.

I grabbed his wrist, searing the symbols that represented my race into his skin, every cell in his body altering as my energy forced itself into him by the same means he had subjected me to only minutes before. He cried out in pain, falling to his knees. I held him tighter, feeling his bones crack underneath my grip, his blood pumping furiously through the thin channels beneath his skin, his lungs held frozen in terror.

"For all you have done, you will suffer this." I said over his cries. "You are separated from your race forever more. The marks you bear will be a symbol of your treason against an ancient deity pact between the very power in my being and with the blood running in yours. If you ever try to hurt me, or mine, again, if you ever seek us as ploys in your wars, the consequences will be far worse than these petty scars." I tossed him aside, my mind separate from my spirit. He clutched his forearm, even as the veins in his body bulged and became purple snakes under his skin.

"You will not get away with this..." He whispered, blood coated eyes holding mine, defiant. He would not heed my warning.

"No. You began this conflict. I am ending it." I took a step towards him, seizing his shoulder.

◆

The moment my skin touched her bone searing surface as I locked my arms around her, she fell cold, silent. She refrained from fighting back when I pulled her away, but whether she had known it was me, I didn't know. The answer to that held two distinct realities, either she had allowed herself to be stopped by any with the ability, or my presence had forced her to by placing myself in the direction of her rage. Each was equally lethal.

In a blur of the man's screaming, Shift's gagging, and Shadow's frantic attempt to flee lest she faint at the sight of him, he had fallen unconscious. In the sudden motionlessness after the storm, everything became eerily quiet.

We stared, speechless. She stood rigid in my grasp, equal to Shadow and Shift, who were equally immobile, their expressions horrified by the sight of the man, completely unrecognizable even to be human. His body appeared to have boiled beneath his skin, but it refused to burst. His eyes were black, even the whites of them lost in the darkness too deep for even me to make a distinction within.

"*What* the freaking *hell*?!" Shift shrilled, staring in revulsion. He took a step back, pulling Shadow behind him in a swift, unyielding jerk. Her only response was to grab his hand with her own, her heartbeat humming against the insides of her chest. Her blank, frightened eyes met mine for a moment, not daring to look at Stargazer.

"What did you *do*?" He yelled again.

I wasn't thinking enough to tell him to shut up. My sole focus was keeping her contained, but I too edged away from the barely breathing mass lying on the ground, as I held her tighter, fearing the fact she could leave any time she wanted.

"Release me." She ordered, remaining perfectly still under my weight.

"No."

"Release. Me. Now." Her words were deliberate, each of her carefully chosen pauses emphasizing the power behind them.

"*No*." She knew I wouldn't let go unless I had to, and for it to come to that, she'd have to kill me. I wasn't letting her go otherwise.

I felt her move in my hold, her back losing its rigidity against my chest and her hands falling from the fists they had been bound in since the moment I had seized her. A softer, apologetic tone replaced the arctic edge of her voice at her next words.

"Dagger, let me right this wrong, before it hurts them more." She whispered.

"I can't let you run."

"And I cannot let him die, not in your presence."

"And if I were to leave?"

She hesitated, turning her head when I tried to look at her.

"…I swear to you, I shall not kill him."

I freed her, heeding the way she wavered, never meeting anyone's eyes. She grazed the man's swollen hand with the tips of her fingers, and just like that, he was normal, his body, down to the perfectly rhythmic reverberations of his heart, returned to perfect health, his gaze as wide and alert as ours were.

"You are to never seek after any of us again, or else I will leave you with a wound far more painful than this memory. Tell your superiors. Tell whoever you please. Tell them what happens when they attempt to domesticate a deity beyond their comprehension. Tell them what you have seen. And tell them if they ever come for us again it will be the world that knows what you now know." She ordered, before turning and walking out of the door with an ease that only added to their terror, a terror I knew that I was spared from if only to parlay on the behalf of all humanity.

I stepped back through the doorway, finding her gone.

"Where is she?!" I turned to Shadow, who retreated at my escalating frenzy.

"…I don't know." She whispered, cowering behind Shift.

"We're going home." He threw himself against me before I could push him aside. The pale walls we were surrounded by a moment later were as much their sanctuary as they were my prison.

"Where is she Shadow?" I demanded again, my voice rising with my fear.

"I...I don't know." She took a step back, pinning herself between my body and the wall, her arms raised to her sides as if in surrender. "I can't – I don't see her. I can't..."

"Then *find her*." I ordered.

"I'm trying to!"

"Hey! Back off BD." Shift put his hand on my chest, placing himself between Shadow and I. "Stand down." He glared. He had shifted back to his normal state, glaring at me in warning. Shadow trembled behind him, her hands clinched against the sides of her head.

"Enough." Her voice cut through the fear laced air like a razor blade, its piercing edge marked by their retreat at it.

"Enough." I said, as the black wind-tunnel-storm like power about him fell still, the yellow tinted wall around Shift and the scarlet throbbing of Shadow's terror filled pain following the path he had set. When the lights around them had dimmed, I fought to find the courage to face them, materializing my tangible form in the midst of the dying anarchy.

"You – *You* – what did you do?! What was that?! What on earth was *that*?!" Only once I looked up did Shift allow himself to explode, his body shaking and weak as he stood, but his mind determined for one purpose, keeping her safe, from anything, and anyone. *He is scared of me*. His very power-life-force screamed it, even louder than his words had.

I closed my eyes to keep Dagger from seeing my blackened soul any longer. I had gone so long without their *fear*. I had fallen into the lie that perhaps I was different, that I was not an ethereal might to be dreaded but a healer to be imitated, and that my resolution of my path was here and it was good. Being accepted by humans was the comfort that exceeded even that of the stars, but another truth was in birth, one so horrid it left me near collapse. *What if this has changed everything?*

"Explain, Stargazer." Shadow had held her peace, but when Shift's accusations had subsided, her single demand was the hardest action I could have taken in that moment.

"...I had to...to stop them. He wished to separate us from each other. I would not permit that. I had to stop them, from trying – from taking any of you." I whispered, fighting back the terrors I had seen in his mind and the terror that had consumed my own. I could not explain to them the drive that had overcome me in the wake of their torment, for the power they had forced into my own was equal to me as to them was flesh forced into flesh, with wounds as deep and scarring as it would bare if it had been my body that had been shattered, rather than my being. I could not share with them the memories that had acted as fuel to their fires, or the still burning presence of their power inside of me as I struggled to heal. I could not make them understand, for to do that would be for them to share my suffering.

I looked at Dagger but refused to meet his gaze, observing only at the shudders of his heart, the controlled expansion of his chest, and the faint power settling at his feet.

"What did you do?" Shift demanded, his hand remaining on Shadow's shoulder, ready to take her to somewhere far from this mad-insanity, though it had been she to have shielded him from my radiation before.

"...I retaliated. I had to fight back. I had to stop him from ever hurting us again. They have to know we cannot be taken, or they will keep trying, and they will attack all we love and hold dear to hurt us, if they are not forced into the belief we are untouchable. I did not intend to make *you* afraid. I never wanted any of you to witness...I simply wanted them to fear us, to fear me."

Dagger started to say something, but I could not give him the chance before I finished what I had spent the last minutes that were as days to my thoughts convincing myself to say when I returned to them. I wanted to be able to speak with him, to be held by him, but I shuddered at the possibility of his reaction. The only thing holding me to the earth was him, if in hope if not truth.

"Please, Shift, Shadow, I cannot justify what I did, but know I did not act lightly… What I did… I warned them, I warned them before you even knew of us, I told them to not test me, that if they did it would result in their suffering, and in their choice to take us, to threaten us, they chose to incite me, and I chose to give in to their violence when they acted upon it towards me. It was when Dagger's life was endangered that I found myself unable to hold back any longer. I cannot pretend I was not wrong, but I acted as I was provoked to act. I will not claim that I did not have a choice – but it was all I could do. I do not ask for your forgiveness; I do not deserve it. I do not ask you to not be afraid of me, because you have a right to be. I am powerful, further so than I have acknowledged to each of you, but stand free knowing that power will never be turned against you, nor any who do not seek to take it from me. I only ask that you grant me the time to regain your trust."

Their silence were as the screams of the ancients.

"…Oh." He hesitated. "What did they do?"

"I had to stop them." I said again, unable to voice it.

"…Are you okay?" Shift asked cautiously. I slowly nodded.

"I am sorry, from the center of my being, for any pain I have caused you, and if you wish to ask any more of me, I ask you to give me time to gather myself. It…it has been a trying set of days, and you all need rest as well."

"No…not right now...so long as we're okay. Next time give us a heads up. I mean – don't go into something like that alone. We – I may not totally understand it but don't make us bail on you again. We don't go solo, remember?"

"Of course." Shift's and her fear ceased when I forced a smile across my face. I could not have been more thankful for that, even if my words no longer came to express it.

Shadow smiled softly. She did not speak, though she did not have to. She simply offered her presence, if only for a long moment, before turning to Shift.

"I need to go tell my mom we're okay, if any of this hits the news I don't want her worrying for nothing."

"I'll take you." He nodded in understanding.

"Can you?"

He looked to me, his expression reminding me of the unspoken requirements of his acceptance of my apology, he would want answers one day, and I would owe them.

"Yeah, I'm good." He took her, both of them engulfed in energy before disappearing.

I turned to leave, but his hand caught my arm.

"What *happened*?"

"More…More…than I ever wanted to."

"What did they do to you, Star?" He pleaded, helpless in his muted rage. He reached for me, drawing me towards him.

"If you trust me, you will not make me answer." I pulled away, freeing myself from the confines of my body the moment he no longer touched it.

Figured Out

"Yes, yes, we just got here. I know. I promise. If anything changes – Yes, okay…He's with Jonny and I. Yeah – no more runs for a couple days at least. We're fine here. …Yep. Love you too." I ended the call, placing the phone on the counter. Shift and I had killed nearly three hours at my mother's, and in that time we had not been able to give or receive any new answers. All we knew was that they had gotten trapped, captured, and after that – well, I wasn't entirely sure I wanted to see it. It was the darkness around Stargazer that scared me more than any vision I had gleaned could have. I had been forced to get out of the apartment, just to be able to breathe.

While I had hung out with my mother and spent the better part of an hour convincing her that I knew her energy well enough to see years ahead, and that the CIA wouldn't be raiding the house any time soon, and then meditated myself into a coma, he had cleared out the entire fridge. I had never known the limits of a grilled cheese before him. His somehow ended up with the entire bottom drawer thrown in the middle. He had told me, one hand cupping his third cheddar/mustard/spam/tomatoes /olives/ onion/ jalapenos and BBQ sauce 'sandwich' and the other wrapped around a gallon of milk, that the weirder the food, the worse the day had been. I had agreed, even if I was still too upset to eat. Or drink the Chamomile tea my mom had made me. Or sleep. Or see anything.

I had finally broke, convincing my mom that they needed me back at the apartment should anything alter during the night, and convincing Shift that his plan of both of us hiding at his sister's or in Anchorage or Aruba or wherever else he had a hideaway set up, wasn't going to help anyone. In the ten minutes since we had gotten back, nothing had changed. Stargazer was gone, or at least appeared to be, and BD had made absolutely no indication he had even noticed our arrival.

"Night everyone! I'm going to bed!" He yelled from his room. He'd given me no warning I was about to be ditched me a minute before. I honestly wanted to go to bed too, but something was bothering me, something more than what is blatantly obvious. Black Dagger was sitting perfectly still on the couch.

Alone.

No one should be left alone when they are hurting. The worst thing you can do is leave someone to lick their wounds when they are still bleeding out, and he was in pain. I saw it on him the same as I had seen it on her, a multihued, dark energy seeping out of their chests and into their bodies like every shade of food coloring dropped into a glass of water, its dark hued reach polluting everything it touched.

"BD..." I sat next to him.

"What?" He asked roughly, not bothering to glance up from the invisible battle taking place on the coffee table

"What *happened*?" It seemed that was the one question no one could answer.

He pushed his hair back from his equally dark eyes, sighing and shaking his head in the first admittance of defeat he had ever offered. There was no explanation, no hurried excuse, he simply sat there, his giant hulking mass of a body impossibly void of any formidability against the terror we had faced.

"Did they...hurt...you?" I asked in a small voice.

"No, they didn't hurt me." He paused. "The fire did. And when the building collapsed. She, she healed me. I don't remember them having a hand in anything."

"And her?"

His shoulders shifted, his gaze narrowing when it met mine as his hands flexed. He jerked his chin in a nod, his jaw locked.

I blinked, stunned. I hadn't expected any particular answer, but I definitely had not expected confirmation. It isn't as if waterboarding would work on her, leaving my head spinning at what they could have possibly done to drive her as close to the edge as she had been, and to leave him ready to murder everyone who had done it.

"*How?*"

"If I had known how or how badly, Shadow, I would have killed him the second we opened that door. I don't know what they did, but they threatened her enough to make her react in the only way she knew how." He looked at me again, this time observing my reaction. "She did not have a choice, no matter what we think… Even then, I don't think she planned to go as far as she had."

"She wanted you to stop her?" It was almost rhetorical. I hoped it was rhetorical.

"I should have before it ever came to this."

"We had no idea they were capable of even holding her-"

"It doesn't matter. They are. Everything I have been telling myself since the first month I knew her is irrelevant – if they know how, then it is only a matter of time before the rest of the world does –"

"BD." He stopped, looking at me. He hadn't realized he was shouting, that his hands were gripping his femurs with enough force to shatter them, or that I was doing my best to not edge away out of instinct. "…We will deal with all that later. I promise, I will find out whatever I can. Right now, that's not important. We all safe, and if Heaven forbid they find us, my mom has always wanted to live on her own private island. All that matters is that we're okay, that she's okay, isn't she?"

"I don't know."

He despised not knowing.

"Is there anything I can do?"

"No. ...How did you and Shift deal?"

"Barely. But we managed. You were gone for nearly three days. We had...we weren't sure what to do by the end of it...before she told me to come get you. Are you sure she's okay? That you are? I could try to find out-"

"Not tonight. Thank you – but you're right. We're all okay, and I can't focus on more than that. Keep an eye on us. If you see them retaliating, we will need a heads up. We may have to go underground for a while."

I grimaced. "Underground" was a sixteen hundred acer forest set in the middle-of-no-where rural Canada with a couple of cabins, a anti-satellite "dead zone" of my own creation, and enough security and supplies Shift had brought in just in case something ever happened to survive the zombie apocalypse. Or, as the care may be, a country wide lock down.

"Yeah. Of course. TGIF...*Right*?"

"I used to think the same thing before all this."

"Really...? You did exist before her...well of course you did, duh." I knocked myself on the side of my head in a B movie rated attempt at mock playfulness, still unsure of how safe it was to leave him unsupervised and hoping my sad try at humor might help him.

He looked at me as if I had finally started speaking Portuguese.

"Oh, it's just I've never, like, *seen* you before Stargazer." I explained.

"I should have guessed that."

"Do you know why?"

"Yes."

"...Will you tell me?"

He thought about it, taking longer than needed to stare through me, but I knew he wasn't seeing a tiny girl with ridiculously frizzed up hair that would take an hour to brush out, even if that's what I saw in the mirror on the wall behind him.

"You don't have to BD, but I'm listening if you want to talk about it."

"I know, but you deserve to know why you're blind. You're lucky you can't see it. It isn't something anyone would want to remember. Being purposeless, having nothing to live for except some scrapped together need to beat the world and keep breathing, even when you can't justify why it's worth it to begin with, that's a prison. That's hell. I was locked in with the key in my hand, but I was too busy pulling at the bars to notice. It's that kind of blind desperation that breeds darkness, Shads, and that's why you can't see it." He kept his eyes on his hands, mainly on his ring.

"Oh."

"Yeah…"

"I've never seen you before, like everything. What was that like?" I admit it, I could have chosen a better subject to distract him, but I had forgotten the original persistence behind my plan. I was leaning towards him, literally on the edge of my seat. The curtain was pulled aside, even if only a little bit, but there wasn't a goofy wizard behind it to greet me, just a man I'd been more wary of than I cared to admit, and a purpose behind it all I needed to know.

"I don't remember it, before them, who I was." His voice was flat, as unfeeling as someone explaining for the thousandth time.

"Do you want me to try to look? I mean I'm still learning but I bet if I followed back long enough I c-"

"No."

"No?"

"I don't need to fight for something I had before, it's gone, there's no getting it back, there's no remembering it, so there is no reason to long for it. I know what I am when I am alone... and I know who I am with her."

I don't even think he'd intended on me hearing him that last part, but it was nice. You would never hear him talk like that. Actually it was rare to hear him talk at all, especially to me, if you want the honest answer. He was so...well ... peaceful, if only for the millisecond it took before reality slapped us both in the face.

"I haven't seen when or where you met her yet, either."

"...Would you believe me if I told you it was doing what we always do?"

"Actually, I think I would." I laughed. "If my mom didn't make me come home most nights, I don't think I could sleep at all. I don't know if I could do it without you all making me sit out sometimes – it's hard to when you know what you could be doing."

He smirked. "Shift tried to warn you about the schedule we keep."

I nodded, looking towards his door, not needing to see the future to know what laid behind it. He would be asleep for days if we let him. He deserved to.

"Did he say anything else?" BD asked. Neither of us had forgotten just how freaked out he had been. We all had been. But I had to make sure they were okay before I took the world's longest sanity saving shower.

"He was more scared of *why* she did that than what she did. He's worried for her. We were both freaked, but we're good, concerned and exhausted as heck, but good."

"That makes two of us... And don't think I don't see what you are up to, doll face." He growled, but he almost smiled when he said.

"What? Me? Up to something? *Never*. Although I think I have you figured out."

"Am I supposed to take the bait on this?"

"First *you* tell *me* what my other gift is, the one you were talking about at Mary's, then I will spill."

"You won't think that is fair."

"I will." *You may not. ...Good thing I can outrun him...*

"You were the..." he paused, and for the first time in ever that I had known him he was puzzled, looking for the right word. "...Event, I guess you could call it that, which got me to admit to her and even myself, that I loved her. It is a bigger deal for me than it may sound and I'm not telling you why." He seemed self-conscious, which was new, to say the least.

"Oh...well." *What do you say after someone says 'you almost killed my girlfriend, but I'm glad you did because this and that happened'? Umm...I have no idea...answer his question?*

"I think that you are in love with her. I didn't think the deal would be fair to you either, but you are in love and that means you do stuff that might be a little bit nuts, like letting a building fall on you."

He became tense.

"What *you* wanted was what I meant. You wanted to keep her safe, even if it meant you possibly dying because of it. You loved her enough to not want her with you, even if she could've saved you. You feared for her, more than yourself, when that ceiling fell through. It wasn't the fire you were worried about, it was her. And when we opened that door, you didn't stop at the energy around her, you didn't even notice it. You should have – I know how you see threats – because I do that too – but you, you just held her..." I trailed off at his expression.

He stared at me, *dumbstruck.*

"How...?" He blinked a few times. Not only had I never seen him look like *that* before, but also I hadn't seen anything in what I said that looked like it could deserve a 'how?'.

Not more problems... I can't deal with anyone else's panic...

"Uh... 'how'?"

"You could see that."

Also in hind sight, I misunderstood that, and he hadn't cared to correct me.

"I saw after the fact. This whole day has been on the fritz as far as being able to see energy goes. I can't promise things will settle soon, so we will have to be careful."

"Agreed."

I debated on talking, and ended up doing it anyway. "I'm...I'm really glad you both are home." It wasn't as all-encompassing as I could have made it, but I wasn't sure I wanted him to know how desperate Shift and I had been – especially in the hours before she had finally reached me. We had barely slept, he had shifted to so many different safe houses and to so many different contacts that I had to beg him to rest or he would have hurt himself. I didn't remember the last thing I had eaten before that night, and I don't think either of us had been able to say more than a few words an hour to each other for fear of breaking down. It was the kind of hopeless insanity you can't put words to, at least I couldn't, not to BD, and not here.

He looked at me, slowly nodding. I realized with a stomach sinking feeling that I didn't have to say more, he knew exactly what we'd faced, he'd been there before. I smiled in what I hoped resembled some kind of reassurance.

The lights and colors in the room increased dramatically, my heart jumping a few beats.

She was back.

I witnessed her adrenaline spike just before I felt the air change. She glanced across the room before looking back at me, attempting to be subtle when she allowed herself to yawn.

"*You* may not need much sleep, but *I'm* going to be out of it until noon - maybe later. I'll keep an eye on things as best as I can." She got up and fluffed her hair, a habit she would never admit to even if faced with videoed proof.

"Thanks Shads, for all of it."

"Promise to not go disappearing like that again and we'll call it even." She started to walk off, pausing after a couple steps. When she turned back around, she wasn't looking at me. "You need to go talk to her… Whatever happened BD, it's not over yet, not for her."

"I know."

I waited until her door closed before I looked to Stargazer's, knowing she was behind it. The memory of her standing in front of me, terrified to even let me touch her, held me there, fueling the fires behind my anger. I cowered in the grey shadow the walls around my mind cast, nearly grateful for its shelter from the manic rage I knew would have overcome me. I refused to move until I no longer needed their false protection, until I was free from it so I could go to her and offer mine.

Upswept

I looked at the frozen-image-of-the-past pictures hanging on my wall. My mind was in a time when everything seemed innocent, simple, when the oppressive ruler called guilt did not weigh upon my every movement. *It feels like only last sunrise...of course my life is one never ending day, but all the same.* I put my hand against one of them. The cold-clear-heated-sand was smooth, unscarred. I thought about what the future would hold, of the sure retribution we would have to deal with from the 'government', the wounds I had caused and the scars I left by allowing myself to be seen in such a state, doing the things I had done, all these things plagued me, but unlike Shadow, the future refused to reveal itself. All I saw as definite was the fact we would not be apart, because I would not allow it. Even in my regret, I did not second guess my choices, I would fight them all over again if I had to in order to protect them.

The volatile nature of that instinct was all too apparent, and it was one thing I had not been warned against, misuse of power, manipulation of it, false beliefs, but never once did I believe I would put so much worth into one thing that galaxies weighed less in their wake than a single molecule of stardust.

I went to the floor-length-windows. As if to mock the turmoil within me, all was quiet, dreamlike, the stars-that-are-of-the-heavens shining through the faint clouds, visible only to my eyes in the yellow-lit mist that fell in impossible slowness over our small section of the earth. I studied the skies, seeing the power shine through that only I could see, where pulsars lit up the sky with a fierce radiance that diminished even the brightest of the living stars.

I heard his steady breathing. He was still awake, alone. Shadow had long before retreated to the confines of her room, falling asleep within moments of her body colliding with the spun-plant-fiber blankets. It took all my willpower to refrain from going to him. The image of his possible rebuke kept my desires chained to the uncertainty of my standing.

All that was quaked within me, leaving me to brace myself against the glass lest I fall.

For a single moment I found myself in alarm at what had overcome me, and then I laughed bitterly at my instant reaction of fear to why that had happened, why it seemed my physical body was prone to weakness, when it was only reflection of what lied within. Anything 'abnormal' I felt had more than enough reasons behind it. I had been violated down to my very core with false light, driven to near delusion and utter exhaustion with the pain of its hammering in me, and barely escaped with my sanity, soul, and their trust.

What I wrought…

I felt my surface cool in anger, for even in my guilt failed to quench the inferno that blazed on.

I will not let any of them suffer – by their hand or my own.

I heard him rise.

When the power-attraction between us flashed, I summoned all the strength-of-mind I could muster and went to the door before he could pass it, throwing it open in a silent-swift motion. The soft grey-iciness of his power brushed against mine, cooling my singed soul in an unseen embrace. His unmoving face caught the shadows that fled through the gaping emptiness of the wall. His eyes reflected the light behind us, holding all they saw in perfect stillness, taking in the room to my back and the state of my own as I looked to him, watching for any sign of his thoughts, thoughts I dare not

416

intrude on, not when there were too many things within that cavern that could possibly hurt me.

He smiled faintly, lifting on side of his mouth upwards, his hands opening towards me in a cautious invitation. I collapsed into him, the habit of constant breathing ceasing as I forgot the memories still searing through my physical form for first moment since they had been born. I had not touched him in this way for what I knew were days-as-eons, and every part of me became whole the moment his arms folded around me.

"Dagger-" I held him as tightly as I dared, the recollection of their horrible-dark-thoughts-plans denying me any peace even in his arms. I buried myself in him, the thin shirt he wore unable to conceal the feel of his skin on mine. Without the means to show my grief in any other way, I found myself weeping against him. The weight of his hand on the back of my head and the stronghold of his arm over my back was all that held me upright.

"They would not *stop*. I begged them, they would not listen – I could not take it any more – I never knew it to even be possible and they-"

"I'm right here." In mirror to his words, his hold on me increased until I knew not if I could ever break away, and knew that I never desired to. "They will never hurt you again. I swear it. …It's all right, Stargazer." He whispered, without any explanation, as if his simple words were enough to prove such an impossibility. I pushed away, staring in disbelief. He warily watched me, seeing the way my throat contracted when I held back my words.

"No. It is not. It cannot be. What they did – Dagger it – it was…it was beyond anything I thought them capable of doing, beyond what I ever believed I could – would act upon. I should not be this content to have done what I did in retaliation. It is *wrong*. I am not meant to be here, no argument I have struggled with can justify it, my morality is one even my kind deem as nothing but a fool's delusion, and those who took us deem me a threat, a weapon, and they – they are *right*. I hate them for it but they called me a risk greater than what this world can overcome and I am one…I can abolish this, all of this, if I wanted, if I was *provoked*. But they did worse. I thought I could never be taken to surrender, yet I wanted nothing more than to give up and not have to fight any longer, not have to defend myself, not have to struggle between my desires. I had given in, still they still would not *stop*. They drove me into madness! I could have destroyed so many, more than I-" His hand closed around my the side of face, denying me any chance to glance away from the intemperate intensity of his solemn verse.

"No. You wouldn't have."

"I wanted to." The confession did not lift the weight of the wanted sin, as so many believe such things do, instead it added to the burden. To hear my voice speak such sadistic desires and know that he knew it to be genuine was as hurting to bear and horrible to witness as seeing him taking from me had been.

"Don't. Don't ever think that what your people did or what you fear you can do, what they forced you to do or even what they accuse you of, is who you are. Heroes, fugitives, vigilantes, revolutionist, anarchists – they can label us however they please, but if we refuse to answer, it doesn't matter. You came here to save us from ourselves…me from myself. You came here with a purpose that they can't steal from you, not unless you let them. I battled the darkness of my own soul for too long to see you lose yourself in yours."

"I wanted him gone from this world." My surface cooled as my being drew all of my power, my defensive-shielding instincts pausing when the aura of his own form of light brushed against me. "I would not have stopped, if you had not come for me."

The tension above his eyes greatened, and he deliberately plunged his head against his chest in understanding, but he did not release his hold of me.

"I will always come for you, Star."

I looked away, feeling my hands tighten against him.

"I know." I had known, a part of me that he alone held had clung to the belief that he would have come back, and it was that part of me that had in turn held me to the earth when all I wanted-needed to do was flee it.

I shuddered, turning back into him, burying all I was beneath the surface of his power. He sensed my shattered nature, his own changing with his fear-unknowing.

"Show me, Star."

I shook my head, the human action all I could manage in my revulsion.

"I'm not the only broken one." He said slowly, his thoughts lingering on Shadow's well-intended warning. I had kept her from seeing, I had to, for such was my pain and such was her connection to me that I feared it would leave her as scarred as I even to witness it. I had every intention of shielding it from Dagger as well, for as I had sworn, my burdens were my own, But he sought it from me, and my desire to shield him was weak against his hold.

I sighed, prying open my mind against every instinct still urging me to shield myself, to reach out to his. He tensed when the first of any clear memories I had since I had ceased the fire's life replayed, those of us being unearthed from the rumble, his seemingly lifeless body, seen only through my inner sight, torn from my side before walls of steel-platinum-carbon-lead closed us apart from each other. Those that followed were none the lighter, even if it was channeled light they had forced upon me. His confusion tainted fury welled at the edges of the visions, and though I kept the memories of the sensations that accompanied them at bay, the lingering of my terror could not be overshadowed by the peace brought from his heart beating next to me.

They stopped the moment he had pulled me away from that man. He knew I had not planned on ceasing there, for there were many others who had seen to what had happened to us, and he also knew it was only his presence that had spared them. Yet, it was not these things I had not wished him to see, it was my surrender to the madness, the rage, the very act of bowing to them by allowing their actions to lead to my own that left me folded against him.

The quiet that followed held no threat, for he still held me and the stillness remained untouched, but I was disconcerted when he did speak, not out of a start at the shattered silence, but because I had been within his mind, and his words seemed to not have come from it.

"No matter what we face, we will face it together. We cannot be the protectors they need if we surrender to every guilt or infamy or cry of unfairness they try to place on us. We can't save them if we fear ourselves. We were put above them, not because we chose it, but because they put us here, they *need* us here. *I* need you here. Be it the will of an Almighty or the will of the masses or our personal rage against the injustice around us, it doesn't matter. We chose to stay here. *You* chose it. We are in a place to save those too blind to see their dangers. This could have been our greatest test or just the start, but whatever it was, you were not alone in it. You will you never be." His heavy, rough voice and his black-soul-smoldering eyes paused my thoughts. When I looked up to him he was watching me without expectation for reply. He touched the circlet I wore around my head as he spoke his final peace. "You belong here. With me."

He kissed me softly, holding me in a way that left me at peace, such a flawless, pale colored still-peace, knowing I was in his arms, and nothing, not of this world or out of it, could hurt me here. I flew up so I might stand his equal, both of us sensing the calm before the storm, treasuring the fading tranquility.

"Stay with me." I whispered. His gaze widened before his mouth crushed mine in wordless agreement.

The enflamed-cerise-stained power looming just beyond reach grew greater with every breath we shared. There was a harsh, fraught edge to his cool touch, his once so precise and careful holds lost under the mountainous pressure of our mirrored powers. How desperately I had hung to the promise of being with him again, of his being erasing all they had done, and how perfectly it had come. He had long before taken my heart, mind, spirit, and even my soul for his own possessions. It would take but moments from a previously granted eternity for the theft be consented.

In the middle of the torrent of current-running sensations surrounding me, I felt the energy of the room go into spirals and the colors turned to deep-strong-bright shades. My hands moved without needing the urging of my thoughts, feeling the icy heat of his skin meld into mine. He chuckled at my explicitly stated desire-impatience, his unspoken consent in the form of a slight smirk, his sparkling gaze blazing. I smiled, feeling my own surface begin to glow.

"Will you still be here in the morning?" His laughter was silenced as I eagerly met his cool lips, my fingers moving down from his throat, memorizing his shape. I got lost in him, for how long I will never know. Every breath, every moment was a hazy-soul-jumping response, to his touch, his power. The magnet - the allurement that existed between us was dangerously close to being triumphant. I wanted every part of him. I wanted to be his. All those things that had haunted me only moments before were meaningless, everything that I was giving him in exchange for own was reduced to only the desire to be as close to him as I could be.

Every part of my mind, body, and even my *heart* begged, no it *demanded,* my consent to him-I-us to continue in what we were doing, wanting-wishing-yearning to do, yet my very soul and spirit knew better than to give in, one I argued against yet could not silence. What he had asked of me was still greater than what I sought from him in those moments, and I would not see myself once more surrender to urges-beyond-me without honoring his vow first.

He kissed my neck, freeing me to speak, but the words to get us to stop our actions refused to form. I did the one thing I then could.

I shocked him.

It took me longer than it should have to realize my head was in her lap and she was running her fingers through my hair, her nails slowly dragging against my forehead. The remaining sparks had dissipated a minute before, but it had taken that long, and then some, for my head to clear.

"Are you hurt badly?"

"No. But I definitely *felt* that." I had gone from, well, to being thrown across the room. All of which I said or didn't leaving me stunned.

"I am so sorry."

"It's not like it was intentional." I went to sit up. She put her hand against me, holding me where I was, her caramel colored eyes calculating my every move.

"It was."

"*Why?*"

"I...I do not know. You don't want to...to wait, until we are married? Was that not the purpose of the ceremony?"

The brush of her mind against my thoughts calmed their cascade. Whatever answer she had sought she found within a few moments. She kept her hand against my chest.

"Even so, many also fail to uphold their promises, but *we* do. I have culpabilities against this race, but this cannot be one of them. I am capable of dictating my actions over this desire, even if I nearly failed to cease in the taking of my last. As you were my catalyst to return me to sanity then, so are you the same now. Why should we allow ourselves to do this simply because your, our, *society* has allowed it, if what we promised each other was to be the vow over it? I do not understand such ceremony, but I will not become a hypocrite, even for you." Her voice softened, her gaze falling from mine.

"I have spent time deemed to be called years among this race, but before I ever came here Dagger, I knew what it was to become as more than oneself, I knew what could be possible, and I knew without even thinking to know that to have such with a human could never be within the holds of reason, but even beyond that, I never believed, even for an instant, that I was of the will to or had the ability to forever love someone so greatly, so completely, that it was not my pity or my aid I gave them, but my very strength and my resolve for living…

I have given more of myself to the people of this place in the last years here than I knew I had, but I gave only fragments of my being, pieces of myself offered to those who needed it because they had not the might or means to help themselves, even if they had the will. It was not out of obligation to those I deemed less than I, but choice granted to those who I knew held the same desire to thrive as I hold. That is what and why I gave.

But to you… You seek all of me, and I seek only to give myself to you, not because of your need, but my own. I want you as selfishly and as fiercely as I want to end those who seek your harm, and that violent desire is more powerful and superior a presence within me than any act of altruism I have ever made, for so great is it that even my hand against you now burns as if it were a star I grasped. But in this, I do not desire to be more than you, or this race, so if I am to become yours, I wish it to be as any of your kind would be." She paused, sighing as she continued. "No matter how you want to see this, it *is* hypocrisy and you know it, Dagger. What good is a dozen vows if we have not promised that which is deemed sacred?"

I did not respond, not for lack of agreement or even disagreement, but because I could not think of how to speak. It wasn't guilt – or even the sense of being reproached – it was awareness. It didn't matter that I could hear whispered conversations for three miles in any direction, in those long moments I couldn't make out the sound of my own heartbeat against the thoughts running through my head.

423

"It isn't that I *don't* want to be with you." She was explaining then, believing my silence to be doubt. "As much comfort as I need, as much as you're my protector, I do not want their intended evil against us to be the catalyst. Not tonight, my love. As much as you are mine, I refuse to let them be the cause. This is ours, we have chosen it, not because all that has happened, and not that we are weary and seeking more than we should. If we have both waited this long, then we ought to not give in to our desires when we have a life time to do what we long for."

Her essence met my consciousness, the copper tint to her gaze fading into gold when she saw everything I was failing to speak.

"You understand." She smiled, her skin glowing faintly.

"No, I agree, I just wish I could say my self-control is as good as yours."

"I wish it was a strong as I proclaim it to be." She said, shaking her head, surprised. "I think it will be easier for both of us if we were to be married sooner rather than later." She smiled a very small, enticing smirk.

"Sunday?" I know it was sooner than considered as 'soon.'

"Sunday it shall be." Even as she said it, her eyes roamed. She put her hands together, trying to focus. "To tempt ourselves would be unwise."

"I should go." It wasn't surrender – it was evasion. No amount of tampering with the neurons in my brain and the hormones in my body could have given me the strength to leave. It was what she had said that did, and the ground beneath my feet was proof.

"I do not deem that necessary." She rose next to me.

I traced her arm, from her elbow to the tips of her fingers, not trusting myself to say anything more.

The room's energies had long since returned to normal, but it was the equivalent of the aftermath of a Hurricane, for although the air then stood still, the vehement turbulence was still present in the undying evidence laying around me, in the memory of what I had felt which had yet to dissipate. Somewhere in the settling of my thoughts I regretted not having made all that I had said *before* then, however I had not known that I wanted to 'wait' until it was brought upon me.

I had I had known every implication of the promise to marry him the second I had made it. It was without angst, and I knew the control it wielded, or second-thought-doubt-fear, it was effortless...or so I had believed until that night. Then it could only be called temptation. Everything I had been consumed by only an hour before was forgotten in the cascade of desires he alone enthused. Not once in my lifetime had I felt what I then felt or wanted what I then wanted, not once had I been as defenseless. Not once had I been as confused.

I wished that I could sleep, for without its forgivingly mindless embrace, I fought my mind for hours. He had been able to leave. I barely managed to stay away. I remained tied by the confides of my physical form; it's boundaries were as chains to the walls around me. If the call to become as I was, as light, was answered and I was no longer held in place I did not believe I could resist any longer. I did not even move, for if I allowed even the faintest waver in my stillness, I knew where I would be

Tangibility may have its rewards but I dare say it certainly complicates things.

◆

The first thing I remember was falling out of bed, hitting the ground and waking myself up at the same time. It worked better than an alarm clock, I'll admit it, but it wasn't the most ego glorifying thing I had ever done. *With my luck, Shads will see it by lunch. Speaking of lunch, I'm starving.* I

425

shifted so I was sitting on my bed. I figured it was around five in the afternoon, or evening, whatever you want to call it. For me it was 'morning'. Norming mornings were more of 'I just kicked butt all night and came back from having lunch in Europe and now I have to go to school'. The afternoon was 'Yay- bed time'. From nine o'clock on it was the start of my 'work day'.

As it was, I had no idea how longer I had been out. It could have been days. I wondered if Shads was up, what she was doing, if she had gone with SG and BD anywhere, if she had been shot at, if she was okay, or if she had snagged a day off to spend with her mom, if they were talking about me, what SG was doing, if she'd gone nuts, if BD had kicked someone's tail for it, etc. Unfortunately I was still out of it enough to throw logic into the same basket my definition of 'normal' had been thrown away in.

I grudgingly got up, knowing if I didn't figure out what was happening I would just lay there wondering and I'd never make it back to sleep. I looked around my room. *If they'll let me-I am so hiring a maid.* I had a habit of throwing stuff around and leaving it where it landed. I knew Stargazer wouldn't approve. Her place could be a prop in a movie or in a magazine, of course buying the apartment fully furnished had helped with that. I had no idea about BD's and Shadow's cribs. Hers acted as the communal watch tower, because of the windows and the fact I could always find them there or on the roof. I hadn't been in the others'. I hoped I wasn't the only slob.

I went to the kitchen in my own special 'science experiment' fashion. Shadow was already in there, and she looked like she'd also gotten some rest, something I was happy to see after the mind numbing panic of the last few days.

She jumped at my unexpected appearance.

"SHIFT!" She shrilly accused, nearly dropping the electric mixer onto the floor.

"Killer cake?" I asked in an animated voice.

"Baking."

"And that's normal for you?" *Sure, kidnapping an alien is apparently a new level of normal, but baking?*

She turned away when I attempted to go for the batter.

"Probably the most normal thing I've done all week." She swatted me with the spoon, then I did get the batter because it was all over my hand. "There's eggs in that."

"So?" While I licked it all off, stared at me in disgust, which was actually pretty funny with the way her nose scrunched up all cute, but I'm getting off topic here.

"That's disgusting."

"Unless you've seen me at a crawfish fest, you have no idea. ...I guess this is like stress eating? Isn't that more of my thing?" Her lack of pink flushed nuttiness and the jeans and t-shirt were proof she wasn't freaking out still, which meant we had to be safe to some degree, but I wasn't about to go all in on the assumption she was actually "okay" – which she'd spent a good ten minutes trying to convince me of before we'd gone to her mom's.

"None ya."

"Really – out of the loop again? Who was the one who totally sided with against BD? Do you know how bad that could've ended up for me? And now I'm looped out over *cake*?" I pleaded, after cleaning my hand. *She hasn't yelled at me to be serious, so I guess she is fine. But really, what's with the cake?*

"We are going to need it later."

"Need it for what?"

"A party."

I had no idea what she was talking about. I would have asked her what she meant, or gone to steal some of the cake mix, but Stargazer showed up a second later, her entrance announced first by every hair on my body standing on end. I hadn't forgotten the surreal and extremely terrifying thing that had happened, the one where I was literally stuck in between to places but partially present at both, held there in a weird state of dual consciousness by some massive force of her power for what felt like hours. My edginess was instinctual, if not totally intentional.

"What are you doing Shadow?"

I looked at her and looked away. She wasn't glowing, but the fact her skin was gold and she had a thing for floor length windows equaled blinking and blinded me, what with sleep still a lingering, beautifully warm cloud over my eyes.

Shadow smiled and then flicked her eyes to me.

At least I wasn't alone in my cluelessness this time, because even SG was scowling.

And, I noticed, keeping a safe distance from us.

"Look, you know I'm not really for all the legality so I am not going to pretend I am, but I am my mother's daughter." Shadow smirked, pouring the batter into a few large pans on the counter. "If you are going to do this, then we're in. I mean it's not like you're both all hung up on normal, so I don't even understand why you want to suddenly conform, but if you're serious, then we're are going to do it right. No one will say I supported the whole paperwork bit, but since that's out the window anyway, ceremony or not, we're going to be a part of it. All the goodies. And invites."

Stargazer seemed stunned for a moment. Then she smiled.

"Very well, Shadow."

"Good, now do you want to clue him in or should I?" Shads asked, flicking an oven mitt in my direction.

I'd probably know more if they had Twitters and I followed them.

"You would think that he would have *guessed* from the obvious, but one can only expect so much from a pure human." Her voice was a half sigh / half 'poor little helpless, pathetic thing'. I can't tell you that *didn't* make me laugh. It was actually funny coming from her. Anyone else would have

428

gotten punched in the side or a catty remark in return. But, I also figured she had her reasons. I happily realized that SG was trying to get back to normal – and no part of me had any desire to interrogate her. I would get my answers from Shads or BD, because if there is one thing I've learned about alien issues, leave them the heck alone.

"Jokes, a new language for you." I told her with a little wit in my own voice. It would be a long couple of days back into the swing of things, and if making jokes helped her feel less isolated, and frankly, helped me not have the thought to shift Shadow and I to Tonga in the back of my head whenever she was around, then we'd both play the part.

She smiled, her eyes like mirrors.

"Yes...if you wish to believe that I wasn't being quite serious, Shift."

I laughed as my eyes scanned the room. I noticed two things: one, BD wasn't there, and two: he should have been. He never left alone, they ditched us all the time, but they would never fly solo. *Especially after yesterday.* He hadn't given me a heads up, other than nodding when I had asked if I should be prepared to take Mary and Shads' mom with us to lay low for a while if anything got too hot.

What did I miss?

"Can be let back in the loop now?"

They both glanced at each other and Stargazer started glowing a little bit.

"Dagger and I are getting married Sunday."

I watched as his face went from shock to a blank gape. He made a sound that mixed 'oh' with 'what'. I giggled under my breath. He thought *I* was the drama queen. He came back to normal a few seconds later. "Seriously?"

"You of all people are familiar with our lack of schedules or control of what the next day will bring to us." She told him lightly.

"Way to give a guy a warning. Well, okay, I mean we still may have to hide out soon but I guess tomorrow won't give them time to zone in too much. ...Where's the groom?" He asked, the question weighted with uncertainty.

We hadn't forgotten the threat she'd made, and neither were we in denial of what it could cause. I'd been up since six that morning meditating myself into and out of every energy channel I could wiggle into, what with the corkscrew the last few days had been. I saw Black Dagger leaving early that morning, but unless Stargazer knew where he was, I was as clueless as Shift. My one real victory had been succeeding in increasing the black-out barrier around our loft, my mom's apartment and Mary's, and three of Shift's hide-outs. Nothing could come in, and only what I approved of could go out, so at least when it came to spies and satellites, we were safe.

"He will be here later." SG said.

"Are you two okay? Are we?" Shift pressed, stepping forward, looking as formidable as he could with his adorably messed up bed head and wearing nothing but sweats and wrinkled old Pacsun tank.

"We will be, ultimately."

I was curious to her lack of details, but I didn't ask her, and I most certainly did not try to see anything. I had spent most of the last day and a half, (all of which Shift had slept through) alternating between hour long showers, meditating, reading, and drowning in hot tea in an attempt to get myself back to level. As long as she too had found a way to get back into her own homeostasis, which I knew she had succeeded in, at least in part.

"Is he safe, wherever he is, or do I need to do a pick up?"

Her pause said more than she would ever admit to us.

"Yes. There are just some things that need tending to before tonight. He is straightening out the repercussions of what happened. I will be joining him shortly. I was to see that neither of you are to leave these rooms today. I will call your mother, Shadow, and alert her to be on her guard as well. We cannot risk anything, not right now. In the next twenty-four hours Dagger and I will see to it any immediate threats are neutralized, until then, Shift, you know where to take everyone should something go amiss. I fear that the percentage of our activity here has narrowed down their search for us, and it is only a matter of time before our city is compromised. We are attempting to stop this, at whatever means necessary."

He gravely nodded.

"Do we get the details this time?"

She dipped her head, the lights around her narrowing in acceptance his question and the mistrust it came with.

"I will not let them find us, but I will not go to the extremes I was forced to before. He will be with me when I meet with the leaders here, when that time inevitably comes, I will be joining him shortly. I may need both of your aid this evening, Dagger and I have an – well what you would call an insurance policy – should they attempt to feign ignorance or innocence."

"Got it."

I didn't share his confidence. Insurance policies were another legality I didn't like.

She turned and went to get something from the built in that was in the living room, leaving us alone.

"We're in deep." He admitted.

"Yep." I said, doing my best to not look into just how deep.

He watched me from his new found perch on top the counter for long enough to make me realize he wasn't eying the icing I was working on anymore. I kept my head down to hide the blush.

"Can I help?"

I dropped the bowl I was holding and only his shifting kept it from hitting the ground.

"I knew I'd get it somehow." He snipped, laughing at my apparent clumsiness, forgetting that I knew how to walk on my hands on a five meter long, two inch wide balance beam four feet in the air and flip back to my feet without flinching years before he could do four hundred pushups with me sitting on his back.

Still, it took me a second to get my brain to jump-start back into operation.

"Uh, thanks. Yeah, sure, that'd be great. I still need to make the other icing." I took in a deep breath and nodded. "I already shopped for it earlier so we won't need to sneak past her."

He gave one of his infamous half smiles and grabbed a gallon of milk off the counter, putting it back in the fridge, totally oblivious.

"So what was with the speech about conforming? I thought you and I were the ones who liked normal."

Or not so oblivious?

"Oh, I do normally, but… they're above it." I managed to make my way over to the grocery bags decorating the table, digging around for the powdered sugar and cream cheese. I didn't plan on going into details, but his uncharacteristic silence seduced me into it. "It seems beneath them, to have to make a show of it, like a piece of paper is somehow more binding than them just being together. It – It is ridiculous that after everything they think they still need to prove it to us, or whoever. I mean, even I can't see them apart, so what does it matter?"

I finally found the sugar, and by the time I returned he had then continued to *load the dishwasher?*

"It doesn't matter – not like that." He said, and his tone was an odd mix of sentimental and serious, a tone that could have been another language, taking in consideration he was the one using it. "I know you're parents kind of jaded you to marriage – " He glanced up from the silverware tray, unsurprised to find my expression less than joyful. "No, I get it,

432

mine were and probably are still a pain to each other too, but it's not about the show, or the paper, not when its real. They – well – Even I don't like institutionalizing stuff. It doesn't go with God, people, relationships or whatever, but to them it's not about that. It's more like they are doing it for each other."

"Because they like normal." I summed up, taken aback when he shook his head, smirking.

"Nah, they just like the idea that there's nothing that could possibly stand against them. Just wait until you see what they will be up to today. I bet SG's already got whatever alien fine print goes with this covered, so all that's left is the human stuff, and whether it makes sense or not isn't really on us to figure out."

"And you just magically understand them." I wasn't jealous. Okay, I may have been.

He shrugged. "When I'm actually given a heads up, maybe. It's just easier to see where they're coming from when you know where their heads are at. You'll see – give it another six months and you'll be able to read them better than I can." He assured me, moving onto the hand washing, leaving me standing there still holding the powdered sugar with no intentions of remembering it was in my hand.

"What's going on?"

"Bout' what?" He didn't even look up at me. I wanted to know if he was secretly laughing over some kind of joke. He had 'trolled' me before, enough times for me to have gone and thanked my mom for not giving me a little brother when I had asked for one.

"You are doing the *dishes*. You are psycho analyzing BD and Stargazer, better than I can and I've known about this for hours. You're practically being humble about it. What *happened*?"

He turned, smirked, and laughed.

"Nothing *happened* to me. I'm just helping you Shads. Give me a hard time on it and I may have to stop." He handed

433

me a plate. I set the sugar down, before fumbling to put it up into the cabinet.

"I'm shocked." I muttered, still wondering when the punch line would hit.

"No you're not, you're just ticked that you haven't figured me out yet either. I'm not just a big shot, wanna be comic-book-superhero with no sense of rules or real responsibility, and no intentions on growing up." He handed me a large bowl he had just washed. My movements were mechanic, lifting my hands, taking it from him, applying the towel, missing a spot, putting it in the bottom cabinet. He'd practically quoted me. No, he *had* quoted me. On many occasions.

"I know." I hoped it didn't sound as defensively guilty as it felt.

"As for the dishes, I did have chores once...and I...well, never mind."

"What?"

"Nothing."

"Tell me!" I put my hand on my hip and tapped my foot impatiently. I had grown used to knowing what was going on.

"You're right – about me, about us, normal I mean. I need this, normal, okay? I know I can be a bit overenthusiastic about how awesome all this is, and try to put it off like it's fine when the person who is somehow both my adopted big sis and my boss ends up getting hurt and raising hell, but I need normal. This is normal. Not fun normal, but normal, and with everything going on, it's nice. Boring or not, it isn't half bad if I get to do the work with you."

"With me?"

He laughed, washing his hands before he turned to me, laying one on the edge of the sink and the other hooked in the pocket of his sweats as he leaned against the counter behind him. "Don't even go there Shads, because we both know exactly what I would say and I don't need to be a psychic to know what you will, so just let it go."

"Oh."

Way to not sound like you've been punched.

"Yeah." He agreed, before his attitude and tone took a turn down Changing the Subject Avenue. "Anyway, what have you seen so far? I need to know what kind of shifting capacity I'm looking at the next few days. If it's just you and your mom and my sis back and forth, I've got a truck load of boxed MRE's to drop off to some missionaries in the Philippines and a few shipping containers medical equipment to go to some refugee camps – but if I need to hold off I can. I don't want to risk anything."

"No, you're good. We're good, I mean." I sprayed the counter, wiped it clean, and then did it again just to have something to keep my hands busy. *I still have to make the almond icing.* "They...whatever is in the works is putting things on hold."

"Okay, cool. She has us on lock down but if you can cover for me, I swear it'll be five minutes, tops."

I nodded.

"Thanks."

"Sure."

He waited, and I knew he was waiting because I could feel him staring at me. I didn't intend to make it sound as irritated as it did, when I demanded "What?" because it seemed to only justify his suspicions.

"I need to know you're good, before I run off."

"Since when do you run?"

"Shads. Seriously. We weren't exactly model citizens of sanity."

I sighed, turning back around to see he had yet to move.

"I'm fine. I just want to make it through the next two days without anything going wrong. After that, you can ask me again, okay?"

He pushed himself off the counter with his hip, taking a step towards me. He didn't look nearly as puckish as he had five minutes before.

"Alright, make things difficult. I get it, you want to deal on your own terms, but you need to tell me if you're not okay, or if you see anything – you come first in all this."

I am horrified to admit this to you, to anyone for that matter, but two things had come of that, the most immediately irritating was that I forgot to breathe and fainted.

"Shads?" He picked me up off the kitchen floor. I saw his distraught face through half closed eyes and wanted the light to just come get me. I would never live that one down, so it would be better just to not live.

I felt a really hot hand on my arm.

Please kill me.

"Did she see something? Is she ok? Is BD all right?"

"All is well, Dagger is safe, and it was not a vision that has rendered her out of touch with herself ...Shadow, focus please." Stargazer said clearly.

Oh yeah, fine, throw me through an emotional blender for three days and top off the milkshake of my mental saneness with him suddenly dropping the play boy act and somehow "focusing" on that is going to help me.

I blinked, letting them both know I was back. I wasn't thrilled about it, but I was back.

"The chemically made molecular compounds within the combined cleansers have caused her to become weakened. She will be back to health with a change of atmosphere."

"Some *Protector* you are. You can almost dodge bullets, but get you around some Clorox and you fall out like a peeled banana." He smiled and his eyes had those laughing little yellow-green glints in them that made me go weak at my knees. Thankfully I was still on the ground. Sort of.

"I guess. Thanks, but uh, you can let me go now." I don't think that he'd even realized he was still holding me up.

"Sorry." He said quickly.

"It's okay." I tried to not blush more. Normally, and he knew this, he would have gotten slapped. "Stargazer, I'm going to have to take you up on the fresh air. Don't worry about finishing up, Shift. We'll get it later."

I don't remember if he responded, only that she was standing at the door to her room, already waiting for me. I went to her, making it look like I had a hard time catching my footing. Once the door was shut, I nearly laughed in relief.

She smiled, revealing something she had hidden behind her back. She handed me an eight-by-ten picture that was framed in something I couldn't identify. It looked like black metal, but it also looked like it was moving. It was warm to the touch, sort of like her skin. I flipped it over and I saw her and Black Dagger both sitting on grass under a big tree. He was staring directly at whoever had taken the picture, wearing his mask, meaning they had been 'on duty.' She was looking up at him, an expression on her face that I had never seen before. Stargazer was the epitome of extremes, hot or cold, blissful or enraged, all out alien or the best of humanity. Then, seemed to be the exception to the never altered rule. She was puzzled, but she was smiling too.

"When was this taken?" They never let the pictures of us get that close. Or personal.

"A short time after meeting him. A child took it and I had him give me its reproductions. There are a few others, but this is the best, because it shows parts of ourselves we had yet to see… I was unknowing. It is the alteration you ponder over. You too are unsure, though differently than I had been."

"Different?" *Other than the obvious.*

She took the picture from me and went to go sit on the ground in front of one of the windows. She set it in front of her, leaning it against the glass. All of which I knew was for my benefit. Sitting was always deliberate.

"I was unknowing of *his* feelings, not my own. You want a form of... friend, which is completely understandable. Often times, those of your kind mistake their needs for companionship as a need for intimacy – a fact that leads to much of the unrest that plagues so many, regardless of age. In their desire for comfort and safety, they sacrifice both ethics and peace for superficial bonds. Though he and I were of those ages most susceptible, your age, he was more than that for me. We were yet to be called 'together' by most, it was different ...for many reasons, than you are with Shift."

"Huh...The only difference I see is that BD doesn't think *teasing* is a form a *flirting*." Lie or not, she fought a smirk. I knew I was doing the same game I had played the night before with BD, and despite her ability to see through me, that day would be the exception. If helping me and my (slightly exaggerated for her benefit, I assure you) issues somehow healed her of her own, then tandem therapy it was.

"You are still learning who Shift is, but so is he. Beneath the many personas he was taught to create or made to grow into, there is still much to be discovered. With Dagger, I knew *everything* of him and yet knew *nothing*. I knew all of his past, yet the choices he made in the present left me baffled and in awe, and I knew all of his thoughts, yet the actions they bore fruit to only had left me seeking more. His mind, it is what was the most changed of him, but I did not see it as such. He was a beautiful mystery I soon fell into."

I blushed and she smiled.

"You sought the reasons behind our conforming to tradition? It is these. Even then, I loved him more than I even acknowledged. He says he isn't one to speak, but when he does, it is something unmatchable. His views, his beliefs, they are faultless because nothing is allowed to sway them, even if he is often wrong in how he sees himself.

We were and are different because we loved and love differently. We did not need the other to feel as we did. Our companionship wasn't based of the needs for the other's approval, but out of an honest desire to see the other in their fullest."

"I don't want his approval." *Okay, maybe for like the first few weeks, yeah, but it doesn't count now – right?* "I just want to figure him out. I mean he can go from hair bands around facets and messing with my friends to delivering vaccines in an hour."

She touched my arm. "I know why you seek these answers, and I know why you chose today to do so, as you equally understand my need to share that photo and these things with you, to feel human, to feel equal in this world again. And for that, Shadow, I am more grateful than I can voice, and I offer you the only answer I can give you in regards to one of the things you seek from me, as for the answers to what happened, they will come when I have the strength to face my own actions once more. This is where my council stands: Do not see Shift for what he appears to be, but by who he is, and do not seek to hide yourself."

I caught myself again remembering what I had seen in that office: a creature beyond anyone comprehension glaring in utter hatred with a look of death on her face and the void of power around her pulling everything within reach into its darkness, that feeling of being sucked in that I recalled so vividly, one that had led to more than a single nightmare. But those images somehow did not belong to the soft-spoken angel kneeling in front of me. I smiled, realizing that the sooner I left it to be, the sooner she could stop having to relive it in our minds and her own.

"I know. I'm glad I can talk to you about this... My mom is kind of biased because she really *likes* him, which doesn't help when every weekend I hear 'oh how are you and

Shift' and 'what did he do today' and 'oh that is so nice/cool/sweet/ weird of him.' I really think that he purposely did that to her somehow. Maybe he is like BD."

A small crease formed between her eyebrows.

"What do you mean?"

"Oh, he just is always so controlled, I get calm too when I'm around him, *now* at least. I think Shift does the same, he likes everyone, and he makes people like him, but BD puts everything into perspective ... I'm really happy for you too, I mean it. Me and Shift and everything else aside, I'm glad you both found each other. You needed him."

I wasn't entirely sure I'd pulled it off.

The softened edges of the aura I sensed around her told me I had, at least in part.

"He needed me more so."

"...Yeah, that's what he said." I replied in a distracted laugh.

Exposure

I stared at the three people on the other side of the steel table, calculating their body language and micro expressions in my own form of mind reading. A woman in her mid-thirties stood by the door, one hand on the gun at her hip and the other near her right ear as she was listening to orders through her ear piece, orders I could hear perfectly. Her posture betrayed the second gun she carried inside her jacket and a third at her right ankle. Her eyes, unlike the others' in the room, were void of any fear, and had never left mine since she had entered. Her heart rate rested at just under sixty-five, but the adrenaline and cortisone I smelled in the air betrayed her apparent calm. The other two who had done the curtesy of making their presence known were both men. One looked like he was from Haitian descent, and the other had a faint southern accent. The darker man held himself like a martial artist, and judging from his much lower resting heartbeat, he was still an active combative. He had introduced himself as Thierry. The last had yet to give his name, taking on the bad-cop persona by saying only four words up until that point and lingering in the corner of the room, his predictable charade only marred by the questioning glance he would cast to the woman every fifteen to thirty seconds.

I had gone to a subset of the CIA's headquarters, at least one of their many small outposts Stargazer had taken from the mind of the man at the Pentagon. It was chosen specifically for its location and personnel – far enough away from where we lived and any major military or government presence, and

441

small enough that any chance of them making a move was limited to what we could handle without any more violent conflict. Anything greater than local backup would require time to organize, allowing us a window of time to escape.

Stargazer had left me there, as it had been our agreement that she not come unless it was absolutely necessary, an agreement that was not to be broken unless I was in lethal danger. I had walked up to the building, which was disguised as a hole in the wall computer repair store, told them who I was, and had requested an audience. I was unsurprised at their shock, but their wiliness was a different matter. They had yet to ask me how I had known who they were, as this subset was designed to be so far into hiding only four people knew of it, so I took their acceptance to mean they had long before sent word of my presence the moment I had been spotted on whatever hidden cameras surrounded the place, and that they would be reinforced shortly.

Thus the reason the Haitian and the woman, who I had heard was named Oksana, had not allowed silence. I waited for their words to be more than repeated demands to know why I was there or time stalling questions, for someone to say something that wasn't a blatant attempt to distract me long enough for Seal Team Six to show up and attempt to take me in. An hour passed, each minute marked with the same predictability as the last.

"You asked for a hearing, so let's hear it." Bad cop muttered.

Thierry inhaled, preparing to smooth the edges of his order.

Unlike the last four times a similar situation had happened, I didn't let him.

"You are all aware that as of yesterday we were declared enemies of the state, and put on every black list of every organization on the tax payroll. You already alerted your superiors and security that I am here, and you believe that because you were told we are wanted, the idea of my capture is a good thing, done for the safety of this country and humanity. I am here to tell you why that is wrong. Myself and Stargazer were detained four days ago. The circumstances regarding it are ones that will not be repeated again, so this is not out of fear for ourselves that I am telling you this. When the people who had taken us, some of whom you know, were unable to force me into consciousness they attempted to torture her as a means to an end, an end that would have led to our submission and the surrender of the location of our allies and the identities of our informants all over the globe. As my presence suggests, they did not succeed.

Their actions are what led to the destruction of the nuclear power plant in Georgia, the hour black out of satellites over the Southern portion of the US, and the shutdown of the NSA base and the signal garrisons at Fort Gordon. Further, there was an isolated confrontation of the man at the Pentagon the task force dedicated to our capture took orders from. I am here to tell you why this happened, and how it is to be avoided, so that nothing and no one else is to suffer."

The woman stepped forward, placing her hand on the table.

"And you expect us to comply to whatever demands you have in order?"

"I am not demanding anything, Oksana. If your bosses once thought selling machine guns to fugitives in hopes of following the trail, only to lose them, or that a plan of home grown terror attacks was a great way to encourage a war on Cuba, then I would think they would want to hear what I have to say."

Her eyes narrowed.

Thierry tensed.

"Good." I stated. "The person you call Stargazer is an alien. Your superiors know that, and they also know she is not the first to come here. Their most blatant mistake was made in thinking that her living on earth gives them jurisdiction over her, and anyone else who is here, for that matter. Their failed attempt to subdue her resulted in the reactor melt down at the power plant. But, if you go test anywhere surrounding the area, no radioactive activity will be present. This is also her doing, as civilian lives are what we try to protect. The only person we held responsible was the man who gave the order for our abduction and her torture – and that is where our retribution ended. If we are left alone, nothing else will occur that puts the authority of the government, any of them, or the lives of civilians, anyone, in peril. However, should the situation arise that we are once again targeted without reason, we will not stop at the one who gave the orders, but all those who took it upon themselves to follow them.

Then, we will go public with every single operative, operation, and assignment we know of, which are many if not most of what you do. It will not be a simple accusation. We will have evidence, and it will be the public who hangs those at fault, not us. If you do not believe me, then I suggest you call your bosses now, since they are watching this interview and are likely scrambling to cover their tracks. I can assure you, and them, that this is futile, because we have seen to it that the truth would not die with us even if they somehow succeeded. We will have this testimony recorded, it will be sent to every public server – worldwide – by midnight. Unless they want more than this testimony shared, they will leave us alone. "

Shadow wasn't that good, but a virus file Shift attached to the video was one Shadow had a direct part in making, meaning its electronic signature could be picked up by her same as she could pick up our organic ones. As I had warned, the video would be viral before dawn. There were no details, because their partial success was best kept under wraps, if only to prevent copy cats in Europe, Russia, and wherever else there was the tech to rival her.

When we recorded it that night, she spoke throughout it, explaining the what's and the why's – and her voice had not faltered until the last few seconds, where in the most human of ways, she had pleaded with the people listening to open their eyes to just how unstable the world is, and how only they had the ability to stop its spiraling out of control. *"I will stand by humanity, as I stand by its pinnacle, and I will never desert it – I only ask that you in return do the same, and stand by that which you believe to be just, to be good, to be honorable, and you fight for these things against an enemy worse than evil: apathy. I beg of you to not succumb to it. There is a battle of principalities taking place – and any place where light is not, darkness will have domain."*

Whether they believed me or not, I did not know. Thierry picked up his phone, the other looked to the mirror, scowling, waiting for confirmation. The woman glared at all of us as a whole, sizing up the room the same as I was. The only break was when I stood up, watching their hands go to their guns, hearing the people on the other side of the wall rise in sudden rapt attention and readiness, sensing the rise in their fear, and waiting for her to appear beside me. When she did, the guns raised, stopping at a forty-five degree angle to the floor when her hold of their minds took precedence over their own conscious control.

It had been plan B, one I hadn't supported, but needed. Time was up.

I didn't hear what she said, her mind was closed in its concentration to subdue them and the various others within the building, but in the minute that followed, their eyes had fallen to the floor. Epinephrine coursed through their blood, pumping fast and with greater force as their hearts pounded in response. Thierry's knees had buckled from under him, leaving him kneeling before us. The other man stood rigid, soaked with sweat. The woman's fingers closed tightly around the weapon in her hand, going white with the strength of her grip. Her skin went from red to grey, before she was released, catching the table to keep from falling.

Star took my hand as the ceiling above us blew outwards. Within a few seconds of being airborne, her thoughts opened.

What did you say?

I said nothing. I showed them the things I had seen, and the events we know of regarding those who hold their loyalty. I showed them what they did to me, and what they were planning to do with us. I will let the truth speak for itself.

You only showed them?

They experienced the memories, if not the actuality.

I don't believe the woman is as low on the chain of command as we thought. She was trained, extensively.

As are we, Dagger. For now, I believe we face an equal opponent.

If the government and the UN were our only concerns, then I would agree with you.

You are still concerned over the group that oversaw the genetic altercations?

They cannot be isolated from all of this. The amount of funding to make me alone would require backing, and the only groups large enough are private sector war lords and governments. If they are linked, they know too much now. You're compromised, in that, we're both capable of being compromised. We can't let them stay in the background-

And I promise you, as I promised the world, I will stand by you, against them, when the time comes.

The Promise

I looked around the large, well lit room, still becoming accustomed to being in it, as I had only entered a similar part of our dwelling a few times. Shadow and Mary were both there, as was Shadow's mother. The Lieutenant's wife had bustled through minutes before, leaving behind a trail of rosy-hued energy and a sense of sumptuousness belonging to these moments that had failed to take root in the core of my being. They were getting ready for the wedding, *our* wedding.

It was not hesitation that weighed on me, nonetheless it was with a false sense of helplessness that I felt the unclear things I did, even if the genesis of their existence laid hidden in the multitude of thoughts tumbling over one another within me like stones down the face of a cliff, landing in splashing chaos into the river below. The infuriation I had with myself at being nervous only added to my inner turmoil, leaving me desperately wishing to be able to see him. Just see him. They did not even have to let me touch him, but to only see him would be to know peace.

However, both Shadow's mother and Mary would not hear of it, a belief they had held fast to since arriving that morning to find Dagger and I returning from the location of downed plane over the far side of the planet. The situation there had been less unnerving than the one Noel had raised, with Shadow following her lead. I knew the scars Shadow bore from wounds yet to heal, and in aims to appease her through honoring the wishes of her mother, whom had put up the largest commotion that I had to obey for the sake of anyone within distance-of-hearing-and-valued-sanity, I had consented.

That surrender seemed petty then. I debated how much of a deceit it would be to reach out to him without their knowing, before deciding against it, even as I felt the energy in the room drop as my skin chilled.

It was the first time in three years where the apprehension of the indefinite came to repossess my mind. I rocked back and forth in the slightest gesture, allowing my body to take on the motions of my stirring energies, concentrating on the undulating waves to calm myself.

I have faced the unknown before, but this is as great a polar difference as a star to the black hole...I know what is to come, yet I am once more standing at the edge of a nebulous looking down at the endless-expanse below. I am not the same as I was then. My name has even changed.... I want to be his. Why am I still apprehensive? I have chosen to be bonded to him, what more could possibly be relevant?

...Premeditation seems to also bear its dark side.

Mary noticed me in the large reflecting-glass she had been standing before, pausing her application of a colored wax to her lips.

"You look scared to *death*. You should be happy! You're getting *married*!"

I put a smile on my face. Unconvinced at my passive attempt to placate her, she glanced at Shadow. I let my eyes lighten, though this also had failed.

I am happy, so much that I currently have to force myself to keep from glowing. It is more than this. I do not like to not know. He was there then too, but rather than being almost source of it as is now, he was the cure. Is he really the source now...or am I? I have 'nothing to fear but fear itself'. That isn't a very good saying I think. Then I would only have more fear of the very fear I feel.

"Star." My sight shot up towards Shadow, in surprise and unexpected pleasure. She smiled and bent down; taking my hands in her own, her touch cool and comforting in the midst of my inner conflict.

The others eyes were on us.

"It is your turn to need to breathe." She encouraged, recognizing better than even I could the foolishness of my apprehension, for even if she could not see its source, she knew the vow I had made and the one I was to make bore a greater purpose than any doubt.

Shadow's mother stared with a puzzled expression when I simply smiled in answer to her daughter's counsel. I had already been audience to an hour's length of her advice the first moment she had gotten alone with me. Her insight was appreciated, if not entirely relevant to I who merely appeared to be human.

"Just remember what he promised, okay?"

He said that he would always belong to me. Whatever the true source of my fear, his words had ended it completely. No matter what, he would always be mine and I would be his. In this hope, I felt myself become so still that even the energy of the room became unmoving, as it got lost in my own.

"You guys only say half of any given conversation." Mary muttered, recognizing how justified Shift was in his judgments of us. I felt her doing something yet again with my hair, the pins made of imperfect metal bending and holding it into waves that I could have done had they told me what it was they wanted it to be. But, and I struggled with each moment that passed to adhere to this when my body was to be manipulated like a falsely-proportioned-doll, I was to be human, at least in part, and such things were of this race.

"Hold still-" she warned, the bent sliver of copper clenched between her teeth. "Ok, perfect...Gosh you look gorgeous."

I ducted my head.

"I'd think you'd be blushing right now if you could." Shadow teased.

"Grant me a few of the spaces of time you call hours."

She flushed. Mary thought it was, in her own thoughts, hysterical, her power flaring as she laughed aloud. I smiled. It was a bit unnerving for everyone's thoughts to flutter back to us in that manner every few minutes. Even more so, my own mind refused to drop those memories and anticipations. Voicing it seemed to be the only way to cure the seemingly unseen pressure, since none present had yet to end it.

"Okay, okay, enough, before someone messes up their makeup." Mary chided, before shoving the group of ribbon tied plants in my direction. "Here. It's about time." Mary said happily.

I took the flowers from her. My hands shook slightly, the appearance of my body taking on the actions of my energy.

"You would think that you're facing the *bad* guys."

"This is not something I grew up expecting, in any form. Not this way, not with these customs. I doubt it will become a reality in my mind until it is a true reality." I explained.

"What do you mean?"

I smiled, realizing then how glad I was that this was as it was.

"Nothing that bear consequence here."

-BD-SG S//5░S░

"I do." I promised her. She smiled, her honey hued consciousness sweeping against mine, her joy rushing over me. She looked up at me, her eyes bright, the stars in them pulsing far past the edged of their gold rims. I was instantly awed and unbelieving of the angel next to me. I was barely aware of anyone else being there.

Only when she said softly, but with all the sureness in the world, and in her case, every galaxy, 'I do,' did I remember the man in front of us as he pronounced us husband and wife. I picked her up, I hearing what I guessed was applause, but only knowing the warmth of her in my arms.

"I have made good of my promise." She whispered so only I would be able to hear. She kissed me again, her exhilaration unencumbered by the people around us.

Shift let out a hoot in the background. I saw out of the corner of my eye that Shadow's mom was crying, with Shadow leaning away from her. We'd invited the lieutenant and his wife, Zach, Mary, two people who ran a rehabilitation center and three who operated one of our closer safe houses, both of which Stargazer funded and we supplied patrons to, and lastly, Shadow's parents. However, as far as her dad knew then she was attending her 'best friend's sister's wedding.' Star had to keep from glowing, as long as he stuck around.

She laughed softly.

"I could scarcely even be in motion previously, I was so nervous." She admitted.

"Why?"

"Does it even matter now?"

I smiled. Her mind brushed mine and she held me tighter. I kept my hands flat against her back, so not tear the silk of her dress, no matter how desperately I wanted to never let go.

I felt someone tap me on the back. I turned sideways slightly, enough so they would know I was listening. I didn't want to be there, not because the walls were closing in, but because the thought of sharing her left me restless.

"Congrats!" Shift shouted, taking the role of the party host with more enthusiasm than it had called for.

I felt Stargazer being pulled away from me by Anna and Noel. She looked to me with an expression of helplessness. She knew I could keep her from being subjected to *them*... But the 'marriage' deal meant the whole thing, including the madness after the 'I do's' from every female attending.

I smirked.

"Go on." I said. She pulled away from them and managed to kiss me again before she was practically yanked from my side.

Shift cocked an eyebrow.

"You let her go huh?" He jeered. My hand flexed. He flinched instinctively and then laughed. I couldn't help but grin back.

"Thanks a lot...*Jonathan*." I said with a little ill humor in my tone.

"Oh, right. We'll be cool soon. Shads' dad is going to be preoccupied in a few minutes - and is tearing into the food right now. I don't think he would even notice." He laughed.

Dagger let me be subjected to the constant chatter and the increasing questions which I made a point to forget. Somewhere in the pastel hued chaos I managed to hold Shadow's gaze with my own. She seemed confused at what I wanted. So consumed was I in the whirlwind within me that I did not even attempt to open my thoughts, I mere tapped my exposed arms.

"Oh...right," she said, smiling, her powers increasing their brilliance as understanding flooded her thoughts with light. "Hey Dad, why don't you go and get the car?" Her father had come that morning, although neither she nor I had expected him to, for the notice we had given was small in length. However, I believed it to be eagerness to accept her invitation for a visit more so than what the invitation was for, and I had convinced both her and my husband -I jumped at that thought, and my surface temperature rose by its own accord- that I could control my "non-humanness" around him, as Shadow had attempted to state insouciantly. I doubted that he would be kept in the dark much longer, for Shadow was facing greater trials in keeping her two identities separated, and though her mother knew all, she still made it a point to not be 'Shadow' around her, yet I knew it would not be long before Shadow and Cynthia knew no divisor.

As soon as he left, I freely glowed. It was a relief to be able to show my true self, and then everyone got to see how happy I actually-truly-beyond a doubt was.

"Mary, Zach, will you mind going with him? He's fine to joy ride for a while but I just don't want him getting lost – I saw it earlier." She sighed when she said it, though I knew what she had been 'playing at'. Both Mary and Zach looked at her, unaware of her reasoning, simply happy to offer assistance into rewriting a future they thought to exist, and then went out to find her father.

I smiled. She winked back.

"What that about Cynthia?" Her mother questioned, not blind to her daughter's antics.

"Tell you later."

His blazing eyes smiled when I met them.

"Come on." She interrupted my thoughts.

I looked at her quizzically. I felt her become slightly annoyed.

"You have to learn to trust me."

I weighed my options. I could be in his arms in only a moment if I wanted, or I could trust her. Against all odds, I would do as Shift would have advised and "humored the physic."

"Oh boy." I quoted her.

I felt a slight pressure on my back. "*What* are you doing?" He was attempting to push me somewhere. Futilely.

"How much do you weigh?!" The pressure increased momentarily, as if he tried to ram me over. I took a step forward. He would've fallen if he hadn't shifted himself to standing next to me. A bandana hung in his hand.

"I know. Look, just go with it okay? I'm drowning with Shads and for whatever reason she thinks this will work. Throw me life saver."

I took it from him, tying it over my eyes. I could see through it, but for my sanity's sake I gave the impression that I could not. High-pitched giggles and very 'wedding like' music began to play in the background. Through the fabric her glowing figure stood in between Shadow and her mother. She looked like she had a similar, meant to be blinding tie, though anyone who was then present understood it was all for show. I knew instantly what they had been planning and what they were doing was about the only way to get either of us to do *that*. She entered my mind, her happiness washing over the room until everything I saw, even through the blindfold, was tinted in gold.

They want us to dance.

Do you want to?

Are we being given much of a choice?

Shads is emotional blackmailing Shift into it. He might take us to Antarctica if we don't, and leave us there.

I would not allow you to freeze.

... No, you wouldn't, but out of convenience, let's not disappoint them.

Of course.

"It worked." Shads was smiling as they spun around the room. If I may, you have never seen a type of miracle until you have seen BD dance, or ice-skate for that matter, now that I think about it. It just doesn't look like it should even be *possible*, but they both were really good at it...the dancing, not so much on the ice-skating.

"I don't think all that was worth it. They don't look like they mind too much Jonny. You and Shads *might* have over done it just a little bit and he could have kicked both of your tails if he wanted." Mary was smiling too, and trying to get in on the conversation again.

"I'm with Mary." Zach agreed, for all his comradery choosing to stand in rank with my older sister. *Now they've ganged up on me!* His parents were dancing too. "Her dad is watching the car outside. We couldn't get him out of it."

"Good, she is still a torch." I smirked, imagining her father's reaction if he walked in. I hadn't made a point to get too friendly with him, mainly to keep up the guise that Mary and I were "Brad's" step-siblings who had flown in from New Jersey, and that Shads and I had only met a few days before. The only reason she was tied to us was that SG had been the coach of some gymnastics team Shads worked with, and with SG's brain fog, he bought it. The cover story had been her plan, and as irritating as it was to waste precious 'brownie point earing' time, I went with it.

"Well, we can't let him have all the fun." Zach commented, and for a second I thought he was going to propose a quick joy ride/drag race, thinking we were still on the subject of cars, but when I looked back it wasn't me he was looking at. "Can I have this dance?"

He asked *my sister?*

I stared, feeling like I'd been punched in the stomach when she agreed, the same chick who had gone with me and my friends to light fireworks on a beach the night of her school's sophomore prom was suddenly willingly dancing in heels.

"What did I miss here?" I demanded. I was afraid my only normal video game partner was about to be polluted my big sister. That'll get any guy freaked out.

"What? Oh, that."

"Yeah. That."

"He asked her if she wanted to dance...*duh.*"

"Well thanks for clarifying."

"Oh, shush. Leave them alone. You're just paranoid. Aw...Look how sweet they are."

What does a guy have to do to get the girl to quit changing the subject for once? *Honestly. And what would I have thinking BD could ever fit in the description of sweet?*

"*Sweet* may be just a little bit..."

"Normal?" She suggested.

"I guess."

"You did a pretty good job at distracting my dad though." She complimented. "I know it's been a ball of awkward. He will be staying a few days so I'll be in and out a lot. I don't think they care, but just so you know."

I took slight hope in the idea she wanted to give me a heads up. Then she kept talking.

"I haven't seen anything with the feds. But I did see that dad will be back in a minute so..." She whispered.

"Time to go?" I had never been to a wedding so I wasn't sure how it all worked and movies are no good to get information from either. There was a bag of rice in the backseat of my car to prove it. Shadow, fortunately, saw me and told me not to do that, that it would make me look ridiculous, which I didn't care about. And that BD would actually throw the rice *back*, which I did care about. Wisely, I decided I would rather not have my first experience with edible shrapnel.

"Not yet, but she is still glowing and he'll figure out the rush from driving the car isn't the thing making the room vibrate, at least once the food runs out." She sounded like she could care less, something I wanted to maybe, if I could, fix eventually.

I saw Shadow standing behind her. She mouthed the words 'my dad is back'. I nodded. Star was, for once, oblivious, her pale gold halo and the soft pulsations of her energy radiating off her skin the source of Shads' warning.

"You need to stop glowing Honey." I cautioned.

"And if I do not wish to?"

"Then you have to keep Shadow's dad from figuring out who we are." I reminded her. She sighed and the light and energy that came from within her stopped, but her arms

456

remained folded against me, the confirmation that her contentment to stay where we were mirrored my own.

"Time for the presents!" I lifted my head from his cool-pounding-torso. I recognized Shadow's piercing voice and smiled, despite the fact that I understood that what she had proposed would mean my letting go of him, even if it was only for a few minutes.

I looked in his eyes, his consuming-fire-soul-light shining brightly. He was smiling, the truest sign of his joy, yet I could not glow, to my displeasure. I did however let the pulsars in my sight expand with my ever escalating joy, if only for a fraction of a second.

"I think we need to put up with this as well." I spoke. He sighed and released me just enough so we could both face our family.

"Okay, well, we didn't really know what to get you guys...so...bear with us." Mary smiled as she spoke. They led us to a small table and each gave us a gift-of-celebration.

I wish that I could recall all that had been given, but only one thing stands out in my mind, not because there was no sign of who the giver had been, but because of the sudden-shock it gave me; it not only mentioned something I hadn't even thought over, but reminded me of everything I had. Us, together. I had never been told with any detail what would come, only that it would be eternal in the sense that ours was a vow I would see fulfilled unto my end, and if that was the sole cost, then I had known I was to pay it for a great time before.

I grasped his hand in mine. His living fire eyes laughed when I inconspicuously showed him to contents of the unmarked package. His only answer was to hold me tighter, denying anyone who was not privy of the content the chance to guess at its purpose.

Sunglasses.

Happiness is

Contentment, completion, peace, love, gratefulness, hope, acceptance, forgiveness: 'Happiness'. If you were to try to explain the sensation of happiness to someone who claims to have never felt it before, or has never accepted it, then it would be pointless. A hundred and ten thousand words or so back I believed that such a thing was impossible. How can you describe something measureless? Something that just comes out of nowhere to find you and at the smallest invite or reason? You can fake happiness, or do as I did and rebel against its entire existence, or you can attempt to buy it (and if it could be bought we could afford it) but you can't, no matter how rich you are or how much you want to. Some people even try to sell it. Futilely trying to get it through material things or through experiences is where many fail to understand it. It isn't tangible so you can't get it from something tangible. Same as it cannot be taken from you, not unless you consent to the theft, as I did for far too long. No one but you and the one to who you belong 'holds the key' to happiness. Happiness is being held in the arms of the one who exists for you and you alone - Your One. To know you are loved forever and without any need for explanation, and that she is yours eternally more.

That is my description of Happiness.

What's yours?

-Black Dagger

Querencia

All who I was had been changed, the mixture of his power and his soul taking me where every second I existed was a part of him, of us, the feel of his touch and the sound of his heart pounding in my head same as my energy augmented and withdrew within me, as I knew what it was to be more than one single being, more than anyone but he now possessed. I was not beyond recognizing that precipitous plummet of power, but I came to know that the chasm it created only came to be so that his own energy could fill it, if not entirely – Yet it was not loss, nor was it surrender. It was as standing on the precipice of present and past tense, looking at what had been and who I had been, and knowing what we then were, knowing beyond any notion of doubt, fear, or hesitation and with the utmost of righteous convictions that we stood together – as we unremittingly would.

Every argument I ever had against tangibility, I take it all back. I laughed in my mind, only then having the concentration to think in ways that can be put to words. I looked for a difference in him or me that he might notice, fearing to let him see anything significant in either of us, but in my carelessness I forsook my search after only moments, giving my attention to much more present matters.

I recognized the heat of her fingers running down my back, the first thing bringing me back to what I was stunned to call reality. The glorious creature whose surface merely scratched at the wonder she contained held me tighter.

"Good morning."

"Good may be a bit of an understatement, however it is a very good morning." She murmured, her voice from just above my head.

I laughed and propped myself up so I could see her face. She was softly glowing, eyes a hazy gold, the stars pulsing in a way that left me unable to look away.

"Have I ever told you thank you?"

"For?"

"Everything."

She smiled, animatedly rolling her eyes.

"You're delirious." She accused, still grinning, glowing brighter, her aura only adding to the heat of the room, the source of it originally the rising sun.

"A little."

"Is that something I can 'fix'?"

"Considering you're the cause, I just hope Shift can take care of things for a while."

I watched the laughter turn to her ever bright glow. "They are well, you needn't be concerned."

"I wasn't."

"Ah, of course you were not." She smiled.

Only then did I notice the slight burning on my arm, the sensation subtle enough to not be blocked by my immunity to pain. I turned to my side, looking to see what the source of it was. She followed my gaze, the light around her ceasing with what we both saw.

She sat up, grabbing my shoulder.

I studied the banded design, following the many sharp curves and twists within it. I realized it was nearly solid, and oddly enough the longer I stared at it, the less I felt it. When I touched my hand to it, it was warm and smooth, like stone, but my nerve endings below its surface were still intact. I glanced at her, reading her pensive expression.

"You have your own energy mark now." She whispered, as if speaking it louder scared her. She met my eyes, hers darkened. "All of my kind bear them. All but... I had no notion such was even possible – else I would have warned-"

"Warned? Why would I need a warning – I can take a surprise." I comforted her, raising my hand to her face. She caught my wrist, cradling my hand in one of hers. The other stroked the onyx like brand. "Why are you upset?"

"You are not...not in pain?"

"No. I take it this has something to do with...?" I left off suggestively, not letting myself fully flashback, or else my mental capacity would take a greater blow. She nodded, her eyes never leaving the band.

"I did not want you to change, to bear consequence. I know not how you can be at such ease, being banded without consent." She shook her head, her eyes closing for longer than the forced habit of her blinking. "I never thought such things were possible between our kinds. It is the physical representation of our bond, my presence within you, as yours within me. You refused to hear my first warnings, but now I see even they were incomplete, and even now you are silent when you must have questions, and if you do not it seems only more troubling. How is it you can have *peace*?"

"Because I'm happy."

I laid back down, knowing her reservations when she hesitated to do the same, her thoughts drifting against my own with the same sensation of her fingers dragging against my sternum. I cradled her next to me, consciously admitting the few times I had openly wondered what this might have been like, and knew my former naivety. No words, spoken, imagined, or even typed, could capture the extremes she'd brought me to, from rhapsody to this perfect feeling of her next to me.

I looked down at her, her expression waiting to form before she could read my own.

I fought the desire to scowl, knowing my unease would be better left internal, for what he had spoken was true, truer than any argument against it I could had proposed. Yet my reservations remained unmoved. I recognized what was different within me, for no two elements may be mixed together so completely that one could expect to retain its might while also granting it to the other, but what of him?

I drifted into light, only allowing my physical body to form again, free of hindrance or hiding, before the glass-expanse-windows, the last set of those that also belonged to the main room. I looked out of them for moments I did not count, though time was now a very tangible dimension of my reality. I had once seen the world below desiring to belong to it, at the greatest of costs. Looking back to him, studying the manner his banded arm braced the weight of his torso against the folds of thin-white-cloth beneath his hand, the angles of his face turned up in the faintest hint of expectancy, his gaze meeting mine without hesitation or uncertainty, I did not think of either of those things.

"Could it be that simple?"

I felt my own power shift at the rise of his, his agreement made with the surest of smiles.

"It is that simple. I didn't ask you before because it doesn't matter. I love you. Anyone, anything, genetic engineering, and power bands be damned."

"Do not damn them yet, Dagger. For if that band is as I believe it to be, you will find everything you value in your abilities to be greater."

His curious-surprise became an action as he rose, coming to stand behind me, his arms once more around me, his sight matching the bearings of my own over the many buildings below us.

"You've made me stronger for years." He said quietly, turning so that his lips might be against the and atop my head. "We will have to be, Star." The tautness of his hold increased, his breathing deepening, matching the constant rise and fall of my energy without fault.

"I know…I never contemplated that I would know what this is, this surrender without defeat. I never once thought I would be here, as I am." I turned back to face him, dismissing the world below for the one that owned it, that was both its son and its keeper. No force below us or power above could have taken me from him, and if I had been asked, I believe that one of them may have already granted me this. "Time cannot hurt us, neither can man nor other creatures touch us, for just as you are my protector, so I am to you."

I have had one person ask me what love is, and it is this moment. It was not the hours that came before it, or the countless spent after, the years it has been since, the chapters you've read, or the books that are to follow. It was this speck of stillness, with neither one of us seeking the other to break it, because we both recognized its greatness. That moment in all of eternity, with her hand on mine sealing it into place, was the redemption of what had been, and was the peace that I would fight to keep in the seemingly endless trial that was to come.

THE PROTECTORS TRILOGY
BOOK II
COMING SOON